THE
DOOM
PUSSY

THE DOOM PUSSY

BY ELAINE SHEPARD

TRIDENT PRESS
NEW YORK

Published by Trident Press, a division of Simon & Schuster, Inc., 630 Fifth Avenue, New York, N.Y. 10020.
Printed in the United States of America

FOR DICKEY CHAPELLE: KILLED IN ACTION
AT CHU LAI IN THE SWEAT AND
GUNPOWDER OF BATTLE ON PATROL WITH
HER BELOVED MARINES

Only the men who flew up north after dark are entitled to wear the Doom Pussy emblem on their left shoulders. In green letters around the border is emblazoned: TRONG MIENG CUA CON MEO CUA DINH MANG. *Translated literally from the Vietnamese this reads: "I have flown into the jaws of the cat of death."*

Most American fliers merely say, "I have seen the Doom Pussy."

CONTENTS

FOREWORD

Not everything in The Doom Pussy happened the way I've told it. But it could have. Certain events have been telescoped, a few names and incidents are fictitious, some of the personalities are composites.

I shall always be grateful to Elmer Roessner, editor in chief of Bell-McClure Syndicate, who gave me my first credentials as a foreign correspondent; to Robert F. Hurleigh, President, Mutual Broadcasting System, who sent me to Vietnam to report for the world's largest broadcasting system; and to Bucklin Moon, Executive Editor of Trident Press. He believed in The Doom Pussy from the start.

THE
DOOM
PUSSY

THE ANGRY PALM TREES

"Secure?" inquired the sentry.

"Secure," replied Pfc Mumpower in his dry North Carolina drawl, at the wheel of the Army jeep. The query was mandatory every time a vehicle reentered the base. The Viet Cong in and around Saigon too often succeed at planting bombs in American conveyances left unattended for even a moment.

Mumpower had collected me at seven that morning at the Caravelle Hotel. I wore an Army uniform of camouflaged jungle green, called a "tiger suit," an Australian Go to Hell bush hat, and shoulder harness and web belt supporting tape recorder, cameras, and canteens. I was scheduled to fly an early mission on a combat assault with the 145th Aviation Battalion aboard the Command and Control helicopter piloted by the CO, Lieutenant Colonel Chuck Honour.

The 145th is the largest chopper battalion in the world. If it were part of a division it would have two companies. It had six: four lift companies, one armed-helicopter company, and one fixed-wing surveillance company.

Mumpower, a lean blond of nineteen, with only the fuzz of innocence on his suntanned face, released the brake and bolted across the courtyard to Honour's quarters. He eased out of the jeep. "Be back in a minute."

Idly I watched the Vietnamese maids and handymen filing through the gate and wondered how many of them were Viet Cong infiltrators, a monumental security problem at all American installations. The women wore white cotton jackets, black trousers, and the inevitable conical straw hats which serve them in myriad ways: as protection against sun and rain, to fan themselves, as a means of carrying laundry and sometimes even vegetables from the market.

Through the mess-hall screen door drifted laughter and the buzz of Army talk. Shortly the men began strolling out to their jeeps, piled in, and drove off to the business of battle.

"The Colonel is on the phone. He'll be out in a minute," Mumpower said as he climbed under the wheel. "I sure envy you this mission. I'm studying to be a gunner. Ought to hack it in two more weeks."

As Colonel Honour strode toward us I climbed in the back so he could sit in his customary place. He was a short man but his shoulders were blade-straight and he was in a good humor because the 145th had just received the Vietnamese Medal of Valor.

"Morning."

"Good morning, Colonel."

We rattled over to Tan Son Nhut Air Base and the 145th helipad. The Colonel went directly to his ship, and I slipped out my side of the jeep to follow him when I heard the high-pitched whine peculiar to F-100s. Turning to watch the ships taxi by on the adjacent runway, I could see the eyes of the pilots above their oxygen masks.

As the third blunt-nosed Supersabre rolled by, I impulsively upped both thumbs in the traditional gesture. The pilot, surprised to see blond hair flipping in the wind on the Tan Son Nhut ramp, did a double take. His eyes crinkled as he held up the thumb of his black-gloved hand in return. When he rounded the corner to the long take-off runway he looked back and waved.

Preflighting his craft, Honour circled it, checking everything. "Doesn't take long," he said. "It's a few minutes' insurance."

He went topside. I climbed after him. He pointed out the rotor head and the large retaining nut which holds the rotors to the mast. "This," he said, "allows the thing to fly. If it comes off we lose the main rotors. At that point a helicopter has all the aerodynamic characteristics of a footlocker. We call it the Jesus nut."

As the Colonel climbed down, a jeep came to an abrupt halt beside us. A young captain with brawny sunburned arms delivered about the snappiest salute I'd ever seen.

"Sir, they have some empty seats on the plane going home today. So I'm leaving a day earlier than planned. I just wanted to tell you how much I've appreciated serving in your outfit."

"You've done a fine job, Kuykendall."

The captain turned quickly and left.

"He had tears in his eyes," I said.

Honour stood silently watching the jeep round the corner. "I've been through this so many times. I guess combat is about the closest you'll ever get to someone. Last mission he flew, that boy's ship had twenty-seven holes in it. He has seven in his body. At his farewell party the platoon presented him with a plaque: 'From the Razorbacks to their Magnet Ass.' "

In covering this brutal, many-sided war, you watch men go through their tours dreaming of home. Then when the day comes to separate from their buddies and commander, emotions tear them both ways, especially if their comradeship was born in moments of danger. Shared perils are a private thing of great depth between them.

Waiting on the flight line was Sergeant Major Dubrey, the senior noncom of the battalion and Colonel Honour's direct link to the enlisted men. Dubrey was a beefy, tackle-type hulk of sergeant with the girth of a sequoia. Completely devoted to Honour, he usually flew with the Boss. As Dubrey began to zip me into my flak vest I read the label inside:

"This vest may save your life. When properly worn it will protect your vital areas against shell or grenade fragments, which cause most casualties."

Next came a fifteen-pound chest protector of laminated steel and plastic, called "the iron brassiere."

Ground crews hover around an aircraft like mother hens. A good crew chief is married to his ship and would rather do twenty-four-hour duty than let anyone else mess with it. There are 1,800 helicopters in Vietnam, operating 75 percent of the time, regardless of weather.

As Honour buckled in at the controls, the crew chief and door gunner fitted ammo belts into their M-60 machine guns. I adjusted my flight helmet and headset so I could hear the radio transmission between Colonel Honour and Saigon Ground Control.

"Helicopter seven three two. Departure from Hotel two. East departure mid-field crossing."

Tan Son Nhut, three miles north of Saigon, is the busiest airport in the world. All day, every day, seven days a week, more than fifteen hundred planes and choppers take off or land on its runways.

Speaking English with a strong accent, a Vietnamese replied from the tower, "Helicopter seven three two. Takeoff approved. Cross at five hundred feet."

We lifted gently from the helipad, hovered over the taxiway and the sod area adjoining the runway, the nose tilted slightly down. Then there was a slight shudder as the chopper went through transitional lift and we soared gloriously.

As we swept away from Tan Son Nhut the neat farmlands below could have been my native Illinois. I momentarily forgot that we were subject to sniper fire of the Viet Cong, or, National Liberation Front, as they prefer to be called. Actually, the soggy rice paddies and sparsely inhabited low mountains covered with thick forest make the countryside an open invitation to ambush, a guerrilla paradise. It was exhilarating to be able to see all around, yet the crew at the open doors seemed so exposed.

The day's objective was to deliver two battalions of troops to a Landing Zone close by one of the Michelin Rubber Plantations northwest of Saigon. It is a new concept in tactical mobility, born out of the peculiar needs of this jungle war.

Honour flew at very low level, just above the treetops. Over the microphone I asked why.

"The VC have machine guns in this area and if I don't fly very high, I fly very low. It's more difficult to hit us. Our exposure time is that much shorter."

We landed at one of Honour's lift companies, commanded by Major Donald "Jug" Haid. Jug Haid's group called themselves "The Rattlers" and their heliport "The Snake Pit." The company's insignia was an angry-looking coiled rattlesnake with a scarlet forked tongue. All the helicopters were UH-1s. The true transport model, which hauls seven to nine men into battle, is called "The Slick," technically "The Delta" or UH-1D. They carry no formal weapon system; machine gunners at the open doors on each side provide incidental protection with M-60 machine guns.

Gunships, however, carry a variety of weapon systems, ranging from quad 7.62-millimeter machine guns to 2.75-inch rockets and 40-millimeter grenade launchers. These are called "The Tigers."

After checking in with The Rattlers at Jug Haid's heliport, we learned that the orders were for Phu Loi, where the other chopper crews and troops were waiting. We would actually take off from Thu Da Mot, a three-thousand-foot laterite strip built by the Japanese during WW II.

The briefing at Phu Loi was cryptic. I sat in the large map-walled tent studying the crews. On my left was a Captain Schaber, who pointed out his new commander, Lieutenant Colonel Louis Williams of Bamberg, S.C.

"The day the Colonel arrived to take over," Schaber whispered, "I flew him to Bien Hoa. With no warning I received a divert to extradite some ARVNs who were in trouble." He pronounced it "Arven"; the initials stand for Army of the Republic of Vietnam. "The area was fogged in and when we landed, nine ARVNs and their weapons piled in on top of the Colonel. It was the first he'd heard of any divert and he ended up with three ARVNs, plus all their gear, sitting in his lap."

"Will there be artillery fire along our flight route?" asked a tall lieutenant from Tennessee.

"Negative, we hope. Can't be sure," replied the spokesman.

A hundred helicopters were lined up nose to tail along both sides of the strip. It is easy to understand the respect and hatred the VC feel for the squat, ungraceful gunships. Rockets and machine guns were mounted prominently on the nose, looking for all the world like phallic symbols. Crew chiefs scurried up and down the line vying for the attention of the fuel trucks. The pilots sat around and smoked and talked.

"I've never understood this," Jug Haid said to me, "but the gunners lie down on the ship's floor and grab a nap before takeoff. Plenty relaxed. You'd think they'd be going over the map checking with the copilot."

"*Cr-a-a-nk!*" echoed up and down the line and when the choppers were churning the men checked their radios.

"Radio check Fox Mike. Alpha One, Alpha Two, Alpha Three. Bravo One, Bravo Two—on to Delta Three." It was repeated on the UHF.

Then Jug spoke into the mike. "Rattlers, one minute. Rattlers, ten seconds. Rattlers, six. Pulling pitch." We were off. He later told me that those words never failed to raise the hackles at the back of his neck.

As we approached the Landing Zone we watched the Guam-based B-52 SAC bombers overhead. In threes the silver superbombers with drooping, swept wings glistened high in the heavens.

"Great hairy Ned on the mountaintop," exclaimed Honour. "Curt LeMay never dreamed that one day his big SAC dairy barns would be used in a tactical bombing role."

The Tan Son Nhut tower announced: "*Attention all aircraft. Attention* all *aircraft. Heavy artillery fire three-three-zero-slant-three-zero.*"

With that broadcast all friendly aircraft in the area were alerted that the B-52s were dropping their 750- and 500-pound bombs. The multimillion-dollar jets demolished the jungle around the LZ, followed by Skyraider A-1Es, which strafed and dropped napalm. The armed choppers went in for low-level fire passes at the immediate trees and a final low-level reconnaissance before the troop-carrying Slicks landed.

It was the first eye-glazing B-52 performance I had witnessed from the air. I had a grandstand seat as the fearful missiles erupted. Enormous flaming explosions were followed by huge clouds of smoke as wave after wave of the giant ships spot-bombed the jungle to secure the area for American-Vietnamese forces waiting to land. Orange mountains of fire and smoke mushroomed hundreds of feet into the air. Only these heavy bombers can seriously damage the fortified network of tunnels the Viet Minh started digging twenty years ago. For years the underground storage chambers and headquarters had enjoyed virtual immunity from serious penetration by the enemy.

The B-52s' ordnance seemed to be exploding directly below us. "Can those B-52s see *us?*" I asked Colonel Honour.

"No," he replied. "They can't see us because we're painted olive drab and blend in with the landscape. You can see them because they're silhouetted against the sky."

I couldn't help wishing the big bombers *could* see us. Leaving the big birds, the dun-colored missiles were not visible; only the results were. Day or night the B-52s aim their loads by radar and get excellent precision with computers. Not until the radar reflection matches the outline of the target area do they let go.

The choppers, like a swarm of orderly bees, retained their pattern. Like armed duennas, the gunships hovered below the Slicks. When the Skyraiders peeled off to bomb and strafe after the B-52s headed back for Guam, I wondered if any of the pilots I'd flown with were among them. Was Cactus Jones up there?

The quartet of fighter bombers alternated their runs, dropping awesome napalm and white phosphorus, called Willie Peter, which burns even longer. Braided columns of scarlet flame and dark smoke shot up from the fiery patches of cleared jungle.

Then I spied the FAC pilot, who flies the Forward Air Controller plane and dictates every move of the prestrike. Like a little wasp sailing through the sky, it stubbornly carries out its role of strike-force catalyzer and coordinator. Though I'd flown on several missions that included the FAC, it was always startling to see the little plane cruising about just above the holocaust.

"They are the wheat-shockin' end."

"Don't tell me you flew with those idiots." Honour said it with the intonation of respect reserved for FAC pilots by all troops involved in the Vietnamese conflict. Only intimates have the privilege of insult.

The tiny craft flew through the smoke at five hundred feet, tootling about as if it owned the universe, invulnerable and without a care in the world. The plane itself has a personality that matches the fantastic mettle of its pilots. On a mission the FAC is a combination boss-mother hen, and all-important to the strike forces.

"The A-1Es are rolling in for their last pass. LZ will be cleared in zero two," the FAC announced to the chopper crews. Its job done, the tiny craft buzzed out of sight.

It was time for the landing. The Slick pilots reduced pitch and in a staggered trail came in low and landed quickly, rotors still turning. To allow minimum time in the LZ, the trail pilot called out "Trail up" even before he was on the ground. By the time each chopper was down, the troops were out and the lead element, or ship, was already pulling out of the LZ. Chopper pilots sweat it if they stay in an LZ too long.

It is difficult for the troops to move quickly. Even from the air you can see why. Rice stalks were visible, flattened and waving from the rotor wash. The green and black-silver fields glistened in the sun. The troops carried rifles, machine guns, mortars, heavy gear, and, knee-deep in paddy mud, headed as best they could for the bordering jungle to secure the LZ for subsequent lifts. Their mission then is to fan out and sweep the area, to patrol, search out, and destroy VC, and assess the damage of the strikes. The Michelin Plantation already had paid approximately a million piasters a year to the VC to remain in operation; in effect the VC owned the area.

We flew back to Phu Loi for lunch. The second element was due to be lifted in at thirteen hundred hours.

"How about some C-rations?" invited Jug as he came over to the command chopper.

"Great."

The men allowed me first choice among the boxes: beefsteak; ham and lima beans; boned chicken; chicken and noodles; and cheese and macaroni.

"Hope there's enough ham and lima beans to go around."

"Me, too," I said. They quickly handed over a box. By now I had mastered the tricky little can opener that hung on my dog-tag chain. We all fell to sitting on the chopper floor, using the toilet tissue in the C-ration box for napkins. For dessert we swapped pecan rolls for cheese and crackers and Pall Mall cigarettes for Winston filters, as we talked over the mission.

"I'd like to go on the afternoon wave," I suggested.

"I thought you were bellyaching about never getting a chance to sleep or write your articles. You said you had to start back at noon," chided Colonel Honour.

"What time do we take off?" I asked.

Then everyone stretched out on the floor for a five-minute nap. The crew chief slept on top of the chopper. Being a guest of sorts, I was offered the narrow nylon troop bench, which had only two metal bars to interfere with complete rest. They struck about at the shoulders and thighs. I was out in one second.

After we all woke up, Jug confessed. "We were putting you on about the ham and lima beans. We all hate 'em and tried to sell you the package."

"Well, I happen to really like them. Always have. Back in Olney, Illinois, we called them butter beans."

At thirteen hundred hours the additional battalion of the First Infantry Division scrambled aboard, eager to connect and tangle with the communists. The First is one of many good divisions in Vietnam. Its troops have a tradition to uphold. They played a very important role in Europe in WW II, especially on D Day. These men of the famous Big Red One held the record of more assault landings than any other US unit in WW II. Everywhere the Big Red One is recognized by its patch—a red-as-a-cut-throat numeral 1 on an all-drab background. The division's unofficial motto is: "If you have to be one, be a Big Red One."

The hundred angry palm trees lifted off, headed northwest to pour fresh fighting men into the LZ. As the snipers fired from the ground, each aircraft that received a hit marked the spot with a purple grenade to warn incoming aircraft. There soon were several markers.

Colonel Honour said, "We don't sweat those single-shot Charlies, or waste ammo on them when we may need it in the LZ."

A greater threat was the 50-caliber-machine-gun emplacement at the edge of the LZ. A gunship swooped low and knocked it out with a 40-millimeter grenade.

"After a CA" Jug Haid said to me, "of course, I hate like hell to see the ground troops get zapped, but it seems a unit commander always feels that the operation is a success if none of his own people are hurt. It may sound parochial, but it's human I guess. You know what my mother puts at the end of every letter? 'Those Viet Cong guys wouldn't dare kill a nice Jewish boy like you. . . .'

"Last week," he continued, "I had six helicopters drop out of the sky in three days. Two mechanical failures and four shot down. Only two pilots were laid up with bad backs. Ironically, I had just talked both of them into extending their combat tours because of their skill. When I visited them in the hospital before they were evacuated, they were arguing the merits of Hawaii versus Tokyo for the swingin'-dollies department."

I filed my reports, grabbed an hour's sleep, and showed up for a 2 A.M. briefing for still a third mission with the angry palm trees. Honour had decided to let me accompany the armed-helicopter group on a night mission.

General W. C. Westmoreland, commander of the US Military Assistance Command Vietnam (known as MACV and pronounced MacVee), was concerned about the mobility of the Viet Cong along the 2,100 miles of serpentine rivers and canals that meander through the lush Mekong Delta south of Saigon. After dark they provide a favorite mode of transportation for the elusive sampans of the VC and their guerrilla barges carrying tons of vital VC war matériel. The Republic of Vietnam must approve any activity on the waterways at night, but the VC take their chances. Any unauthorized movement after dusk is assumed to be unfriendly and fair game for Operation Lightning Bug.

"It's sort of a Rube Goldberg contraption," explained Captain Bill Fraker, co-pilot of the craft I had been assigned to. "But a very effective one. We 'requisitioned' the lights from other aircraft. They pick up any canal movements, and the gunships immediately zero in for the kill. It's always a sporty proposition because thirty caliber and fifty caliber machine guns are mounted on the VC sampans. The Lightning Bug makes a juicy target, so we vary its altitude from mission to mission. The glare makes it difficult for the Charlies to calculate the distance."

One of the most important items of discussion at night strike briefings is H & I fires, the harassment and interdiction the friendlies or ARVN may be carrying out at the same time. Operations usually knows the ARVN plans and informs the chopper pilots on Operation Lightning Bug to stay out of such areas. Equally important is the location of any friendly patrols or river boats.

Captain Glenn Smith conducted the briefing.

"We will leave here with rotating beacons. I will fly at five hundred feet in ship thirty-six. The gunship, thirty-four, will be at seven hundred to a thousand. ARVN-FM forty-five point three frequency tonight is Ghost Dance Control."

After more instructions about rolling in on the target, we picked up our helmets and other gear and headed for the helipad.

Honour walked with me to the chopper and checked my seat belt.

"I think I should warn you. These are our diciest missions. It's your decision, but you know, the boys don't always come back."

I realized he was too professional a fighting man to dramatize unnecessarily, but I didn't see why he had to say it out loud.

"About the last thing I think of is growing old."

"Well, nothing can be more sudden, vicious, or lethal than night fighting. I think some of you correspondents see more action than the troops. We take time off now and then after several missions."

The three choppers cranked up to take off for Duc Hoa, where there nearly always is pay dirt. Just before liftoff, SLAR (Side Looking Airborne Radar) reported illegal traffic in the area, two good returns or big blips on his scope, moving northwest north of the horseshoe.

En route we maintained fifteen hundred feet. As we approached Duc Hoa, Smith let down to the deck. The other craft stayed at altitude a mile behind. We were over land but proceeded upriver when the Lightning Bug, with its cluster of seven aircraft-landing lights strong enough to light up a supermarket opening and mounted on a maneuverable pod, exposed two motor launches slithering along the jungle stream. Each pulled two sampans.

On the prow of the first stood an old woman who looked like everybody's Chinese grandmother. When the light hit her she lifted a BAR bigger than she was and squeezed off a few rounds before Smith released four 2.75 Willie Peter rockets. Then Fraker fired the 40 millimeter.

The old woman reminded me of the Russian communist I had interviewed in Moscow, Mme. Ovsyannikova, editor-in-chief of *Soviet Woman* magazine, a fifty-six-year-old grandmother who had served four years in the tank and infantry divisions of WW II. When I asked her how many people she had killed, she lowered her head shyly. "I am an excellent shot."

Smith called the Lightship. "We've got some big ones."

"Roger. I have you in sight."

Smith slipped in behind the Lightning Bug and its powerful airborne searchlights, which was at six hundred feet, picking up the launches just as they tried to pull off the main river into the mouth of the creek to take cover in the clusters of water lilies and reeds. They were out of sight behind the overhanging tree branches when Smith came around again. This time he lined up on the creek at three hundred feet and fired twenty Willie Peters at the point where the creek and the river intersected. A huge secondary explosion blossomed among the trees. As the launch's fuel tank exploded, Smith pulled off and the other copter came in. "It's all yours," he said. "Just drive around and shoot the same area."

"Roger. I have the fire in sight. I'll be in position."

Immediately the second copter started a right-hand orbit around the target at five hundred feet. The Bug and Smith moved off outside its circle to set up a pattern which would keep it and the target in sight. This gunship was equipped with 50-caliber machine guns firing incendiary and tracer bullets.

Smith broadcast to its gunner. "You're on target. Let's go."

The tracers ricocheted higher than the helicopter and out of sight into low clouds. After fifteen seconds of firing, a series of five explosions illuminated the area and left no doubt that the sampan's cargo was ammunition. Smith radioed the 50 ship.

"Well, Fox Mike Delta. We've blown 'em up," probably more suitable for the ears of a woman correspondent than, "Fuck Me Dead. We zapped 'em."

"Roger. Shall we keep shooting?"

Before Smith and Fraker could answer, the Lightning Bug broadcast: "If both of you aren't needed over there, we've just received information that a village of Viet Cong are having a big celebration. They did a lot of damage to a Special Forces camp and now they're throwing a victory ball."

"Well, by God," Fraker answered, "we'll just go over there and furnish some fireworks for that little jamboree." These guys didn't know when to quit. A minute ago we'd been on our way *home*. I sat between the door gunners and hated being so scared.

The clatter and roar was deafening. Riding high in the air with bombers or fighter pilots seems remote and impersonal. Search patrols with the infantry can turn out to be a walk in the woods. But this was petrifyingly real and the helicopters so much more vulnerable than I'd ever understood before. I could have reached out and touched the armament and at first I wasn't sure whether the tracer bullets were ours going out or the Viet Cong's coming in.

The Charlies can be disciplined enough to withhold ground fire in order to conceal their position from air attack. Not tonight. They returned our fire instantly. Our crew chief fired while the right-door gunner reloaded. Then a bluish light changed the night into day for miles around. The explosion illuminated the entire countryside.

"Man, we're getting it from everywhere now," broadcast the lightship. The Bug and the 50 concentrated on the target while Smith returned to the creek and our gunner fired his sixty rounds of 40-millimeter.

Whatever the gunners on our chopper had hit must have been an important ammo dump. It burned with such intensity that we could still see it half the way back to Tan Son Nhut.

Expecting to be back at the base within minutes, I began to regain my composure. Then, another revision of plans—this time by instructions coming in from Ghost Dance Control: change our course and go to an isolated outpost to evacuate a wounded ARVN.

We put down on an unlighted pasture. The headlights of an automobile flicked on just long enough for the ARVN to be lifted aboard by corpsmen. The only conversation I heard was: "Get the litter back as soon as you can. We need it."

The ARVN was in civilian clothes. Dark as it was, I could see that he kept drawing up his good leg. I reached down to touch his knee to see if it was cold. As soon as my hand touched him, he grabbed my wrist in a wet, icy grip and held on for dear life during the rest of the journey.

When Smith put us down gently at a quiet corner of Tan Son Nhut, in the area where we were supposed to have rendezvoused with the ambulance we'd radioed for, it hadn't arrived yet. We had intended to exchange the litter still needed elsewhere for an on-the-spot stretcher. No stretcher. No ambulance. Our crew chief and gunner laid the boy down on the tarmac and started back for the chopper. Smith's schedule called for him to debrief quickly back at 145th Headquarters, refuel, rearm, and go on another strike tonight. He couldn't wait for the medics.

Fraker climbed off.

"You go on. I'm staying here with him."

As the chopper lifted off, the two figures on the ground grew smaller and smaller—the helicopter jock from Little Rock keeping vigil over a fellow soldier, a Vietnamese peasant.

Two

THE WEIRDNESS

SWALLOWS YOU AT ONCE

It was sometimes difficult to remember what New York was like, how my apartment looked, or to visualize matrons at the Colony around the corner, complaining about the color of the lemon in their martinis. I had been in Vietnam for two months. And it was about six years to the day since Elmer Roessner had sent me out on my first newspaper assignment, Moscow.

This go-around was for Mutual, the largest broadcasting system in the world. Mutual was the first network to send a woman to cover the Vietnamese war. Also, Sid Goldberg, editor in chief of North American Newspaper Alliance (NANA), had asked me to file for them. A foreign assignment is about the best thing that can happen to a correspondent, but nothing will stunt your growth quicker than simultaneously trying to shoot pictures, tape shows, file at the Telex, and broadcast to boot.

Throughout those six intervening years I had been on two assignments of several months each in the bloody anarchy of the Congo, covered the shelling of Quemoy, had a return trip to the Kremlin, and attended the incipient revolution in Haiti. In the palace at Port au Prince I managed a private audience with the President, "Papa Doc" Duvalier during which I asked to see the "beauty parlor" (torture chamber) and his voodoo altar. That annoyed him greatly.

I had also been at the Aswan Dam celebration when President Nasser played host to Khrushchev, the little man of preposterous energy who exhausted his bear-shouldered bodyguards as he tore around at top clip patting his medium paunch as if to reassure himself that it was still there.

All over Saigon I kept running into reporters I'd last seen in places like Pugwash, Litwit, Slopsybob, Banana, Swat, Coquihatville, Hofuf, or Ferkin. Much to my embarrassment, the *Washington Evening Star*'s Richard Critchfield reminded me of the time in Rawalpindi when I had committed the gaffe of belting a local gendarme. It was during the visit Red Chinese Premier Chou En-lai and Foreign Minister Chen Yi made to Pakistan, and I had traveled for two days and three nights to get there. My arm was still flaming from my recent immunization shots, so I kept telling the guards I'd stand where they indicated, but please not to touch me. When this five-cent Firpo grabbed me from behind and happened to pinch my cholera shot, by reflex action I whirled and clipped him with a right cross that Billy Conn had spent an hour teaching me at a party one night after the Sugar Ray Robinson—Randy Turpin fight.

"My God," said a colleague, "women are barely out of purdah over here. You've disgraced the guy in public."

I was staying with the ranking American diplomat and his wife. He was on the horn most of the night explaining the incident. Luckily he sided with me. Not like one Pakistani-employed Englishman who worked in public relations, looked like a disgraced British colonel, and kept repeating, "But it simply isn't *done!*"

Getting harpooned to head off outrageous and exotic plagues like cholera, smallpox, yellow fever, typhus, paratyphoid, and bubonic plague, besides being stabbed with gamma globulin to offset hepatitis, is still part of the preparation for most overseas assignments. In the case of Vietnam it is also necessary to travel to Washington if you want a visa for longer than seven days.

I spent the last day in New York with my niece, Lindy, a nature girl whose idea of a nice place to live would be the eighth floor of Abercrombie and Fitch. She didn't have to read Thoreau to discover it's more satisfying to step to your own beat. And that to do so frees one from fear. We walk a lot for exercise but it was Lindy who brought home the manual of Royal Canadian Air Force exercises as a hint for me to keep in shape for the more rugged assignments.

Sometimes I think she figures my opportunities to watch history in the making are a cross between an absorbing nightmare and a top-ho vacation. My one regret is that I can't take her along on these trips. She's been with me since infancy and is a very entertaining companion, possessing wit and an infallible ear for false notes.

At three-thirty we strolled back from the Central Park Zoo to the apartment, collected my cameras, tape recorder, and other gear. Going down in the elevator, Lindy said, "Maybe the Marines will want to dance. Do you know how to do the Frug and the Watusi?" There in the lift I got a one-minute checkout in the shadow boxing that passes for today's dancing.

"I want you to give my best regards to every single Marine you meet," said Lindy. "Please?"

It has been her *idée fixe* since she was a little girl that the Leathernecks were the elite, supermen, God's greatest invention, a race apart. I never knew where the idea originated, but she has been carrying on about them since she was two.

At the weighing-in counter at Kennedy International Airport I busily engaged in the old dodge of outwitting the excess-baggage hawks. I had packed the heavy objects—traveling iron, dictionaries, bottles—in what I refer to as my shoulder purse. It requires a certain amount of savoir-faire and skill to hoist it off the floor and toss it casually over your shoulder without having your feet fly out from under you, arousing suspicion. As I airily tried it the first time, my arm almost came out of the socket.

The rather practical Lindy called out in a clear voice, "Will somebody please help my aunt with her pocketbook?"

By the time Pan American landed us in Honolulu I was surfeited with food. When the hostesses learned I was on my way to a war, they brought me three steaks after I'd gorged on caviar and polished off more than my share of champagne. The wine would help me sleep, for I was determined to arrive rested in Saigon. Two pillows under my ear and a blanket up to my chin, I was about to doze off when I noticed the couple directly in front of me. The man was dignified and looked familiar. Then I recognized his wife, the former Haru Matsukata, granddaughter of a distinguished Japanese prime minister in the 1880s. I would forgo the nap. Here was a chance to interview the single most influential architect of our policy toward Japan in recent years, US Ambassador to Japan Edwin O. Reischauer.

He had just left Pacific Commander in Chief, Admiral Ulysses S. Grant Sharp, and a top-level policy meeting in Honolulu, where those present sounded like a Burke's *Peerage* of the military and included Chairman of the Joint Chiefs of Staff General Earle G. Wheeler and General William C. Westmoreland.

The Ambassador and I sat all nicely pressurized at 35,000 feet. I opened my notebook to a clean page, and persuaded the Pan Am flight engineer to run my new tape recorder for the interview.

"I stress to the Japanese people the advantages of a 'partnership' with America," he said. "That we should agree on fundamental objectives, yet maintain independent views and judgments. It is impossible for an advanced country to be neutralist. The Japanese must stand up to be counted in world councils and work for peace, not passively wait for it."

He says classical Marxism is our enemy and he attacks it with such finesse that the word is never mentioned. Because of his knowledge of their language, the Japanese listen respectfully when he speaks.

With the time differential in our favor, Pan Am had the interview in Mutual's hands in twelve hours.

In Hong Kong, the most modern and affluent city on the mainland of Asia, I could only make connections with Air Vietnam by laying over two nights. Hong Kong's four million are perched on the edge of Communist China. Hong Kong's economy is so successful that Red China's trade with this British colony accounts for about two-fifths of its hard-currency earnings. Red China claims the treaty with England is unfair and will "be renegotiated in due course," possibly sooner than the thirty-three years yet to run.

This little plot of earth, traditionally a free port, is the capital of the most dynamic community of Asia, and the last testament to nineteenth-century capitalism. The Russian press refers to bustling Hong Kong as that "stinking urinal of capitalism." If the turbulence of current conflicts changes the picture, it certainly will mark the end of an era in every sense of the word.

Mike McCrary of the *Hong Kong American* and a reporter from the *South China Morning Post* dropped by to interview me.

The view from the Mandarin Hotel compares with Istanbul or Acapulco. Sitting in the Lookout Lounge, Walt Kelly, creator of Pogo, and I fielded questions from Hong Kong newspaper and radio reporters. He had just come from where I was going and the Pogo strip no doubt was reflecting his Vietnamese adventures. The Asian conflict was getting saturation coverage.

At Hong Kong's Kaitek Airport I sat on a coffee table, facing four young Marines on a bench. They were scheduled for the next military flight. I told them, "My niece will be delighted to hear that you Marines are the first men in uniform I've met." Right away they wanted to know what she looked like. As I started to answer, a tall captain rushed up to them. "That C-130 just went down. I don't know if they drove it into a mountain or dropped into the bay. There may be some survivors."

The four young Marines sat very still. Some of their buddies had been aboard a plane carrying American servicemen back to Da Nang after a week's R & R (rest and rehabilitation).

A hostess approached to say that I was the only passenger not aboard my Air Vietnam flight to Saigon. The Marines stood up and walked over to help me pick up my cameras and other gear. When they saw the typewriter they asked if I was a reporter, then said, "There sure is a lot of horse hockey in the papers about pickets and guys that don't think we belong over here."

"Millions don't picket," I said as we walked to the gate.

After a moment they called out, "We'd sure like to talk some more if you ever get to Da Nang."

"I'll be there."

The boys turned left and headed back for the terminal.

On the Hong Kong–Saigon leg of the journey there was the usual variety of nationals aboard. One garrulous American woman with interesting paunches under her eyes was lecturing her seat partner on the vagaries of US politics. She wanted him to know that certain weak-kneed senators in Washington no more represented the majority than did the weirdie-beardie sit-in specialists. She said her destination was Bangkok. "But I'd sure like to stop off in VEETnam and watch one of them Buddhas burn hisself."

A Spanish gentleman across the aisle asked me if I had known President Kennedy. Anyone who travels must have observed the incredible *Weltschmerz,* or world hurt, over his death. He muttered, "It was no accident. Those things cannot happen without the approval of someone very high up."

Aware that it is useless to argue with foreigners on that subject, I turned to the Oriental lady on my right.

"I am from Taipei and firmly behind President Chiang Kai-shek," she said. "Everything that communism stands for is loathsome to me. Yet I am Chinese, and when the Reds on the mainland make technological advances I cannot help being secretly pleased." Then she added, "Their successes please me because none of us can ever forget the signs the English used to put up at the better clubs and restaurants in our country—'No dogs or Chinese allowed.'"

The last hour on the plane I talked with a Marine pilot. He was fascinated by what had been done in Vietnam with the old reliable C-47, now called "Puff the Magic Dragon."

"Man," said the colonel, "when they made that one back in the thirties they really came up with an airplane."

He asked if I had a match and I fished out a packet from the Carlton Hotel in Kuwait. I hadn't worn my tropical jacket in months.

"You must do a lot of traveling," he said. Then, suspiciously, "You a reporter?"

"Yes."

"Some newsmen have been giving the Marines a real shafting. When I walked down the street in New York people stopped me to ask, 'Do you Marines really shoot old women and kids?' "

"Not all the press allow their prejudices to match their impressions."

He perked up a little. "But some of the accounts of the war are so inconsistent. I wonder if the reporters are covering the same scrap."

"Sometimes objective reporters turn into political zealots during a sticky war. If you think certain newsmen have been unfair, don't let it get you down. Ignore them. Marines have a psychological advantage because of past performance. Don't blow it."

The FASTEN YOUR SEAT BELTS sign came on.

"There's old Tan Son Nhut," said the colonel.

I looked down at Saigon's international airport, which not only handles stupefying amounts of commercial traffic, but is also a vast military base housing hundreds of warplanes and helicopters. One of the most chaotic in the world, with more traffic than San Francisco, this airport moves a million pounds of cargo daily. It is two-thirds surrounded by thickly populated suburbs of Saigon, all within easy mortar range of the runways. Fifteen thousand civilian employees meander around the base and security is a nightmarish headache. Terrorist bombings are always a threat for the complex of buildings which includes radar installations and barracks for US Air Force men as well as Vietnamese Air Force and other military personnel.

"I've heard encouraging reports about Prime Minister Nguyen Cao Ky," I ventured.

The colonel grinned. "You can say that again. At least flying men think he's a good troop. If anybody said anything against him in front of an American pilot, they'd probably get knocked flat."

We left the plane and were caught up in a swarm of humanity in a country that is a snarl of conflicting religions, cultures, tribal beliefs, and politics. Some families preparing to board outgoing aircraft carried turkeys, ducks, chickens, piglets. Most had plastic diapers tied around the fowls' rear ends as a sanitary precaution.

As a Navy bus drew up, a big American sergeant tugged his buddy's sleeve. "Come on, Crunch. Let's git on into town where they got cold beer and clean sheets."

Three Marines climbed in after them. "Let's stop by the PX. I need some lighter fluid and socks. Only thing they got left in Da Nang is hair spray and Kotex."

CBS commentator Charles Collingwood said hello and good-bye to me, his hitch in Saigon finished.

As I pulled up in front of the Caravelle Hotel, Paul Schutzer, a *Life* photographer, was just dismissing his driver. We had been on two overseas Eisenhower Presidential tours together, in the Middle East and South America. Paul greeted me as if continuing an interrupted conversation of an hour ago.

"Hey," he greeted me, "the first thing we gotta do is get you some Army gear. You're supposed to dress just like the troops or you'll get pinked in the patootie faster. Come on; Tim and I'll take you over to the black market."

We threw my bags into the room at the Caravelle first. I wanted to nail that down. Accommodations are the toughest thing to come by in Saigon, especially at the Caravelle, where most of the press is billeted. Then Tim Page, a British photographer, cranked up his Yellow Peril, an ancient jeep painted egg-yolk orange and looking somewhat like an illuminated bedpan, and we took off into Saigon's formidable traffic for the charcoal market, where, for cash on the barrelhead, you can purchase anything from a battle helmet to a carbine.

You need no identity card or introduction to do business in the dark, cavernous market; just someone to get you there, then you walk in and flash money. In any one of a dozen seven-feet-square hidey holes the customer can select dappled camouflage suits, regulation Army web belts, shoulder straps, canteens, waterproof ponchos, a hammock for sleeping in the jungle, heavy wool socks, and what we called "comboot bats," with a steel plate in the thick soles to prevent the sharpened bamboo sticks planted by the Viet Cong from piercing your feet.

Paul, the compulsive shopper, bought a complete set of everything he already had; Tim tried to explain to the proprietor what I needed. As the transactions progressed, the black marketeer tossed each purchase over to his tiny wife, hunkered in the corner. She deftly wrapped each item in a dirty newspaper, then secured the packages with knotty, second-hand twine.

The irony is that some of the gear is available *only* in the black market. The shopper pays in local currency—piasters, or p's, in soldier slang. I stuck my foot into three pairs of wool socks to see if that would make the oversize Charlie Chaplin boots fit any better.

Next came accreditation. The first step in collecting a packet of necessary cards and press passes is a trip to the Vietnamese press center. There endless information is recorded about your past, correct age (which confession I consider morbidly unfeminine), birth place, occupation, parents, employers, *and* intentions. You also surrender a few small passport-type photographs. Mine had been taken in a hurry about ten years before, and I looked like a wounded nun. The polite, handsome young Vietnamese studied them and me rather carefully, then told me to come back in a couple of days.

The next procedure is presenting your VN accreditation to two American sergeants, who put you on a press list and later issue you a PX card. Later, script, or toy money, is obtained at the base post offices. The idea is to discourage illegal money-changing. Later it was forbidden to have American green on your person.

Though I eventually was given a slip of paper permitting me to be on the streets after hours in the interests of a story, nearly everyone observes the curfew, which fluctuates, depending on current crises. Americans are told not to loiter at curbside, and windows are crisscrossed with tape against explosive repercussions. Army and Navy buses shuttle between American installations with strong steel mesh bolted over the windows to keep out grenades. Around the clock the VC hate, hunt, and harass Americans. They have poison hypodermic needles that can stab silently in a crowd. Cigarette lighters left on restaurant tables have been found with the wick set to ignite a high-explosive charge. And in suffocating heat Americans drive with the windows rolled shut; your clothes may look as if you'd showered without undressing, but better that than having your head blown off.

"It's all part of Saigonitis," people say. "You relax and then some friend gets zapped and you start being cautious again."

The terrorists, who on Christmas Eve bombed the Brink Hotel, where American soldiers live, have infiltrated Saigon in battalion strength and could paralyze the city if their commanders so wished. But this would probably bring on retaliation-clobbering of Hanoi from the air, and the VC care less about terrain as such than about winning over the people. Any significant destruction of Saigon's facilities and buildings could alienate citizens who otherwise might go along with them.

Nevertheless, the threat is always there, particularly when Charlie suffers serious reversals, and morale lessens among VC troops. Charlie feeds on headlines. Any sensational explosions within the city reap a bumper crop of propaganda for Hanoi; momentum is the life blood of any revolution. Also, such headlines increase VC or North Vietnam bargaining power at any eventual bargaining table. Saigon citizens often feel like fish on a chopping block.

The elevator was not functioning the night I dined at the Brink. We climbed endless stairs to reach the dining room and our route took us briefly out on a balcony at one of the higher floors. As we walked across, shouts greeted us from below. A cluster of Saigon children were in the courtyard cheering wildly at each soldier, as if just seeing an American was the most exciting event of their lives.

The day following the Lightning Bug mission, I flew with Lieutenant Colonel Don Page of Redlands, California, in his FAC spotter plane. He was looking for VC from the air and visiting Special Forces camps. Usually the first step in covering this war is to take a taxi to it. Cab drivers are not cleared to enter the military section of Tan Son Nhut, so I hopped out and waited to hitch a ride the rest of the way after showing my credentials to the Vietnamese sentries. I ended up in the section harboring helicopter groups. As I stood on the flight line talking with the chopper jocks, I noticed a man standing in front of a helicopter armed for takeoff. Without warning a rocket misfired and caught him in the neck and shoulder. Flesh torn away, vital arteries severed, he writhed on the ground. Within five minutes a doctor attended the man, crazed with pain but still conscious. He stitched, clamped, operated right there on the runway.

"I hope you reporters realize what the medical men are doing over here," said a soft-spoken, intense young man. "At Chu Lai they worked like men possessed—amputating, dressing wounds—the sweat pouring off them. Some just wore shorts. Only way you could tell they were doctors was the stethoscope hanging around their necks."

I met Colonel Page in the top-secret map and plotting room, where a centralized control system has been installed. The men in charge are in constant contact with every ground-operating location and every aircraft at all times. Their goal is constantly to cover the country with small flights of craft, awaiting only development of a target. They call it an air umbrella.

"In the majority of targets we've hit," said Page, "we've probably killed more Viet Cong than the ground forces. For the records, we have destroyed more VC than the ground forces by a three-to-five ratio. It has been apocryphal for years that you have to win a war on the ground. Our air power here has held a bigger gun to the heads of the people than the VC have. Orientals are realists if nothing else. They recognize our power and are coming over to us by the thousands. Given half a chance, Premier Nguyen Cao Ky will build a stabilized government. He is one-hundred-percent anticommunist and dedicated to reforming his country."

As I got into a flak vest, Page fastened his gun belt, and we climbed into the tiny, one-lung craft with me riding tandem.

"The American and Vietnamese air forces," said Page as he prepared to take off, "fly approximately four hundred overall sorties a day. In one twenty-four-hour period there were six hundred eighteen air strikes. We're going to double that soon." Page was Special Projects officer of the TAC center where the in-country war was run.

"The name of the game," he continued, "is to act quickly. To keep pace with the reversal in Viet Cong fortunes, we have to respond to more fleeting and small-type targets. We have to put bombs on any target in the country within ten minutes of the request. That's where the Forward Air Controller comes in. So many FAC flights occur, it's almost impossible to count them. There are forty-one operating bases."

When he motioned it was time to take off, I asked, "How do you spot the elusive Charlie from the air?"

I had checked and adjusted my headphones and mouthpiece so we could communicate and I could also listen in on his conversations with Tactical Air Control Center as well as with other airborne FAC pilots. "Can't the VC listen?" I asked.

"Sure, they can listen. They have the equipment and they try to jam radio communications between pilots, or mislead them. Some speak surprisingly good, natural-sounding English. Our methods of locating them are varied. For one thing, the South Vietnamese have no rhyme or reason about how they bury their dead—in rice paddies or fields, any which way and at odd angles. On the other hand, the Viet Cong are tidier. So we can usually tell if they are or have been in an area. After a battle they try to take their dead with them, even drag them off the battlefield with butchers' meat hooks. If VC leave bodies behind it means they're in real trouble."

After takeoff and once across the river, our ring of security ended. We could be fired upon by snipers at any time. Below, chopped-up roads were clearly visible—standard VC harassment. "The Charlies don't always stay in the jungles. They live in villages with the people, hiding behind women and children. The VC fortify an area, depart, but with every intention of returning. There are about ten thousand of these villages. If a village that should be full looks empty between three and six P.M., you can be sure VC are hiding there, as invisible to the eye as worms in an apple. Or if we see only women and children we know something is wrong, that a VC group is hiding. And when we fly low and the women and children do not look up, this also is not normal. They must have been so instructed by the Viet Cong."

Page pointed out more roads cut up by ditches or blocked by big trees placed there by the VC. Such obstacles do not hamper VC troop movements since they employ elephants or carabaos to transport their heavy equipment. But it makes roads impassable for American-Vietnamese tanks and trucks.

The radio static was like the sound of frying bacon as we flew over Zone D, the traditional Red stronghold. Their exceptionally well-concealed headquarters had not yet been located by the "friendlies." Zone D is fifty miles long and thirty miles wide, completely forested.

"Those who have been there," continued Page, "cannot remember how many turns they took in the jungle, but we'll find them one day. Prisoners report arms and supply shortages, bad health, and a loss of morale and momentum, vital to the success of their plans. When we do locate and bomb their headquarters it may well be a decisive factor in ending this grisly business."

As we approached Song Be Special Forces Camp, Vietnamese and livestock scattered, surrendering their promenade so Page could make a landing.

The highly trained and superbly disciplined men of the Special Forces at Song Be wear their Green Berets with jaunty pride.

"I feel sorry for the Charlies if they come here again," Major Jack Fatum of Columbus, Georgia, told me. He was in command of the B Detachment at the compound.

Song Be, literally "Little River," is the capital of Phuoc Long Province, which means "Happy Dragon." On May 11, 1965, one of the bigger actions involving Special Forces took place here. The VC penetrated the compound's defenses and threw satchel charges of explosives into the mess hall, killing three Americans and wounding thirteen. The fighting was fierce; there were hand-to-hand battles with knives.

Fatum showed me the defenses the base had since build up: 60- and 80-millimeter mortars, complex underground communications and defense posts, barbed wire. The jungle had been cleared in the surrounding area by the Montagnard tribesmen, or "people of the mountains," as the French called them. Powerful floodlights and stacks of ammunition had sent the morale of the men soaring.

On the wall of Fatum's office was a "measle" map. The areas were marked with colored pins—blue for secured, diagonal lines for undergoing security, green for cleared, black for destroyed or abandoned, plain square box for contested, and pink for VC-controlled.

I asked so many questions the Major said I sounded like his wife, Tina.

"She's always writing me full of suggestions. She wonders why we don't hang little bells in the trees all around, to alert us of approaching VC. She says I shouldn't play my tape recorder at night because I might not hear them sneaking up."

The other officers laughed but I could see how pleased they were that their women worried about them.

Ever since the bloody May 11 debacle, the Special Forces had expected the VC to strike again. Sentries slept in foxholes.

"We're ready for them this time," Major Tom Brogan of Leavenworth, Kansas, told me. He was senior adviser for the 9th Regiment, 5th Division.

The VC had also shot up the big refrigerator in the mess hall. The men now had it decorated with a Combat Infantry Badge and the Purple Heart.

"They'd better think twice about attacking us now," said a grinning Captain Jess Hodges of Camp Hill, Alabama. He pointed to a plaque on the wall. Printed in old-English type were the words:

YEA, THOUGH I WALK IN THE VALLEY OF DARKNESS, IN THE SHADOW OF DEATH, I SHALL FEAR NO EVIL. BECAUSE I AM THE MEANEST BASTARD IN THE VALLEY.

A Vietnamese soldier rushed up as we talked. Word had just come in from B-2, a normally reliable source, that the VC had been sighted on a trail in the area with a hundred elephants transporting heavy North Vietnamese equipment. Colonel Page and I ran for the FAC plane. The report had come from a Montagnard, or "Yard" as the soldiers call them.

"They can't count beyond ten," said Page, "so the hundred is probably an exaggeration. But if they're in the area we'll find 'em. Somebody's going to have elephant meat tonight."

As we flew over the jungle, the FAC received a hit in the right wing. Page immediately dived like an arrow to locate the attackers. I couldn't help thinking the natural thing was to run, but that is not the FAC's function. Page curled out of the dive, then flew the plane on its side to present the smallest target for ground fire. My face rested against the window. I could take a nap if I weren't so scared, I thought. I was sopping sweat wet. Page went in to fire smoke rockets, made contact with some Navy F-8 fighters, advised them of the location, and then we got the hell out of there.

When I got back into town I stopped by Minh's, where one of his tailors, a little Chinese fellow, was stitching up a Churchill-type jump suit for me. Wong was the only male in the place permitted to conduct fittings for women.

"No lights today, missy," he announced.

There were a few candles spaced about the tiny store. In the dark dressing room I climbed out of my battle gear and into the basted coveralls. Into a little pile in the corner went money, credentials, and the bubble gum I carry for kids. Then I stuck my head through the curtains to signify that I was ready. I needed the outfit too much to postpone the fitting.

Wong toddled in holding a candle. He marked, pinned, and fussed with one hand, holding the dripping light with the other until I took it from him. By squinting my eyes I could dimly see my silhouette in the mirror.

"Now, as long as you have these darts coming in under the shoulders, Wong, you might as well have them end at the proper places." I indicated strategic points. "Give me some pins, I'll do it."

"S-s-s-s-s-E-E-E-E-WWWWWWW." Wong sucked in his breath and shook his head violently. "No, missy."

Wong kept sucking in his breath, shaking his head, and crawling around on the floor until he found what he was looking for. A piece of chalk. He came up for air and indicated I could mark my own chest. Pins? Never!

I tried sitting down. The suit nearly cut me in half.

"Wong," I laughed. "You've got a lot to learn about women's crotches."

Back in my room at the Caravelle, I hung up Major Fatum's green beret which he had given to me, with the request: "Wear it only when you're with us." Then I typed and taped by a hard-to-come-by kerosene lamp. The dispatches had to go out first thing in the morning. One never knew when there might be a power failure, so everybody kept a supply of candles or a lamp.

Some of the contrasts in Saigon bordered on bizarre idiocy. Australians, Koreans, Filipinos, New Zealanders, Vietnamese, and Americans grimly engaged in war, while others carried on as if oblivious to the deadly serious turmoil. Dressed in fatigues, bush hat, and shoulder harness supporting cameras, canteens, and tape recorder, I frequently shared the hotel elevator with a chic French woman in tennis shorts, with rackets nestled cozily in the crook of her arm. She always whistled softly as if anticipating the sets to come on the neat courts at the Cercle Sportif.

There were precious few nights and days off for the fighting men. Reporters sometimes ran into trouble when they least expected it.

That morning, as taxis and buses sailed along the highway to Bien Hoa, a Pulitzer prize-winning Vietnamese television cameraman got unlucky. Seven VC opened fire on his automobile and blew out the tires. He put the accelerator to the floor and came limping into Bien Hoa on shredded rubber and clattering rims.

There was a knock on the door.

"Come in," I called. When they are in their rooms, newsmen leave their keys in the lock on the outside, a custom which seems to have originated at Shepheard's Hotel in Cairo during WW II.

It was Molly Wells from across the hall. "How about borrowing that lamp if you go out, girl?"

"You bet. I have to go to the PX in a little while. I'll drop it by your room. You look fresh and perky. How do you do it with no rest and all the excitement?"

"I attribute what looks I have to sleeping with the windows open, eating leafy vegetables, and trick lighting."

"I'll be over as soon as I've finished, Mother."

Molly was a fashion consultant who selected fabrics for New York designers. The past few months she had been in the Far East, and operating out of Saigon.

She had intended to keep herself unattached, but then Colonel Jim Hall, commanding officer of a unit so secret it was a feat just remembering what all the initials stood for, courted Molly steadily and stubbornly.

One day she was startled to return to her room and find a G-2 type waiting there for her.

"Don't be alarmed," he began, showing his credentials. "You're a friend of Colonel Jim Hall's, I believe."

"Well," she said, "he's got more shoes under the bed than I have, if that's what you mean."

Shyly Jim had moved in on her, carrying, in his briefcase, one shoe at a time. And his uniforms, as well as some civilian suits, were hanging in her closet.

"I don't want to frighten you, but you may or may not be aware of the extreme sensitivity of his highly classified work here. The VC have an exorbitant price on his head."

He produced a snub-nosed pistol. "Keep this in your purse for emergencies. That's tantamount to an order."

He excused himself and left Molly standing there with the gat in her hand, the first she had ever handled.

When I stopped by with the lamp, Jim and Molly had just opened a can of smoked oysters and a bottle of Dom Perignon.

"Traffic's a little light in here tonight," I observed.

"Have some champagne," Molly answered. "What have you been writing about? The good guys or the nasties?"

"I'm doing a background piece. I'm fed up with reading so many items about 'The Girls on Tu Do Street.' It sounds as if it were one big raucous debauch—that when the bars close they belch forth battalions of snockered GIs."

"The girls here are lovely," Molly added. "Those high-collared tunics with the long paneled skirts split to the hip, the high-heeled sandals *tak-tak-tak*ing along the sidewalk. When their tunics are secured to their bicycle fenders—and they *all* ride bicycles—they look like rare, beautiful butterflies sailing down the avenues.

"Instead of punching up the action on Tu Do Street, why doesn't the press bear down on VC atrocities?" Molly asked. "They fight a pretty depraved, sneaky kind of war."

"Agreed," I said. "But photographs are hard to come by. I'm working on a story now about documented VC terror tactics. Young men who refuse to join the VC ranks are emasculated, their genitals stuffed into their mouths. Small children with plastic bombs under their rags are sent out to beg from American soldiers. To buy protection for members of her family, one young Vietnamese woman was ordered out, with a hand grenade concealed in her coiffure, to flirt with a group of Yanks. The VC are masters at the art of imposing iron discipline through unlimited terror."

"The treatment of prisoners is one of the most controversial aspects of the war," Jim said. "On both sides."

"The VC have no intention of allowing us to publicize how many prisoners they have tortured or murdered."

"The worst pictures I've seen," Jim said, "were of twelve-year-old recruits chained to their machine guns by the retreating VC. I wonder how many people realize what a frightening capacity for violence the Viet Cong have? A man in the Special Forces was captured the other day. The VC removed his Green Beret, spat on it, then jumped up and down in glee as they poured molten lead into his ear. He had gone to the village to help the people help themselves. The village chieftain was friendly to him, so the VC decapitated the chieftain and threw his head in the latrine. Yet when US Marines level a place held by the guerrillas, some reporters send out stories picturing the Marines as 'heartless bullies.'"

"My God," Molly said. "You get a feeling this thing over here is swinging back to all the barbarities of the ancient world. A few weeks ago a group of Green Berets went into the village of Dak To, forty-two miles northwest of Pleiku. The villagers welcomed them. One day, during the absence of the men of the hamlet, the Viet Cong sneaked in, grabbed all the children, and cut off their hands. The atrocity was compounded because of the Buddhist belief that if your body is not intact—if there is an ear, finger, or limb missing—you cannot enter heaven when you die."

Almost daily a combat reporter takes the measure of men putting their lives on the line. I have always considered the way a man wins or loses at poker or how he handles his liquor as rather infallible yardsticks. But watching a man face torment and danger can furnish an even more probing estimate of his manhood.

In Vietnam my first combat air mission was in a Douglas A-1E piston-engine fighter, where cockpit temperatures can reach 140° F. plus. The Skyraiders are wedged into available places all over Bien Hoa Air Base, wings folded as a reminder that the A-1E was designed as a Navy carrier plane.

The VC despise this stubby, tough, counterinsurgency fighter bomber which carries its own weight in ordnance, remains over targets for extended periods, and is capable of a greater and more varied bomb load than the B-17 Flying Fortresses of WW II. It can drop napalm (jellied gasoline), phosphorus bombs, 500-pound demolition and 260-pound fragmentation bombs, and a 500-pound Daisy Cutter with an attachment to detonate the bomb before it buries itself in the soft soil of the Delta.

Captain Donald E. "Cactus" Jones flew for the 602nd Air Commando Squadron, a unit stationed at Bien Hoa, the huge bastion sixteen air miles northeast of Saigon. It has the longest runway in Vietnam and is a training center for the Vietnamese Air Force (VNAF). Four Vietnamese Ranger Battalions patrol the area, while the Royal Australian Regiment guards the perimeter. The mission of the 602nd is to train Vietnamese pilots in counterinsurgency operations and augment the strike capability of the Vietnamese Air Force.

"The Vietnamese make cracking good pilots," Jones told me. "The main problems are language and their size. Some of them are so small they have to sit on cushions in order to reach the rudder pedals of the American-built Skyraider."

Other pilots on our mission were Cactus' commanding officer, Major Oscar Mauterer from Gillette, New Jersey; Captain William H. Kyle, Medfield, Massachusetts, and Captain George Pupich.

After a quick bite in the mess hall, we started for the flight line, where Captain Michael Holsinger, the information officer, introduced me to Major Charles C. "Vas" Vasiliadis.

The Major was from Huntington, New York, and a guy who must have thought he was literally a bird and sent over to win the war all by himself. Vas had 420 missions racked up, more than any other fighter pilot at the base, and was putting in for transfer to F-105s. A handsome, fantastic man, he wrote daily to his wife, Joan, and to his sons Douglas, four, and Mark, one and a half, a little ankle-biter whom he had never seen. If Ho Chi Minh is counting on men like Vas to get tired and discouraged, he is making a fundamental mistake.

The 602nd averages 750 combat sorties per month. A-1Es are credited with destroying VC sampans, bridges, dams, foxholes, bunkers, gun emplacements. Normal targets are VC structures, troop concentrations, supply areas, land and water vehicles, and pack animals. Their anti-personnel weapons spew out buckshot-size pellets for hundreds of yards around. "That Cactus usually hits what he's shooting at," said Major Mauterer.

Maximum gross takeoff weight is 25,000 pounds and the variety of ordnance carried includes, besides the 500- and 260-, 750- and 100-pound general-purpose bombs, 120-pound fragmentation clusters. The aircraft is an excellent and accurate dive-bombing platform, can operate in poor weather, and with its armor in vital places, is capable of absorbing a lot of punishment from the ground. Cruising speed is 180 miles an hour, and up to 350 miles per hour is possible in dives.

"It's a real stalwart bird," said Cactus, "though some of the guys call it a dump truck with wings." Jones is from El Paso and as he sat checking last-minute details before the mission, he drawled, "Now this is the gadget that unlocks your harness and your seat belt. If we get hit and I instruct you to bail out, you release it first. Then push that hydraulic button to open your side of the canopy, stand up and dive for the right flap."

My parachute had been placed in the seat earlier. I would sit on it. All I could think of was the tiny opening I'd wiggled through without a parachute. How did you dive out in a hurry with a cumbersome chute on your back?

"A certain anxiety will see you through," Jones answered. "The main thing to remember is to dive straight back at the wing flap. You won't hit it, but aiming for it will cause you to miss the tail."

As the four Skyraiders with full bomb loads prepared for takeoff, Jones hit the starter button, the straight stack Wright engine started barking, and we taxied onto the runway. Minutes later, bristling with bombs and ammo, we sliced through low-hanging cloud cover, curved into the sky to 5,000 feet and headed for our rendezvous with the O-1E, or FAC plane. Their pilots work closely with ground forces, and literally look under trees and bushes to ferret out Viet Cong or structures hidden from the higher, faster strike planes. Because of the low clouds, we let down again to 1,500 feet for better visibility. Strike pilots, cruising at 180 miles an hour, do not like to fly missions at this altitude because of ever-present sniper fire.

An hour out of Bien Hoa we made radio contact with the FAC and proceeded to the prearranged target—but we never got there. As I sat tightly hunched, completely harnessed in straps and securely locked gear, helmet and headphones in place, I heard the FAC pilot call: "I've been hit."

He had. Four times. Often the VC are reluctant to fire first and reveal their position, especially to the Bird Dog FAC. But this time, for whatever reasons, perhaps an excitable new recruit, they had gone after the FAC, the eyes and ears of the strike aircraft.

FAC radioed the Skyraiders to call a divert to the new target and abandon the original one. The brave little craft dived and marked the origin of the ground fire with his smoke rockets, then directed the A-1Es in for the kill. "Hit one hundred meters south of my smoke," he broadcast.

The Skyraiders, one by one, climbed, peeled off, and using a variety of angles to confuse the Charlies, went in for their first bomb run. "That ought to keep their heads down," Jones said.

During the briefing I had told him that I was once married to a pilot and had flown a couple million miles. I hadn't bothered to mention that I had never been up on a dive-bombing mission.

He roared toward earth at almost four hundred miles an hour, released his bombs, and climbed skyward in a sickening, gut-pulling reversal of direction. The gravity pull, or Gs, is tremendous for an uninitiated passenger. My body weight was comparable to several hundred pounds. I could scarcely lift my camera.

"Please, God, don't let me black out or get sick or be any bother to this busy man on my left," I prayed.

Again and again we climbed, then dived. The 20-millimeter cannon shells rattled my teeth as they blazed from the four 20 mike mike wing guns and we strafed at what Jones later told me was treetop level, sometimes lower. We were "cuttin' 'em off at the pass," as the pilots say.

Jones put his plane through a dizzying variety of maneuvers to reduce the chances of our being hit by the tracer fire or bullets from the automatic weapons spitting at us from below. With enormous relief we observed the FAC, hit in both wings, fly safely away from the immediate danger zone.

I stole a glance at Jones. The Gs had distorted the flesh on his face, now the color of putty. I didn't know it until later, but blood vessels had burst below my right eye and the dark-red patch lasted for a few days.

"If I'd known it was your first combat flight in an A1-E, I'd have flown a little more conventionally," Jones said later as he explained how to beat the G forces. Just before the plane commences the climb after a dive, you relax your throat but tense the rest of your body in a simulated grunt, which helps to prevent too much blood from rushing downward and away from your brain.

During the preflight instruction, or briefing, there had been a certain amount of understandable tension or seriousness. The debriefing session, with mission completed, was far more relaxed. Horseplay and idle banter reappeared. Everyone was glad to be back alive, experiencing the sheer joy of survival. Slit-eyed from lack of sleep before the mission, I had become one startled, wide-awake combat reporter as soon as we were in action. Now normalcy slowly oozed back because of the contagious camaraderie in the map room.

Kidded Jones, "She nearly talked my ear off on the way to the target. I never heard a peep out of her on the way back."

I retorted that I was afraid he was going to make one more damned dive. I wondered if I'd ever—for I fully intended to go up again—get used to the god-awful feeling of being cooped up in so small a space with all that heavy gear. I literally had not been able to move an inch in any direction. I remembered that my head itched, straps dug into my collarbone, my fanny ached, the noise was unrelenting, my back muscles burned, and I was petrified that Jones would guess my stomach was queasy.

"By the way," I asked, "what was it you were saying just before that first pass over the target?"

"I said," Jones replied, "that if we get hit, and I tell you to bail out, don't say 'What?' or you'll be up here talkin' to yourself."

Three

BIEN HOA

(PEACEFUL SHORE)

Covered with mud and weariness, thirty men of the Big Red One slogged through the baking heat and slime back to the base. Hoping to flush out Viet Cong troops and locate major arms and weapons caches in the sweep, they had searched in vain. There had been no contact during the day-long operation.

Some shucked their uniforms, crusty with sweat and dirt, and showered and shaved before sacking out; others merely shed their heavy field packs, jungle knives, and M-16 automatic rifles, and collapsed onto their pads in the row upon row of huts and tents. They were too exhausted to think of cleanliness, but not too tired to clean and oil their M-16s, formerly known as the Armalite. A weapon more coveted than a steak or a woman, it can best the rapid fire of the lightweight rifles used by the VC and North Vietnamese in close jungle fighting. It was the aim of the commander of the US forces in Vietnam, General William C. "Westy" Westmoreland, that every soldier there be armed with one.

The tall general with the piercing black eyes was a superb commander and usually got what he wanted. He was a brilliant field general and was fast becoming a legend to his troops by showing up in person at every trouble spot. He took his chances along with his men. The closest shave was at besieged Ashau when ground fire riddled his Caribou on takeoff. Four men around him were wounded. The best rifle in the world was none too good for his soldiers. The M-16 could fire wide open at 750 rounds a minute and puncture both sides of a helmet at 600 yards. If its deadly shell hit a man in the ankle the explosion would shatter his whole leg and the shock would likely kill him.

The snack bar was filled with airmen, Seabees, Marines, and other troops. I pushed my Australian Go to Hell bush hat off the back of my head and let it hang by the chin strap.

"My God, a round-eye," gasped a Seabee.

I climbed onto a vacant stool and ordered a jumbo-size milk-shake and two hamburgers. Beside me sat Pfc Paddy Newman. Obviously he didn't need to shave yet, though he was trying to swagger a bit to appear older. He was smoking a cigar so big it might have been smoking him. He was uncommonly handsome, with great brown eyes, rosy cheeks, and a deep tan.

"Do you have a special girl back home you write to?" I asked.

"Oh, I write to a lot."

"How many is that?" I asked, pulling out my notebook.

"Well, three in Spokane, and one in Okinawa. Gee, lady, are you interviewing me? I've never been interviewed before."

"What outfit you with?"

"Second battalion, Ninth Marines. I've wanted to be a Marine ever since I can remember. A real professional Marine."

"How did you get in so young?"

"Well, it's something my parents knew I wanted. They signed the papers because they knew if they didn't I'd go later. It would only be a year wasted."

"What are you doing in Bien Hoa?"

"I'm going to Bangkok tomorrow for some R & R."

"That's a great place for it."

Now that his dream had come true and he actually was in a Marine uniform fighting a deadly serious war half a world from home, did he feel fulfilled and content?

"No, ma'am," Paddy replied. "It's not as rugged as I expected. So I'm going home when my tour is up. I'm going back to school to study automotive engineering at some Eastern college if I can get in."

I had ordered one more hamburger than I could handle.

"Here, Paddy, you're a growing boy."

"OK, ma'am, thanks a lot," he said and immediately went to work on it. I noticed he had begun a letter to his folks.

DEAR MOM AND DAD,
  Tomorrow I'm going to Bangkok for some rest and relaxation. I'll be there a week. The guys say it's a swell place to shop. Would you like some jewelry, Mom? . . .

I stopped at the door to look back. A real professional Marine? Dear God, a boy of seventeen is professional at nothing.

A tall officer from the Combat Information Office stopped me at the door. "Miss, we've received information that there may be trouble here tonight. All the reporters have been alerted. Instructions are that no matter what happens, you're to remain in your room. Under *no* circumstances are you to come out in the open. Understood?"

"Understood," I replied. If a baby-faced Marine could handle his assignments, I couldn't have them thinking a mere woman would louse up the routine.

I went over to the flight line. Shafts of sunlight reflected off the glistening fuselages of four US Air Force B-57 jets, poised at the end of the runway for takeoff. Four other B-57 Canberras in their parking places on the ramp were ready to start engines. The crews were completing their preflight, securing parachutes, locking shoulder harnesses, fastening helmet chin straps, checking myriad dials, knobs, and buttons on instrument panels, and adjusting their oxygen masks.

I waved to Lars Hansen. String-bean tall, with improbably blue eyes, Lars looked like Gary Cooper, could drive a golf ball farther than Sammy Snead, swam like an otter, and drank his liquor like the Minnesota gentleman he was. His fiancée's picture was tucked in his wallet.

Lars had put in for a concentrated tour in order to get home sooner for his wedding. He had one day to go and like most short-timers, the tension showed in his face.

Lars was a charter Doom Pussy pilot, who had flown more than his share of night missions over North Vietnam, and was immensely popular with the 13th Bomb Squadron. Only men who flew up north after dark were entitled to wear the emblem on their left shoulder, an embroidered head of a big yellow cat with pointed ears and a black patch over her right eye.

The left eye glowed an evil green, and clenched in her jaws was a twin-engine aircraft. For the pilots of the 13th, CANBERRA NIGHT FIGHTERS was printed in white over the top of the emblem. In green letters around the border was emblazoned: TRONG MIENG CUA CON MEO CUA DINH MANG, which re-translated into English reads: "I have flown into the jaws of the cat of death."

American fliers simply say: "I have seen the Doom Pussy."

There were tall tales of the Puss of Doom scratching on the canopy of the night fliers' airplanes to be let in.

"When the radar-controlled searchlights lock on you, when technicolor is exploding all around you, and those red-hot tracer slugs are hosing your ass off—man, you've seen the Doom Pussy," say the troops who fly the treacherous black velvet skies. The Russian surface-to-air missiles (SAMs) are too often diabolically accurate.

The insignia of the 13th and the 8th, a sister squadron of B-57 Canberras, is the oldest of any unit on active duty. It is worn over the right breast pocket of flight suits and depicts a skeleton named Oscar holding a bloody scythe with the inscription: THE DEVIL'S OWN GRIM REAPERS. The men like to refer to themselves as the Grimy Rapers. I walked over to talk to their CO.

"The DPs are hairy sorties," he said. "It isn't just the SAMs; the chances of being hit up north are always twenty times greater than over the South. You're almost guaranteed a hot time if you go north. B-57s are the A-1 of the jets. Twenty-four Canberra sorties are as good as fifty by fighters. They really do the damage. I've commanded both."

"Intelligence reports seem to verify that the Viet Cong share your opinion, Colonel," I replied. "Old Charlie harbors a special hatred for the Cranberries."

The eighth crew of the mission at this point developed mechanical problems and had to abort. Captain Sandy Cole, the only Negro flier in the outfit, and his navigator, Lieutenant Barney Lowe, saluted as they walked by toward squadron ops to report the malfunction of their Canberra.

"Cole is an expert and daring pilot, one of the deadliest on a strafing pass," the CO said. "He could drop a poached egg on a hamburger in the middle of a thunderstorm."

We walked down the flight line and talked of the rendezvous that the B-57s would have with the FAC, the little one-lunged, ninety-mile-an-hour aircraft whose mission it is to locate the enemy, fire his Willie Peter to pinpoint the target, and then call in the Big Boys by radio. The motorized butterflies were maddeningly tantalizing targets for the VC.

"No one over here is more respected than those guys," the CO continued. "Most of them are converted jet jockeys. The switch couldn't have been easy for them, but somebody has to locate the bad guys. Those FACs can tell if the grass is bent one way or another. One day they noticed that a former open space was forested, so they reported that guerrillas had moved trees to camouflage a supply dump. Air observation is playing a large role in this war."

We watched a Navy F-8 Crusader make an emergency landing. The pilot parked it next to the row of B-57s. All aircraft except the four at the end of the airstrip were parked wingtip to wingtip, with bombs pyramided behind the planes on the ramp. I looked at my notes as I walked over to a stack of sandbags, then sat down behind them to shade my camera and reload.

The strike forces' target that day was the VC entrenched along the Mekong Delta in South Vietnam. President Johnson had ordered suspension of air strikes over Ho Chi Minhland for a few days to determine whether wily Uncle Ho, communist leader of North Vietnam, might sidle up to the conference table in the interests of world peace.

Vaaaaaaaaaaa-rooooooooooommmmmmm!!!!

A mortar shell, lobbed from a Viet Cong patrol 500 meters away, lucked in with deadly, unexpected accuracy, detonated the two 750-pound bombs shackled under Lars Hansen's wing. The heads of Lars and his navigator, protruding above the canopy rail, were blown off.

Rubber fuel bladders in above-ground storage had been ripped apart. The JP-4 gushed to the lowest point through the drainage ditches and instantly ignited. The Navy F-8 pilot was blown to a liquid-fire death.

Like a string of grotesque Chinese holiday firecrackers, the detonation triggered a holocaust of 260-, 500-, and 750-pound bombs aboard the ten B-57s, fifteen A-1E Skyraiders, and the Navy F-8. A four-foot-deep outlined imprint was all that remained of Lars's aircraft. Men in the other planes were blasted to bits, as were maintenance personnel working around them. One hundred and three were severely wounded. Twenty-seven died.

A helicopter crew chief, waiting for his pilot to take off on a reconnaissance mission, had had elementary instruction in the intricacies of chopper flying. He jumped aboard and tried to lift the craft away from the inferno. He got eight feet into the air, only to plow into the next helicopter, like a drunken duck.

Sandy Cole was cut in half. Navigator Barney Lowe, walking two feet from Cole, took shrapnel across the face. It blew away the bridge of his nose. He dropped in a heap on the tarmac, his bloody face inches from the lower half of Cole's body. A sergeant threw him into the back of a truck and drove off. The line chief, a senior sergeant, was wounded six separate times as he crawled from the ramp.

Jimmy Washington, a giant-size B-57 crew chief, proved superhuman in the emergency. After the first explosion, the six-foot-five-inch Negro leaped and cleared two rolls of barbed wire. He looked back over his shoulder and saw a ground-crew man too short to hurdle the concertina. Washington ran back, reached over the rolls of barbed wire, and lifted his body to safety.

The remaining ground crews stampeded in Jimmy's direction and without hesitation he threw his big body over the barbed barricade.

"We climbed right up his gahdam back and over to safety," a dazed survivor said.

The men at the end of the runway, ready for takeoff, cut engines, abandoned aircraft, and took shelter in a nearby rice paddy.

"I considered takeoff," the flight leader said later, "but changed my mind when I saw debris flying through the air across the runway."

His decision saved all their lives.

It was quite a baptismal debut for Captain Danny Sudds, who was on his first mission.

"My God," he muttered in a strangled voice, "are they all like this? I didn't give a big rat's ass if the lead did take off. I wasn't *about* to with all that shit in the air."

"Love to you and Dad," wrote Paddy the Marine, before folding the letter his folks would never receive.

A J-65 engine, severed from an aircraft four hundred yards away, hurtled toward the snack bar and concluded Paddy's brief professional career in the dirt and the danger of an alien land, on the outskirts of Bien Hoa, "Peaceful Shore."

Cleaning up the base involved defusing scores of bombs. Many were equipped with special tamper-proof, delayed-action fuses, designed to go off twelve to 144 hours after being dropped in enemy territory. Explosive Ordnance Demolition teams, in a daring attempt at demolition, began defusing them by hand and also by shooting at them. The presence of live bombs scattered about the ramp delayed recovery of corpses. Except for the iron-nerved EOD, the area was a no man's land.

In a hootch, three battle-seasoned warriors, Reggie, Jake, and Crunch, slept through it all. They had put in two months' patrol in the steam-bath heat of the jungle and were due to go next morning to exotic old Hong Kong for some R & R—or A & A (Ass and Alcohol), as they put it. Long before the explosion they had launched into a little premature celebrating which soon developed into an epic debauch.

With the first round of drinks they began discussing a two-week-old article in a stateside newspaper about postpubescents strutting in front of the White House and demanding that Americans withdraw from Asia *at once*. The hoisted placards had announced:

WE REFUSE TO DIE FOR VIETNAM.

"What *would* those slobs die for?" bellowed Crunch, a leathery Texan whose handshake was a paralyzing grip that could bring most men to their knees. So completely homely he was handsome, he had great ears that stretched out like an alarmed elephant's.

Reggie, a member of the elite First Battalion of the Royal Australian Regiment, was a veteran of guerrilla-style war. He was a typical Aussie, all man to the marrow, who had seen action against the Japanese in the jungles of Borneo. After WW II he spent twelve years helping the British put down communist insurgency in Malaya. (And no one recognized Australian know-how better than the Viet Cong. A captured VC document contained the clear warning: "When engaging the Australians, watch your flanks with special care.")

Reggie had a well-developed thirst for hard liquor, was a bit creased around the eye sockets, and looked like a debauched Oxford don. He was astonished that a "bunch of nuts running around with silly signs" could receive such lavish national publicity in the States.

"Why don't those blokes just bug off? Or, come over here and picket the bloody Charlies?"

Jake, an Alvin York-type sharpshooter from the loblolly flatlands of Georgia, was as ugly as Crunch. His face looked like an accident of flowing lava. The more he drank, the madder he got, and the madder he got, the more he—like his two buddies—drank himself into a state of inoperative bliss.

All three were solid eccentrics. In their time, on their buccaneering ways and days, they had eaten fricasseed bullfrog, bush-rat pie, monkey brains, and hippopotamus sweetbreads. Today they were having a satisfying feast of formidable variety. Reggie had squirreled the groceries from God knew where.

Crunch shoveled from a tin of tongue with a dagger. Jake spooned pâté de foie gras with an ivory shoehorn and guzzled a pint of red eye as he cursed and railed, Army style.

Jake and Crunch fought with the US 173rd Airborne Brigade and had seen plenty of war, but they spent most of their off-duty hours with the "diggers" of the First Battalion. The primary mission of both outfits was to guard the Bien Hoa base, when they weren't out on battle maneuvers.

Jake and Crunch once again apologized to Reggie for the gaffe made by Senator Fulbright when he recently visited Australia and deeply offended the Australians.

Upon his arrival in Canberra aboard his special US DC-8 aircraft, Fulbright had been asked, "Do you have any views on Australia's commitment in Vietnam?"

Replied the chairman of the awesome-sounding US Senate Foreign Relations Committee, "No, I don't have any views. I was not aware of Australia's commitment."

The Australian reporters clued him in.

Then Fulbright inquired, "How many troops do you have there?"

"About a thousand," he was told. (The number has since quadrupled.)

"About a thousand?" asked the Senator. "We have, I think, one hundred and sixty thousand."

Tactfully the newsmen reminded him that on a population basis the Australian contribution was comparable with that of the US. Australia's entire army totals twenty-seven thousand.

Fulbright maintained an unenthusiastic silence. If it was a sarcastic put-on, his game packed a double jolt. The Aussies are proud people. One sure way to get under the skin of men renowned for their soldiering and friendship to America would be to feign ignorance not only of their feats but even of their participation in the war. Veterans of both world wars declare that the Aussies are the bravest men God ever made.

Taking deliberate advantage of his important-sounding Foreign Relations chairmanship, Fulbright's remarks while a guest in the Australian capital were unalloyed arrogance.

Jake and Crunch hastened to assure Reggie that the Senator sure as hell wouldn't get elected in Texas or Georgia.

Ribboned throughout the bull session, which was replete with alcoholic solutions of the problems of power politics, were short bursts of song from Reggie, who knew the lyrics of every dirty ditty going. Snorting in scorn at people who duck a fight when national or personal honor is at stake, he rendered a number he considered appropriate. He threw back his head and let go in a voice quavering wildly on the high notes:

> There was a young maiden, so pretty and small,
> Who married a man who had no balls at all.
> No balls at all
> No balls at all
> A very short penis
> And no ba-a-a-allllllllllls at a-a-a-llllllll!

As all three joined in a paroxysm of righteous indignation, Crunch brought a mighty whack of approval down on Reggie's back. It was

now his turn to top Reggie. Crunch had seen action in what he called
World War Twice, and had picked up some dandy refrains in Yur-
rop. His singing voice resembled distant thunder rolling in and he
almost ruptured an aorta going through a few short practice hoots.

His offering was a little folk song dedicated to "misguided dissi-
dents." With elephantine delicacy he put down his tin of tongue and
burst forth.

> The next time you walk over Westminister Bridge,
> Look out for an old man asleep on the edge.
> His chest bears a placard and on it is writ,
> "Be kind to an old man who's been blinded by shit."

Jake ran around the hootch laughing like a legionnaire gone stark
in the desert.

After hours of settling burning world issues and gulping dynamite
till they were glassy-eyed, the three men fell into a sound stupor
while, outside, the rescue units cleared away debris and carried on
the search for corpses.

Clark Air Base, Republic of the Philippines

Sixty miles from Manila sits Clark Air Base, the tremendous US
installation that occupies 157,000 acres in Pampanga and Tarlac
Provinces and is the chief base for air supply of Vietnam. Near Clark
Air Base, the two B-57 Canberra jet squadrons have a "numerical
place," a blood bank called Club 21, where they congregate for a
wake when their buddies go down.

On the ceiling each squadron member has written his name in
carbon from lighted candles. When a member fails to return, someone climbs up on a bar stool and encircles the name. Many of those
present proceed to get dead, falling-down, knee-walking drunk. It
is too dark to notice if they should cry. (Those who have flown with
the deceased usually do, inside and out.) There is no logic to the
system of rewards and punishment in combat.

Many of the pilots and navigators live off base from Clark. Near
the town of Angeles City, thirty minutes from the flight line, is a
modern motel-like housing compound, Barangay Court, their home
during sixty-day relief from combat flying at Da Nang, the sprawling
northern base for American-Vietnamese troops in South Vietnam.

Since there are approximately thirty-five Canberra men living in
this one court, they pooled their resources to rent unit number 21

and turn it into a club. The name of the more famous New York watering hole came naturally.

The two B-57 squadrons, the 8th and the 13th, pull a sixty-day flip-flop rotation between Da Nang and Clark. There are never more than half the members present at the Club 21. The men on duty there always tip their glasses with the knowledge that half their number may be eye to eye with the Doom Pussy at that very moment. Many crews have been caught in the jaws of that cat of death.

The Club 21 has, besides a bar, a stereo, a TV set, a pair of cushioned bamboo lounges, and a corner table with a lamp fashioned out of a magnum whiskey bottle. The walls are covered with B-57 pictures, patches of the units, colorful certificates and mottoes, and crew photographs. The room is eighteen feet square and has an adjoining coeducational powder room. Suspended from the ceiling is a chandelier displaying color prints of nude swinging dollies from *Playboy* magazine. As the contraption slowly and subtly rotates, breasts point in every direction.

But the night they circled Lars Hansen's name was not a time for girl-watching. Smash Crandell picked a fight with a full-bull colonel who he felt showed insufficient respect for the deceased.

"It's impossible not to feel emotional about somebody you've flown with," said Smash, a six-foot-four hulk of a man, and the only navigator of the 13th with the rank of major. He had flown on the first mission into North Vietnam.

Smash was a tireless party thrower. He was always having one, designing one, or appointing committees with explicit entertainment chores. The boys had dubbed him "our own Elsa Maxwell" and the "Mesta of the Southwesta." His houseboy was the best cook on the base and Sammy's enthusiasm for blowouts even surpassed Smash's. The most recent had been a celebration when Smash received a gong, the Distinguished Flying Cross, pinned on by no less than General John P. McConnell, Chief of Staff of the US Air Force, when he stopped at Clark on a recent tour of the Pacific.

Smash's eyes were large and gray, his light-brown hair an unruly mop of curls above a chubby face bearing a misleading air of indestructible innocence. He had a lopsided grin, the craziest giggle in the Air Force, and the most amiable disposition until someone foolishly shafted a pal. It was pointless to suggest that he confine a scrap to someone his own size. There wasn't anyone. Smash's loyalty knew no bounds. His wisecracks and normal good humor were potent morale factors for the men in the 13th.

Sitting around the Club one night, Smash recommended his favorite Monday morning pneumonia cure. "Gimme a big bowl of bread and bourbon every time."

From across the room an itinerant officer, known as Beanbag, in a bellowing foghorn voice, began needling Smash. "Heroes. Heroes. What about a solid gahdam failure for a change? Wouldn't you guys like to hear about a solid gahdam failure?"

Marty Keller, who thought the guy might have been seized by a suicide complex, took him aside. "Lissen, you animated bass horn, you're welcome to stay on condition you zip your lip."

Marty, a former Marine foot soldier with a stand-up crop of short sandy hair and three Purple Hearts from the Korean action, was now one of the sharpest jocks in the 13th. Next to flying he liked to talk. "They say war is killing, pillage, and rape. How come I'm not getting any of that P & R?"

Beanbag, who ranked Smash a couple of notches, was in a surly mood, and underneath his jolly exterior, Smash was, too. He had just sent off a couple of Dear John letters, then received two himself, and claimed his schedule was "dicked up like a Mongolian shot card." Besides, his ex-wife had just requested a check for an operation. There was one too many short fuses in the room.

Beanbag then made a crack about a pal of Smash's in the Special Forces. "Those Green Beanie guys are overrated. Too lazy to work, too nervous to steal."

Marty stepped in again. "Listen, old cock, you've heard about the cross between a parakeet and a tiger? When I talk you better listen."

The troublemaker's gourd had been caught in a bucket of tequila all afternoon and he was about nine feet tall.

"Too much publicity," he continued. "Misplaced stallions who—"

Smash felt obliged to smartly lift the fellow's Florsheims off the tile by his necktie. With a short lethal jab of balled fist he dispatched him eight feet across the room, where he stuck to the wall, then slid to the floor like a sandbagful of Jell-O. Blood spurted from his face, so a pilot from Montgomery went to the bathroom to get some Alabama Kleenex.

Beanbag was out for thirty-six hours and the inside of his lip required sixteen stitches. If he had died, which Smash's commanding officer was sure he would, there would have been a court-martial. The commander, Smash's best friend, was furious. "For Christ's sake, you spin around like the button on an outhouse door. If you've got to deck a guy, don't pick on some weenie from MACV."

Next day Smash received a note from the Japanese girl he had

Dear-Johnned. "Oh, babee," she wrote, "when you loved me my glad was very big." He read it while sitting with some buddies in the Officers' Club during the Hour of Happiness which begins at four o'clock daily at CABOOM, the initials for Clark Air Base Officers' Open Mess.

"Hey, Smasherino, heard from Mercy Belle lately?" asked Marty. Some of the mail Smash had been receiving the past few months could compete with the best-read ever to come down the US mail pike.

The story began when he had absent-mindedly gone through a wedding ceremony a couple of years before while snockered one Saturday night in San Francisco. Slipping out of the knot was expensive but Smash was eventually able to untangle what he called "the whole nine yards." He therefore smoldered like a sullen bull when Sears Roebuck sent him a bill for eight hundred dollars run up by his "ex." Smash fired back a sharp little rejoinder mentioning his single status and his lawyer's address.

An employee in Sears' credit department handled the complaint and decided that Smash was for her. She inundated the post office with messages for her own hand-picked fighting man.

Smash answered periodically. He couldn't resist the wild improbability of it all. At first it had been:

DEAR MAJOR CRANDELL:
So you were recently divorced! It would be nice to have someone to write to. My ex-husband was a sailor. He traded me in for a younger model. I am thirty-four with three children. Is it too forward for me to write? I do hope you answer.
Sincerely,
MERCY BELLE MEATY

P.S. I'm really *not* this formal but I have been told that I must not always laugh and make jokes. So I sincerely try to be sedate. Hard to be polite and not be me. If this letter is stiff and rather nauseating just remember it's from everyone trying to make me over, and that, dear Major, is a job.

The letters soon warmed up.

DEAR SMASH:
You answered my letter! I was afraid after I'd written. What do I have to lose except my job? But who cares if I can find someone to make me feel better? I am five feet seven, weigh 140, and have very

kissable lips. My former husband was a really fine man but got himself into trouble and went to prison for rape. I waited for him but when he got discharged he drank very hard and heavy and kept forgetting where he lived.

I am considered attractive. I like to laugh. I watch my drinking because I get loving and that can be dangerous. I like Scotch, gin, 6% beer, and an occasional cigar. Tiparillo.

I'm lying here in bed right now. Wish you'd write more often. After all, I picked you. And I always have good taste in picking men. For God's sake take care of yourself. I just found you.

Don't ever sign your letters again "Your pal." I don't need a pal. I need a lover. So there.

Loads of love,
MERCY BELLE

From then on every letter indicated that if they ever met she would collapse in passion on the nearest flat surface.

HI, HONEY:
My feet are cold. Wish I had someone to warm them. I'll go get a blanket. Excuse me.

I'm back. Got a piece of celery while I was up. Care for some? I am lonely. Sure I like sex with a correct partner. But I don't want you to think I am an easy mark. Hurry home, honey.

Went out for a little while tonight with my girl friend and her beau. Some men found me rather attractive, but aloof. They told me: "Any man that owned or had me really had a lady." Believe me, I get so lonely that it's tough being a lady.

My son is telling everyone we have a major. What sports do you like? Couch checkers? By the way, lover, will you please type your letters? I can't even read your signature. No offense, but gee whiz.

I bet a dollar to a doughnut we can make some wicked music together. I'm very discreet but I don't mind saying I like to be loved and love back. Do you think I'm over-affectionate? It's all for free. Doesn't cost a cent.

I can't wait for you to fix me a gin and tonic. That's a passion drink. Not that I'll need it. I seem to have a one-track mind. That's what I get for reading *Fanny Hill*. I dream a lot. I need you.

I admire you men over there. I'm enclosing some poetry I made up. When I get the writing bug I go to town. I think of you constantly, dream man. Sleep tight, honey, and remember in those photographs I sent you I only wear nighties in front of the camera. They make more washing and ironing and I hate ironing, my love.

MERCY BELLE

The poems were all about her decent Christian heart and how she and the kids would wait for him forever.

Smash's best friend and the pilot he flew with, a veteran of WW II and Korea, who had served in every B-57 wing in the USAF, was known in flying circles around the world as Major Nails. His and Smash's combined weight was 460 pounds and when they entered restaurants or nightclubs together people mistook them for tag-team wrestlers.

Nails was a compact 240, had played professional football, and could still do one-arm pushups till you got tired just watching. A swashbuckling type reminiscent of WW II fighter pilots, he was as colorful as the 13th's past history. An avid sportsman, he was the first American in over thirty years to win the skeet and trap-shooting championship of Great Britain.

Strangers regarded Nails with a mixture of envy and respect. He could outdrink, outshoot, outtalk, and outsing anyone. His rich baritone continually prompted suggestions that he train for the opera.

Spread a little sunshine was Nails's creed and he preached it with a braid of psychology, the sunshine-spreading, and a generous sprinkling of bull roar.

Nails had that rare quality of communicated excitement and whether he showed up five minutes, five hours, or five days late, the room became electrified. His walk resembled a military penguin's, the shoulders ridiculously broad, the fiery-bright black eyes blazing with continual amusement. He was a natural clown with a compulsive necessity to be applauded. He would have them laughing before he walked through the door. In him boiled a great zest for life, tremendous energy, and a Rabelaisian passion for loving, eating, talking, drinking, deer hunting, flying, and endless good fellowship.

He was a consummate ham and never pretended otherwise. Any compliment or attention paid him, he soaked up like syrup on a dry waffle.

When General Earle G. Wheeler, Chairman of the Joint Chiefs of Staff, visited Da Nang Air Base, the squadron commanders stood smartly in front of their respective aircraft as he came down the line. Two steps beyond Nails, Wheeler did a double-take, backed up, leaned forward, and had another look at the tag above the major's left pocket.

"Hmmm," he said, "that's a rough-sounding name. Is it your real one?"

"Yes, sir. It is."

"Well, I like it. I like it," said Wheeler.

Nails was as tickled as a Little Leaguer who had just grand-slammed with Koufax pitching. Strangers would have thought kind words were unknown to him.

If Nails found a companion who could sort out the wisecracks and throw them back, the new friend was in for an exhausting marathon of bull slinging. Nails could sling it with the best of them.

He had been a boxer, horseman, practical joker, hunter, fisherman, landowner, husband, father, and lover, who had logged more time bedside than airborne. Nails claimed to have been all of twelve before he had carnal knowledge of a woman. From then on he couldn't be sure he was Prince Sure Shot of the Mighty Fornicators until he had at least tried them all.

They hung Silver Stars on Smash and Nails the same day. Nails wrote to his father, known as "The Moose," and the only one to ever top him at almost everything: "Maybe the heavyweight twins will turn out to be the most decorated warriors on the campus."

Nails and The Moose were rivals and buddies, and double-dated when Nails was not away at war. Each despised sentimentality, but were frequently sentimental. They were precise, irresponsible at times, yet forever charming. They lived by the Sioux Indians' credo: "Never condemn the brother until you have walked in his moccasins for two full moons."

The Moose's shoulders were even broader than Nails's. Just the sight of father and son discouraged many a brawl. Their friend Harry Brahm gave me an example.

"At the Shamrock Club in Pocatello, Idaho, it was nineteen hundred and ought forty-six and Nick Lucas was playing "Tip Toe Through the Tulips" on his magic guitar. Nails had just walked out of the gaming room in the back and Moose was making a play for a blond in a silver fox chubby. Enter, five cowhands. Four of them eased into a booth. The fifth one copped a feel from the blond and the Moose backhanded him across the room. The cowhand hit the floor and the four in the booth stood up simultaneously. Moose and Nails took one step toward the booth to catch the four coming out —and they all sat down again just like they got up.

"The bartender reached for his SAP and for a minute it looked like he was going to use it. Then he nodded to the bouncer in the Roy Rogers shirt with a badge on it. He tossed the guy out that was having a siesta on the floor. It was all over in about thirty seconds. Moose and Nails turned around and ordered another round of drinks."

Nails was a Jack Mormon of Welsh and Italian descent. He

crooned into the hot mike of his Canberra on the way to a target. The dicier the sortie, the louder he bellowed bawdy ballads. Nails hated to let his true emotions show for fear it might tarnish his image.

Most crew members had their own system of keeping the pucker string taut. Salty language has been practiced since the beginning of warfare.

On one Sunday mission Smash had the ADF (Automatic Direction Finder) switch on, the means by which an aircraft can tune in a commercial station. Richard Evans and the Mormon Tabernacle Choir were on the Armed Forces Radio. Knowing that Nails's mother had belonged to that same choir for nineteen years, Smash hollered into the mike, "Damned if that ain't fine music to bomb by, hey, Nails?"

Nails had his own private means of communing with God. When he pulled out of a pass and realized the murderous ground fire had missed him again, he would look heavenward and say, "Thank you, Hubert. Now I'll take over."

If a new young troop seemed intimidated by the perils he faced, or threatened to behave like a candy-ass, Nails would tell him, "Now look here. You get five hundred seventy p's a day, free airplane rides, all the bombs you can drop, and daily excursions to foreign countries. What the hell more could you want?"

Nails was in his element as a dedicated combat leader, squadron commander of the 13th. Even as a little boy he had had a hunch that he would grow up to be a leader. There never really had been the slightest doubt in his mind. He hadn't lost a man in combat and urged his squadron not to press a target if the antiaircraft fire was too hot.

"Unless the friendlies have their ass in a crack, no target is worth a man or a bird."

His system was based on a stringent economy—plan well, fight well, and hurt the enemy the most by inflicting maximum damage at the least possible cost. "Don't duel with ground fire. It is not economically feasible to trade aircraft and crew for quad 50s. Even McNamara and his band without an IBM machine can figure that one out."

The day after Lars Hansen was killed, Smash and Nails's two-month duty tour and training missions at Clark were over. They and the rest of the squadron packed their gear to get back to the business of war at Da Nang, or Dang Dang Next the Sea, as they called it.

They climbed into the pickup van for base operations, filed a clearance, then preflighted while the ground crews loaded. When the tower gave them clearance, Nails eased the throttles forward and watched the instruments as the two jet engines stabilized at full power. The gauges were in the green, so he released the brakes, began his takeoff roll, announcing as he always did, "Stoney Burke coming out of chute number five."

Four

HARRY'S HOG HAULERS

BLAST THEIR ASS is printed on pencils and personal cards of Lieutenant Colonel Harry Howton's crews, who call themselves Harry's Hog Haulers. (Combat crews seem uncommonly concerned with their own derrieres or those of the enemy.) Harry is commander of the 311th Air Commando Squadron, stationed at Da Nang. His is one of four squadrons of the 315th Air Commando Group, with headquarters in Saigon under the overall command of Colonel George Hannah.

The men who fly the ten-year-old twin-engine C-123 Providers keep open the vital lifeline in Vietnam. Besides Harry's Hog Haulers, there are Styron's Stallions and the Teeny Weeny Airlines.

The Air Commandos fly the aerial highways on relief and supply missions and land in the jungle on primitive dirt airstrips about the size of a blacksmith's apron. The Commandos go into battle in unarmed cargo planes with two pilots in front, livestock in the rear, and one of the crew whistling "Can't We Be Friends" over the intercom.

The Viet Cong try to make sieves of the big, lumbering aircraft that were originally built as gliders, with engines added as an afterthought. All missions are flown through the constant harassment of ground fire. If the load is a bellyful of AVGAS, dynamite, or thousands of rounds of ammo, a direct hit could explode the whole business. Typical cargo might include concertina, rice, ammunition, people, mail, troops, hogs, cement, spare parts, ducks, chickens, or cows, bound for bases or Special Forces in remote outposts, boondocks, or "boonies," military slang for just about as far from civilization as you can get.

Many of the Air Commandos are former supersonic-jet fliers or off the flight decks of SAC bombers, but all were handpicked for the job of piloting the high-winged, twin-engine assault transports with the tall, upswept tail and huge cargo doors at the rear that yawn open to disgorge paratroops, jeeps, trucks, or bulldozers. Some of the boys who fly the reliable old craft carry personal gag cards reading: A SUBSONIC, FIXED WING, CENTURY SERIES, ASSAULT TROOP CARRIER. YOU CALL. WE HAUL.

I had caught a ride to Da Nang in a T-39, the snappy little executive-type jet. I was going on a mission with Harry's Hog Haulers. As we waited our turn to land, the pilot explained, "Da Nang is the world's busiest airport with only one runway. Fifteen hundred landings and takeoffs on peak days besides two extra traffic patterns for helicopters at the edge of the airstrip. Something lands in Da Nang every twenty seconds."

As we flew the pattern, waiting for permission from the tower to let down, he continued, "Three emergency landings are coming in. Pretty badly shot up."

Ground crews sprayed the runway with foam as we watched from the flight deck.

"This is routine up here in Da Nang," he said. "In a day it's commonplace for ten or eleven to come in with in-flight emergencies or battered by ground fire."

Da Nang Air Base sits on sandy terrain just outside the big port city of Da Nang, which is in Quangnam Province and was formerly named Tourane. On the east is a lovely harbor and the clear blue-green China Sea. Heavily forested mountains of seven thousand feet rise on the west and are clogged with guerrillas, tigers, elephants, and monkeys. One hundred miles to the north the Seventeenth Parallel divides South Vietnam from North Vietnam.

Once little more than a provincial airfield, Da Nang today is a vast US fortress swarming with planes. A wing of the Vietnamese Air Force, VNAF, also is stationed there. Some of the Vietnamese pilots take turns flying the government civilian airline, Air Vietnam. Thus, a pilot flying a commercial plane from Da Nang to Saigon one day might have been piloting a B-57 or Skyraider on a strike against the Viet Cong the day before.

Colonel Franklin H. Scott, commander of the 6252nd TAC Fighter Wing, sat on a powder keg at this crucial air base nestled among three mountain ranges. His job embraced all Air Force activities and the operation of the airdrome. Under Scott's supervision was one of the most powerful air armadas ever assembled in Southeast Asia. The row upon row of warplanes fenced off by low concrete revetments or sandbags represented an astonishing assortment. Rarely has any single airfield been utilized by such a variety.

There are some thirty types. The wing inventory ranges from the

O-1E Bird Dog, or FAC spotter craft, for visual reconnaissance and fighter control, to the WW II C-47 Gooney Bird or Skytrain, for logistic support. In Vietnam that old workhorse has become a weird sort of fighter. Almost thirty-five years old, it has been modified and outfitted with the newest gadgets, including six-barreled "miniguns" of 7.62 caliber each firing six thousand rounds a minute. Known as Puff, the Magic Dragon, it has proved very effective in close air support by delivering heavy fire against Viet Cong ground forces.

There are also propeller-driven A-1E Skyraiders; F-105 Thunderchief fighter-bombers, one of the classiest planes in the inventory; B-57 Canberra jets for air-to-ground strikes; the U-10 liaison and courier single-engine plane; C-123 Providers, for intratheater cargo and airlift, as well as flare support; the HH-43 Husky, a helicopter used for fire-fighter and rescue operations; the CH-3 chopper, which comes in models A, B, or C, a big, long-range rescue craft with a two-ton cargo capacity; the F-4C Phantom, with its 1,600-mph-plus rating, put out by McDonnell as a versatile fighter-bomber jet; Lockheed F-104 Starfighter, used for air cover and air-to-ground strikes; F-102 Delta Dagger interceptor jet for air defense; the HU-16 Albatross for over-water air-crew rescue; C-130s, which transport troops and cargo, and drop flares for the night strike forces; and—mentioned as little as possible, if at all—the famous U-2, which carries on regular reconnaissance flights throughout Southeast Asia. There are modified C-130s serving as 7th Air Force Airborne Command Posts. The duties and specifications of the latter remain classified.

In a typical month at the base, operations average more than fourteen hundred radar approaches by aircraft and one thousand transient-aircraft turn-arounds; from three to four million gallons of fuel are supplied to thirsty planes plus thousands of tons of bombs and ammo.

With all this activity resting on the shoulders of Colonel Scott and his staff, his twenty-six years of service in the Air Force comes in handy. Strategic Da Nang, the most northern VNAF-USAF installation in South Vietnam, is a base that the VC itch to obliterate. They would pay a fantastic price. And if North Vietnam were to risk an air attack it would almost certainly bring on massive retaliation, including a flattened Hanoi.

A spidery network of trails leads out of Laos and Cambodia along nine hundred miles of Vietnam boundary. The Viet Cong guerrilla who has infiltrated via the Cambodian or Laotian border from Ho Chi Minh's training bases in North Vietnam looks just like the Vietnamese peasant in the South. They wear the same black cotton pajamas and conical straw hats and speak the same language.

Colonel Scott assumed command July 8, 1965. In the first week there were three calamitous incidents, including a B-57 aborting on takeoff. The craft blew up and burned at the end of the runway. Scott, nearby, had his sunglasses blown off by the concussion.

"The second night, the VC hit me," Scott said later in his Greenville, S.C., accent.

Security then was undeniably loose compared to its present tightness. When the VC dead were stacked up after the attack, one corpse turned out to be a Charlie who had been driving an American officer for three months. Another was a twelve-year-old hawker of newspapers who had roamed the base at will for weeks.

One of the maids was stopped at the gate toting a bucket of water. A check revealed that below the first inch of water was a false bottom filled with plastic explosives. "There," said Scott, "you have a picture of this battle. The old lady with a bucket of plastique challenging our supersonic jets. The ambassador calls it the unholy trinity—subversion, terrorism, and classic guerrilla tactics."

When the VC hit the second night, six planes were destroyed, two C-130s and four F-102s. All received direct hits. The attack was a heavy mortar barrage, and ten to twenty VC had infiltrated the base and laid satchel charges.

Scott was caught between Marine and VC fire. "One side was shooting in front of my car, the other behind it."

Now when visiting brass pass through Da Nang, they kid him about his first week's baptism by fire. "Did you ever find your sunglasses, Scotty?"

Colonel Scott is reluctant to admit that in his early flying days he could cut up with the best of the boys. When he flew his plane behind a waterfall, then buzzed the diamond and broke up a baseball game, General "Hap" Arnold fined him five hundred dollars. But today Scott has the complete respect and confidence of the ground crews and flying warriors at Da Nang and no American officer in the theater enjoys a closer rapport with VNAF. Prime Minister Ky presented him with a prized war souvenir, a captured AR gun, manufactured in Red China, and had the five-and-a-half-foot firearm mounted in a big red-velvet-lined glass case before he gave it to him. Only General Westmoreland has received a like gift.

Harry Howton proved always good for a story. Harry's wiry, gray-streaked blond crew cut protruded defiantly forward even when wet with sweat. Before a mission his face was comparatively unlined but after a sporty flight, or dicey situation as the Colonel called it, that face could look like a navel orange packed too tightly in the crate. In his Birmingham drawl Howton spewed corny humor like an honest slot machine. "Well, skill and cunning will triumph over suspicion and ignorance every time."

Harry's squadron had not lost a plane. The VC had the usual 80,000-piaster price on his head, dead or alive, and the middle-aged pelican was working his third war—World War Twice, Korea, now this one.

"The same pros always show up for the action when there's trouble," he said. "And the same gahdam termites crawl into the woodwork in headquarters jobs, rated pilots evadin' the action. They're called seagulls. You know why? Because they can only eat, squawk, shit, and stand on one leg at the bar. You have to throw rocks at 'em to get 'em to fly."

Besides a few Vietnamese, livestock, and food supplies, Harry's manifest that day included me. We were going to several Special Forces camps.

"You're a mighty snazzy chicken to be hanging your fanny out coverin' this cockeyed hassle. A lot of those Saigon philosophers report on the war without leavin' the Caravelle Hotel. You've got a lot of sand, gal."

"Political factors are important, too. Besides, some of the fellows have to be there to do daily live broadcasts."

"What's the matter with your foot?"

"An accident. They're taking the stitches out in ten days."

"Well, I want you to stick two flak vests under you today. No sense gettin' your butt shot off. I see you already got on your iron brassiere."

As Harry slipped into his flak vest he handed me his latest *carte de visite,* struck off in wavering type.

HARRY'S HOG HAULERS

HARRY HOWTON	LT.COLONEL,USAF
World Traveler	*International Lover*
Renowned Gourmet	*Last of the Big Spenders*

The reverse side read:

Any chance to crawl in the sack with you tonight? If so, keep this card. If not, kindly return it, as they are expensive. I am not as good as I once was, but I am as good once as I ever was.

P.S. You don't have to say yes; just smile!

As Harry checked last-minute details with the copilot, the passengers stood at the cargo door listening to the loadmaster's routine little speech, which I now knew by heart. Only the destinations were different. "We will land at Hue, Quang Ngai, Aloui, Dong Xoai, Khe Sanh. There is no water aboard. You can drink from your individual canteens. No toilet facilities except a relief tube for the men. And if you get airsick, *please* try to *hit* the containers aboard for that purpose."

One little Vietnamese, a brand-new recruit hitching his way to Pleiku, got queasy just listening to the speech. He looked very unhappy but determined to complete the trip.

I walked around to the front of the plane to climb aboard. Harry had invited me to ride in the navigator's seat, on a swivel a few feet above the passengers, adjoining the flight deck. Like a barber's chair, it had an adjustment lever permitting it to swing forward, backward, or to the right. It originally was intended for the navigator, and had a desk large enough for my typewriter.

Before climbing aboard I noticed Smash and Nails walking up the flight line. Smash spied an Army nurse waiting on the ramp to board a plane. Never one to let a sugar, or sug, get away, he walked over to whisper a little sweet talk.

Most of the men look magnificently male in their flight suits—a one-piece affair with neck-to-below-crotch zippers and pockets everywhere. The climate in Da Nang is worse than the underside of hell and most men go unzipped to the navel.

Flying crews have been glamour boys since the beginning of flying machines. As far as Nails and Smash were concerned, they had grown accustomed to having women flock around them in romantic vertigo as if they were blue-ribbon studs from outer space.

Smash handed the nurse his card. "Have one. I got a double order and I've got to pass them out before I get fired or promoted or all of the above."

SMASH CRANDELL   MAJOR, USAF
Social Lion —— *Captain of Industry* —— *Connoisseur of Fine Booze* —— *Big-game Hunter* —— *Boudoir Athlete* —— *Art Critic* —— *Assistant Fighter Pilot* —— *Poor Man's Magellan* —— *Bon Vivant* —— *Conversationalist Par Excellence* —— *Raconteur Extraordinaire* —— *Gourmet* —— *News Analyst* —— *Warmonger* —— *Temporarily Unemployed*
                    (not necessarily in above order)

The nurse looked back as she reluctantly boarded her plane. Nails and Smash walked in the direction of Harry's C-123.

My typewriter was already aboard. Hanging around my waist was a bandolier of tape recorder, Polaroid, and Rolleiflex; over one shoulder, a Nikon and a bag of film; over the other, tapes and two water canteens; on my wrist was a Rollei sixteen.

"She looks like a gahdam Alpine milkmaid," Nails said.

"Hmmmm," hmmmmmed Smash, "I wonder who's rattling *her* knickers."

I pretended to ignore their scrutiny as Staff Sergeant Nathaniel Jones of Dayton, Ohio, a slim-hipped, nimble Negro crew chief, checked to see that I had on my flak vest. He had already followed Harry's instructions and placed two flak protectors on the seats.

I climbed aboard to the navigator's seat, unzipped my Olivetti, and went to work.

"Watch them cows," hollered Harry to the loadmaster. "It's a real dicey situation trimmin' this motorized Spam can with a bull runnin' loose in the back end. On drops we have to kick 'em out, two to a crate and pray the chute opens. Otherwise, it's instant steerburgers. The ASPCA back home wouldn't like that."

As the noisy 123 barreled down the runway and aimed for the sky, the engine noises were deafening and a little alarming to the uninitiated. Some newly arrived ground troops smiled weakly as they gripped their carbines.

Airborne, Sergeant Jones explained the technique the pilots used for short strips—sometimes called riding the stick-shaker. "In order to get this beast into a short slick strip they use an approach speed indicator on the dashboard that's tied in with a stick shaker that shakes the control column more rapidly as they near a complete stall. Since the 123 has about the stall characteristics of a streamlined lead brick, this bit of ingenuity starts a warning about five to seven knots before the bird is about to become a free falling object. On these strips it's pretty vital to be at the absolute minimum airspeed to keep from running out of airpatch and completely ruining your day."

I appreciated Jones's pains to explain.

"Now, on takeoff the same system works on getting the bird in the blue. On climbout they want to climb as fast as possible to get as much ozone under you as you can. Now that you're fully checked out on this Century Series Spam Can I'll go back to my duties."

There were no navigational aids at the landing zones in the remote outposts, and sometimes no airstrip, just a drop zone which must be located visually. Crews contend with tricky mountain winds and short, narrow fields with improvised surfaces, and the obstructions require the highest pilot proficiency, particularly during rainy seasons with low ceilings and poor visibility. Visual flights are made in conditions much lower than minimum standards in the States. Actually, there are no weather minimums in combat. There is plenty of dead-reckoning navigation and no room for error. Every crew member assists in visual identification of the position. "It's real easy to become disoriented in a chop-it-and-drop-it high-rate descending turn with no reference except clouds and green-jungled mountain slopes," Harry said.

It is commonplace for loadmasters and crew chiefs to peer out the side windows or the open tailgate to be of assistance.

Every crew member is fully aware that mechanical failure or a forced landing can mean coming down in hostile territory. Jones squatted on the flight-deck step, earphones clamped to his head, eyes darting from left to right. Any ascent or landing from or into South Vietnamese–American-held air bases is subject to VC snipers. Machine guns, mortar fire, or even a well-aimed rifle shot can be fatal to a passenger or crew member. All the latter wear .38s and an ammo belt and carry an M-16 rifle. Soldier passengers carry submachine guns or carbines and ammunition, and a jungle knife hangs in their hip holsters. The area surrounding Quang Ngai airstrip is so studded with VC, who fire so regularly at incoming or outgoing aircraft, that the American crews refer to them as duty snipers.

Harry spiraled in for a landing around a couple of thunderstorms and their bouncing turbulence. With engines roaring in reverse, flaps full down, we pitched and skidded down the airstrip. Cargo started pouring out of the yawning rear almost before the engines stopped turning.

"The natives are downright inhospitable around here," Harry announced in his slow southern accent. "A real sporty piece of real estate. Coupla months ago the VC showered down on one of my birds right where we're parked. Didn't kill anybody—coupla boys got messed up from fragments and they ventilated the aircraft pretty good, but Joe Rogers and I whipped in here with some of the quick-fix types from maintenance at Da Nang—patched up the control cables and hydraulic lines and the boys flew it out about four hours later. They were right lucky—number two was running and one of the guys had leaned down to put his camera away when a round went right through his headrest. I told them to take the rest of the day off when they got home but they got another bird and went back to work."

Lumber, two priests, cement, a cow and four pigs were off-loaded. "Fill up that deuce and a half," hollered the loadmaster, soldierese for two and a half ton truck. Chains of Vietnamese and American soldiers passed out the load, Quang Ngai passengers sprinted down the tail ramp into the downpour while hitchhikers for the next stop stood under the wings waiting to come aboard.

I moved to the back of the plane for the rest of the journey, and after the Vietnamese troops scurried aboard for the next leg of the trip, a tiny civilian Vietnamese couple, carrying an infant, timidly climbed the ramp. The only two vacant seats faced across the aisle. A soldier and I moved so that they could sit together. The mother lashed her seat belt to include the baby.

Harry started the engines as the loadmaster pulled in the rear doors. Taxiing rapidly down the rutted, steel-mat-bumpy strip, he swung around quickly and wound up the engines. Our 123 pounded down the strip and up, like a grapefruit seed squeezed into orbit. When the No Smoking and Unfasten Your Seat Belt cardboard signs were taken down, I screeched into Sergeant Jones's ear. "You sure don't mess around on the ground at Quang Ngai, do you?"

"Hell, no," he replied. "Didn't you know they were firing at us?" He pointed to a knoll below us.

"Do you have a name for the hill?"

"Nothing I'd care to repeat," he growled.

As I looked over at the Vietnamese father, his chin slumped down on his chest. I nudged Jones and pointed. He scooped up his long interphone cord, went over to investigate. Perhaps the passenger was ill.

He was dead. A sniper's 30-caliber rifle slug had punctured the plane's underbelly and come up through the flak vest on the seat directly beneath him. It had penetrated his right buttock, passed through vital organs, and lodged in his shoulder.

The baby opened brown eyes wide, whimpered to be fed. The mother, a petite woman with exquisite features, stared up at Jones beseechingly. In that second, high above battle-weary Vietnam, it seemed that all the hope and despair of the world were etched in her face.

"Get those zipperheads off the runway," Harry called over the radio to the Special Forces camp at Aloui. Natives and animals were strolling about the airstrip as if it were Central Park.

Aloui was one of the many camps in Vietnam that stand like an island in a sea of terror. The Special Forces assigned to them—called

"Sneaky Petes" in Army argot—are superbly trained, dedicated, and they fight like lions under attack. The senior adviser at Aloui, T/Sgt. Eugene Shepherd of Buchanan, Michigan, met our plane and supervised the unloading. He beamed.

"We think of old Harry as Father Christmas without the beard," he said after we were introduced. "His troops bring us luxuries paid for out of their own pockets. Do you know what a piece of ice can mean to a man out in the bush? Neither bullets nor monsoon weather can keep Harry's guys on the ground. Here they come with lighter fluid, shoe polish, Scotch tape, and envelopes. We've seen Harry break out of the fog at two hundred feet in this mountain country when we hadn't seen a plane in days and days."

We walked over to Harry. "Do you think the young lady would like to meet the rest of the men?" Shepherd asked.

"That's what she's here for," Harry replied.

They escorted me down six steps to the underground bunkers, which are about the size of a prison cell. Here the men lived, ate, slept, and communicated constantly with Da Nang. The radio was manned around the clock. It was their sole link with the outside world.

"What do you do for relaxation?" I asked two communications advisers, Sergeant Henry Zielinski of Los Angeles and Sergeant Barry Keefer of Clarksville, Pennsylvania.

"We think up names for the rats who play football on the tin roof all night," Keefer replied. "Our favorite is Clod, because of his clumsy footwork."

Zielinski walked over a few feet to check on the charcoal-fired hibachi. Their generator was out of whack so they were cooking on the hibachi. To men stationed out in the boonies, the United States is the Land of the Big PX and the All-night Generator.

"Maybe I'm a little safer over here than in LA," Zielinski said. "Sounds like they're playing a little rough in Watts."

"Why doesn't the press report more VC atrocities?" Shepherd interrupted. "Seems like some reporters come over here, pencils aquiver, just to help the agitators at home."

"The Charlies are clearly losing the war," I said, changing the subject. "That is why communist sympathizers are accelerating their protests. All that uproar on the campus actually represents less than one percent of the undergraduate student body and an even smaller fraction of faculty members."

"Haven't you heard about the VC torturing civilians beyond recognition?" said Keefer. "And you can't find a South Vietnamese family that hasn't suffered directly or indirectly from Charlie's terror and brutality. The Charlies don't give a big rat's ass about respect for ancestors, the old people, or the sanctity of the village."

"They've got a real cute trick now. The Cong fasten deadly-poisonous bamboo krait snakes to the ceilings of caves to lash out at Americans on search parties. And what about that teen-age girl who was kidnapped and found next day, the torso mutilated, her breasts and head chopped off? On what had been her stomach was a sign: 'Death sentence to the enemies of communism.' We never saw anything in the papers about that."

"Go to it, Willie," said Keefer, then turned to me. "Willie Van Cleve's our professor. He's got a couple of degrees."

"Some of those newspaper guys picture Ho Chi Minh as a sweet old Bolshevist. Who the hell's side are they on?" asked Willie.

"Well," I replied, "in a democracy every shade of opinion has a right to be heard. Some of the protestors at home are genuine pacifists or conscientious objectors who refuse to kill another human being under any circumstances. Some of them have volunteered for the medical corps in wars they protested. But you've got a genuine beef about the others who have jockeyed themselves into influential positions in the protest movement. They are rooting for the Viet Cong. They want Uncle Ho to control all of Vietnam. They want Peking to dictate the peace. Although they see no reason for North Vietnamese citizens to voice their preference in government leaders, they're hollering the house down for free elections in South Vietnam."

"Yup," said Willie. "Liberals can get pretty damned illiberal when faced with opposing views. Don't the people at home know that Mao Tse-tung preaches that power flows out of the barrel of a gun? By God, the Cong are brave, tough, vicious, and full of tricks. Ho Chi Minh says, 'To wound one American soldier is to remove three from the battlefield, because two have to carry him to the hospital.' And why doesn't the press lay off the Marines? Marines are sent in to search out and destroy the enemy in villages saturated with VC shooting from behind the skirts of women. And then pickets at home scream bloody murder when the jarheads don't hold their fire because of the women."

"Christ," said Harry, "they'd be dead fools if they did. And some of those VC dolls shoot pretty damn good themselves."

"Why don't those creeps who write crank letters to American widows have the guts to put on a return address?" Willie asked.

"I'd ship 'em a gahdam Claymore mine. What kind of punk sends heckling letters to a war widow?"

Harry looked at me and tilted his head toward the door. "It's gonna be a sporty proposition gettin' out of here. Thanks for the coffee, fellas. See you next trip."

The men stomped and bent the beer cans flat. The VC use cans and whiskey bottles for Molotov cocktails. As Shepherd walked with us toward the plane I heard one of the boys behind us say, "I'd like to get a bead on one of those Vietniks at home marching down Main Street carrying the Charlie flag. I'd shoot the living shit out of him."

The pressures on troops in combat are constant and severe. Nobody could order them to talk like Little Lord Fauntleroys. The only guys who could top the Americans at colorful language were the Aussies. They had it developed to a breathtaking art.

Next we flew supplies to the village of Dong Xoai (rhymes with "wrong's why"), the capital of the district of Don Luan. A tall young Negro, Captain Hurl Taylor, Jr., of Richmond, Virginia, 5th Special Forces Group, Detachment A-342, was in command of the Dong Xoai camp. While we talked at one end of the mess hall, his executive officer, Lieutenant David Rittenhouse of Reno, Nevada, was making pies.

Protocol dictates that the local district chief rank the Americans at these posts. In this case it was Major Nguyen Con, who had survived the vicious Viet Cong attack the previous June. Beginning on the ninth, the battle had raged for two and a half days in the tiny district capital, fifty-five miles north of Saigon. They had been buttoning up for the night when the radio crackled in Con's darkened home. A sentry on the unfinished airstrip at Dong Xoai blurted, "The Viet Cong are everywhere."

In minutes communist mortar and recoilless-rifle fire turned the night air into an inferno. Clad in breechclouts and steel helmets and armed with Chinese flame throwers and grenades and automatic rifles, the VC shock troops cascaded out of the ground fog. They slaughtered women and children they found in dugouts. The camp was then only two and a half weeks old and very vulnerable. The VC were at their peak in the sector and very strong. Everything on the base and in the village was leveled except district headquarters, where the last stand was made. There were 100 percent casualties, wounded and dead.

"It was comparable to the Alamo," said Sergeant Douglas Sapper from Mount Vernon, Illinois. "Eight hundred friendlies, an airborne battalion, and the 52nd Ranger Battalion were flown in to support the camp. By chance some landed in the middle of the VC regimental reserve, who were completely dug in all the way around. Those friendlies were annihilated in twenty minutes. About thirty pilots of the 602nd swept in under cloud cover to napalm, rocket, and strafe the VC. Those guys flew sixty sorties in support of us. The A-1E pilots received three Silver Stars and two DFCs for the job."

"Don't forget the B-57s," added Rittenhouse. "It looked like those Skyraiders and Canberras were wired nose to tail when they dived in to let ole Charlie have it. They really turned the tide."

One chopper-borne relief force was wiped out. The US planes dropped napalm and white phosphorus, and blasted the VC with cannon fire, but the VC had hung on. Then Army Brigadier General Cao Van Vien, commander of South Vietnam's III Corps, elected to land forty troop-laden choppers onto a soccer field adjacent to the compound. It caught the VC by surprise; they were dug in throughout the jungle clearings, anticipating relief forces would land there.

To leap from a helicopter under fire—carrying full battle packs that would give a mule a hernia, including five hundred rounds of ammo apiece—and go charging pell-mell toward the entrenched enemy is everyday fare for well-trained ARVNs. They are quick to pick up technical know-how in training and are very good artisans. It is marvelous how quickly they learn to handle American weapons, their American instructors claim.

"Along the defense perimeter lay twelve disemboweled children," Sapper said. "One of our guys was found burned to a crisp, his dog tags soldered to his bones, and his charred pet monkey even in death clinging to his back. When the relief troops came in and saw the dead they vomited. Several heads were scattered in the church."

"We didn't win, but we didn't lose. We salvaged two buildings," said Rittenhouse, still working on his pies. "There was one Cambodian on our side who fought like a devil. He was stackin' 'em up like cordwood. He was credited with one hundred killed for sure; how many more we just don't know."

Outside the mess hall I could hear a soldier singing lustily to the tune of the "Battle Hymn of the Republic":

Jesus walks upon the water
He's the lifeguard at our pool. . . .

"There was a VC woman commander. We killed her," said Sergeant Lamar Sale, who was wearing fatigues with "Garcia" embroidered on the breast pocket. "What kind of pie you got there?"

"Apple," Rittenhouse replied, turning to me. "You gotta learn to do everything out here."

I went over to the sink to wash my hands. "Where's the soap?"

Rittenhouse pointed to a can.

"But that's scouring powder."

"Out here it's soap."

I found that it worked very well.

Sergeant Sale hoisted himself up on the kitchen table. "My mother is always writin' letters tellin' me what to eat. Salvation through spinach and other livin' foods. Be sure to have plenty of meat and vegetables. As if I could march right down to the supermarket. Cheeeeeee-rist. Our Vietnamese cook—you compliment her on her stew and it's stew three times a day for a week. *Un-buh-lievable!*"

In the savage June battle the South Vietnamese fighting man demonstrated that he could stand up and die with the bravest. Too little is written about the 300,000-man Army of the Republic of Vietnam, the ARVN, and the 6,500 men of their Marine Corps, who slog through waist-deep Mekong Delta mud. Their six battalions of airborne brigade have also fought well in battle. The Australians call them "bloody good troops," high praise from men who have the right to appraise. The 42nd and 44th Vietnamese Rangers are considered easily as good as their Marines. They are in the Delta area. VC avoid them like the plague.

The French used to call Vietnamese women *"douces comme les mangues"* (sweet as mangoes), but many of them know how to fight beside their men. One such was the casualty, the woman lieutenant company commander, mentioned by Sergeant Sale, in the bloody Dong Xoai battle. On the friendlies' side in the same encounter was the wife of Private Nguyen Van Ngoc. While he was pinned down by enemy fire, she stuck by his side and, ignoring cross fire, streaked back and forth supplying him with fresh belts of grenades and bullets until they both were wounded.

On my first day in Vietnam I had heard about the pistol-packin' thirty-eight-year-old "Tiger Lady" in the Mekong Delta who was the wife of Major Nguyen Van Dan. A mother of six, with the rank of master sergeant, she packed a pair of 45-caliber automatics on her hips. She often accompanied the 44th Vietnamese Rangers, nicknamed The Black Tiger Battalion, into battle, and won three medals for combat heroism. She fought alongside the troops in full battle regalia, including a polished steel helmet marked with her sobriquet, "Tiger." In the vagaries of love and war, her old man rubbed her out one night when they scuffled over a forty-five she brandished because she thought him overly attentive to another woman.

Captain Taylor drove us a few miles up the road by jeep to visit one of the hardy, independent mountain tribes called Montagnards. These dark-skinned "people of the mountains" are mostly of Malayo-Polynesian origin, stocky, with thick lips and wide noses. Their friendship is of utmost importance in the war. They live a Stone Age existence in the mountains and wooded foothills but they know the myriad trails and places to hide the chow, and control the High Plateau, which borders on Laos and Cambodia. They worship the sky, earth, water, animals, and the spirits of the trees. The women weave lovely cloth of Latin American-type designs. The men hunt with poison-tipped arrows.

"These are Sten," Captain Taylor said. "They are not as cultured as the Rhadé in the central highlands around Pleiku, but much more politically organized. The Rhadé are the biggest and most powerful tribe."

South Vietnam's 700,000 "Yards" amount to 12 percent of the population, but they are in the majority in seven of the forty-four mainland provinces and always have claimed the right of eminent domain to their vast mountain and jungle hinterland, which makes up one-third of the country's land mass.

They are settling today for some kind of representation in provincial governments, their own zone of military operations, and government support in medical supplies and food. Their grievances must be negotiated directly with the Vietnamese, even though they have had a special relationship with American Special Forces for years. The Vietnamese traditionally look down on the Yards as *muoi,* or savages. But Prime Minister Nguyen Cao Ky's administration is attempting to come to terms with them.

The Montagnards feel friendly toward the American troops and toward the Catholic missionaries and French plantation owners, all of whom wield a wide influence over the primitive tribesmen, economically and culturally.

The Montagnards file their teeth, wear loincloths, and among their superstitions is the women's reluctance to marry any man with a limb missing. They adore their children. Mothers warily allowed me to hold their babies; one of them was only two weeks old.

The stench in their thatched-roof longhouses was overpowering.

"It comes from about a hundred years of living this way," said Captain Taylor.

One couple was so old they moved like arthritic sheep. Every rib in their skinny bodies could be counted. The husband's loincloth had slipped its moorings, revealing scant pubic hair. The wife's bosom was old and withered flat and her loincloth identical to her mate's. One had to pay attention to determine which was which.

All around the sun-bathed compound, beautiful, bare-breasted young women balanced baskets of grain on their heads. At first they were shy about posing for pictures but quickly changed their attitude when I, in a spirit of "when in Rome," peeled off my army shirt and joined them. They were delighted with the sixty second color Polaroid prints I gave them.

Sitting down with them on a mound, I passed around Coca-Cola I had hauled out of my shoulder bag. Their grins couldn't have spread wider. They tilted back their heads, guzzled, came up for air to belch, then drained the bottles too quickly and belched some more. We were having a whale of a time until a little Montagnard boy of five came over to size me up.

I hadn't noticed him until he smiled and said, *"Num*bah *one!"*

I quickly grabbed for my shirt. As soon as I got the last button fastened, he snorted:

*"Num*bah *ten."*

With roads and railroads scarce, and vulnerable to ambush by Charlies, and usually impassable because of heavy rains and floods, the old Providers carried a heavy load. Even when conditions are fair, aerial supply in a combat zone is challenging, particularly in the northern provinces, because of the strategic situation, low ceilings and visibilities of the monsoon weather, plus rugged terrain. The peaks of the Annamite Mountains spear the heavens at almost ten thousand feet and the valleys are steepsided. The dense foliage sometimes reaches two hundred feet in height.

"That kind of canopy could easily swallow an aircraft and reform over the wreckage to hide all the evidence," one of Harry's Hog Haulers said. "When the weather's number ten we use the old canyon flying technique.

"To get into the site you zigzag along the base course. When the bird enters steep-walled valleys in the high mountain areas it requires plenty of coordination from the entire crew. You should never go into a canyon or valley unless there is another way out, in the event it is inadvisable to continue straight ahead. Airplane trouble, deteriorating weather, and ground fire are all factors that make it mandatory to have alternatives."

A few of the canyons are wide enough to allow a 180-degree turn, but it is sometimes necessary to use a steep bank (60 degrees), maximum power, and flaps to reduce stall speed. If an aircraft is flown down one side of the canyon to permit more turning room, it is often exposed to unnecessary ground fire since Charlie likes to concentrate in the valleys of known routes during the bad-weather season and take shots at low-flying aircraft. Early in the war the VC realized a certain FAC pilot repeated his daily trips through a certain valley. They waited for him one day on each side of the canyon. As he approached, both sides started firing to form a curtain of bullets. He barely was able to duck out in time.

The C-123 crews rarely use free-fall techniques when making air drops because troops and camp buildings crowd the drop zones. Parachute techniques from very low altitudes are used to minimize the wind drift.

On one mission to Hiep Duc, the drop zone (DZ) was on the side of a hill in a bowl-shaped valley with higher terrain surrounding it on all sides. Unpredictable gusty surface winds shook the 123. Harry flew the pattern and when turbulence increased, his copilot monitored the instruments, prepared to take control of the craft instantaneously should Harry be hit by ground fire. The navigator controlled the drop signals and the loadmaster, the Special Forces paratrooper, and the flight mechanic rapidly prepared bundles for delivery after each pass, because the pattern was quite tight due to the terrain. Flying into Hiep Duc with a gross weight of over 52,000 pounds, and at a low drop airspeed, left no reserve power to speak of. Harry said it would be mighty convenient to have more horsepower, especially when flying with a heavy load.

"We lose an engine about now, it could create a very interesting situation." About the only choice, if an engine suddenly lost interest in further toil, would be to jettison the cargo as fast as possible and strain to get to lower terrain in the valleys.

One reason ground fire is common on air drops is that the Special Forces camps are located in areas where the VC operate, and another is the necessity of making repeated passes. When Charlie does open up, the 123 drops a smoke grenade and the ground troops at the camp lay down mortar fire a few meters behind the smoke along the track of the aircraft. The pilot always makes sure not to fly over that same area on the next pattern.

Harry went into landing zones I would have thought no sane person would attempt, certainly not in civilian flying. At Khe Sanh the elevation was 1,600 feet, the pierced steel plank (PSP) runway 66 feet wide and only 3,200 feet long. The surface was laid over laterite clay and the rain had soaked the field, causing clay to ooze up through the holes in the PSP. It was so slick Harry couldn't get nose-wheel control or braking action.

How the pilot manages these things is never very clear to a hitchhiker. The winds at Khe Sanh were strong and everchanging. (That is SOP.) "Gets right interesting," according to Harry, "with quartering twenty-five knot tail winds on final approach and the touchdown end of the runway, with a ten-degree upslope, being only two hundred feet away from an 800-foot gorge. Keeps you too busy to appreciate the scenery. Dicey at times. A real hairy piece of airpatch."

"We're now four clicks from the Laotian border and ten miles from the demilitarized zone separating North and South Vietnam," he continued. "The altitude and the seventy-five-degree climate here at Khe Sanh are number one."

Second Lieutenant Louis Pincock of The Dalles, Oregon, was the ranking US officer. He said, "I'm probably the only second lieutenant in Vietnam who commands anything."

Tall First Lieutenant Nguyen Van-Sy was CO of the post.

"He and his troops are Nungs—Chinese mercenaries—who guard us Americans. Our lives are literally in their hands," Pincock told me.

Like the Gurkhas from Nepal, who have earned a reputation for soldiering surpassed by none, the tradition of the Nungs is to fight to the last man. The Nungs are hired by Special Forces in South Vietnam as bodyguards. Even US Ambassador Lodge has one assigned to him. Getting 3,500 piasters a month, the Nungs are 25 percent better paid than Vietnam regulars. Nung officers have a graduated scale up to 8,000 p's which means "found pay" or "cash at the table" as they say in the Army, since it includes room and board. Part of the Nungs' duties is training young Vietnamese troops.

"Out here in the boonies, when a Nung is assigned to guard somebody," Harry explained, "he takes it seriously, even to sleeping beside his charge."

Taller than Vietnamese, the Nungs are ethnic Chinese from North Vietnam and lower China around Nanning. They fight for the sake of fighting and have done so as mercenaries in Vietnam and China for centuries, back into the warlord era. They fought with the French and when colonial rule ended the majority moved to South Vietnam because they disliked communism. They live mainly in Saigon or the Cholon area. They are not the type to lose their heads in battle.

I sat on the floor of beaten earth in their thatched-roof longhouse and taped a broadcast. They were cheerful in an aloof way. Some checked their laundry, strung from wall to wall, others seemed interested in the tape recorder. All were courteous as only Orientals can be. With military aplomb, a few continued with their naps instead of joining the ones crowded around an American reporter hunkered on the dirt floor, fiddling with a Japanese Panasonic purchased in New York.

The men called their post the Taj Mahal because the buildings were better constructed than at other posts, and they had planted small gardens. One wag was nurturing a plot of marigolds, two feet by four, with a sign on a stick reading: AEROSPACE FLOWERS HERE—TYPE MARK II.

"The brass wasn't around when construction was going on so we jazzed things up a bit," explained Second Lieutenant Charles Carroll of Delmar, New York. Carroll was based out of Okinawa with the Special Forces in Vietnam. His operation was called Civic Action (CA) and Psychological Operation (PO). He had done his Reserve Officers' Training at Syracuse University. Carroll was executive officer of Detachment Alpha 101.

"The Bru tribes of the Montagnard here are being given a written language for the first time," Carroll continued. "It will resemble Vietnamese and will have twenty vowels and forty consonants. Two missionaries are conducting the translations. It is a very big status symbol to the Brus."

The men at Khe Sanh were proud of their camp. Ditches lined with corrugated tin curved throughout the grounds. "In case of attack the troops can move without exposing themselves to the enemy," Pincock said. "The tin prevents mud from slowing us down."

As our 123 lifted from the primitive strip and climbed out of the narrow valley, I wondered how many enemy eyes were watching from the jungle.

One passenger Harry picked up along the way pictured exquisitely how pathos can work both ways in this exotic, high-stakes war, in which some peasants hark to the clanking siren song of communism, and others cling to their dreams of peace, dignity, and a desperate hunger for national identity. Tales of great courage are not rare in Vietnam. And one saw every day more vignettes than there would ever be time to report.

A nineteen-year-old fine-boned Viet Cong nurse, captured by the Marines, sat wide-eyed in the C-123. She was clad in black pajamas, a maroon silk shirt, the traditional sloped straw hat, and rubber sandals. Unable to figure out the mechanics of her bucket-seat belt, she thanked, with her eyes, the big sergeant who tucked her safely in. With strange sleepy trust, she put her head on her Marine captor's shoulder. He was big, like so many Americans over there, and she was petite. With correctness and tenderness, which many American women take for granted, he assumed his protective role with rather military precision.

As the C-123, engines thundering, became airborne, the young nurse's eyes, under lowered lids, rested on a rubber-encased American Marine's body we were carrying back. The girl continued to stare at the dead American four feet from her on a stretcher.

Perhaps she had been shanghaied into fighting for Mao Tse-tung's and Ho Chi Minh's holy writ. Possibly she truly believed fanatically in Marxist-Leninist theories. Which, was her secret.

It must have been her first experience at flying, and like some sensitive children on a first roller-coaster ride she got sick. She indicated her condition by touching her tummy with Oriental daintiness. The Marine understood. Gently, as if handling an errant kid sister, he handed her a plastic bag and held her head. I wondered what her punishment would be when she was turned over to the Vietnam authorities.

The body of the Vietnamese who had been killed by a sniper's bullet was removed at Da Nang, as well as that of the Marine. The least desirable duty of pilots is to ferry corpses that have lain too long on the battlefield. The crews often wear respirators on these missions and the aircraft won't smell the same for weeks if they are not sprayed to saturation with wintergreen. Med-EVAC crews stuff Vicks VapoRub in their nostrils.

I went with Harry to the hangar, where he wanted to check on an airplane. The ground crews were banging on engines and whistling despite the strength-sapping heat. The place was abuzz with the latest VC incident. Some of the guards around the base had been given three hours' leave to go to the PX. When they returned to duty, in more than half the one hundred foxholes there were small brown paper sacks, each bag with a deadly poisonous bamboo krait in it. Some Viet Cong worker had just trotted around dropping snakes in the foxholes.

"Sometimes I think the Charlies know more about the activities around here than we do," said a sergeant. "We caught one the other day drawing diagrams of the whole joint."

I walked over to the water cooler to fill my canteen. A bulletin board was almost solid with pictures of shapely pinups wearing no clothes to speak of. Above them was the church-service schedule and weather charts, maps, and personnel listings.

Then Harry took me to lunch at the DOOM Club. DOOM stands for the initials of Da Nang Officers' Open Mess just as CABOOM at Clark Air Base is an abbreviation of Clark Air Base Officers' Open Mess. One careless reporter, afflicted with bone-deep pessimism over the chances of anyone defeating Premier Ho Chi Minh's communist soldiers, had taken a look at the sign and without inquiring, filed a story reporting that the morale of the men at Da Nang had dipped so low that they had even named their club "Doom." When a couple of other distorted stories on Da Nang were sent out over the wires, Colonel Scott closed the base to the press, except by invitation or escort. No one could blame him but it was tough on the other correspondents.

Harry and I stood in line at the cafeteria-style counter. Out of the corner of my eye I saw Smash and Nails enter the Club. They were so big you couldn't miss them. Harry said the ground crews kidded them with suggestions about carrying one less five-hundred-pound bomb so they could get their Cranberry off the ground quicker.

I had removed my shoulder harness and the web belt supporting the canteens and other gear. But in combat fatigues a woman's figure definitely is hidden.

"Do you suppose she's got bad legs and no waistline?" I heard Smash say.

"Who knows? But she's an aloof little snit." Harry and I walked over to the beverage table for some iced tea.

"I got another letter from Mercy Belle. Wanna read it?" Smash asked Nails. "She's a large-hearted gal so I'm sure she wouldn't mind."

My Darling Navigator,
    I treasure your two little notes and I've stopped dating everyone else. Aren't human beings a funny race? They generally can think of only one thing at a time. Sweetie, you arouse me. When will our bodies touch? That would be divine. We could have many good loving years together. My daughter is gone and it feels so good to strip completely and sleep between the cool, clean sheets. It would feel better if you were here to snuggle. I could keep you tired and happy.

The kids say hi. You seem to have aroused the whole, entire family. Somewhat. Love forever.

MERCY BELLE

P.S. For God's sake I just received another note from you and I couldn't be any happier if you had sent me some sex airmail. Do you realize I have an inferiority complex? But I bet my sex angle can't be beat anywhere. I believe in pure, wholesome, unadulterated, free, no-holds-barred sex. I'm going to stick with you forever. Glued to you. You'll probably need a glass navel so I can see where I'm going. My father says if I ever met a man I could love I would kill him. Don't want to go that far, but want you to be well spent.

I have a continual sex urge but have found ways, alone, to relieve some of the physical pressures.

My doctor says that's why I giggle all the time. He says I'm over-sexed and underserviced. I am not a tepid fire, but a burning, desirable, needed woman. I want to make your fire burn. Am I brazen? One of my favorite sayings is: there are two things I like hard and one of them is ice cream. Need I say more? Daddy, my prayers are all for your hot breath on my neck and your strong hard body pressing against me. Completely, eternally,

MERCY BELLE

P.P.S. Scotch and sofa, anyone?

"She sent me a present the other day," Smash said. "An ashtray. It's printed clear across the middle with big red letters: S-E-X."

"Wait till the cleaning woman hears about *this* one?"

"She called me at Clark and you should have heard her. Said I was fouling up her life by making her so passionate. Jesus."

"Seems she's given *you* a harrowing dose of hot pants."

"Yeah. She does sorta stir the juices," Smash said, looking like a conscientious rooster. "Here's her picture. She's sort of a plump Ava Gardner."

The photograph showed a siren half-lying on a couch. She had a bee-stung pout, big gray eyes, and a waterfall of dark hair cascading over her shoulders. A chiffon negligee had been slipped down off both shoulders to just above an overloaded black lace brassiere.

"It's a cardboard world," Nails ventured.

Harry invited me to come along on the afternoon's mission. He seemed at home nowhere but in the sky. When some of his squadron presented him with a silver bowl from Bangkok for his wife, Frances, the accompanying note read: *"We know what you'd rather have had. But we couldn't afford an* Airborne *command post."*

Harry took to the demanding aspects of bush flying like a sunflower to the sun. Harassed by record monsoon floods, mountains, continuous hostile fire, narrow, rough, slick pierced-steel-plank and sod landing strips, night-and-day tactical emergencies, long hours, inadequate housing, mediocre food, and no navigational aids in the mountains, Harry's 311th still had a zero accident rate.

It doesn't always work out so fortunately. When a C-123 crew of the 309th Air Commando Squadron searched for a sister ship that had vanished in bad weather on a flight from Pleiku to Tuy Hoa, they searched until it was too dark to see anymore. There was no trace of the lost ship or its passengers. The search party skimmed the beaches, scoured each ravine, and circled every island. There was nothing.

"We went back to Nha Trang," said First Lieutenant Al Mac-Whinney, "and thumped down the landing gear. It was dark. We were hungry, and each of us had things to do. There is no time for mourning, not here. You hear the news, look at your boots, shake your head, and go back to work."

Airlift is vital to the prosecution of the war effort and equally important to the support of the Civic Action and Disaster Relief programs. Flights out of Khe Sanh carried many tons of coffee, a mainstay of the Montagnard economy. During the November, 1964, flood, when 7,000 were killed, the 311th moved 4,174,630 pounds of relief supplies and 1,358 passengers in 632 relief-support flights. Only the Australians were as eager as Harry. They scarcely blew in from Down Under and touched ground before they bounced into operations and banged on the counter. "OK, mate, where's the next mucking load?"

Harry said one big porcupine snarling up the course was communications problems with the Vietnamese. The air crews must communicate over many matters; for example, off-loading, on-loading, briefings of passengers, no-smoking regulations, and authorization to ride. This usually is done by gesturing, pointing, shouting, and charades in general. It's frequently ineffective. The Vietnamese national is naturally bewildered when he is refused a ride due to weight limitations, especially when he can peek into the aircraft and see vacant seats. How can he know the reasons are sound? To him it could be nothing but American arbitrariness.

"I've seen it happen a hundred times," I said. "But I understood the caution and the rules better when I flew one day with the Fangs. They had a captured VC guerrilla they were taking back to headquarters at Da Nang, and for some reason he had not been thoroughly frisked. When the chopper was forty-five feet off the ground, the guerrilla reached for his crotch. The alert crew chief noticed the furtive movement, picked the guy up, and threw him out of the helicopter. When the guerrilla hit the ground he blew up like a minor ammo dump. His plan had been to take everybody aboard to kingdom come with him. The crew and I were pretty thankful that our guy was on his toes. But that crew chief would probably be condemned as a bully by war critics at home."

"They ought to climb down out of the bleachers and come over here for a grandstand seat," Harry said. "We have to inspect VN credentials, travel orders, or ID cards to determine authenticity or validity. I wish Washington or somebody would step up the crash language courses for the troops and smooth out these daily situations. It's a rough language to get the hang of."

"Ambassador Lodge has been pushing that for years, not just for troops but for State Department employees and all government workers."

"The biggest bellyache, as I don't have to tell you, is the telephone. Routine intercity administrative calls—well, hell, it's easier to reach outer space. A short call can take thirty minutes just to get connected through that turtle switchboard. Communications in Vietnam are solid proof of man's ability to do things the hard way."

Harry echoed the gripe of all when he ground his teeth about the creaking telephone system. The military has a Tropo-Scatter System, which cost approximately twenty million dollars to install and bounces off ionosphere. It ties in long-line connections to various military headquarters and operations throughout the area and requires a heavy energy source. Within it are a number of local switching systems with code names at the various bases. The first step is to get in touch with Tiger. It is SOP to hear some red-faced soldier shouting into one end of the phone, "Hello. *Hello.* Tiger? Gimme Bluebird. Bluebird? What? *Copperhead?*"

If it isn't a top-priority call he is likely as not to be disconnected a few times before completing his conversation, especially the Aussies, who have a language barrier, what with their idioms. After waiting for hours to get the line, the Aussie may say, "Tiger? Give me Peacock. Peacock? This is Lightning."

At this point the local operator breaks in. "Is everything all right, sir?"

"Yes, mate," answers the Aussie, "I'm through," which in Australianese means "I have my party, thank you."

"Oh, you're through? Fine," says the operator, and promptly disconnects him.

Wherever you go you can hear press, fliers, sergeants, sailors screaming into the mouthpiece of some maddening phone. "Weasel? Falcon? Thumbnail? Condor? Bloodhound? Mockingbird? Eggplant? Puma? Backache? Typhoon? Penguin? Alarm Clock?" For newsmen calling in a story from the field, it would be easier to dictate under water.

The existing system for Saigon is called Post Telegraph and Telephone System, PTT. It is the nationalized agency that handles post-office operations, telegraph systems, and the telephone company. It is the AT&T of Vietnam, the national instrument that provides all communications. Calling outside from the Caravelle Hotel, which incidentally has only four trunk lines to handle its hundred rooms, involves first getting the hotel operator, then either local or long-distance Tiger, even if you only want to call Tan Son Nhut. Soon you're plugged into four or five switchboards and it takes only one indifferent operator to throw the monkey wrench into the whole nine yards.

I once asked the Caravelle operator, who I thought was also Information, for the number of the Filipino Embassy in Saigon. The next thing I knew I was magically connected to Clark Air Base, with no one to talk to.

Some of the best news to come down the newsmen's pike occurred when it was announced that cable traffic from Saigon would be facilitated by the introduction of a special Telex operation run jointly by the Vietnamese Telephone-Telegraphic Office and RCA Communications, Inc. The two key Vietnamese officials chiefly responsible for the new Telex were Buu Mghi, director of the National Press Center, and tall, good-looking, bi-lingual Nguyen Ngoc Linh, director of Vietnam Press and one of the Prime Minister's most reliable assistants in charge of press relations.

That afternoon mission of Harry's Hog Haulers included livestock and a batch of raw Vietnamese recruits, who marched aboard in civilian clothes, patched but starched Sunday-best-fresh. They clung together as Sergeant Jones demonstrated to them the strange new seat belts, for this was their first airplane ride. They were going to Kham Dum, where the late President Diem planned to build his summer palace; it is now a camp where civilian troops receive vigorous training from the Nungs and Vietnamese officers.

The Vietnamese lads huddled together like school chums, sleeping on each other's shoulders or laps, and unself-consciously putting their arms around each other. I remembered the ten cardinal rules issued to a battalion of US Marines involved in a pacification drive near Da Nang. Number seven read: "Recognize that hand-holding among Vietnamese males is a custom of comradeship in South Vietnam and not an indication of homosexual tendencies subject to ridicule and mockery."

The young recruits stared in saucer-eyed wonderment at everything new. They watched Jones, a Negro, swap backslapping stories with an Australian officer and two American majors in the back of the plane. If they had heard or read of race prejudice in the United States, the Vietnamese were not seeing it here. There is no race problem among fighting men. There is simply no time for it. In Saigon, the Negroes congregate in one section of a side street and supply the bar owners with records of the music they prefer. But they swear they are not there because of discrimination. "We just naturally gravitate, man." There is absolutely no foundation or sign that Negroes are being drafted to fight out of all proportion to whites, "liberal" rumors to the contrary. I've seen white GIs from Southern states quite happily taking orders from Negro officers and NCOs.

As usual, the air-conditioning condensation began to leak in torrents. Jones whipped out his water-repellent poncho to make a tent for some of the boys, then tore up cardboard boxes to shelter the rest. As Harry hit turbulence, one of the youngest, an uncommonly handsome youth with an angelic face, turned green with nausea. Jones was there in a flash with a small brown envelope containing a plastic barf bag, then distributed more to the others.

I had seen so much drama, heartache, tragedy, and farce in the months of covering the scene, that at times it became an oblong blur. Suddenly my eyes rested on Harry's big, muscular arm as he prepared for a landing. Sunburned and hairy, sinews rippling, it was an awesome hunk of muscle.

But what held my attention, what I never had noticed before in millions of miles of flight, was the gentleness, the fingertip gentleness of the pilot as he handled the flight controls, throttles, and switches of his aircraft. His hands moved with a surgeon's precision or as if they were caressing a little bird.

Five

SAIGON PHILOSOPHERS

"Idiot! Idiot!"

Each time this outburst rent the air I tried to sink lower and lower on my side of the pedicab for two, called a *xich lo may* in Vietnam. And I swore that no matter what the transportation crisis, I would never again share a vehicle with Brody Claud. The target of his abuse was a Vietnamese *phu xichlo,* making his living the hard way. Perhaps he didn't know English, but even a baby would understand the tone of voice.

Brody was not typical of foreign newsmen in Vietnam. He was intensely conscious of himself, blindly oblivious to the feelings of others.

"Now how could you let that happen?" snarled Brody minutes later at the military spokesman conducting the press conference. "Are you gonna let it happen again?"

An American pilot mistakenly had bombed a demilitarized zone and Brody was leaping at the chance to highlight and emphasize any defect in US military exercises. (At that time US forces were still scrupulously respecting the neutrality of the DMZ.) The incident was six weeks old but this kind of bastardized parliamentary debate often substituted for combat reporting. And Brody was not much given to traveling outside Saigon. While he howled for weeks to learn the identity of the "guilty" branch (Army, Navy, Marine or Air Force), the South Vietnamese were far more realistic. They say simply, "This is war."

JUSPAO, Joint United States Public Affairs Office, occupies a heavily reinforced building on the corner of Nguyen Hue and Le Loi, a couple blocks from the Caravelle Hotel. At four-thirty daily, the press attends a Vietnamese briefing. At five o'clock, the Saigon press corps ambles over to JUSPAO, show their press passes to the sergeant on duty, and then navigates the labyrinth of corridors to the briefing auditorium.

Portly and affable Barry Zorthian, whom *Time* calls "the information czar" in Vietnam, is minister-counselor at the US Embassy. Harold Kaplan, former cultural attaché at the US Embassy in Paris, is the witty, knowledgeable spokesman for JUSPAO. He usually leads off the briefing with political information regarding Ambassador Henry Cabot Lodge, Prime Minister Ky, or visiting US Congressmen —who at times descend on the area in near battalion strength. Then officer spokesmen for the military, using brightly lighted and annotated maps, discuss the handouts that have been presented to the newsmen at the door, and elaborate on action in the field. The briefing more often than not disintegrates into a shouting match, especially when the military spokesman refuses to discuss a classified operation. The daily sessions soon were known as "The Five O'Clock Follies."

Shortly before I departed for Vietnam a Washington official told me, "The communists consider this a war for the minds of men. The military is actually secondary. It is a new kind of war for this day and age; different from Korea and World War II—different from anything in our current recollection or thinking. It is ten percent military, ninety percent psychological. We can win or lose through mass communications. This is a war of words as well as bullets."

It is all very well for reporters to be spurred by curiosities which know no restraint, but absolute one-sidedness in reporting is a waste of time for reader, listener, and writer. Newsmen whose private convictions lean far, far to the left, claim more conservative newsmen are "politically immature." The conservatives gag over what they consider the "slanted observations without foundation or perspective" of the extreme leftists. Each group suspects the other: saber-rattling jingoists on the "government team" or Red nuts on the "Peking team." A reporter feels an eerie obligation to be discreet in selecting confidants in South Vietnam. For the clash of opinions among some newsmen can become wide and deep. Reporters can get intensely personal about the war and, at times, ridiculously suspicious of one another.

It is a pleasure to hear writers like New Yorkers Murray Kempton and William F. Buckley—men capable of respect for the very *opposite* point of view. I have found few events more stimulating—or useful—than listening to such men, poles apart and uncompromising in political convictions, giving an object lesson in courteous dialogue on television appearances on "Firing Line": Murray a soft-sell, brilliant, pixie cynic and Buckley a wickedly incisive wit on the highest level.

In a March 17, 1966, speech, Representative Richard Ichord, Democrat of Missouri, hinted that censorship may be necessary, as he attacked the "negativism" and "destructive criticism" in which so many newsmen in Vietnam engage:

"If the news media do not demonstrate the responsibility and the voluntary self-restraint of which I know they are capable, then we must be prepared to consider some form of wartime news censorship, which would include a more stringent policy toward accreditation of correspondents, a limitation in access to battle zones, and a scrutiny of the copy filed."

It would have to be a new type of wartime censorship, because this is a baffling, challenging, new kind of war. In past conflicts there has been field censorship at the front and voluntary censorship at home. But in South Vietnam the United States does not control a theater or a front. Besides, it is South Vietnam's battle, and censorship would have to be under the control of the Republic of Vietnam. That could result in an intolerable mess. In March, 1966, there were 360 accredited newsmen in Vietnam, 141 of them US citizens, 67 Vietnamese, 24 British, and 26 Japanese. The rest are Koreans, Filipinos, New Zealanders, and transient correspondents from Canada and other countries. The number later passed the 500 mark.

A voluntary withholding of stories about troop movements and tactical information is requested of correspondents. Statesmen's background briefings normally include material not for attribution. When spokesmen felt that some reporters violated confidences or filed classified information, they resorted to withholding information. These reporters then claimed they could no longer trust government sources and reveled in writing pieces that irritated officialdom. It was equally annoying to foreign correspondents who hold back on news as requested, only to find it printed by reporters on the home front.

In modern war, officials regard some news as a signal to the enemy and feel that they cannot carry out their duties with the desired precision if newsmen persist in tipping the diplomats' and generals' mitts about planned maneuvers or explicit casualty figures.

Should newsmen send back "superpatriotic" stories, or should they call the shots as "they see" them? Are they supposed to be an extension of government policy, Americans first and reporters second? This question never seemed to come up to any significant extent during WW II. True, that was a declared war and people at home were making companion sacrifices. They cared about WW II and thirsted for encouraging information. To have written negatively about American fighting men and generals in Europe, Africa, or Asia would have been considered in most quarters as bordering on treason.

Representative Ichord also said: "The problem, bluntly stated, is that neither in terms of adequacy of journalistic coverage nor objectivity are the American people being given a complete and fair picture of the Vietnam situation by the communications industry."

Strenuous objections were occasionally voiced that many US newsgathering organizations have hired stringers or part-time correspondents, ostensibly, to avoid the expense of sending a full-time representative, knowledgeable about the area. And there had been a great flap in Washington about some reporters who were not American citizens and had established reputations as being antimilitary prior to their arrival in Saigon, filing for American wire services and networks.

When Senator Thomas Dodd, Democrat of Connecticut, visited the war theater, he said he realized that the press is traditionally cynical, iconoclastic, and in general disrespectful of officialdom. "They recognize no sacred cows and this is the way it ought to be. But extensive coverage of the self-immolation carried out by the Buddhists in protest against the Diem regime reached the saturation point in sensational news." Why, wondered Dodd, was little or nothing written about the self-immolation of High Priest Thich Nguyen Ty in Binh Dinh in protest against the communist occupation of *his* pagoda?

No conscientious reporter wants his mind to travel in the approved rut, he clings to the statement of the late Hugh Baillie of UPI: "Freedom of information is the greatest modern cause for which man can fight."

When you share and try to relate the dreams, frustrations, loves, ideals, and dicey missions of the men in the air, on the sea, or on patrol, and join them in the rugged humor that sustains them under the pressure of combat, it is hard to be impersonal or wish the enemy well.

In Saigon, some of the newsmen who were antipodal in their beliefs ranged from iron-jointed conservatives—who were usually optimists and felt we should not "deprive our fighting men of the absolute confidence of home-front support that combat troops always ought ideally to have"—to extreme liberals, who felt our presence in the Far East was turning into a diplomatic and economic liability. American Embassy officials ordinarily listened to playbacks of what was being reported in the world press.

"I don't listen any more," one of them said to me. "The stuff they're reporting is irrelevant. They broadcast or report on a battle here, or a mission there, and all they get is a cacophony."

Some members of the Saigon press corps appear to have nerves of steel and a complete lack of fear. Others are scared witless. But to do their job thoroughly they must go on patrol in the slimy jungle, get shot at on the beaches, accompany airmen on perilous strikes, and often sleep on the wet ground with the assault troops. Their stories frequently ring with authenticity because the reporter was *there*. The ones who attempt to sum it up without ever leaving Saigon often get rockets from their foreign desks back home because their accounts do not jibe with the eyewitness stories.

Not so, Robin Funk and Jim Wilson, CBS's star sound engineer and cameraman, who crashed in one helicopter, were shot down in another, and kept going back for more stories. Or Tim Page, veteran combat photographer at twenty-two, wounded three times in Vietnam. Nor *Look*'s Sam Castan, the brave young man who put his life on the line and lost it. No one was more vocal than Sam about a combat reporter's place being in combat.

The legendary forty-five-year-old Charlie Black of the *Columbus* (Georgia) *Ledger* lived in the field with the First Cavalry Division. He could outmarch some of the younger soldiers and used the M-16 automatic rifle and .38 he carried. "I don't want there to be any doubt about whose side I'm on," Black said. He left Vietnam with three notches in his belt.

Paul Dean, *Arizona Republic,* made friends everywhere. He not only got good stories, but was blessed with the unpurchasable talent of being on the spot when drama was about to break. And Paul was almost as good a storyteller as AP's winsome leprechaun, Hugh Mulligan, who has managed to persuade the N.Y. office to send him back to Saigon for several hitches.

ABC's popular Lou Cioffi, a top television reporter, went out on every big one his schedule allowed. Jack Foisie, *Los Angeles Times,* who had known Ernie Pyle and even looks like him, missed very little action in the field.

But no one dived into the thick of it more often than newsmen of the Republic of Vietnam. Of eight reporters killed to date, five of them were South Vietnamese. The miracle is that the score wasn't higher. NBC's tough little Vo Huynh, thirty-five, handles the camera while his brother mans the sound equipment. Vo has been at every major battle and is a legend among his colleagues.

"I've been lucky," he says. His NBC bureau chief, towering Garrick Utley, twenty-five and the son of Chicago newcaster, Clifton Utley, has high praise for Vo and knows more than luck is involved. Garrick has been on some rough ones himself and had fallen victim to malaria while on patrol with the Marines. Many other newsmen have been in more operations than the average soldier. A dozen have been seriously wounded and over a hundred have been nicked.

Jimmy Breslin, the wild Irishman of the *New York Herald Tribune,* was assigned to the theater for only a few weeks, but he saw a lot. His vivid accounts of the little man were enlightening and entertaining. Charlie Mohr, *The New York Times,* was grazed in the leg on patrol when a Marine tripped over a booby-trap wire. His *Times* colleague James "Scotty" Reston experienced a crash landing at Da Nang. Jim Lucas, *Scripps-Howard,* called it the "worst reported war ever." Preferring to share the life of the soldiers, Jim seldom was seen in Saigon. He was bounced out of a jeep one day and was hospitalized for a few weeks.

Arnaud de Borchgrave, Bill Tuohy, and Bill Cook, of *Newsweek,* covered every bullet-spanging dust-up with eyewitness accounts. *Leatherneck, Pacific Stars & Stripes, Air Force Times,* and other military journals naturally provided full coverage of the big and little stories with variety and detail for their readers. Tim Page twice hit the jackpot with gory, firsthand battle pictures for *Life* magazine. And it would be difficult to dispute that *Time's* Frank McCulloch is the most knowledgeable military reporter regularly in Saigon.

A handful of newsgatherers were making their first interesting money stringing for a number of newspapers or broadcasting stations. The majority of them were out hustling honestly for good stories. The others scarcely left their hotels or apartments, yet sported exotic submachine guns on occasion. Sometimes they wore custom-made gun holsters, extra-wide-brimmed hats (which the soldiers dubbed B. F. Skypieces) and fancy knives curving in thirty different ways. The worst of these was Brody Claud, the liar of insane proportions who approached all subjects and questions with an open mouth. He sported a foxy mustache, Adler lift shoes, and had all the backbone of a well-boiled icicle. Innocent of any foreign reportorial experience prior to Saigon, he now was stringing for just about every known organization—much of it on speculation—outside the major wire services, and also broadcasting for a few US stations. As the busiest bachelor in town, he was buying his Vietnamese girl friends diamonds and hair sprays, and hiving money for the first time in his life. And he was a slow man with a kind word for US servicemen, particularly officers.

Irascible Brody blew in to the briefing wearing a brand-new commando outfit. He had dipped one leg into the bathtub to give it that lived-in look simulating perilous jungle forays. Weeds were stuffed into his left elephant boot for atmosphere. It was difficult for colleagues privy to Brody's habits to keep a straight face.

With galling monotony and windy chaos, Brody specialized in attack—inside good, strong, well-guarded government buildings. As if engaged in some kind of varmint hunt, he shouted, "Awrite, awrite, now just a minute, just a minute. Was there two or three bodies? My papers and stations want to know about the corpses. Not so fast there, changin' the subject, Colonel."

The colonel's neck muscles twitched but he restrained himself handsomely. To be spokesman at the briefings is not an enviable role.

"Well, what's the answer, Colonel? Don't stall. I'm not in the Army, you know."

The colonel replied, "Watching combat or being in it is vastly different from getting a report secondhand. Why don't you go out to the real battlefield and find out in person? Sir."

Brody was beyond insult. "Now there's no need to be derisive, Colonel."

When it was announced that the commander in chief of the Veterans of Foreign Wars, Andy Borg, would arrive the following morning and be available for a press conference, Brody threw back his head and hooted, "Who needs *him?* Who's calling the press conference?"

Brody's impertinence and heckling of the long-suffering information officer, who after all did not write the rules, proved too much for Keyes Beach, an expert analyst on Far Eastern matters. Keyes had covered Asia for the *Chicago Daily News* for twenty-one years and was one of the most respected veterans of the news media. Keyes got up and walked out, muttering, "I have more respect for the press corps than to be associated with that!" A few others followed him.

After the briefing a little captain cornered Brody in the hall. "You're the biggest fake in Saigon. I don't know why you've got on that breakaway costume. Show me a record, a manifest, or proof of any kind that you've been *anywhere* outside the suburbs. Do you know what they call you at headquarters in Honolulu? Toadie Fraud."

His job was something between a nightmare and a pipe dream. The nightmare part was because he had convinced himself that the American military were following him twenty-four hours a day, quite the height of his hallucinations. Waggish MACV officials, learning of Brody's fears, exhorted him to try and get home earlier.

"You keep us up so late tailing you, Brody."

After eight straight months of reporting by osmosis, Brody finally ventured five miles out of the Saigon city limits to tape a show for a radio station he'd just picked up. Nervous as a demented Pekingese, he barked, "And that colonel better have me back in an hour or he might just be a *captain* in the morning."

On this maiden trip to the fringes of war he was to interview a group of ARVN soldiers and American advisers who were part of an outfit that had suffered 100 percent wounded or dead in a recent battle. In a cheap fictional atmosphere of making news to set men aflame, Brody wheedled, "Now looka here, sport, while I'm recording and talking to ya, would one of your guys shoot off a pistol so it'll sound like we're on the battlefield?"

One of the American advisers quietly quoted Emerson to himself: "What you are thunders so loud I can't hear what you say."

The granite facts are not easy to come by in Vietnam. The effort to collect them requires plenty of digging. The majority of newsmen, impartial, disciplined, conscientious, careen around the country like highly trained bird dogs uncertain of the scent. The oddballs trying to make a name for themselves in headlines report events out of propor- tion and perspective. Sometimes the trouble lies back at the foreign desk. One London newspaperman received a cable from his editor requesting an exposé on racial discrimination in the US Armed Forces. Another wrote a solid piece which stated in essence that the United States not only had good cause to be in Vietnam but even had a fair chance of winning. His editors fired back a rocket accusing him of failing to be objective, and informed him that they had altered his copy.

Some newsmen in Saigon complain about the public-information setup. Others consider it the best possible under the circumstances. The bitterest brouhaha to date erupted between Arthur Sylvester, who has the unenviable position of Assistant Secretary of Defense for Public Affairs, and a reporter employed by CBS.

The reporter had produced a TV sequence putting US Marines in a bad light. The reaction was immediate. The reporter then, in print, claimed that Washington officials had warned his network that if they didn't get him out of Vietnam "he's liable to end up with a bullet in his back." The reporter also quoted Sylvester as saying: "Newsmen should be handmaidens of the government."

Sylvester replied in print that perhaps he shouldn't be surprised at "such self-created quotations" coming from a reporter who had so distorted US Marine Corps activity that "he has won the undying contempt of the Marines." And "incidentally," Sylvester added, "that reporter is the only man I ever heard refer to another man, especially a newsman, as a 'handmaiden.' "

In the States I have queried CBS officials. None recalled any Washington threat that reporters might be "shot in the back."

If the story was false it involves the most foolish form of self-advertising. If it is true—even in jest—that a newsman's life was threatened, his colleagues should unite behind him because freedom of the press would be at stake. I would scramble to be the first in line.

If the American public is ill-informed, scores of newsmen are doing their best to correct it and feel their responsibility fully. Though his reports are often at odds with his paper's editorial stand, *The New York Times* columnist Cyrus L. Sulzberger has consistently called for US firmness in Vietnam. He wrote: "It takes two sides to negotiate, and what the other side makes plain is that all it wants is total victory. What the Viet Cong and Hanoi want is peace at no price, and what Peking wants is no peace whatsoever."

Qui Nhon had been just another seaside town, a lovely fishing village, before the 7th Marines and an Army transport company arrived early in the war. Now it is a critical port. The town straddles two major highways, Route 1 (running north and south) and Route 19 (going east and west, to connect with Pleiku in the Central Highlands). It is in that area that the war could be decided in a showdown.

Aboard the USS Boxer, the Flying Cavalry of the world's first airmobile division came in to port at Qui Nhon. Some of the troops choppered off the amphibious assault ship; others marched off an LSU to shore, with the Stars and Stripes held high; then came the Guidon or unit emblem of the First Battalion, 9th Cavalry Regiment, and last, strapping soldiers toting a hundred pounds of gear in their duffle bags.

Most of the men looked formidably fit and itching for battle. Close up, taking photographs, I saw in some faces fear of the unknown, but they were ready to fight in places with names the majority of them couldn't pronounce and had never heard of before.

From the moment they saw a four-star general and a distinguished-looking civilian watching them come ashore, the soldiers' faces lighted up with pride. And one tough-looking sergeant was the first to pass the word: "Westmoreland! It's the gung-ho Old Man himself!"

"Yeah. And ain't that our American Ambassador?"

General Westmoreland and Ambassador Lodge were standing at

the shore's edge. The Ambassador was in shirtsleeves with a snap-brim straw hat pushed back from his forehead. Westmoreland, his four stars gleaming, wore knife-sharp starched khakis.

Both are six feet tall; they towered above the Vietnamese mayor at the refugee camp we visited half an hour later—Dong Ciang, which was teeming with goats, pigs, people, ducks, chickens, and baby calves. The refugees, who have fled from the Viet Cong, are given a few piasters a day and are taught carpentry, modern farming, and trained as blacksmiths, masons, barbers, and tailors.

The refugees streamed to these camps by the tens of thousands because the Viet Cong had broken the near-sacred rule of the great text on guerrilla war, Mao Tse-tung's *On Protracted War,* reiterated in *People's War, People's Army* by his remarkable Vietnamese communist pupil, General Vo Nguyen Giap: *Popular support of the guerrilla movement must never be endangered until the final victory.*

Over and over the VC had promised the peasants that there would be *no* VC taxation and *no* VC conscription. As the going got rougher for the VC, taxes were levied till the burden became insufferable. Universal military service was proclaimed for all males between eighteen and thirty-six, and then the VC began rounding up boys as young as twelve. Shocking photographs taken by American photographers showed the bodies of some of them, still chained to their machine guns. The VC had made sure the children could neither desert nor retreat.

By February, 1966, the number of sullen peasants fleeing from the VC "liberated areas" reached 800,000, about one-sixth of the population that the VC had controlled at their high point in the summer of 1965. This exodus began to leave the VC areas seriously short of hands to till the crops; the rice supply formerly available to VC tax collectors diminished dangerously; and the pool of conscripts was drying up. Not at all surprisingly, the VC propaganda machinery began shrilly to denounce the refugee flight as "an imperialist plot." Potential popular support is indeed being alienated daily, excepting the possible 15 percent of genuine communist converts in such "liberated areas."

The reporters invited to cover the day's activities included: John Maffre, *Washington Post,* Charlie Mohr, Jimmy Breslin, Bill Tuohy, Jack Foisie, and AP's chief Vietnam correspondent, Ed White. On the flight to Qui Nhon, Jack shared with me his cold, foil-wrapped, charcoal-cooked steak from the previous night's dinner; he carved it off with his Swiss pocket knife, a chunk at a time.

The next day, in Ambassador Lodge's outer office at the Embassy, we taped my interview with him. On his first tour as Ambassador to Vietnam, during John Kennedy's Presidency, the Ambassador's wife, Emily, had been exceptionally well received. She visited hospitals and schools, and mingled with the people in the market places. But she had had to leave when all dependents of American military and diplomatic personnel were evacuated the first week of February, 1965, after the bombing at Pleiku. The wives were sorely missed. The inducements Lodge was alleged to have employed to get the ban lifted were definitely imaginative. The story goes that Lodge invited visiting senators to stay at the Embassy residence, then deliberately arranged for routine matters to go wrong. The highballs had no ice, red wine was served with the fish, butlers spilled water, and there was far too much salt in the salad. Lodge murmured apologies for the chaos by explaining, "Everything would be all right around here if Emily were back."

When I asked if he anticipated a reversal in the ban he thought not. "And no exceptions as far as Mrs. Lodge is concerned."

For President Johnson to select Lodge, a Republican, for a second round in the bloody and dramatic hot spot, seemed an extraordinary political act.

Lodge replied, "I didn't accept as a Republican, but as an American. I don't think anybody asks, when you go to see the soldiers, whether you are a Republican or a Democrat. I accepted the President's offer because a great many young Americans out here, just at the beginning of their lives, are in positions of danger. I wanted to help if I could. This is the most important place in the world at the present time, not only for Americans but for people everywhere who value their freedom."

Ambassador Lodge had retired the previous year from the Army reserve with the rank of major general. I asked how significant he considered combined Vietnamese-American air power in the recent reversal of Viet Cong fortunes. "Air power," he said, "has played a tremendous part. The B-52 strikes, for example, provide a saturation of Viet Cong strong points and redoubts which could not be reached in any other way. Places like Zone D north of Saigon and the Camau Peninsula were never entered at all in the days of the French colonization. Air power is an utterly vital element of the struggle. But sea power, land power, civil and political aspects, the economic and the social, the doctors and teachers—all play a decisive part. It is a political-military struggle. All these programs must be braided together. Mao Tse-tung, the patron saint of the Viet Cong, says that war is politics with bloodshed and politics is war without bloodshed, and these are the two wings of statecraft."

I mentioned that the communists regard America as the sole major obstacle standing between them and world conquest. "What more can be done, Mr. Ambassador, to enlighten 'unwitting communist accomplices' who picket the White House, who say in effect, 'Don't say harsh words to the alligator as he prepares to swallow your friend. It will only make him madder.' "

"That," said Lodge, "is like the story of the two men who were sitting in a restaurant and one of them said to the other, 'Don't look now, but a man is making off with your overcoat.' I wouldn't worry about the people who are picketing the White House."

"Some of our soldiers over here worry about it," I said.

"Well," he replied, "a lot of them don't. I think President Johnson has done a remarkable job educating public opinion. There has been a tremendous increase in the amount of understanding in America about what's at stake in Vietnam. Today I think there isn't a single person of goodwill—exempting a few screwballs—who doesn't know why this struggle is important. Some don't know yet how we're going to resolve it, but honest people can discuss that. We certainly discuss it out here. But nobody of goodwill in America is in doubt any more as to why it is important for us to be here. Recent polls prove my point. I think the people who willfully act as though they didn't understand why we're in Vietnam are really people we can disregard."

The Ambassador felt that those behind the clamor of the "US peace bloc" were not as interested in a long-term solution as they were in the mechanics of protest.

That afternoon General Westmoreland presided at a briefing in MACV headquarters. These briefings are conducted for what some call the "inner circle" of the press corps. The General told us that the next day's operation, involving battalions of the 173rd Airborne Brigade and elements of the Royal Australian Regiment of Infantry, was going to employ non-nauseating tear gas if necessary. It would be launched either by grenades or by a device known as the "Mighty Mite," a fifty-pound instrument that was originally a fumigating device but was later used to force tear gas under great pressure into Viet Cong tunnels. The briefing of the forthcoming exercise not only was not for attribution; it was of the greatest secrecy. After the B-52s softened up the densely wooded jungle of Zones C and D, our troops would go in.

There had been what H. L. Mencken might have called "a geyser of pish posh" in the world press the first time US troops used such gas. When Secretary of Defense Robert S. McNamara visited Vietnam the previous July and was asked about the prospect of using tear gas in future operations, he gasped, "Oh, my God, I do not want to go through that again."

The Red Chinese leaders are tirelessly committed to spreading their "hate-the-USA psychosis" around the world. They are determined to organize global opinion against American "intervention in Vietnam," and to convince the world that we are using "poison" gas in Vietnam.

The Red Chinese who have never been deterred by facts noisily clamor that Americans employ "poison gas" of the CS and CN variety. In truth, the CS is a simple tear gas and the CN is tear gas plus a vomitory agent. But in a twinkling Peking can produce faked photographs, bits of gas-impregnated clothing, and highly circumstantial evidence and melodramatic personal accounts to support their accusations. To back these up they summon fellow-traveling "independent scientists," mostly the type who parroted germ-warfare charges in Korea. Their monumentally ambitious propaganda program surpasses anything dreamed up by the Nazis' Joe Goebbels or the Kremlin's controlled press.

General Westmoreland directly and simply explained that "on a case-by-case basis" he intended his troops to use tear gas as a means of flushing the Viet Cong and their followers or hostages from tunnel structures without being forced to use more lethal grenades or bombs. "Tear gas," he said, "may be used on the operation if the local unit commander feels that its employment will assist in accomplishing the operational requirement with fewer casualties to friend and enemy alike. It is anticipated that the use of tear gas will be restricted to small areas where the enemy is holed up in bunkers or trenches."

I walked back to the Caravelle with Lou Cioffi. "I've never met an officer with more dignity than Westmoreland," I said. "He makes things clear and looks you in the eye. I like that. By the way, did you see that story in *Newsweek* quoting Communist Chinese Foreign Minister Chen Yi as saying: 'We will not hesitate to participate in a just war, whether it be classical or nuclear. We will not hesitate to use our atomic weapons to defend ourselves. We fear nothing.'"

"The fact that the Chinese are taught to hate us around the clock is nothing new," Lou said.

"It gripes me that we're supposed to care so much for world opinion. There is no way for us to be universally popular. The US is too big, too rich, and too powerful."

"Well," replied Lou, "you remember what Prime Minister Sir Robert Peel had to say about public opinion. 'It is a compound of folly, weakness, prejudice, wrong feeling, right feeling, obstinacy, and newspaper paragraphs.' God knows what he would have had to say about *world* opinion."

"De Gaulle claims that a great country worthy of the name does not have any friends."

"You know, it's going to be interesting to see what the historians have to say about him in twenty-five years. He's an imaginative, methodical statesman of the first magnitude. He may offend his allies and enrage other countries by breaking the rules, but thanks to him, France now again enjoys world stature and is an important diplomatic power. Paris is a clean and proud city for the first time in decades."

"And you can't say his French diplomacy hasn't worked, whether people like it or not. There was something magnificent about wartime de Gaulle fighting Churchill and Roosevelt for the right to control the destiny of France. Would any good Frenchman have done otherwise, or less?

"It is surprising how many people acknowledge him as the towering statesman of the century, more so than Churchill. Others wish one of those plastic bombs had got him back in the fifties when his enemies tried so hard. I think his strength is the ability to discern the inevitable and then exploit it. He wouldn't dream of allowing sentiment to hamstring him."

No sooner had I arrived back at the Caravelle to shoot a cable off than the ABC crew came dashing out of their corner suite on my floor. "They've hit the My Khan again."

I ran back to get my camera and caught a ride with Pete Kalischer of CBS.

The My Khan restaurant, where the food is excellent, the view and the breeze pleasant, is moored in the Saigon River and connected by a gangplank to a busy pier in the downtown area. Near the gangplank stands a small green kiosk where curios and souvenirs are sold. A Vietnamese woman had approached and quickly put down a paper sack behind the kiosk. When a policeman blew his whistle, she fled into the night.

The explosion, thirty seconds later, blew out the back of the kiosk but only shattered a pane of glass in the My Khan as the South Vietnamese, French, and American customers dived under the tables for cover. There was no panic, and the manager, Phan Sanh, said, "I do not understand why the terrorists are so drawn to my café."

He was unduly modest; the picturesque floating restaurant is a favorite GI eating place, dubbed the "Claymore Café" since the attack on June 25, 1965. On that well-remembered evening two Claymore mines were set off at the height of the dinner hour, and another triggered to explode just as the panicked customers scrambled in horror for the ramp. The secondary mine, across the street, was aimed directly at the exit. Eighty persons were injured in the June blast and forty-two killed. (The Claymore is a directional mine —a device which, when detonated, spews out a broadsword of steel pellets that mow down everything in range. It hurls half-inch steel balls in directed arcs and is a principal defense of US camps in Vietnam. Though the Viet Cong type is far cruder, it is just as effective and lethal.)

Air-conditioning is a status symbol in Saigon and the Caravelle really drove it into the ground. Constantly I typed wrapped in blue blankets. The icy blast from the high vent kept the heavy lined draperies beside my desk billowing night and day. Charles Klensch and two of his ABC crew climbed on chairs and taped a piece of cardboard over the vent. That worked for an hour before it was blown halfway across the room. I got tired of sneezing and decided there was probably a poker game going on in the CBS suite on the second-floor corner, so I went down to sit in. I was accepted now, but it's never easy.

At first they squirm and say, "We don't play with women."

"I don't either," I reply quickly.

You could say the table was makeshift. We had to hold it up with our knees. It had no legs and was covered with the traditional gray blanket. The games often lasted till seven in the morning because somebody's always behind.

"Deal faster," cry the losers.

Lou Cioffi has velvety black eyes, wiry gray hair, and a humor that never deserts him unless a competitive network is shot with outrageous luck and beats him to a story. Lou is crazy about his wife and kids who live in Tokyo and he had just returned from one of his frequent visits to them.

The game was table stakes—the only way to play poker.

In one of the biggest pots, Lou was dealing. He flipped out the cards, bending and turning them over with a sharp snap.

I had queens wired in five card stud and a pair of threes showing with one card to come. Lou had a king and an open pair of fives, with another king in the hole. One player had already folded a queen of hearts.

Jack Lawrence felt good with two tens and one of Lou's kings showing and a ten in the hole. The bets were getting interesting.

With everybody in, Lou snapped a card to Jack.

"A deuce, no help."

Then he sent one skittering over the blanket to me. It was the case lady.

"Two pairs," Lou announced, and gingerly flipped over a fifth card for the dealer. A big five of diamonds. Lou studied my queens and threes, Jack's pair of tens, and felt almost princely with his trio of fives and the regal hole card that paired his open king. Almost. Both he and Jack are good, thoughtful card players. Lou bet his fives and kings. Jack felt he had to raise or get out. He raised. Then it was up to me and I shoved in my whole stack. Lou didn't feel like folding a full house and called. Jack looked at the monumental pot and figured how much he had in it already and paid to see my queens full.

Lou's olive-skinned face didn't change color. He just tossed his cards in the air and said, "Gee, it's good to get away from the family and back here with you guys."

One of the more hair-raising episodes of Saigon occurred a few days later when three volunteer doctors risked their lives to remove a grenade lodged in a Vietnamese farmer's back. In a daring operation, Major General James W. Humphreys, a fifty-year-old Air Force surgeon from Richmond, Virginia, and head of the US Operations Missions (USOM) public-health service in Vietnam, removed an egg-size American grenade from fifty-two-year-old Nguyen Van Chinch.

The two-star general volunteered for the job and asked for other volunteers from the US Aid Mission's health department. Several responded. Humphreys, a thoracic surgeon, selected Dr. Tony Brown, a young British anesthetist, and Colonel Daniel C. Campbell, another Air Force surgeon. The Americans volunteered to perform the operation after Vietnamese doctors said they were unsure how to go about it.

Chinch had been struck in the right side of his back the previous Sunday in Longan Province, south of Saigon. The grenade was thought to have been fired at a distance of about eight yards from a US M-79 launcher; it failed to explode but lodged in the small of his back. It never was learned who fired it but spokesmen said the grenade launcher could have been a weapon captured by the VC.

Whoever fired it was irrelevant; the infection around the wound was getting worse and worse. Nobody had touched it for days, because of the gravity of the situation. The grenade could have exploded at any time, particularly during the operation. This particular type of grenade arms itself after it has traveled a distance of twelve yards, which means that it is ready to explode at any time after that.

Chinch was confined to an isolated shed in a tin building separated from the main building at Choray Hospital. The impact had not broken any bones and after two or three days Chinch wanted to go home.

"That of course was out of the question," Humphreys said.

"If he had stumbled on the street or hit a bump in a taxi, the sensitive fuse of the grenade could have been triggered. If he had blown up he could have taken a half-dozen passersby with him."

Chinch's bed was placed in a corner of the shack with sandbags about ten feet high around it on two sides. Meanwhile the medical team began reading up on the M-79 grenade to try to figure out how best to handle it during the operation. Every precaution was taken to protect the doctors if the grenade went off during surgery. The operating table was enclosed by sandbags, with a small aperture left through which they could operate.

The team of doctors was up most of the night before the operation, practicing with a special set of instruments especially devised for the delicate operation by Captain Jack Faircloth of New York, who was Humphreys' aide. One was a six-foot-long steel arm with a scalpel attached to it rather like an outsize fountain pen. With this Humphreys planned to reach carefully through a slit in his bullet-proof glass aperture and cut the skin away from the grenade. The other instrument was a pair of tongs on arms slightly longer than those attached to the improvised scalpel.

Original plans called for a walled bunker with a small porthole through which Humphreys would operate these mechanical arms. At the last minute USOM delivered a square of bullet-proof glass.

When the doctors were ready, Chinch gingerly arose from his bed and eased himself over to the operating table. Holding his breath, he lay down with infinite care. The most dangerous part of the exercise began when Dr. Brown stepped up to the table and without hesitation injected anesthesia in the area of the grenade. That done, Brown walked away and the bunker was walled up. A sand-filled ammunition box had been placed below the operating table for Humphreys to drop the grenade in. When the General had completed his part of the operation, cutting away the skin, Colonel Campbell took the tongs on the long arms and gently lifted out the grenade and even more carefully deposited it in the ammunition box. Immediately a sandbag was popped over the box and the five-minute drama was over.

However big the story, each broadcaster was allowed only ten minutes on PTT, Saigon's only radio station. If you spilled over into someone else's allotted time, the little Mama-San who ran the whole shebang would march right into the sound-proof room and remind you of the rules. Frequently the static from the earphones was so bad you couldn't hear yourself talk, though engineer Dick Rosse in New York might say you were coming in wonderfully. And if you could hear New York, they often couldn't hear you well enough for the broadcast to be commercial. But Dick always had some cheerful comment that was encouraging for the morale of a correspondent struggling to be heard from the other side of the world.

Saigon's station was reminiscent of Marconi days, but they managed well with what they had. One boy who worked there had been caught in the My Khan Restaurant explosion. For months his right arm was in a cast but he wore a perpetual smile and never once complained.

The stitches had by now been removed from my foot but the swelling wouldn't go down so I wore thonged rubber sandals. I thought it would look silly to wear one combat boot and one sandal but Brody Claud needled me about it whenever our paths crossed. "Trying to attract attention, huh? Just like a woman, wearing those foolish things."

CHECK ALL FIREARMS AND DICE AT THE DESK reads the sign at the entrance of the Saigon USO Club. It is frequented by far more American soldiers, sailors, airmen, Seabees, and Marines than the dark little bars on Tu Do Street. There is a jukebox, occasional live entertainment by a Vietnamese jazz combo and a singer, newspapers, magazines, and a long table with a great roll of brown wrapping paper and balls of twine for the men to package gifts they have bought for families or sweethearts back home.

It was a favorite eating place of mine, with plenty of familiar food. Waffles, scrambled eggs, banana splits, gallons of milk, roast chicken, chili, jumbo-size milkshakes, and assorted sandwiches. The

Vietnamese short-order employees hollered orders to the bustling kitchen help and obviously delighted in seeing how fast they could move the line of hungry men.

I joined two young airmen at a table—twenty-two-year-old Joe Warmter, Airman First Class, of Hyde Park, New York, and Airman First Class Gary Whitney, twenty-six, of Orlando, Florida. I put my scrambled eggs, pancakes, and milk on the table, handed the tray to a waiter, and asked them where they were based.

"At Bien Hoa, the unlucky place," they said and recalled the horrors of the blasts there that had cost so many lives and planes.

"There are a lot of good guys there, especially the Australians, but we're in Saigon for some R & R," Warmter said. "The mortar shelling goes on every night around Bien Hoa. Either they're shelling us or we're shelling them, or both. It's tough trying to get any rest. When I can't sleep sometimes, I think of what I'm gonna do when I get home if I ever meet one of those street demonstrators."

I told them about Inez Robb's column suggesting that street gangs and discontents who beat up helpless old people and children be brought over to fight the Viet Cong.

"Well," said Whitney, "it would be a standoff. Those punks don't like to get in a scrap unless they have the advantage in numbers. They and old Charlie could overpopulate the world in no time at all, waiting to outnumber each other."

Warmter added, "I'd like to see those so-called pacifists who parade the gold-starred blue-and-red flag of North Vietnam along American streets go straight to Hanoi. They deserve each other. Nobody on our side would want to go into combat having to depend on any of those characters."

"I'd like to stay and talk longer, but I have to get ready for a luncheon appointment and pick up some film and tapes at the PX," I said. "Hope you enjoy your R & R."

"It's always good to talk with someone from home," they said. "And good luck to you. Maybe we'll run into you in Bien Hoa."

The Navy PX in Saigon is next to the Ambassador Hotel. I fished out my various identification cards for the Marine sentry. Recognizing a face is not enough; strictest security measures require that everyone, including men in uniform, show their ID card at every entrance to any military installation.

In front of me three warriors stood clutching a bulging brown paper bag. They turned out to be Jake, Reggie, and Crunch. "Can we take our jug in with us?"

"Sure thing," replied the guard.

Servicemen coming into Saigon can take their booze into night-clubs or bars and save money by ordering setups, so some of them tote it around with them all over town.

As the trio marched in to explore the wonders of familiar state-side articles, the guard remarked to me, "Some of the troops are in for the weekend from Bien Hoa. They've been out on some rough patrols. There'll be no holding them tonight."

Sunday is the biggest day but the PX is usually also mobbed on Friday, payday. Each shopper must show his PX card at the cash registers, which are manned by doll-like but very business-like Vietnamese girls. Card holders are allowed six bottles of liquor per month and six cartons of cigarettes.

A Negro captain stood in the long double line. His basket was loaded with shaving lotion, BVDs, a monkey wrench, and two bottles of pink champagne.

"Hold your horses," said a wide-eyed sergeant, who was arguing with his buddy over the merit of certain brand names. "She's a round-eye. Maybe this lady speaks English."

So I trotted around the aisles helping them choose laundry bleaches, insect spray, boned chicken, spot remover, argyle socks, and Dixie cups.

One of the hottest items in the post exchange is hair spray. Some is bought as a gift for local girl friends, but most of it goes to the seven hundred maids in government quarters in Saigon, as an inducement to keeping the floors well scrubbed. Very few Vietnamese girls have hair blowing in the wind these days.

A six-foot-tall, graying, handsome major of the Special Forces had collected sour-ball candies, Fudgies, shampoo, mouthwash, shoelaces, shoe polish, lighter fluid, Kleenex, and a whisk broom in his basket. He asked the cashier to include a pen from the collection in back of her. "What kind, sir?"

"No matter. Just as long as it writes so my wife can read it."

Reggie, Jake, and Crunch looked over the well-stocked shelves. A sailor nearby selected a magazine and walked away humming.

"Oh, balls," growled Crunch as his jaw dropped slack. "The bastard took the last copy of *Playboy!*"

I found little or no time for the cocktail circuit in Saigon, but I'm glad I was able to accept one invitation:

The Secretary of State
for Psychological Warfare
Requests the Pleasure of Your Company . . .

The affair was in honor of a group of men traveling on behalf of President Johnson, and included Dr. Frank Stanton, president of the Columbia Broadcasting System.

For the party I wore the only cocktail dress I'd brought to the war. Stanton said, "I'd never have known you were the same girl who was at today's press conference. I turned to the man on my left and asked, 'Who's *that?*' "

Small wonder. I had been on an FAC mission and particularly wanted to catch that day's briefing and there had been no time to change when I raced in from Tan Son Nhut. I slipped into JUSPAO in a bush hat, fatigues still soaked from the heat and the mission, my Charlie Chaplin beetle crushers, and hair an indescribable mess. As far as I know, my face was dirty, too. I had stood in the back and didn't know who all was there.

During his visit I managed a few private talks with the CBS president. He is completely understanding of the everyday difficulties which are par for the course for most newsmen in Vietnam.

"The responsibility of broadcasting in collecting the news has never been more important or more challenging than now."

He spoke of the frustrating character of the conflict. "It is like no other war in our history and against an enemy like no other we have ever fought. Furthermore, it is on the opposite side of the world, in an unfamiliar land, against a highly motivated enemy, who is wily in tactics and ruthless in purpose. And the United States is fighting in double harness. We alone cannot call the turns . . . an openended, unpredictable war."

I asked what he thought of the criticism of the press in some quarters. He said, "The newsmen over here have to resort to persistence, ingenuity, and sheer guts to get the picture home. For a newsman's pains—and I use the word literally—he is attacked more often than he is praised, as if he were inventing the events he reports."

Stanton mentioned that some people evidently would like only the good news reported.

"The stark face of war is never pleasant to observe. I know how frustrating it is to you reporters not to get behind enemy lines and report the ruthlessness with which the VC tyrannize innocent villages, raid and murder and terrorize, and brutally throw into discard the standards of conduct by which, even under war conditions, civilized men have lived for years."

It was a tonic to talk over dinner with this gentleman. And he is full of surprises. The president of an incalculably rich network travels economy class when he flies. I didn't ask why. But I'll wager he meets more interesting people that way. It is easy to imagine him making a spot check on what programs the passengers watch and why.

"Lunch at the Prime Minister's palace at noon," Captain Nguyen Bao had said on the phone. On arrival, snappy sentries admitted my car, and at the foot of the Gia Long Palace steps the protocol chief received me. They're very long on courtesy and good manners in Vietnam.

Ushered into the lounge for preluncheon cocktails, I was greeted by the soft-spoken Prime Minister Ky. Ky speaks fluent French, and his English is full of idiomatic slang. The only son of a small-town North Vietnamese schoolteacher, he was born in Son Tay, just west of Hanoi.

The luncheon surprise was the presence of Ky's entire deputy chiefs of staff of VNAF, as well as Brigadier General Albert Schinz, USAF adviser to VNAF, who hails from Ottawa, Illinois. There were thirteen in all.

Tall, handsome Lieutenant Colonel Tran Van Minh, Ky's deputy commander in VNAF, said to me, "You are not seeing the real Vietnam. Come back in a few years and you will find how we really are. The war blurs the image now."

I replied, "I've found your people look like fragile dolls yet they have an incredibly stiff spine under monstrous circumstances. The Vietnamese are a fatalistic race who bend but do not break and, more amazing, have not given way to xenophobia. I find them hospitable, quick-witted, and gentle. I do look forward to returning when the war is over. The mystery to me is the Viet Cong's callousness and contempt for family feeling. All the South Vietnamese I've spoken to resent this bitterly."

At eight-thirty that morning, General Ky had presided at commemorative services at the Saigon Zoo, honoring a great Vietnamese hero, Le Loi, who in 1433 had led a ten-year battle against aggressive Chinese. Later he had become a soldier king.

"It was supposed to be a formal, reverential ceremony," Colonel Minh said, "but General Ky was startled to find himself the center of a squealing mass of teen-agers waiting at the entrance. The general understands children very well—has six of his own. He is a little disturbed at the moment because his oldest son likes to earn his own money by shining shoes and selling newspapers."

General Ky walked up to us. "It was bad enough when I was an

Air Force general," he said, "but it doesn't look so good for the son of the Prime Minister to be out hawking newspapers."

Like Ky, most of his staff had attended Air Force training schools in the US, and like him, they were all young, and local heroes.

When the Viet Cong attacked the American compounds at Pleiku, 250 miles north of Saigon, and with mortars and rifle grenades killed eight Americans, wounded 126, and damaged or destroyed twenty-one aircraft, Vietnamese and American pilots next day struck north of the seventeenth parallel for the first time. General Ky himself led the raid, bombing North Vietnam military bases to avenge the American deaths.

Returning from the mission, Ky and his men received a heroes' welcome at Tan Son Nhut Air Base. Every one of Ky's two dozen planes had been hit by enemy ground fire—Ky's three times. Yet only one plane was lost. "The pilot bailed out over Da Nang Bay and was rescued," Ky told me.

Schoolgirls hung garlands of flowers around their necks, and the following day at Tan Son Nhut, flowers and medals were placed on the flag-draped coffins of the Americans who died at Pleiku. General Westmoreland stood at attention as they were put aboard a plane to carry them home. The Vietnamese pilots were awarded medals for their bravery.

Ky never relinquished his role of VNAF chief when he assumed the duties of Prime Minister. His flying colleagues idolize him and he enjoys the close friendship of many American pilots. He has flown hundreds of combat missions. As a major in command of South Vietnam's 43rd Air Transport Squadron, Ky was chosen as the first pilot to carry out secret "black flights" over North Vietnam. For three years he and a group of American and Vietnamese fliers who called themselves the "Dirty Thirty" dropped saboteurs and guerrillas into North Vietnam at night.

Today he and the men of the 83rd Detachment at Tan Son Nhut wear black flying suits with purple scarves and call themselves Than Phong ("Divine Wind")—the local equivalent of the Japanese kamikaze of WW II. One of the reasons Ky's men love him is that if they are promoted, Ky personally presents the new insignia and pay increase in the presence of each man's family.

Ky's detractors claim he is too prudent to get far away from his men and the immensely important key branch of the service which has more or less ensured his political position.

Ky reserves a takeoff strip at Tan Son Nhut, open at all times. Planes and crews are on twenty-four-hour alert. If a would-be successor became coup-minded, Ky's pilots could be over Saigon within minutes.

Sitting beside the Prime Minister at luncheon, I asked about the Dirty Thirty and how they got their name.

"We started out wearing black flying suits so that if we had to bail out over the North, we couldn't be spotted so easily." (The Americans who flew with the Dirty Thirty say they didn't have too many uniforms and were in the air so much that they rarely found an opportunity to send their flight suits to the laundry.)

His basic training was in Rabat, Morocco. Then in 1958 and 1959 he attended the Air Command and Staff College, Maxwell Field, Montgomery, Alabama. It was there he polished his English, which heretofore had been self-taught. He was twenty when the first Vietnamese pilots were recruited.

He can be excused some prejudice when he says that air power has played a paramount role in reversing VC fortunes.

"With harassment from the air, we are taking a heavier and heavier toll. Because of these attacks, the people in the villages are less and less inclined to harbor VC.

"But I cannot honestly share the opinions of those who optimistically predict the war's end in a few months. It is a complex political situation here. You do not build a society even in five years. However, because of our recent successes in the air and on the ground, people are coming over to us by the thousands. If they continue to see the light, it will hasten the day when we can begin to build that society. That is the hope and the dream I have for my people."

Six

THE DOOM CLUB

Today the Viet Cong lobbed mortars at Chu Lai and at Marble Mountain, so named because it is of pure marble. They destroyed aircraft and flipped satchel charges into helicopters. VC suicide squads with canvas bags of dynamite strapped to their backs swarmed into the base. They came dressed in ingeniously camouflaged getups even to live ducks on their helmets. Chopper pilots used to say, "You've never seen anything funnier than trees sprinting across a rice paddy." Today the enemy came dressed in tiger skins, pajama tops, and brief shorts. They did little damage to the SATS (transportable, quickly assembled Short Airstrip for Tactical Support, with a portable catapult of launching and recovery capability).

On Marble Mountain, Marines patrolled cautiously, stumbled onto a booby-trapped mine, and three men died on the spot.

The VC's motley variety of uniforms reduced the usual difficulty of distinguishing VC's when they infiltrated the American-South Vietnamese positions.

Vietnamese and American fighter planes chewed up the enemy with rockets. "I'm gonna kiss the first flier I see if I get out of this alive," one soldier told me.

A Marine Corps helicopter flew over the action. The crew saw twenty VC crossing a river carrying children as shields. The Marine Corps spotter plane then passed the word to "abandon strafing" of the boat. As soon as the barge reached shore the VC threw the children in the water and machine-gunned them.

One Marine stepped into the steel jaws of a giant bear trap planted by the Viet Cong. The teeth were three inches long. Four companions tried to pry open the rusted, rancid pincers. The Marine sat snorting cigarette smoke like a dragon.

Leading his squad up a knoll, one VC officer was hit. Yet he kept coming. He was hit again and lost his rifle. The third time a bullet struck, he slumped to the ground with his back to the Americans, but as he went down he motioned to his men to keep charging. "The SOB had guts," an American GI said later.

The VC are ingeniously equipped. They carry Chinese and Russian machine guns and mortars. They also have a vicious variety of traps and pits laced with poison spikes. They fight with arrows, barbed spears, flying maces, jagged knives, slings, coils, and spear launchers. In the Happy Valley of Song Con, ironically so named because it is VC-infested, a battalion of First Cavalry captured and dismantled one of the oddest gimmicks yet. It was a giant crossbow rigged with an eight-foot bolt to wing helicopters.

While hand-to-hand fighting raged, Med-EVAC cruised above the battlefields in search of wounded. Theirs is a seven-day job, twelve hours a day, every week of the year. Their raw nerve under fire has earned them the reputation as "the gamest bastards of all." Their big Huey choppers have a capacity of ten stretchers, and they have evacuated thousands. Their mortality rate is staggering—over 20 percent killed and 50 percent wounded, though their unarmored ships' noses are clearly marked with red crosses.

"Makes us a better target for Charlie," joke the men for whom it is everyday fare to operate through a hail of tracer bullets.

I rode in the ambulance carrying some of the wounded to Da Nang Air Base, and spoke to Lance Corporal Joseph Fredericks, who lay on a stretcher, his leg and arms full of shrapnel.

"They killed my platoon sergeant," he whispered and turned aside, hiding tears in the crook of his shoulder.

"Where are you from?"

"I'm Canadian," he said. "Montreal. I volunteered."

Seven of the wounded managed to walk onto the C-130 turboprop aircraft that would fly them to Clark Air Base in the Philippines and the antiseptic haven of a modern hospital. Three Negroes were among the wounded.

One of them, Sergeant Linfred Moore of New York City, was receiving tender care from the medics.

"These sergeants are the backbone of the forces over here," he said to me. "God, they're brave. They hardly ever complain. Just keep telling you that the guy next to them is worse off and to help him first. And it's amazing how soon they want to get back into battle. It's not bravado. It's the real thing."

Sergeant Moore had some terrible, undefinable wounds, and a bullet had pierced his lung. He was put on the plane last. I thought Sergeant Moore a very brave man when I bent over to speak to him and he said in a barely audible voice, "If your reports reach New York, please say to my wife, Dorothy, that I'm all right."

"How do you feel, soldier?" I asked a teen-ager already aboard the C-130.

"I'm just fine, Ma'am," the young man replied.

"He'll live," the medic whispered to me, "but he'll never father a family. He's under heavy sedation now."

I thought of Chairman Mao Tse-tung's guerrilla strategy: "The enemy's rear, flanks, and other vulnerable spots are his vital organs. And there he must be harassed. A guerrilla moves with the fluidity of water and the ease of the blowing wind."

The old communist knew that successful guerrilla activity is adapted to the weather and actual battle should be avoided except on favorable terms. The doctrine he preaches is that deadly minuet he has taught all communists operating in the East: "Enemy advances, we retreat; enemy stops, we harass; enemy tires, we strike; enemy retreats, we pursue."

And Hanoi and Peking advertise quite openly that they reckon on ultimate victory—that Vietnam is a showdown of global implications.

On the 130, the wounded were strapped tightly to stretchers which were securely locked to metal posts. The men were arranged in the plane's center in two vertical rows. These men were patient, courteous, stoic, and valiant. I felt like a ghoul climbing about the aircraft to shoot pictures.

"I hope you understand. This is my job. Good-bye, good luck, and God bless you." Then because I wasn't equipped with their dignity and knew I was going to bawl, I walked to the back of the plane.

As I started to climb off, an arm reached up to assist me.

"There's no need to apologize," a voice said in a spirit of helpfulness. "These men are very grateful to have someone telling their story. They respect you for being here. They know there are a million better places to be."

It had grown dusk and I looked up. The voice belonged to one of the big fellows who had been at lunch at the Doom Club that day.

"My name is Nails," he said. "I know yours."

Nearby, a C-123 was taxiing up to park. As it came to a stop several passengers off-loaded, wringing out their jackets and shaking their heads briskly. The air-conditioning system had leaked like Niagara during the flight.

I spied one portly officer with a walrus mustache hanging from his nose like a horseshoe. He appeared to be dry until he turned around. He must have been sitting in a bucket-seat pool of water. The entire seat of his pants was one dark blob. My pent-up emotions escaped in an unladylike whoop. It struck Nails funny, too. We stood there and roared until we were helpless and leaning against each other.

"Are you going to Harry's promotion party tonight?"

"If you're going to be there, I am," he replied quickly.

I had left one of my cameras and some other gear with Harry. He had taken it to the on-base trailer he shared with Nails and five others. Nails drove me there in his jeep.

"Well, howdy, Nails." Harry grinned at us. "I see it didn't take you long to catch up with our girl. By the way, how'd it go up North last night? Did you get into the camp of the enemy and heap calibers of fifty and napalm upon the heads of the hated Cong?"

"Rog. The Red Baron lives to strike terror again in the hearts of the hated Charlies."

"Really waxed their ass, huh?"

It was a three-bedroom trailer with a shower-bathroom and a combination living room and kitchen, a few notches above what some of the personnel occupied. More trailers were on order for other pilots and crews, who were sleeping in stacked-up bunks in buildings that can best be described as Early Uranium Boom.

The telephone rang. It was Nails's friend Bill Bunting on the Tiger line from Clark Airpatch. He said that he had found a transient stewardess in Nails's house.

"Great," Nails hollered back. "Buy her some booze, pat her on the butt, and keep her around. I'll be home in a few weeks."

You soon catch on to Army parlance in Vietnam. An airline stewardess is a stewardi, or stewie; DP means Doom Pussy; Hickam Field in Honolulu is Hickalulu; Cheap Charlie's in Saigon is a good place to eat; roger is rog. The rest of the troops' off-beat vocabulary is laced with cuss words employed singly and in unusual combinations that would not please their pastors.

Turning to me, Nails asked, "Are you gonna wear that baggy outfit to the party, Gertrude Globetrotter?"

"I don't have anything at the Press Center except a clean camouflage jump suit."

"You're a girl. Let's see if we can make you look like one."

He called Smash, who was at the Doom Club. "Hey, there, Smasherino. We need something for the lady reporter to wear to the jamboree tonight. Think you can hack the course so we can get her out of these Mickey Mouse double-breasted bloomers with the auxiliary pockets?"

"I think so, Major," said Smash. "We don't sweat the nickel and dime stuff, do we? I'll get ahold of something to show off the body if she's got one."

He showed up in five minutes with a tablecloth from the Officers' Club. Nails ferreted out one of his blue-and-white-striped civilian shirts and I ducked into the bathroom to try them on.

Like polite boys, the men turned up the radio, made loud talk, and rattled ice-cube trays so that I could have some semblance of privacy.

Captain Gerald "Chris" Christeson dropped by to speak to Nails.

"Sir, the mission was scrubbed after we were airborne so we flew out over the water and killed a few fish before landing." He was invited to join the group but elected to go back, write to his wife, and come over later.

"What time did you get off today, Nails?" asked the Chicken Hawk, another of Harry's roomies.

"It was an early one this morning, over the target at six-thirty and sunrise scheduled at oh-seven-fifteen. It made it on time. The first pass was into a mountain and it was blacker than looking up a Mau Mau's muumuu. Four hundred knots at fifty feet and all cans on target."

Smash had some fresh mail from Mercy Belle. News from home was too scarce and life in a combat zone too rugged not to share with the boys her prescriptions for unending pleasures. She was now writing *"per avion"* on the envelopes, and was developing a slightly inaccurate obsession with all things French, although a little confused in the grammar and spelling department.

BON JOUR, BED BUDDY:

Wish I knew how to write to make you so hot you wouldn't think of anyone else but me. I want to grab you, have us dissolve and make mad French love until hell freezes over. Here I lay nude. My full round breasts aching to be kissed. . . . I want to show a side of me in these pages. Mainly the bare side. Say la vive!

Now I have a joke for you. What do you get if you mate a prostitute with an elephant? Give up? A two-ton whore who will do it for peanuts.

So many things I want to say but I don't want to sound vulgar or chance repulsing you. Do you mind long letters? It takes a while to explain that sex is free, fun, and fulfilling. I will never turn you away—morning, noon, or night. You got that? What I need is one good full-time man and sex, sex, sex.

I got another raise, honey. I'd give a year's pay to get my hands on you. You say in your letters you do not indulge in sex for sex alone. Why do you indulge?

Thanks at last for the snapshot. Who's the fellow with you? The one with the big gun? My gal friend flipped over him. Is that Nails?

Your own loving,
MERCY BELLE

"Well, how about it, Nails? Do you want to write to her girl friend?"

"Better than sittin' around crackin' your knuckles," Harry drawled.

"She's really shot in the ass with you, Smasherino," Nails grinned. "I got another one."

"Well, be a good troop, let's have it," suggested Harry.

HI, DADDY,

I am aching to feel your hot hairy body against mine. Eyes closed, I can visualize each move we make. From stem to stern, port to starboard. I can make you just about the happiest most contented man you ever heard of. I have a pair of full, tender, caressing lips. I have a few other things that are full, tender, and caressing, too. I've never made French love all the way. I stop just a second before and you take it from there.

Nails grunted. "Now that would smite the heart mute."

I won't ever let your interest dwindle if I can get my hands on you.

Sears is having a sale today so must get to work early. Good God! I got the phone bill. It's a sure thing I won't be calling overseas again. Much as I love you I can't afford to go broke and not even get a solid pat.

What a hell of a way to live this is. Thousands of people sleeping and loving together right now that hate each other and here we are thousands of miles apart.

Let's get serious and talk about sex.

The mucho the better. I need some good old-fashioned loving. Make me happy, darling. I'm getting all hot and bothered again. Constant thing with me.

Your passionate MERCY BELLE

"That big old gal is ready for some rib-rattling clutch butt," said Nails.

Smash had the sad look of a heartbroken basset hound.

"Yeah. But she's not *here*."

"No, but in her own way she is contributing to the vegetable bin of history."

"Your friend seems to have some pretty fancy cravings," added Harry. "Judas Priest!"

I showered, then stood on a stool in front of the small medicine-cabinet mirror and practiced wrapping a loud, striped bath towel around me. It was just too thick to work, so I settled for the table-cloth. Then I rolled up the sleeves of Nails's outsize shirt to just below the shoulder, tied the shirt-tails in a knot below the bosom, and eased into the trailer living room.

"Well, very good, Pee Wee," said Nails. "Now let's all go down to the village pump and get our front feet in the trough."

With Harry leading the way, I marched grandly into the Doom Club on the arms of Smash and Nails, with PROPERTY OF US NAVY printed large and legible across my bottom.

Harry made a droll speech and then invited me over to the microphone. "This little lady has packed enough adventure and excitement into her life to satisfy ten women," he said by way of introduction. "She whips around the world playing follow-the-leader with real live leaders. She reels off names of heads of state the way you'd reel off a grocery list. She's interviewed 'em all and covered the major news events of the past six years. The bloody insurrections in the Congo, floods, revolutions, and uprisings. Let's hope she comes through this one without getting her ears pierced. One of her male colleagues told me, 'Don't let that blond hair fool you; she's a big-league, front-line reporter.'"

I checked the all-important safety pin holding me together and stepped up on the small podium.

Nails was casing the situation and Smash volunteered an appraisal to him.

"Ankles of a thoroughbred. But that's a long tablecloth. Wonder if her legs run all the way up to her ass?"

"This is my first undeclared war," I began. The reaction was a groan as if I'd stepped on a collective gouty toe.

"Didn't you fellows know that formal declarations of war have gone out of style?" I continued. "The Japanese didn't think to tip us off before Pearl Harbor. Surely you remember that the donnybrook in Korea involving fifteen nations was and still is called a 'police action.' France, Israel, and Britain never got around to a formal announcement when they decided to cream Egypt in 1956. That was the year that Hungarian teen-agers fought for freedom with fists and stones against Soviet tanks which rolled over them. The Russians hadn't bothered with the formality of any declaration. Washington correspondent J. John Eller estimates that our country has sent armed forces into conflicts a hundred and twenty-five times without the endorsement of Congress or a formal declaration of war. You guys are now slugging it out in number one-twenty-six."

Then we sat around swapping stories. I told them about the time in the Congo that the UN Irish troops kidded me that the flesh of a woman was more succulent, therefore the Congolese had me at the top of the menu. The newsmen promptly put together a television show called "Eat the Press."

Lieutenant George Lyddane, a rosy-cheeked pilot from White Plains, New York, told the famous story about everybody's favorite comedian, W. C. Fields.

Fields and his three buddies, John and Lionel Barrymore and Gene Fowler were sitting around with their beaks in the tankard, getting hot under the collar at the thought of the Japs and the Germans in WW II. Fields had a hammer he used to belt some spot on the globe where the war was going well for the nasties. Then he stuck colored pins in a gaudy map in all the wrong places like Peru and Madagascar. Their hatred of the enemy increased with each drink and vice versa. About four o'clock, in full battle mood, they piled into a car and drove down to enlist. At that time, besides being well along in years as well as booze, they were all suffering from some incapacitating ailment. They took along Lionel's wheelchair, in case he got an immediate overseas assignment. His brother John helped him from the car to his chair, after which they all pushed him in. Inside, they filled out the required forms with many startling entries. Fowler outlined somewhat more military experience than General MacArthur's, John Barrymore gave his age as eighteen, and Fields requested duty as a commando.

The woman at the recruiting center, after her initial shock at the sight of them, looked over their references and asked, "Who sent you? The enemy?"

A toy black cat, which the boys named their own Doom Pussy, faces in to the mirror until men on a mission return safely. She is then reversed to look into the bar. As she stood with her back to us, the boys started their favorite game, spontaneously as always.

They unwind from the tension of combat in many different ways. One caper is to yell "Dead Bug." The last one on the floor buys the drinks. "Rock the Boat" consists of wrapping your legs around the barstool and seeing who can rock back the farthest without falling over. "Dead Man" calls for locking your feet around the rungs and seeing who can be first to fall backwards to the floor while still sitting on the stool.

But by all odds the favorite is the most childish, and it happens at almost all of the parties, especially when men have just returned from a combat strike. It is simply a shirt-tearing contest—an Our Gang debauch.

Harry's party was swinging along at a booming clip when Captain Chris Christeson, the one who had to drop his bombs over the water before landing at Da Nang, remarked that he was wearing his favorite shirt, a sporty number with green-and-white vertical stripes.

"Bee-yootiful," agreed the two ornery friends with him, and promptly tore it off his back.

There was no question that reciprocation was in order, which is exactly what occurred, leaving three men with bare chests, all sputtering graphic expletives.

The game had originated six months before. The ground rules were fairly well established, as Nails explained to me. "No female guests are included, no resistance will be offered when accosted, but all sorts of sly little tricks to save shirts are OK."

The shirt posse began making the rounds of the party. Several men took off like striped baboons to hide their shirts under the seats in their jeeps. After all, a dollar T-shirt is nothing compared to a ten-dollar Thai-silk job.

Nails sat with another major and me in a corner. No one in the squadron wanted to deshirt Nails, since he was their commander. But Smash was called in by a Forward Air Controller spotter pilot, and performed the task with a flourish. Nails and the FAC pilot noted that Smash's shirt was gone, so attacked his shorts, determined to render him bare-assed. Luckily the shorts were of a heavy and stern stuff and the only result was a few bruises.

The name of the game is "Get Everybody."

There were five Navy carrier pilots as guests. Four had been taken care of. The fifth, a full commander, pretended to be incensed at this "childish behavior." "I'll wreck the place," he growled, "if anyone so much as touches me."

Thirty seconds later he smiled sheepishly as he looked down at his bare, hairy chest.

Harry, who loved the game, was bleeding on the shoulder. There were a few threads knotted tightly around his neck that were interfering with his breathing. He nearly garroted himself loosening them to wear as a headache band. "This is one way to see Asia without actually filing bankruptcy," he chortled.

Executives on Madison Avenue seek weekend relief from the tensions of big business with sail boats and foreign cars. Men half a world from home engaged in the death game escape the pressure with their shirt-tearing contests and salty war songs.

Finally it was time for dancing and a chance to practice what Lindy had taught me in the elevator the day I left New York. Major Gerry Hamilton, a grandfather from Philadelphia with five children, the oldest a cadet at the Air Force Academy, dropped a coin in the jukebox and invited me onto the small floor. He was about my height and wearing a dazzling orange flight suit. He was passing through Dang Next the Sea on his way back to Clark and the 8th Bomb Squadron, of which he was operations officer.

I thought it too risky to bounce around the floor in my break-away outfit, so we trooped back to the trailer so I could put on my fatigues. I liked Gerry's so well that I asked how about trading, since we were almost the same size. For the next hour I danced my fool head off.

Colonel Robert F. Conley, an old pal of Harry Howton's, was there. Under his command at Da Nang was the Marine Air Group Eleven, comprised of F-4B Phantom IIs and the F-8 Crusader all-weather jet fighters. Conley was very proud of his flying Marines. "They can make those planes do everything but stand up on their hind legs and beg."

He invited everybody to his club for the next bash.

We took dozens of pictures and had a marvelous time until old Beanbag oozed in. He wanted a shot taken kissing me. The guys tried to smooth his feathers at first, but it was no use. Nails asked what it was he had in mind.

"Just one picture with me kissing the lady," he mumbled.

Nails short-circuited that argument by putting on his incredulous look and inquiring, "In the *face?*"

The subject somehow got around to Sukarno and his problems in Indonesia. Opinion was rather uniform that Sukarno was a bad one. Then Beanbag piped up, "Oh, I don't know. It might be nice to work for him. He offered *me* a job."

"Yeah," squelched Smash, "but who would want to be a houseboy?"

Nails earlier had offered to drive me home. "Let's get out of here before a *real* bourbon front moves in."

We went to collect my things. Nails fastened on his .38 combat

Masterpiece and ammunition belt. Off base, military are required to carry a weapon for protection, especially at night.

By now I was paying the price for all the dancing. My bad foot throbbed and was quite swollen. "I'll take you over to Doc Hightower," Nails said.

The men on the base swear by Jim Hightower, a young captain who looks after them like a mother hen. One of the constant problems is diarrhea: very dehydrating, dangerous and inconvenient for flight crews.

There were two boys in Doc's office. One of the men had sat around in wet bathing trunks and developed a nasty case of heat rash in his crotch. In Vietnam's tropical climate it is almost impossible to get rid of, and the itching and discomfort can be unbearable to a man cooped up in a fighter plane for hours.

Hightower scraped and bathed my foot, then bandaged it tightly. He lectured me soundly for waiting so long to have it treated.

"And it should have been bound tightly in the first place," he said. "Now. Use this germicidal soap twice daily. You're very lucky. Because, if that cut had been a sixteenth of an inch higher, you'd have had a severed Achilles tendon and plenty of trouble. You should have stayed off it for a while. How did the cut get infected?"

"Well, I think it was when I was off with Harry's Hog Haulers on a trip to Ashau. We were taking some cows up there, and I guess I stepped in it."

We drove to the flight line after giving the sentry the day's password, then stopped by the 13th's operations office.

"I had six Doom Pussies tonight," Nails said. "I want to check on them."

On his desk was a printed card.

DEAR SIR:
    IT SHOULD BE BROUGHT TO YOUR ATTENTION THAT THERE IS A FAG-GOT IN YOUR OUTFIT. TO AVOID SCANDAL, I THINK YOU SHOULD DIS-CHARGE EVERYONE. IMMEDIATELY. HONORABLY, OF COURSE.
P.S. I LOVE YOU.

Nails thought it very funny and was unconcerned with what weenie might have put it there. Also on his desk was a letter from his daughter, Dee. A Vietnamese cobbler had made her a pair of riding boots out of elephant hide. She had sent an outline of her foot but Nails was worried that they might not fit.

DEAR DADDY,

I received my elephant boots today and I love them. They just fit so I won't have to share them with my sisters. I sure hope you make it home safe. I'm trying to get good grades so I can get a horse someday.

I really love my elephant boots. They're the best present anybody ever gave me. I wouldn't ever wear them riding, only to church and school dances. Love,

DEE

P.S. Be very careful.

We piled into the jeep and headed for the gate.

I try to be handy with a typewriter and a camera, but I'm a navigational imbecile. I could not direct Nails to the Press Center at I Corps, several miles on the other side of town from Da Nang Air Base. The more we inquired, the more confused we got since Nails had never been in that area before. Few of the combat crews left the base, and rarely at night.

As we tooled around, the fuel-gauge needle bobbed ever lower. We finally found Museum Beach, but in the dark I could not locate the sharp turn in the wiggly road that led to I Corps.

We talked as if we'd known each other for years.

He told about a favorite college professor of psychology at the American Institute of Foreign Trade, Phoenix, Arizona, where he had completed graduate studies in Foreign Relations.

"When someone asks about my education level, I usually tell them that I've been exposed to a lot, retained very little. The old man, the professor, summed it all up as far as I'm concerned: 'An educated man is one who does not believe a great many things that are not so.'"

Then Nails started talking about women. "I've met many, but never one, not one, I was convinced would be faithful if I were away for six months. Is that so difficult for a woman?"

Not to change the subject, but genuinely concerned about the petrol situation, I said, "Perhaps you could siphon some gas out of the Associated Press jeep when we get there. The fellows are good eggs."

"Can't do that without an Oklahoma credit card," replied Nails.

A lot of the troops' cracks sailed right over my head, but I thought I knew what an Oklahoma credit card was. I remembered a hairdresser at RKO in Hollywood who came to the studio every morning during WW II, when gas rationing was on, complaining about her husband. "Every time I go to take a douche," she growled, "my old man has the tail to my hot water bottle out siphoning gas out of my car into his."

By the time we lucked onto the turn in the road that took us to the Press Center, Nails's tank had been reading empty for half an hour. We waited at the gate for the combination sentry-gardener Vietnamese gentleman to undo the heavy padlock, and then drove in.

It is impossible to make a quiet entry into the place. The courtyard is covered with gravel. All the network and wire-service jeeps were parked in neat diagonal rows in front of their respective quarters. The lights were on in the press office. George Esper, a young reporter for Associated Press, dashed out.

"Our bureau chief called from Saigon tonight. He and Hugh Mulligan said your interview with Ambassador Lodge was released today because your network is putting it on the air tonight. Ed White said to tell you he's sending it out on the AP wire because he considers it a damn good interview. UPI is doing the same, and I think Reuters, too. Congratulations."

"George, this is Major Nails, commander of the 13th Bomb Squadron. Nails, George Esper, Associated Press."

"How do you do, Major."

Nails stepped out of the jeep to shake hands. George had been out on a patrol when I had come in from Saigon. He wanted to know if I had brought any letters for him. George seemed to get mail from girls in every state of the Union.

"It's in the bottom left-hand drawer of the office desk," I said, and then Nails escorted me to my little room.

Originally rooms at the Press Center accommodated three men, sometimes more. On arrival in Saigon at the beginning of my assignment, Special Services, who arrange for reporters to go out in the field, told me that the Da Nang Press Center was filled up and that they could not give me a room because I would displace three or more male reporters.

But Colonel Jim Williams, ISO (Information Service Officer) at Marine headquarters in Honolulu, met me at an American Broadcasting party for Malcolm Browne at the Caravelle, and listened to my problem. He instructed the ISO in Da Nang to turn over a tiny office in the Marine Office Building at I Corps to all future women correspondents.

It was in the complex of male reporters' rooms. Their digs were elegant compared to mine. It was about seven by eight feet and filled with swarms of angry mosquitoes. The only toilet in the building was coeducational. It was up a step and not only was there no lock; the door wouldn't even stay shut. So with my knees bumped against it, for lack of space, I kept a death grip on the knob.

But I was still very grateful to Colonel Williams.

Nails stepped inside the room. I excused myself to run over across the courtyard to ask George about an execution of Viet Cong guerrillas I had heard about at the party. I was afraid he might have gone to sleep before I could find out what time I was supposed to get up.

When I returned I found Nails had hung up his gun belt on one of the three clothes hooks and was lounging on my bed. One arm was flung in studied carelessness above his head, as if he were the last bonbon in the box.

"Come here," he wheedled.

"You put your gun back on."

"In a minute. Come here first."

"No."

"I want to kiss you."

"No."

"Why not?"

"Because I like it too much. I wouldn't sleep."

That seemed to catch him flat-footed.

"Nails, the fact that I danced more with you tonight than the others does not constitute an irreversible overture. And the fact that I've shown you my quarters does not automatically imply that we fly into bed."

"Now, honey, gahdamit, sit down a minute."

I sat on the barest edge. "Nails, you're out of gas."

"I'm *what?* Oh. The jeep."

"What will you do?"

"Stay here."

"Now listen. Any woman reporter practically feels like a den mother up here. But I certainly didn't come to Vietnam to be a sexual samaritan."

"Come down here. Lean over just a little bit."

"Nails, I was up till five-thirty this morning. Tucker and another Marine next door taught me to throw jungle knives at their slanting board. It took me that long to get the hang of it. That's the board out there propped up against the water tower in the courtyard. We've probably awakened them and they can hear every word. Please go."

I held out his gun holster and belt studded with ammo. "Nails. You're being very difficult."

For some reason known only to a Mormon airplane driver, that hurt his feelings. He stood up, put on his .38, and walked the three feet to the door. I followed him down the hall to his jeep.

"You didn't have to say that about my being difficult."

"But you *were* being."

Early next morning I was paged to come to the Marine office telephone. It was Nails.

"Hello dere, Sapphire. Dis is da Doom Puss."

"Hi. How did you get home?"

"I slept in a ditch."

"No."

"Yup. Ran out of gas two blocks from your place. Parked, pulled out my poncho, and slept with my .38 in my fist. Good thing I did, too. Seven different times somebody tried to dismantle the jeep and make off with it."

"How do you feel?"

"I'm taking my annual flight physical today. So I'm listening to music to take physicals by and soaking up a bit of Old Sol in front of the trailer. If the blood pressure blows the mercury out the top, I can blame it on sunstroke and get a rematch with Hightower next month."

"How about my going on a B-57 mission?"

"I'll fix it. But you go with me, Pee Wee. Nobody else. You can ride in Smash's seat."

"I'm ready any time."

"I'll let you know. Meanwhile don't let your Munsingwear seize on you."

"I have to get back to Saigon soon."

"Smash and I haven't taken any leave yet. We're coming down there to see you."

"Fine. It will be a pleasure to show the big city to the heavyweight twins."

Two days later the Marine band played the Air Force hymn as, one by one, four men stepped forward on the tarmac to receive decorations, pinned on by Colonel George Hannah, commander of the 315th Air Commando Group, which consisted of Harry's 311th, two squadrons at Tan Son Nhut, where Colonel Hannah is headquartered, and another squadron at Nha Trang, which now is the double enclave of Nha Trang and Cam Ranh Bay, a major entry port for US supplies and troops into Vietnam. Since the days of Marco Polo it has been an important way station for navigators. The port developed at Cam Ranh Bay has the best natural harbor in Asia except for Yokohama. Now there are two deep water piers and over a million square feet of storage facilities handling three thousand tons of military cargo each day. The region is hemmed in by mountains and crawling with guerrillas, but Nha Trang has one of the most beautiful beaches in Asia.

Colonel Hannah is a very correct soldier, impeccably starched at all times, but has a wry humor. When we talked of the price on the heads of many American officers in Vietnam, he said in his hot-biscuits Knoxville accent, "I hope the VC guy who has the file on me likes Southerners."

Captain Beryl J. Rankin, of Maplewood, Louisiana, Captain Gary W. Goldenbogen, Gates Mills, Ohio, Staff Sergeant Ernest E. Bryant, Gary, Indiana, and Staff Sergeant Robert L. Sloane, Monticello, Florida, stood at attention as the citation for five clusters to the Air Medal was read:

> The following air-crew members have distinguished themselves by meritorious achievement while participating in sustained aerial flights as a combat-crew member in the Republic of Vietnam. The airmanship and courage exhibited by these men in the successful accomplishment of important combat-support missions under extremely hazardous conditions demonstrated outstanding proficiency and steadfast devotion to duty. The professional ability and outstanding aerial accomplishments of these men reflect great credit upon themselves and the United States Air Force.

All of the four beamed at Colonel Hannah with quiet dignity and returned his handshake firmly. There is a little less reserve and rank-consciousness among officers and enlisted men in the Air Force than in other branches, perhaps because flying men have the deepest respect and genuine affection for ground crews. It is reciprocated in full.

Later Smash told me about his arrival in Saigon.

"The B-57s had been deployed in Bien Hoa since October, 1964, as a threat. We flew road-recee missions, which meant flying up and down the main roads at about two or three thousand feet watching for VC roadblocks and so forth. This was in South Vietnam. It was kind of a candy-ass war for us and the A-1E Skyraider pilots at Bien Hoa wouldn't let us forget that they were dropping bombs."

"What's a candy-ass, Smash?"

He looked at me for a minute. "A candy-ass is a—is a—a *candy-ass*," he explained. "Well, anyway, we had quite a few false starts before our entry into the active war and most of the guys were pretty anxious to do something and get the A-1E jocks, who'd been carrying the whole load, off our backs. Then Nails arrived, and the

Flying copilot with Lt. Colonel Chuck Honour on mission to Dong Xoai. Chuck was CO of the 145th Aviation Battalion, a crack helicopter pilot loved and respected by his men. He was killed three months later over Bien Hoa.

PHOTO BY S/SGT DOUGLAS SAPPER

Da Nang: Nobody enjoys his own stories better than Lt. Colonel Harry Howton, CO of the 311th Air Commando Sqdn, whose men call themselves "Harry's Hog Haulers," one of four squadrons under the over-all command of Colonel George Hannah's 315th Air Commando Group.

After early morning interview, Prime Minister Nguyen Cao Ky prepares to take off in his official helicopter from lawn of sand-bagged quarters he occupies at Tan Son Nhut with lovely, swan-necked wife, "Miss Mai."

PHOTO BY LT. COLONEL WILLIAM KREPS, USAF

PHOTO BY CAPT. MICHAEL HOLSINGER, USAF

My first bombing mission. Pilot: Capt. Cactus Jones, 602nd Command Sqdn, Bien Hoa. Cocky smile faded when A-1E Skyraider swooped over target.

USAF OFFICIAL PHOTO BY S/SGT JAMES THEALL

Thumb up in traditional gesture before bombing mission in B-57 Canberra Jet with Major Nails, CO of 13th Bomb Sqdn at Da Nang. We took three hits.

On the bar inside the Doom Club sits a stuffed cat, turned to wall when bomb sqdn crews are on night strikes over North Vietnam. Night flights over enemy territory are referred to in official bulletins as "Doom Pussy Missions."

PHOTO BY BEN FORDNEY, U.S. EMBASSY

Exclusive interview for Mutual Broadcasting System with Ambassador Henry Cabot Lodge at U.S. Embassy in Saigon.

An ARVN soldier is pleased with magical Polaroid shot taken at Ashau.

PHOTO BY LT. COLONEL HARRY HOWTON

Photo by Eddie Boaz, S/Sgt, USAF

Unloading pigs at Khe San while outgoing passengers wait. Vietnamese woman and child are VN camp commander's dependents going out on leave.

Interior C-123 Provider. Harry's Hog Hauler's typical load at Da Nang includes ammo, ducks, chickens, concertina, rice, people, mail, cement, cows and spare parts.

Photo by Eddie Boaz, S/Sgt, USAF

Spoiled after instantaneous rapport with babies of 64 countries, I was consistently rejected by wailing Montagnard tots. Col. Honour and Capt. Taylor are amused.

PHOTO BY S/SGT DOUGLAS SAPPER

PHOTO BY CAPT. HURL TAYLOR, JR. III, SPECIAL FORCES

The Montagnards' co-operation could throw the war one way or the other. They control the High Plateau, know the trails and places to hide the chow.

At water's edge, Qui Nhon, General Westmoreland and Ambassador Lodge proudly watch the First Cavalry Division (Airmobile) come ashore.

Press scramble to photograph "The Flying Horsemen" wading ashore at Qui Nhon carrying their flag and a unit Guidon.

Surrounded by Nails and Smash.

first thing the base commander asked was, 'You ready to go fight a war?'

"Nails fully opened his canopy. 'Hell, yes. The Grimy Rapers are ready any time. Which way?'

"The commander implied that the deal would be that day. We had been faked out before, and took it with a grain of salt. However, two days later we got a frag order directing us to bomb the jungle area six miles east of the town of Bau Ngua. That's thirty-five miles east of Bien Hoa. We were afraid the thing would get changed, but two hours before scheduled takeoff time we got word that another coup had been pulled off in Saigon—another 'guest president' was in. But the field at Tan Son Nhut was isolated. Tanks were already on the runway. Vietnamese A-1Es were making dry passes at the field. If there had been any intention by headquarters to stop this initial air strike, there was no possibility of changing it without radio or telephone contact.

"We waited and waited, expecting changes or cancellations, but they didn't come. It was finally time for us to take off on the first air strike in South Vietnam by a jet. We taxied out of our parking space just like we knew what we were doing. As we taxied down past rows of parked aircraft, the ground crews formed a solid mass of men as if they were lined up for parade. They were giving us thumbs up and throwing their hats into the air. It made us feel damn good. Hell, these are the guys who load the bombs and fix the planes. How the mission works out means as much to them as it does to us. It made me very proud."

"How did the mission go?" I asked.

"Like a breeze. We got to the target area and located the little gray FAC buzzing impudently around down there. Beautiful. Our first big deal and we hadn't blown it yet. FAC said the target was a VC command post, and marked it with smoke rockets. After dropping four seven-fifty-pounders we heard a big secondary explosion, meaning we'd hit an ammo cache. FAC said he'd received heavy ground fire several times prior to our strike, but we still hadn't drawn any that we knew of. Ground fire often is invisible in the daytime. You can be shot down without knowing you're being shot at. As for the FAC pilots, I don't know any braver men. Many of them are topnotch fighter pilots. Naturally they'd rather be in a fighter plane. But somebody has to scout around looking for the bad guys."

The unrelenting heat in Da Nang literally seizes you by the lapels in the noonday sun. Most of us called it Sauna City. I had just finished photographing and interviewing some F-104 pilots who had unloaded their bombs on a mission up North, and was walking over to my jeep parked close to the ramp, when someone called to me. It was Brigadier General Schinz, the thirteenth guest at Premier Ky's luncheon a short time before. As Schinz descended the steps of a T-39 jet, he motioned me over. "The General would like to say hello."

"The General" turned out to be our nation's number-one airman, John Paul McConnell, Air Force Chief of Staff. He was accompanied by four-star General Gabriel "Gabe" Disosway and other members of his staff. Born fifty-eight years ago in Boonesville, Arkansas, McConnell has a sun-wrinkled face and a southern drawl. He became Chief of Staff in February, 1965, but had been Vice Chief of Staff since August, 1964. He was in on the ground-floor planning of the huge American air buildup in Vietnam since its inception. He had served in the China-Burma-India theater in WW II, and is married to the former Sally Dean, a WAC he met in Ceylon.

How long did McConnell think it would take USAF and VNAF to immobilize the North?

"To put war-supporting industries out of commission and blast supply routes could be accomplished in less than two weeks. And that is without top effort. This does not mean attacking civilians, of course. But supply routes can be repaired, so you have to go back and knock them out again."

How effective did he consider the B-52 bombing?

"These bombers have penetrated into places that have sheltered the Viet Cong for years. Whether you catch the VC in the caves and tunnels or not, at least their installations have been demolished and they no longer have a base in which to hide. I am completely satisfied with the B-52 performance."

(That air assault was taking its toll in real damage, hurting the economy and scuttling morale, was confirmed in the dispatches of Soviet correspondents in North Vietman.)

After a few words with Lieutenant General Joe Moore, deputy commander for air operations of MACV and commander of the 7th Air Force, who was accompanying General McConnell and his staff on their inspection tour, I climbed off their plane.

While top US brass frequently tour the war area, diplomats of a dozen countries circle the globe trying to hammer out an understanding with Ho Chi Minh. And people all over the world wake up every morning hoping that the break is about to come—for the gentle people of tiny Vietnam, for the daytime farmers-nighttime Viet Cong, for the ARVNs and the men from five countries who fight along beside them. Meanwhile, the war is seeping across to Thailand.

In an American officers' mess at Pleiku hangs a framed quotation
from a Rudyard Kipling poem:

> The end of the fight is a tombstone white
> With the name of the late deceased
> And the epitaph drear:
> "A fool lies here
> Who tried to hustle the East."

The stubborn courage of squadrons like the Fangs played a major
role in the reversal of Viet Cong fortunes in the summer of 1965.
Their commander, Major Erwin Cockett, was a living legend among
his men, especially after the day when four of his metallic eagles were
shot down deep in VC territory. The rescue teams got there in time
to pluck the chopper crews out of danger, but Cockett elected to stay
on the ground and cover their getaway. After that his men's feeling for
him bordered on undisguised worship.

"He is the most magnificent of men," his colonel told me. "When
there was little hope of getting crews out safely, when the chances of
success literally were one in a million, Cockett invariably found that
one and made it work. Superlatives often are wide of the mark, but
not in this case."

Cockett had grown up in his native Honolulu with Al Chang,
photographer for *National Geographic* and, later, Associated Press.
Both had fought in the streets as kids, got safely through the Korean
War, and now it seemed as if Cockett had been preparing all his life
to command and lead these men in Vietnam.

That night I was invited to a party for Cockett and his departing
Fangs, who were being rotated home. The men whooped it up with
funny speeches and loud guffaws. A captain played the guitar and led
the singing. "OK, what gear do we start in?"

To the tune of "Jesus Loves Me" they bellowed:

> Lyndon loves me, this I know,
> McNamara tells me so;
> Yes, Lyndon loves me . . . Yeah, yeah, yeah . . .

In another corner a quartet harmonized:
"Rock of Ages. . . . . . Cha Cha Cha."
Cockett walked by. "That really opens me up."
"Mouthy little bastard, isn't he?" asked one of his buddies.
The lyrics to "Jesus Loves Me" had changed to:

Ho Chi loves me, this I know,
Hanoi Hannah tells me so;
Yes, Ho Chi loves me . . . yeah, yeah, yeah.
Say, hay, hay.

At the height of the festivities a quiet chap from Palmer, Alaska, joined me. He had arrived the month before and already was missing his family sorely. There are men in Vietnam who are terrified of dying and some who itch for battle. Robert Harris was somewhere in between.

"These guys left a hell of a record for us replacements to follow, but I'm sure we'll make it. There are a lot of trite phrases but I don't think any of them capture the full meaning of what a man's feelings are—toward his enemies, his comrades, or even himself. I don't feel that any of us Fangs are any different from any American soldier or any civilian over here who's involved in the conflict."

I interrupted. "The rescues and strikes the Fangs have pulled off border on the fantastic; returning alive so often verges on the miraculous."

"The guys here tonight undoubtedly would hoot at what I'm going to say. But I know it exists deep inside us."

"What's that?"

"A basic, fundamental, implicit belief in America. In the way of life of America. What our critics call flag-waving. But regardless of how it's said, or how some of our group are cutting up here tonight, *this* is the reason they're over here sticking their necks out."

Harris was thirty-one years old and for ten years had been married happily to a girl named Sally.

"I've been here barely a month," Harris continued thoughtfully, "and much as I love my wife and my kids—I have three—and much as I want to be with them, I'm not sorry I'm where I am."

Al Chang drove me back to the Press Center. I sat in my little room making notes and batting at hit-and-run mosquitoes. The men I had watched die, kill, bomb, tell bawdy stories, get drunk, cry, quarrel, and make up—all of them moved me deeply. I wondered how long you had to be in the business to develop the rhinoceros-like hide reporters are reputed to have. I don't see how anybody can be hard-boiled about a war. Because of the greed of a few men for power, thousands have to be separated from their families. I wondered about Eric Sevareid's remark: "Communism is not so much a way of life as a political technique for seizing power."

I walked over to the dining room to see who still was up. Chet

Walker, a free-lance writer, was smashed out of his mind, and laboring on a magazine piece he said had to go out in the morning. Chet's wife was in Bangkok. Chet wished he were there, too. He had three Scotches lined up in front of him, and he looked like a dissipated cherub.

Chet's torch was no secret to the press corps. Nor were his wife's fickle ways. She was having an affair with a minor diplomat from the British Embassy.

"I'm doing a piece on Thailand," he said. "You know, it's bad enough to be cuckolded in Bangkok, but rendered doubly odious by onomatopoeia."

Marine Major Dean Macho gave me a copy of the Ten Commandments issued to Marine battalions involved in a pacification drive around Da Nang. Besides number seven, explaining the Vietnamese custom of male hand-holding, they were:

1. Wave at all Vietnamese.
2. Shake hands when meeting people whether it be for the first time or upon subsequent meetings.
3. Respect graves, tombs, and other religious buildings or shrines.
4. Afford normal courtesies such as deference and respect to elders, respect for authority of the village and hamlet officials.
5. Give the right of way (on roads or paths) whenever possible.
6. Treat women with politeness and respect. . . .
8. Keep your word. Be slow to make promises, but once made do your best to keep them. Remember, though, promises involve a command decision. Your commander must be given an opportunity to rule in such a matter.
9. Enter into the spirit of bartering without abuse, and respect the local methods for conducting business.
10. Return what you borrow, replace what you break, and avoid unnecessary "liberation of local items" for your personal or unit's use.

Lieutenant General Lewis Walt's Marines were adapting to the country's ways as well as adding Chu Lai and Da Nang to the roster that once included the Halls of Montezuma and Belleau Wood, just as Ia Drang Valley became a battle page added to that of the airborne men with a background of Bastogne.

"The South Koreans certainly are a big help over here," I said to Macho. "They get along very well with the Vietnamese. I guess it's natural since they have similar Oriental cultures. The Koreans strictly observe the local customs and make a big project out of the basic courtesies of Vietnamese society."

"Yep," Macho said. "They're good troops all around. Fantastic soldiers, and their casualties are the lowest of any combat men over here. The Charlies hate their guts, even more than they do the Aussies or us. They're deadly at close combat. Those cats are unsurpassed in judo and karate. Did you know the kill ratio of the Korean Tiger Division in South Vietnam is over sixteen VC to one Korean?"

"They know what they're fighting for. A victory could expedite unification of their country. That's why forty-five thousand of them are backing up the demarcation line where the fighting ended twelve years ago. They know the score. It's the first time in Korean history that they've sent troops outside the country to fight. They don't forget that the communist attack in 1950 came dangerously close to wiping them out altogether as a nation. Anyone who claims that anticommunism among Asian nations is just a reaction to American propaganda should talk to any adult Korean who's lived through the nightmare of a communist invasion and occupation."

Korea has exported over sixteen million dollars' worth of goods to South Vietnam and expects to double that in 1966. South Korean technicians are hired by American engineers and contractors at salaries ten times higher than those paid in Seoul, and Korea has the highest priority status as a supplier of war materials to South Vietnam.

A Korean soldier receives $1.50 a month in Korea, $30 in Vietnam. Death benefits to their families, starting at $800, represent about eight years of income at their present national level. Besides the increased income is the additional incentive of occupying a rather privileged status and experiencing the comparably adventurous position. It's a far cry from their former xenophobic stand.

"Their folks at home are real proud of them," Macho said. "Korean newspapers carry headline stories of their superiority in night fighting and effective tactics in close jungle combat. They're a real hawk nation."

"Makes you feel kind of secure when you're with them," I added. "Not like wondering if some of the friendly friendlies might switch to unfriendly friendlies when you're not looking."

Seven

TEQUILA, THE PINTO JENNY

DEAR PEE WEE:

I'll be stopping in Saigon with the Nail for a couple of days. Then on to Bangkok for four days R & R (B & B?) the day after.

We've got a visiting colonel sharing the trailer these days. I don't think his sense of humor is in step with us keen guys.

We have established a pretty good rapport with the Marine F-4 fliers here at Dang Dang and have been attending both O Clubs. Last night we had the social event of the season when we took a posse of ten Cranberry troops to the other side of the base to their club. We got there about eightish and found them playing dominoes, etc. Dick Ryan didn't ring their gong or blow their Ooga horn, which means you want to buy a drink for the house, in the conventional way. He kicked the gong (eight feet into the air) and jumped up and bit the Ooga horn to blow it and the party got going.

The CO of the outfit thought this was all so great that he kept the club open an extra half hour past closing—until ten. Then we all came over to our club and the festivities really got under way.

The party progressed and we got to the shirt-tearing bit. This time, though, they didn't stop at shirts. We wrote a new song entitled "Ryan's Pork Is Hanging Out."

I was stripped to my shorts as the Officer of the Day said, "I'm going to have to ask you gentlemen to leave."

We told him to go ahead and ask. And he did. And *we* said, "Get f——."

As he streaked for the phone to call old Eisenwhateveritis, I told him to explain that Smash did it and the good colonel would understand. I guess he had no sense of humor because they called out the Air Police riot squad.

Balance and timing is everything, I always say, and I played it just right as I left the front door in my shorts just as the Keystone Kops came up the street with their helmets and their little billy clubs.

Back at the trailer we rounded out the evening with a Marine knife-throwing contest at the front door and a wrestling match. The visiting colonel got upset and got out of bed and chewed a little.

Ralph just laid in bed and hollered "Quiet!" every few minutes. We told him to shut up as he was bothering the partiers and he finally did.

You know, I really do need an R & R. Write if you get work.

SMASH

Smash and Nails flew their Canberra to Tan Son Nhut and went to the Officers' Club to see about a ride into town. There is a terrific car shortage among American personnel stationed in Vietnam, although it is horrendous to envision more cars on the streets of Saigon. The traffic easily rivals the unbelievable, cacophonous uproar in Tokyo's streets, which includes the motorcyclists the Japanese have coined a word for—*Kaminariyoku,* meaning "thunder breed." To dart across a Saigon thoroughfare requires the stamina of a Karachi camel and the daring of Wrong Way Corrigan.

Harry the Hog Hauler was in Saigon that day for the weekly staff meeting with Colonel Hannah. He invited me to lunch in the Caravelle rooftop dining room, on the ninth floor. I let the switchboard know where I could be reached and Scotch-taped the same information on my hotel-room door. Midway through lunch, a call came. It was Nails; he sounded exuberant.

"Where are you?" I asked.

"In your room."

"Come on up for lunch."

"We're in our flight suits."

"Great."

When the two good-looking outsize gorillas made their entrance, waiters materialized instantly and tripped over their own feet bowing the fly boys to our table. Many an appreciative eye was on them as they crossed the room in the gray K-2B flying suits with the awesome-looking Doom Pussy patch on the upper left sleeve, the Devil's Own Grim Reapers emblem above the right breast pocket, and the Command Pilot or Master Navigator wings on the chest.

"Where have you been—bucking head winds?" I asked.

"We ran into some of the boys at the bar at Tan Son Nhut," Nails answered, grinning.

"How's your mail-order romance going, Smash?" Harry asked.

"How can I tell from here?"

"I think old Mercy Belle drinks Tiger's Milk all day long," Nails commented.

"I have a surprise for you, Nails." I excused myself and went down to Robin Funk's room on the fourth floor, where I had left my tape recorder, a Japanese Panasonic about the size of a compact, square pocketbook. Back in the dining room I put it on the table. "I made an extra tape of one of my shows. Want to hear it?"

It was "Mail from Home" and included the letter from Nails's daughter, Dee, about her elephant boots.

When Dee's letter was played, Nails stopped eating, and his face took on the look of a man who has just been decorated. Unashamed, he let me see his eyes cloud.

"Where are you staying?" I asked.

"Smash took a room down the hall on your floor. My gear is in your room."

I assumed he was joking. The Vietnamese floor boys couldn't guard the press's quarters more carefully if we were government officials. They certainly were not going to admit strangers.

I had some calls to make, so Nails escorted me downstairs while Harry and Smash continued lunch. In the small foyer off my room I stopped in my tracks. There, big as life, was Nails's B-4 bag.

Mon Dieu and *Choi Hoi!* With his persuasive ways Nails could defeather birds and talk cautious chamber boys into unlocking ladies' quarters. I remembered Smash telling about the day they had visited the 2nd Air Division Headquarters for an investigation of the B-57 that had burned at the end of the runway and blown off Colonel Scott's sunglasses. Before they ever got around to discussing the accident, Nails sold the Flying Safety Officer some real estate in Utah and a shotgun from Hong Kong.

Nails had arranged the contents of his shaving kit so that they lay alongside my cologne, bobby pins, malaria suppressants, and lipstick. In the closet his clothes were hung here and there between mine. With the barest touch of shyness, he volunteered, "Don't you think our stuff looks nice that way—all mixed up together?"

"My, aren't you the sexy devil!"

I laughed when I saw a bottle of brandy on the desk beside my typewriter. But the touch to end all touches was what had been done to my bed, a king-size that had been accomplished with two large twin beds. Quite clearly Nails had reached below the sky-blue linens and blankets and, with his handkerchief, had secured the legs in a tight double knot. Was he going to start roaring like an ape man for his mate?

He just sat there looking virile, mannerly, and sweet-tempered; his eyes, almost as black as his hair, were a little too suspiciously innocent beneath level brows.

He poured two brandies and said, "I think you are saddled with all manner of Victorian hangovers about man-woman relationships."

"You can't stay here, if that's what you mean."

"Now don't try to drown me in respectability."

"You were pretty presumptuous, plunking your things in here."

"You need someone to call the shots. It'll take quite a man to make you feel like the woman you're capable of being."

"I'm leaving with the Prime Minister and his wife for Kuala Lumpur on a state visit and I have a million things to do. We're going on the PM's plane as part of the official party, but still the red tape is unbelievable." I made a deliberate pause. "You and Smash are a few days late getting down here."

"I've been a little busy, too. I tried to call you the other afternoon but the Tiger line was tied up. I had to be at chapel at five. Yes, we lost one the night before and both guys burned—two of the best—Bud Tollet, blond nice-looking new major, and Leon Smith, a dark-complexioned pipe-smoking captain type."

These were the first men Nails had lost.

"I've got all my new crews checked out now as lead pilots, and all are night-qualified except four. I have a hunch we'll be flying nothing but Doom Pussies in the future."

"If I get home first do you want me to call Bud's and Leon's wives?"

"Maybe. We'll see. By the way, I got a letter from Lars Hansen's fiancée. She says she wishes she was ninety years old. She really loved that guy."

Nails poured a brandy. "I've told you about my old man, The Moose, haven't I?"

I nodded. I felt one of his famous stories coming on—he was lapsing into his raconteur mood. And nobody's a better audience for good yarns than I am.

"I had just returned from a three-year tour in England with a seven-month TDY at the University of Omaha. I was reassigned to Hill Air Force Base, which is close to The Moose in Salt Lake City. I'd been there about a week when Moose and I cooked up a deal to go to the Golden Spike Horse Show sales. The summer before, he had bought a horse for the number-four boy by his third wife, and was contemplating buying another for his number-three daughter, same wife.

"We had a few shots of booze at my apartment, then we stopped off at the BOQ and then at the Hill Stag Bar for a couple more. This is when I started bugging the old man with, 'C'mon now, Pop, gahdammit, you promised *me* a pinto of my very own about forty years ago. How's about it, Pop? Can I have a pony? You've bought one for all your other kids.'

"I ran this act into the ground and the old boy was getting a big charge out of the routine. We arrived at the horse show and looked over some of the stock before going into the ring, where we seated ourselves in the bleachers. We watched the auctioneer sell twenty or thirty horses and in the meantime, I'm still giving him the 'C'mon, Pop, buy me a pony' bit 'All those other little bastards have one, and I've waited forty years.' We were drinking out of paper cups, Seven-Up well laced with booze. Needless to say, we were having a hell of a time.

"I slipped out of the bleachers and went around the corner to hit the men's room. Fifteen minutes or so later, as I elbowed my way through the crowd, I noticed a jenny in the ring with four little kids sitting on her back. She was a pinto. Black and brown spots on gray, and a couple of ears that looked at least eighteen inches long. The kids were in the act to demonstrate her gentleness. The tail-end kid slipped down off her rump and crawled between her hind legs and under her belly. Then the kids rode her around the ring a couple of times as the auctioneer started the bids off with 'Who will go fifty dollars?' "

It obviously was Nails's favorite story. I moved my chair a little closer.

"Well, I was coming back through the crowd on my way to my seat up in the bleachers when I looked up at the place where old Moose was sitting and saw him with a smile on his face like a wave on a bedpan. He went the fifty and I caught the big eight-by-ten glossy at once. *I was going to get my pony.* I eased back into the crowd to watch the old man have his fun, and the bidding kept going up in five-buck increments.

"It got to sixty-five dollars. The old boy was right in there. He and a couple others. But nobody went for the seventy-dollar pitch and the auctioneer said, 'Who will make it sixty-seven fifty?'

"The Moose rose to the occasion in fine style. Yep, I was going to be the proud owner of a pinto pony three and a half feet tall and with the longest gahdam ears I ever saw.

"I stalled around and didn't go back until they had got her out of the ring and back to the stables. When I did show up, The Moose asked me, 'Where in the hell you been, son?'—he usually calls me Stromboli—'I just bought you a fine pony and you missed the whole action.'

"I played it straight. 'Naw, I don't believe you. Forty years I've waited for a pony. It's not so easy to pull *my* hind leg.'

"When the show was over Moose lined up at the cashier window and paid for my pony and got his receipt. But I couldn't get him to show me the pony. 'We'll get the truck and come back in the morning. In the meantime you better get home and get things fixed up to take care of her.'

"The last thing he said before he took off for Salt Lake was, 'I'll see you in the morning and you be ready to go with me back to the Coliseum, son.'

" 'Thanks, Pop. I'll be ready bright and early.'

"About seven-thirty the next morning the old man rolled up in his truck and I was all suited up with the Stetson hat, Western boots, and fancy suede jacket. I had a rope and halter and was playing the act right up to the hilt. Moose had called the auctioneer and tipped him off to put Tequila into a special stall to go along with the gag.

"I zapped the hell out of them when I ran up like a tickled kid and threw my arms around Tequila and gave them the 'Oh, boy, just what I've always wanted, a real pinto!' I never once let them get the idea that I thought she was a donkey, just the finest pony I ever saw. To this day I've never told Moose I saw him close the deal.

"That was almost five years ago and I still have her back in Utah. She's been one hell of a fine female-type donkey.

"I took her one time to Flaming Gorge to pasture her for the summer at my dad's place, where he and a couple of his business associates have forty head of horses.

"They had a big palomino stud in a corral when we unloaded Tequila, and she ran right up to the corral fence to rub noses with the stud, and spooked that little man so bad he tore down half the fence and cut out like a tornado. This stampeded the rest of the horses and we were two weeks rounding them up and getting them back to the ranch.

"This act came off a second time a few weeks later and we finally had to bring her back to Salt Lake City, where she is now, in a pasture of her own. I'd like to give you a ride on her sometime. Do you think your Lindy would like her?"

"We both would. Doesn't the legend have it that Tequila all began when lightning hit the cactus? Lindy's friend Ceci Winston has two little white burros. They think they're people. They get you between them and nearly reduce you to mash trying to be petted.

When the girls were still in boarding school, Lindy and I used to go up for weekends. At night, whenever there was a full moon, Ceci and her brothers would wake us up and we'd all go lolloping about out in the daisy field because it was so beautiful. The donkeys would be out there having moon madness."

Crunch, Reggie, and Jake sat at a table in the Green Apple Stereo Club, their three jugs planted solidly between their tankards. They were in town for some A & A. One petite Vietnamese girl was almost invisible in Jake's bear hug. He had made a fairly astonishing leap over the language barrier.

The Green Apple was chaired by a Mama-San who looked like a mixture of every ethnic culture that ever had passed through the Orient. Her place was like all the others except that the girls were prettier. The club was long and narrow with tables along the walls and a service bar across the back. A dozen B-girls invited customers to buy them Saigon tea, which was just that, tea.

Among the patrons was Alby Skurnel, bullet-headed, with an undershot jaw, beefy neck, short on stature, long on shadily-hived money. Alby had come to Saigon as a middle man, to knock off a big share of loot through bribery. He was devious as a crab, one step forward, two to the side. In the sudden death world of the big deal, Alby tried always to hang around a chalk horse.

He had gotten his start as a young hood out to clip the queers. Agreeing to drive with them to some secluded area outside New York City, he would pretend to be a willing love partner. When the homosexual got his head down, Alby would deliver a paralyzing blow to the back of his neck and roll him.

Alby was more at home with the transparent shirt crowd, but in New York the Skurnels now lived like bloated, tattered title royalty. His wife, Pottie, a former Ziegfeld chorus girl, tried to buy her way into second rung society with her husband's bank account and a sharp elbow. The first social-climbing step was to give Sunday brunches. Her ultimate aim was to meet an honest to God maharanee or be photographed next to a bona fide big shot. Six fairy press agents charged her ten thousand dollars after they'd squirreled her into a charity ball, hired a cameraman to stand by, and signaled her to rush up to General Douglas MacArthur on one of his rare public appearances. The pictures were planted in a national magazine. And the Skurnels were on their way like corrosive leeches on a tinsely garment.

"Now that we're up we gotta look respectable," Pottie told Alby.

Her attempts to amputate their former identity required lots of money and time. In Club 21 one night Pottie loudly chided her husband, for all to hear, about his bad table manners and ignorance of the wine list. Both had grown up in neighborhoods where eating out meant having a bologna sandwich in the garage. Now, Pottie spent what leisure time she had sorting her jewelry and trying on her chinchilla burnooses.

In Saigon, Alby prowled like a modern carpetbagger. If specifications for telephones to be installed were white, weight two pounds, and the Vietnamese couldn't meet those requirements, Alby was relieved. Houses in Hong Kong, Manila or Japan were available to deal with. He preferred the Chinese. "The Chinese keep their mouths shut," Alby said.

He was a craven coward and uneasy in intrigue-ridden Saigon, but that was where the money could be made. He was happier in New York where Pottie had installed a secretary with a crisp, British accent and his office was in the American Climax Building. Alby considered that name the greatest thing going.

Two tables down at the Green Apple sat Major Tors Nordstrom, an old and solid pal of Nails and Smash. This short, stocky, balding Swede resembled the late Joe Penner, the "Wanna Buy a Duck" comic. Tors, a fighter ace with six enemy planes to his credit in WW II, could count among his decorations three Silver Stars, six Distinguished Flying Crosses, twenty-six Air Medals, and six Article Fifteens. (The latter is the next thing to a court-martial.) He had been a major for nineteen years.

"Probably always will be," Smash had once commented to me, "unless he gets one more Article Fifteen." Tors didn't take too kindly to military discipline but could keep his feet after a drink.

Like a tomcat on a petting party, Alby tried to force two B-girls to sit on his knee. Tors eyed him with distaste.

"He's fuck-struck," observed the Swede to no one in particular.

Five young Vietnamese who had been loitering around the door of the club peered in. Finally one of them entered. He was in his late twenties, handsome, and he swaggered. Dressed in an American golf shirt and well-creased slacks, he stole a glance at Tors as he passed, then took a table at the back of the room near the bar and ordered a Coke.

Mama-San whispered to Reggie, "Viet Cong."

"Why don't you kick him in the nuts, Crunch?" suggested Jake.

"I would, but the little bastard probably has those Botany 500 britches full of grenades," Crunch replied, and poured himself another hooker.

At roughly this moment Nails and I were at Luong Phan's tailor shop picking up some name tags Nails and Smash had ordered. A Chinese salesman took Nails aside excitedly.

"Yesterday a Vietnamese ARVN colonel came in here and wanted to order name tags exactly like yours and Major Smash's."

"How did he know about us?"

"My sales book was on the counter. He turned the pages and stopped at your order. He said he wanted the same names and rank, plus your Command Pilot wings and Major Smash's Master Navigator wings. Of course, I refused to make them for him." The Chinese lowered his voice. "I do not believe they were friendlies. It is no secret that the Viet Cong have infiltrated even the elite Vietnamese Air Force."

Nails thanked him and we left to meet Smash at a local tonsorial emporium.

"I don't want to sound melodramatic," said Nails, "but we've been told that around here in Saigon it is inadvisable to wear the red baseball caps we wear in Da Nang. Or anything showing the Grim Reaper or Doom Pussy patches. The VC know damn well who's bombing up North at night."

Outside the barbershop was the sign COIFFURES. Inside, it looked like a ladies' beauty parlor. Colognes, perfumes, sprays, brushes, combs, and bobby pins lined the mirrored shelves. Most Americans enjoyed getting the full nine yards that is included in the French barber's repertoire.

Smash was in the front chair. A barber had given him a trim, shampoo, and shave, massaged him from waist to ears, then trapped his stubborn curls under a hairnet to keep them pasted flat while they dried.

"What the hell's that on your head, Smash?" Nails asked.

"That's the gahdam ninth yard," shot back Smash, grinning.

"Well, when he gets through, come on over to the Green Apple bar next door," Nails suggested. "Pee Wee here has a few details concerning her trip with the Prime Minister to take care of so I agreed we'd meet her back at the Caravelle later on."

Tors spotted Nails as soon as he stepped through the Green Apple door. He was holding a glass in each hand as the wings of a dove encircle her young. He put the glasses down and hit Nails a violent blow of affection on the back that echoed up through the roof of Nails's head.

"Come here, you overweight sonofabitch. You owe me a drink." Nails sat down and ordered a round.

"A guy over at Second Air Division tells me they've upped the ante on you and Smash. The VC's price on your butts is now a hundred thousand p's apiece. I told you if you kept dropping bombs on those little guys in black pajamas you'd hurt their feelings. They never could take a joke."

Nails excused himself to go to the men's room. Alby was in there and immediately struck up a one-sided conversation.

"Whadda ya think of these slant-eyed babes? Pretty good, huh? I've had all kinds all over the world. Knew that English actress, Margot Flowerpot in London. She went for the sodomy bit. Gorgeous-looking tomato. Say, if you're ever in New York look us up. The wife gives open-house Sunday brunches. She loves to meet new people. Here's my card."

Nails had a card of his own that he carried for just such emergencies. Without a word he handed it over and left for his table. On the card were two words in print so tiny they were scarcely legible:

```
┌─────────────────────────────┐
│                             │
│                             │
│         BULL SHIT           │
│                             │
│                             │
└─────────────────────────────┘
```

A dozen Vietnamese gradually had materialized in front of the club. A few of them entered. Mama-San nervously approached the table where Jake, Reggie, and Crunch were buying Saigon tea for four of her best girls.

"I think we should call it off for now," she suggested with an imperceptible nod toward the newcomers. "I don't like this." She knew how very unusual it was for Vietnamese to come into her place. Instinct convinced her they were Viet Cong terrorists.

"Who do you want us to take care of?" Jake asked, then decided they were wasting good R & R time. "Mama-San, how about some more soda?"

One of the Vietnamese took a long look at Nails. At no apparent signal all of the Vietnamese men in the place paid their tabs and headed for the door. The last one reached into his pocket and pulled out a grenade.

As the VC pulled the pin, Jake, not as drunk as they thought, sprang from his table, grabbed the grenade, and hurled it into the street. In almost the same movement, he kicked the VC in the face, breaking his neck and shattering his teeth, then took him by the seat of the pants and hurled him through the plate-glass window.

Smash, next door, had heard the explosion. He threw aside his copy of *Paris Match* but didn't bother to remove his hairnet or the powder-blue smock. As he reached the street he saw a VC de-pin another grenade and hurl it into the club. Knowing his friends were inside, Smash hollered a warning and galloped toward the action.

The grenade exploded in back of the bar. Two B-girls were disembowled. Plaster fell everywhere.

"The bastard spoiled my drink," growled Crunch, then headed for the street to catch himself a VC.

Alby Skurnel smoked his cigar right through the label and tried to hide behind Mama-San. He was caught by shrapnel in the right temple and died instantly. His greedy little eyes stared upward in stark terror and disbelief. Mama-San pried loose the death grip of his fingers on her *ao-dai*.

Smash had seen the fellow who threw the second grenade sprint for a 4-CV Renault. With four strides Smash reached the tiny French automobile. He buried his knee into the door and, with one ham-size fist on the roof, flipped the car over on its side. The right side doors were not yet closed so two guerrillas were pinned beneath the escape vehicle. Gasoline from the fuel tank sloshed onto the hot engine and instantly ignited. As Smash made it to the curb, the car exploded.

He blocked the getaway efforts of the remaining VC. One look at the giant Smash and they ran screaming back into the Club, where Reggie hurled a well-aimed bottle of Ba Muoi Ba beer, braining the first one.

"Ruin our A & A, will you?" he snorted. "Gahdam dick-head."

Tors, a Karate black belt, kneed another in full flight and heaved him in back of the bar. Crunch, uncorked a haymaker which connected with a VC's adam's apple and lifted him into the air. He returned to the tile floor like a stone.

The other four headed for the stairs and the balcony but Nails overtook them as they reached the top steps. The one nearest him reached for something in an inside pocket. Nails didn't wait to see if it was a grenade. He hit the man so hard he sailed straight off the balcony and down into Smash's arms. Smash pitched him through the blown-out front window into the gutter.

These were the first VC Nails and Smash had ever encountered face to face. On air strikes, their high-speed passes precluded any detailed look at people on the ground, and most of them were dug in deeply anyway.

One guerrilla on the balcony drew a hypodermic needle from his pocket. He waited for Nails to come to him; and not seeing the palmed needle, Nails moved in. But Reggie had seen the gesture and speared the needle artist in the ear with his kris.

The remaining terrorist on the balcony slumped to his knees as the White Mice, the alert, efficient, white-garbed Vietnamese police, entered. The situation was in hand.

Kicking the rubble aside, Jake suggested that they all have a drink. "Who's your funny friend in the breakaway kimono?" he asked Nails, glancing at Smash's hairnet. He took another look at Smash and added respectfully, "No offense, fella."

"Will somebody please close the door?" requested Reggie.

But there was no door—no front.

Then Nails took a look at Smash's getup, swept the aisles with imaginary palms, grabbed two long-stemmed carnations off a table, and bowed. "What is your pleasure, luv?"

I was sitting with Molly and Jim in Molly's room when they all filed in to fill me in on the tussle at the Green Apple.

"Hell, Smash, if old Earthquake McGoon could have been here it would have been perfect," said Tors.

Earthquake McGoon was another of the vanishing breed of bush pilot, a great, huge, fat fellow who flew C-47s. "To three-point-land a gooney bird you have to pull the yoke back far enough to stall in a nose-high attitude," Nails explained to Molly. "Old Earthquake had too much stomach stickin' out so he had to wheel it in. That's as if it were a tricycle landing gear, a wheel landing."

Molly was pouring the drinks and hauling out of her closet small cans of pork and beans and cheese which Jim had provided from the PX for picnics like these.

"When Earthquake was flying during the Nationalist-Communist fracas in 1949 he was shot down over the Chinese mainland and captured. 'OK,' said Earthquake, 'if you want me you gotta carry me!' He refused to walk."

"Well," continued Smash, "after about fifty miles those five coolies carrying all of Earthquake's three hundred pounds set him down and gave up. 'Go on back,' they motioned. The next time he was shot down he wasn't so lucky. His dollar nineteen went into a flat spin over Dien Bien Phu and straight in. He was the best troop there ever was."

Tors was a firm believer in taking the top six inches off Hanoi and would have put his grandmother in the lead plane if it would have helped. Apply the power where it pinches. He railed about the handicapped Merchant Marines, who were not permitted to fire back even if fired upon while unloading cargo.

"And it's a hell of a thing to have to watch the Charlies shoot at our troops, and just let them fall back into the sanctuary of Laos or Cambodia."

"But this is the tinderbox of the world," said Molly. "If we flattened Hanoi or Peking, the Reds could retaliate by grabbing India."

"It's the side that has the staying power who will come out on top," said Tors. "The art of winning is outlasting the enemy, even for a second. I don't know that we could say we're winning right now, but we're sure as hell not losing. We should press every advantage, just as the VC do. The nearer to triumph revolutionaries get, the tougher they become. I say swock 'em now. We've got 'em by the gonads. Why don't we squeeze?"

Nails decided a little entertainment was in order and broke out with some of his choicer ditties.

I was sitting beside Tors. "How long have you known the Red Baron?" I asked.

"Forever, I think. He's everybody's favorite drinking partner and buddy. He's got more friends than any guy I ever met. He's got 'em all over the world. You mention 'B-57' at any spot on the globe where there's fliers, and whoever you're talking to will shoot back, 'Do you know Nails?' Did you ever hear what this big old ox squadron leader did at the SAC air base in Blytheville, Arkansas, about ten years ago? He got up a Mickey Mouse Club. I mean a club with grown men. Transient fliers who dropped by the club for a drink used to flip when at five o'clock the bartender solemnly hit the gong, turned on the telly, and handed out the Mickey Mouse hats. Members slapped them on their heads just like the kids in the studio audience were doing.

"They went through the whole thing, with Nails leading the caravan, marching around the officers' club, singing all those little-kid lyrics. You can imagine the effect. The hats with the big ears, each guy a fat cigar in his kisser and a jug of beer in his fist. With drums rolling in the background to marching music, the MC, Jimmy Dodd, would open:

Oomph oomph oomph oomph
Oomph oomph oomph oomph.
Mickey Mouse Club! Mickey Mouse Club!
Who's the leader of the club that's made for you and me?

"And the members across the nation, the kids in the studio audience, and those apes down in Blytheville shouted back in chorus:

M-I-C-K-E-Y M-O-U-S-E.
Hey there! Hi there! Ho there! You're as welcome as can be!

"Nails and his pals would hold their steins in the air.

Come along and sing the song and join the jamboree!

Here we go a-marching and a-shouting merrily:
M-I-C-K-E-Y M-O-U-S-E.
Mickey Mouse. Mickey Mouse!
Boys and girls from far and near, you're as welcome as can be!
Come along and sing our song and join our family.

"There were a few more interludes about how they played safely, looked both ways when they crossed crossings, rode their bikes carefully, and played a little, worked a little. It was a sight not to be forgotten. From time to time the flutes would tootle and they would get back to the theme song.

"A couple of full-bull colonels passed through Blytheville and got so caught up they wanted to know how *they* could get some hats. Nails made up some kind of membership certificates. Very official. And the next thing we knew, he had chapters at bases all over the country. Headquarters was called The Mouse House and Nails was president. Everything that crazy weenie does is contagious. There's a whole catalogue of yarns, all of 'em true."

"I hope the producer of *Strangelove* never gets hold of that."

Molly, who had come over during the stirring rendition of Mickey Mouse, interjected, "Why, didn't you know? It's just possible that Dr. Strangelove lives in Peking."

Nails walked over to our side of the room. He pulled out a cigarette lighter and, with it, Alby Skurnel's card. He started to toss it in the wastebasket, then turned to Molly. "Ever hear of this character?"

"I regret to say I have," she replied. "Real slime. Anything that will stand still is his meat; in spite of all his money, the best he could do for a full-time mistress was a charming one-eyed girl with acne. Since that's a little humiliating for him, he tries to build his ego up by claiming he scores with women who wouldn't step on him. You'll see him look around a party and pick out the best-looking girl present, to claim he's just come back from a shack-up with her somewhere. Sometimes he goes so far as to credit himself with a whole season."

"Well, whoever he was, he bought the farm at the Green Apple today," Nails said.

"That's a shame."

The Caravelle switchboard wasn't functioning and I went over to JUSPAO to use their phone. I tried always-cooperative Major P. H. Stevens' office. He's with Special Projects for the Army and as usual was on the horn himself. So I walked across the hall to try his US Navy counterpart, Commander D. W. Madison, a very handsome fellow and absolutely unflappable.

The Commander was sitting there with a vacant look on his face, and presently he explained, "I picked up the phone and asked for Tiger to give me Bloodhound and for the first time since I've been in Vietnam the connection was made immediately. I was shocked stiff and forgot what it was I was calling about."

Sometimes our mail was sent to the American Embassy and re-routed to JUSPAO. A letter from Lindy was in my box. His Holiness had visited New York. "The Pope's visit caused quite a stir, needless to say," she wrote. "The security precautions were massive. There were so many policemen on duty and all store windows on Fifth Avenue were boarded up—it seemed like a city readying itself for a siege rather than preparing to welcome the Pope.

"New York reporters are a pretty special breed, but this time they outdid themselves. As the Pope left Cardinal Spellman's residence, Bill Ryan solemnly announced—'The Pope is now leaving Cardinal Spellman's *restaurant.*' And that was just the beginning!

"That evening the Pope celebrated Mass before thousands at Yankee Stadium. On television it was wondrously impressive. On the radio the newscasters did a good job, but being creatures of habit, the reportage sounded a little incongruous. 'His Holiness is now leaving the dugout—The Holy Father is approaching the pitcher's mound.' At any moment I expected to hear, 'And here comes Pope Paul sliding into home plate! Hang on to your beanie, Father.'"

She had visited her friend Jan Burns in Dorset, Vermont. "In the front yard is the flagpole, up which we proudly run Old Glory every morning, and there she reigns supreme until dusk, when she is gently and respectfully lowered and put to bed."

There was the latest news on the baby orangutan at Central Park Zoo, with its little ears and red hair. Its mother had run out of milk and would let no one near her offspring to feed it. The hippos had a new baby. "Nothing could put you on a diet faster than a glimpse of mother and daughter in repose."

"Tomorrow I trundle off to Ceci Winston's house. Or should I say zoo? They certainly qualify. At present they have two raccoons, a seven-toed cat, a German shepherd, Fluffy, the Golden Retriever, a family of ferrets, a kinkajou, a box turtle, Samantha the goose, a mischievous crow, guinea fowl that perch in the treetops and honk if strangers approach at night (watch fowl?), a hog-nosed snake and, oh, yes, a praying mantis that dropped in a week ago."

Lindy reminded me to "zig and zag" and not to stand on the bomb-bay doors, and sent her love to me, and to the Marines, and to the "adorable Aussies" and to the fliers I'd been describing to her, and "please tell all the soldier boys how proud we are of them."

> P.S. I read in your copy of the *Overseas Press Club Bulletin* that Dickey Chapelle is going to join all you newspaper nuts in Saigon-land. If you see a parachute floating in, you'll know she's arrived. What a gal!

In his best New England tradition, Ambassador Henry Cabot Lodge coped with the psychological and economic problems of warfare in Vietnam. As head of the entire American mission in Saigon it was up to him to wrestle with current affairs, as well as try to anticipate problems that might arise. Having spent a number of years at the United Nations, he had had plenty of experience with negotiating techniques of the communists.

Uppermost in his mind always in the delicate and complicated business was to be prepared for the conference table with a clear definition of the terms of a settlement that would protect the vital interests of free people and the Republic of Vietnam.

But the Ambassador found time from his busy schedule to dutifully entertain in honor of Mary Martin, star of *Hello, Dolly,* and leading members of the cast. Bureau chiefs of leading magazines, wire services, networks, and newspapers were invited. The Embassy was packed with as many guests as it could comfortably accommodate—military, diplomats, and assorted citizens of Saigon.

At the side of the American Ambassador in the receiving line, Mary Martin was graciousness itself. That she was thrilled with the honor showed plainly in her expressive brown eyes. I taped a half-hour show with her.

Mary sang for the guests because she wanted to; no one demanded it. And though no applause could ever match that of troops, she was received with great enthusiasm as was Martha Raye on her tours of Vietnam.

The hit of the evening was the host. Mr. Lodge sang "Some Enchanted Evening" with Mary Martin, then she soloed with "I'm in Love with a Wonderful Guy," directing her lyrics to the Ambassador. Lodge rendered a spicy number in seven languages that brought down the house.

But the *Hello, Dolly* producer decided to milk it for a headline. As he was leaving the country, he called in the wire-services reporters, whose mass audience David has always appreciated, and blasted Ambassador Lodge. His pique, he said, was that the entire seventy-one-member cast of *Hello, Dolly* had not been invited along with the leading players. He claimed that Mary Martin had been imposed upon, that the Ambassador had got a lot of free entertainment, that the press there were of the most obscure origin, and topped it off by calling Lodge a "washed-up Republican."

Ambassador Lodge did not allow himself to get drawn into retaliation. His marbles are for other games.

A batch of mail was waiting for Smash in Da Nang, most of it from Mercy Belle. She still was featuring *Per Avion* on the envelopes.

MY BIG DARLING PARAMORE CHEREE,
Did you get the snaps? Disappointed? I warned you I'm not much. Hell in bed, though. One pair of attributes show in the pics. OK? *Write!*
I often close my eyes and make believe you are here. This doesn't get the job done like the real thing will. Oh, well, say la vive. You oversexed he man.
I don't fraternize with my neighbors, consequently they know nothing about our personal lives. It upsets them so they asked us to move.
Can you feel my breasts against your back, honey? Mmmmm. Nice. Things are beginning to look up. I love it. Radio is playing "First thing in the morning and the last thing at night." Sure puts me in the mood. I'm sending you the record.

Am I giving you too much sex airmail? I am much too nice to be alone and waste all this lovely talent. Sex I got.

Did you know I work for two Jewish men? I have never worked for Jewish people before and believe me they are really wonderful. Both of them have accents and I can hardly understand what they say. Their pet word is schmuck and I ken to what they are saying. Excuse the way this letter is composed, but say la vive.

I wish you would write more often. I don't recall having been obnoxious. I tried calling you in desperation, but the message was that you were TDY in Bangkok. What a lovely, lovely word!

Darling, don't you want to feel my lips caressing you? My breasts pushing against your chest? Then climax after climax? All this you want to give up before you've even had it? I'm probably just getting you heated up and sending you into the arms of some broadie over there. Oh, well, no one is perfect. I am becoming quite anxious.

My nickname used to be Jinx. I wish it were Minx. I read everything about the war in Vietnam and those poor boys. Sorry that your friends were killed at Bien Hoa. I read that you were giving the Cong hell. There was a report of two of our men being executed to compensate for the three that we shot. I'm no war expert but this doesn't sound to me as if we're winning. Where will it all end? Sure makes the old adage "Ours is not to reason why, ours is but to do or die" make sense.

There is nothing I wouldn't do to hear from you. You just name it and baby I'll do it. Anything. Even to going all the way. That will be an accomplishment for me. Sounds interesting though.

I have everything planned for you when you get here.

The kids go off every morning at 7:15 and that gives us until 8:15 for "breakfast." Then I come home for "lunch" at 12:30. Then from 5:30 on we are strickly on our own. There is a bed on the third floor, two on the second, a couch in the living room, and a bed and couch in the so-called rec room and a cot in the basement. Any place in the house that the mood strikes you I can be ready and able in less than five seconds. How does that sound to you? Like an oversexed female?

I pray that you'll be safe. Take care of yourself. I am patiently waiting for you. In the flesh.

Desperately,
MERCY

Nails was watching Smash, who sat with his chin in his hands.

"Whisper to me, sweet lips."

"God. The first thing in the early pearly morning and the last thing at night. Beds all over the gahdam house. The whole nine yards."

"You've got a hell of a pen pal there, Smasherino."

"Quick connection before dinner. Kids go off at seven-fifteen . . ."

"Sounds better than a kick in the ass with a frozen mukluk."

Smash was tearing open another one. "Christ. It's from her daughter."

My mother speaks very highly of you . . . and it's all good. She hasn't gone out with any other men since you. She likes you. She tells me this. I never read her letters because I don't want her reading mine. So if you write to me she won't see it. Do you really like her or are you just building up her ego so you can break it down again?

She really likes you. She really needs someone like you, to love her and help her. She has been hurt so many times. I really want to know what kind of a man you are. Do you like kids or what?

I am ten years old. It is very lonesome around here for Mom and us. We are hoping you will come. It will be nice. I don't like boys and men too much because of my father. But for some reason I think I like you. Maybe because you've filled Mom's loneliness patches with writing her once in a while, and all. Thanks for helping Mom. I can't write letters like her but I try. Well, I have to take a shower. Please write to me. Please call me "Fifi," Mom says.

DOTTY MAE MEATY

P.S. Hope to see you soon.

"There's nothing behind 'Fifi' but a shove from Mother," said Nails. "Good blood. Good bone."

Smash was having some apprehensive twitches as he opened the next one.

BON JOUR YOU BEAST,

Are you going to answer Dot's letter? I keep thinking of that terrible disaster at Bien Hoa. Terrible. This war, or whatever term they are using for it, is affecting too many people. Chaos. I read all the papers now that I have found you. I feel compassion for those who feel it's necessary to rule the world and must do it by violence. I feel no contempt for what you are doing. It must be done and our reasons are for freedom for all, not to rule the world. This reading the papers to see if you are on the list is like eternity. I am not trying to be obnoxious, just anxious . . . to know.

I guess if the papers told us the whole story it would cause mass hysteria in the States. Boy, do I need somebody to help keep me warm. Sure that's a proposition. How about that?

I cut out the piece in the paper about your friend Nails, but the damn fools didn't mention your name. I'm writing my congressman about that. We were short-changed. Say la vive. I feel so awful about Lars and your friends getting killed. Pity about the human race and their desires to hold all power regardless of costs. So childishly stupid. Like little kids in kindergarten fighting for ownership of the blocks. All this so women can be alone and children fatherless. So that parents can feel that all the training and heartaches of raising him were for nothing. Darling, I'm praying that you have strong sex urges and do not suppress them.

But don't wear yourself out over there before I get a chance to show you my qualities. I can't wait to meet you. Am I a lark to you? Four-flushers are nil in my book. Got my black negligee and peignoir all ready. Are you sure some little blonde isn't taking care of you? First we should get acquainted physically, mentally, and emotionally. It's your body and soul I'm interested in, honey. My nude body against yours. I love you, miss you, kiss you, caress you, undress you, night after night.

Nails: "What are you groaning about, Smash?"

I will understand if you are sleeping with other girls, honey. You're human, far away, and lonely. I understand. I've been down the road. *Really* I have. Just don't get interested in any individual piece. Are you getting to know me through my letters?

Are you a big T-man? I'm 38-C cup. See, it's the little information that counts. I know that wasn't a question a lady asks a gentleman but I'm the type that gets right to the bottom of a problem.

I go around telling people all I know about navigators and what they do and how they couldn't fly the planes without navigators even if they had Nails the best pilot there is. I'll always be waiting when you return. I'll be at the front door. What's your favorite drink? One part man, one part woman, stir and shake? What's your favorite sport so I can bone up on it? After sex that is. God how I need you. Not for just a one-night stand but from here on out. Comprehend?

Do you dance? The close, slow kind? I will never forget you. Dottie is anticipating the letter from you. She hopes you like kids because she is one. Keep your zipper zipped.

Your own
MERCY

P.S. I'm thinking again. In bed. Upside down. Mmmmmm. That's a winner. I'm for it. Vive la France. Keep some for me.

Smash was perspiring freely. There was an extra sheet in the envelope folded many times and tucked in a corner. He took that out.

DADDY LOVE,

Here I am in bed again. With only my panties on, and I have to sleep with my daughter. Good God, honey. Come and get me. When I think of what we're going to do together it's almost more than I can think of. I'm even having trouble writing about it. I would rather _____ than anything in the world. I've had a few drinks and am hot to trot. Ready? I want to be your Happy Hour. Kiss me. Unbutton my blouse. There we go again. If you can't trust me, who can you trust?

I would never lie to you. But sure expect to lie down with you. I have a fabulous imagination. You will love me.

I have a hunch you like fudge. I'm going to make a batch up every day and mail them to you.

MERCY

Nails looked at his friend. "What is it, Smash?"
"I think I'm going into sugar shock."

Eight

THE PRINCE AND THE
PRIME MINISTER

"You must return one day and see our beautiful country when we are not at war," said demure Mme Ky, the twenty-three-year-old wife of the dashing Prime Minister.

I had just been admitted to the Kys' living quarters at Tan Son Nhut Air Base. The road leading directly to their home is guarded by machine guns, and their three-bedroom ground-floor quarters sandbagged. Beyond the front door of the compound is the armed Alouette helicopter flown by the Prime Minister, and a well-kept lawn on which two fawns, Bambino and Bambi, nibble. Compared to a palace the Kys' home is primitive. The Vietnamese Air Force redecorated it when the Kys were married, but the Kys insisted on paying for it.

"On the installment plan," explains Mme Ky. "With payments every month." In Vietnam this good example was as unprecedented as the Prime Minister's cutting his own salary in half when he took office in July, 1965.

Ky is twelve years older than his wife, who is known to her friends as Miss Mai. In their spacious drawing room are numerous photographs of the General (as Ky prefers to be called), and an oil portrait of him in his flying suit dominates one wall. A dozen bird cages line one side of the room.

Besides Vietnamese, Miss Mai speaks superb French, good English, and fragmentary German. Her hobbies are dress designing and photography. On my first visit, she got out her Polaroid and we compared notes on how to get the best results with color.

On Ky's last birthday the party drew to a close with the Prime Minister at the microphone, his arms around Miss Mai, singing sentimental love songs to her. He also writes poetry for her, she told me. They met at an officers' ball and fell in love on sight. Daily he sends her pink roses. Their uncommon good looks and devotion to each other add to their popularity.

"Whatever people may think of him as a politician, my husband loves his country very much," she said. "His sweetheart is the Air Force, and of course I am jealous. Even the nights that we can be at home—and it is so seldom—his sweetheart joins us."

I told her that I had once been married to a pilot. "In America it's the same. The men stand around in the kitchen and 'fly' while the wives sit in the parlor and discuss babies, formulas, and servants. All their wives soon learn that the adrenalin of fliers pumps differently from other men's."

The Kys have a television in their home, and use it at times for a baby sitter. Their favorite stars are John Wayne and Gary Cooper. Miss Mai has a black flight suit, a revolver, and an ammunition belt. She likes to demonstrate how fast she is on the draw.

Ky has five children by a former marriage, and the latest addition to the household is a chubby doll born just about the time General Ky began to figure in the world press as leader of the world's most strife-torn country. Miss Mai explained to me that her baby daughter's name is Ky Duyen, which means "Wonderful Story of Love," but that when she is called just Duyen, the name means "Charming." Miss Mai's voice is soft as temple bells.

The Prime Minister's helicopter landed on the turf outside the door. It was nine in the morning. He had already been to his office in Gia Long Palace but was returning to change clothes for a trip to an outpost. He held his daughter for a moment, kissed his wife, and strode with his waiting aides to the official chopper.

Miss Mai, the baby, and I followed, said good-bye again, then retreated to escape the considerable updraft from the clattering rotor blades. The deer were so tame they reappeared in minutes, but would allow only Miss Mai to touch them.

Before her marriage Miss Mai worked as stewardess for the national airline, Air Vietnam. Her father was killed fighting the French. A graduate of one of the finest French schools in Vietnam, she is now taking English lessons from an American girl and is boning up on world history and politics.

On November 12, 1964, when Ky married this lovely girl, who was born in Hanoi, he was Air Vice Marshal and commander of the Air Force. The Vietnamese soldier is among the poorest paid of fighting men. One of Ky's first acts after the governing military junta named him Prime Minister in April, 1965, was to double the soldiers' pay. Ky is stubborn, and his bravery as a combat pilot is a matter of record. Whenever possible he likes to smoke out his enemy—political or military—face to face. He uses idiomatic English learned during his two years at US staff colleges. He is a far stronger man than skeptics at first suspected.

"I am not as young as many people think," he once told me. "With communists at our backs, and the corruption we have inherited from former regimes, we have to solve our problems quickly. So many of my people are so wretchedly poor and hungry that they think they have nothing to lose by listening to the Reds' empty promises and alleged ideals.

"As for the Vietnamese character, our people have been fooled so much for so long by insincere leadership that they think they must camouflage and don't always dare tell the truth. They have found in the past that to tell the truth can hurt them. Like many other Asians, they have a monumental inferiority complex, impossible for a Westerner to comprehend. They are patient and courageous; and I think they know that I am honest. Many politicians regard it as standard procedure to get rich in office. I do not."

Ky has never denied that security is a serious problem in Vietnam. "With two or three guerrillas," he acknowledges, "the enemy can terrorize a stockaded hamlet. Defense against terrorism is difficult."

When Senator Robert Kennedy suggested that the National Liberation Front (political arm of the Viet Cong) be included in any postwar Vietnamese government, Ky countered that it was unclear exactly what Kennedy had in mind. Was the Front to be included before or after the election?

"The next American Presidential election will be in nineteen sixty-eight. It seems a little soon to begin the campaign," Ky commented disdainfully. "Is it good to use the destiny of twenty million people as an issue in the campaign?"

Later, writing to Kennedy, he explained that the Senator's ideas were not helpful and outlined his own proposals and plans.

By October, 1965, American officials in Saigon were finally looking with favor on the responsible manner in which Ky and his government were tackling major problems. The budgets for all of Vietnam's forty-three provinces were being approved. Vietnamese press briefings were now being conducted daily in the manner of American press conferences—previously the briefings for both US and Vietnamese actions on the battlefield had been done by Americans.

In one of my conversations with Ky he told me, "My wife would like me to go back to the Air Force. When peace comes, that is what I would like to do."

Prime Minister Nguyen Cao Ky and his wife had been invited to Malaysia by Prime Minister Tunku Abdul Rahman Putra Al-Haj. Included in the official party were five Vietnamese correspondents. I was the only foreign reporter, possibly because I had told him about being in the Congo with the United Nations Malayan soldiers during 1960 and 1961 when they were rescuing missionaries and other whites from the marauding gangs who called themselves Leopardmen. The only son of the Prime Minister of Malaysia, Lieutenant Tunku Ahmad Nerang, had been among the officers stationed at Kindu, a Congo hot spot ringed with machine guns of hostile and unpredictable Congolese, and I eagerly anticipated a reunion with these men. That's one club you can't belong to unless you've been there.

State trips can be a lot more monotonous than they sound. But not the one with the Kys. Dazzlingly beautiful stewardesses in turquoise or canary-yellow *ao-dais* glided up and down the aisle, serving the party of forty-two. The white pantaloons and high-collared tunics slit to the hips are famous for flattering the feminine figure.

A queen or first lady is always half the show, and Mme Ky was a knockout in her gun-metal raw silk tunic, with a single strand of matchless black pearls around her swanlike neck. The hostesses were all aflutter as they served her because they knew that before her marriage she had been a stewardess.

A man with a style and flair that make his critics call him such things as "off-duty playboy," "hot-shot pilot," and "reciter of long tearful poems," Ky was impeccably dressed in a faultless dark business suit and a black-and-white tie with small checks.

What was different about this trip right off was that the PM was up in the cockpit at the controls of the chartered Caravelle, flying us to Kuala Lumpur. I taped a show while airborne and said, "Some detractors claim that Prime Minister Ky's flying suits are too flamboyant and that his lavender scarf, his wife's favorite color, is a pretension. Make no mistake about it, the Vietnamese love the whole performance and it's what *his* people think that matters."

High-ranking passengers on the trip, all snug and pressurized at 35,000 feet, included the Deputy Premier Lieutenant General Nguyen Huu Co, and Brigadier General Nguyen Chanh Thi, powerful commander of the Vietnamese I Corps, who had long been considered a potential rival to Ky. Just as Ky is popular with the American Air Force, Thi, understandably, is well-liked by US Lieutenant General Lewis Walt, commanding the III Marine Amphibious Force in Thi's area. There are no flies on either Ky or Thi.

Prime Minister Ky had thwarted the gossips when he invited Thi to come along in the official party to Kuala Lumpur. General Thi accepted. He couldn't very well refuse. Whatever the rumors, I decided, he can scarcely bag the throne while he's out of the country with Ky.

Like old-style Chinese warlords, the generals in command of the four corps areas had virtually unlimited power in their areas when Ky became Prime Minister. The corps commanders make allocations of money and appointments, and all military decisions must be coordinated with them. In Thi's year of command he had exercised his prerogatives to the fullest. "When General Thi spits, the people in his area swim" was a popular saying.

To cement their power and influence, the corps commanders appointed friends or relatives as district and province chiefs. With the incessant turnover in corps commanders in coup-battered Vietnam, only one of Vietnam's forty-three provinces has had the same province chief for more than two years. The populous province of Gia Dinh has had six province chiefs in a period of thirteen months—much to the Viet Cong's glee and benefit. The tragedy is that the province chiefs, mostly military men, have no training or background for the challenging and complicated tasks of administering a civilian government. Often they are shamelessly corrupt.

General Ky does not have the powers of a military dictator. All major governmental decisions are made collectively by a committee composed of representatives from the Saigon military district, the national police, and past and present commanders of the four Army-corps areas. Their sessions are top secret and not even an Army stenographer is permitted during their deliberations. Though the meetings are chaired by Major General Nguyen Van Thieu, whose title is Chief of State, rumors persisted that they were dominated by General Thi.

Thi had long been the most independent of the corps commanders and a master of coup-making. He had led the Vietnamese paratroopers in the abortive coup to oust Ngo Dinh Diem on November 11, 1960. When it failed he sought sanctuary in Cambodia. Both publicly and privately Thi had spoken scornfully and skeptically of the junta regime of Ky, yet there were those who insisted that he was Ky's biggest booster, and certainly Ky's insurance for staying in office at the time.

Thi's detractors said his interest in the survival of Vietnam was secondary to his ambitions and accused him of ignoring the central government authority repeatedly. Thi had a variety of connections. Two of his four children were attending school in the United States and living with the family of Sam Wilson, director of field operations for the Saigon Mission of the US Agency for International Development. Perhaps most significant of all, the agitating, militant, ever-plotting monks and some of the students of the northern city of Hue worked tirelessly all over Thi's area to strengthen support for him.

To needle Thi, Ky used to tell him he should not bother getting coup-fever, that the premiership is a tedious business. Ky's strategy was based on his knowledge that Thi is a theorist with grand ideas about solving problems but impatient about compromises on minor challenges day to day.

Thi turned on the charm as soon as the FASTEN SEAT BELTS sign went off, and streaked up the aisle to greet the press with a handshake, as, up front, the Prime Minister piloted the big airplane.

"Enchanté, enchanté," he said when he reached me and the only Vietnamese woman reporter aboard. The former paratrooper told me that upon our return to Saigon he would like me to fly to Da Nang with him in his plane and do a story about his troops.

He asked me how I liked the Da Nang area. I told him that that was where I got my best stories.

"Does the heat bother you?"

I said that anyone who had spent two winters in Istanbul has a tendency to appreciate the sun.

"I advise my troops to skip the soda pop, cold beer, and highballs and drink nothing but hot tea. When I tell this to Americans they think the cure sounds worse than the curse."

(US Marine Corps regulations provide that each Marine carry two one-quart canteens at all times. In hot climates troops lose one pint of water per hour, which must be replaced. It's better to chuck a little gear than to short-change yourself on water. The humidity is thick as peanut butter and the temperature goes to 130 degrees.)

I had been aware that Ky and Thi had for many years been close friends, and had heard that they even look alike. As I talked to this controversial figure, I saw that indeed both were thin, dapper and moustached.

I also remembered what I had heard the first day I arrived in Da Nang: "There will be no end of trouble if Ky sacks Thi."

I played Vietnamese blackjack during much of the trip. The game differs from Las Vegas style in that everybody deals his own cards off the bottom of the deck, making in unnecessary to worry about anyone's cheating. It would be well nigh impossible.

At Kuala Lumpur International Airport, Prime Minister Tunku Abdul Rahman Putra Al-Haj greeted his Vietnamese counterpart. Sixty Royal Malaysian soldiers of the Recognizes Unit, or Recco, were reviewed by General Ky. Most of them were Sandhurst graduates, looking quite snappy in their white coats and black trousers with yellow stripes down the sides.

Since Malaysia and South Vietnam are two countries committed to the same aims, security was light at the airport. The Royal Malaysian Band, in blue and white, played both national anthems. The Tunku addressed his visitors in a spirited speech about "the death struggle going on in Vietnam against ambitious communist aggressors" and added: "Malaysia had to face a similar problem when we were threatened by Indonesia."

Prime Minister Ky replied to the "honored sovereign of Malaysia" by comparing their similar historical evolution and their concepts of freedom and human dignity, and pledged his life and the sacred honor of his country to overcoming the "modern, brutal neo-imperialism called communism, threatening the ancient peninsula." He expressed profound gratitude for Malaysia's sympathy and assistance, and for their expert anti-guerrilla training of Vietnamese troops—their expertise had been gained from twelve years of fighting communists.

Poised and at ease on her first state visit, the first lady of Vietnam captivated her host country's people much in the manner of Jacqueline Kennedy on her first tour abroad with President Kennedy. Malayans called her Mme Beautiful Charmer. She visited homes for underprivileged children and hospitals for the blind and handicapped, and presented checks to these institutions.

At a state dinner for fifty, I watched her on the dance floor. She was wearing a gown of lavender silk and matching pointed-toe satin slippers. Her jet-black hair was piled high in a magnificent coiffure. It took the Tunku about one minute flat to teach her the *gronget,* or *joget,* a swinging dance that is his favorite and that he performs with the gusto of a teen-ager.

While she was dancing I noticed a slender and beautiful Malayan girl apparently at a loss as to how to stay close enough to the visiting first lady. All evening this dainty figure, clad in a tan ankle-length tweed skirt and orange sleeveless blouse, had literally been shadowing Mme Ky.

"Who is that young lady?" I inquired of a guest.

"It's supposed to be a secret," he replied, "but as long as you're so inquisitive I'll tell you. She is the bodyguard assigned to Madame. In that black leather bag on her arm is a little pearl-handled revolver."

If she was the sole security guarding the first lady of Vietnam, it was a grand testimonial to the friendship and faith of the two countries.

The people of Malaya are uncomplicated and as naturally care-free as children. No country has a gentler face than theirs. Over five thousand varieties of orchids are indigenous to the land. Innumerable species of butterflies, including the exquisite black velvet ones, flutter in and out of open windows. There are rolling hills everywhere, even in Kuala Lumpur.

Nevertheless, the capital is rapidly expanding and the calm facade is deceptive. Twenty-five percent of the national budget goes for defense. British warships bob in the harbor and off the coasts and the uniforms of Commonwealth soldiers are seen everywhere. Malaysians live under the constant threat of a pincer movement from a northward-moving Indonesia and a southward-marching North Vietnam and Red China. Would-be invaders see as ripe fruit ready to be plucked the rich farmlands of this country, the rubber plantations, the tin mines, and the natural resources of Sarawak and Sabah. (Malaysia is the world's biggest supplier of rubber and tin.)

Despite Indonesian threats of invasion, real-estate values have remained high instead of dipping. Merchants are content. In economic strength and stability Malaysia is second only to Japan, Australia, and New Zealand.

Measures to provide for greater per-capita income are being given priority consideration in government planning. And often the people quote what is being said in Singapore: "It is too late to change the way of the man who draws the ricksha; but his sons will drive a motorcar."

General Ky's talks with the Tunku centered on formation of an anticommunist military alliance of Asian countries, an alliance first suggested by Nationalist Chinese President Chiang Kai-shek. Other matters discussed included the forthcoming, if ever, Afro-Asian conference. High on the list were the Indo-Pakistani undeclared war, and—of painful interest to Malaysia—the situation in Indonesia, that hostile neighbor whose national rallying cry was "Crush Malaysia."

"This is a critical and anxious period," said the Tunku, "but we are vigilant and prepared to defend our political independence and territorial integrity to the end."

In his after-dinner remarks at one private affair for the Kys and the official party, the Tunku said:

"The Prime Minister of the Republic of Vietnam seems to have everything going for him—youth, good looks, and an exceptionally beautiful wife. He is only thirty-five, which makes him the youngest prime minister in the world—except for me." The high-born leader, who is in his sixties, chuckled. "My hair is not as black as it once was, but neither is it as gray as it should be." It is easy to understand why he is renowned for his charm and wit. I was looking forward to our interview, set up for the next day at his home.

The Tunku (there are several tunkus, but in Malaya just one The Tunku), a gentle, even-tempered, amiable man, was born a prince—although only rarely does it seem to occur to him that this is so. He has an aristocrat's mystique of dignity and a great personal elegance. His self-assurance is balanced by an innate kindness.

The Tunku and the Indonesian leader Sukarno were brother Moslems. Sukarno's actions caused the Tunku heartache and many troubled nights. The two men were simply not on the same wavelength. The Tunku, a devout man, respected womanhood. He was guileless, not especially scholarly, and had been a playboy in his youth. Though he started out as a seat-of-the-pants politician, he transformed himself into a master statesman and the father image of his country. He was what all Malayans would like to be.

Sukarno, who by his own repeated admissions was one of the all-time egotists, had acquired an unsavory notoriety. Such condemning words as "lecher," "liar," and "opportunist" were commonly used by Sukarno's adversaries and critics in describing him. He was, in a word, the epitome of too many things the Tunku loathed.

The Tunku felt his role deeply. He was proud that he had been able to obtain independence for his country in 1957 without slitting any white (British) throats. Malaya, the "Happy Corner," treasures three sturdy assets—national prosperity, the Prime Minister, and the legacy of the British government. From England the Malayans inherited reliable administrative machinery and an organized system of trade and economy. Malayan independence was gained with a minimum of bitterness and little perceptible or lingering British resentment.

An abrasive situation exists in Malaya because 37 percent of the population is of Chinese origin. If the Chinese were ever to achieve power in Malayan politics, the country could quickly become communist-dominated. Traditionally contemptuous of foreigners, the Chinese Malayans are visibly proud of their five thousand years of civilization. They look down their noses at the less educated, *dolce far niente Malays*.

Rich and resourceful traders and entrepreneurs, the Chinese are ruled by a government almost entirely Malay. The Indians are in the same fix, but since they represent only 15 percent of the population, they are no problem. So far the situation is under control due to the general prosperity. Besides rubber and tin exports, iron ore is increasingly exported; there is an endless market for it. Crops have been diversified and the life of the little man is—by Asian standards—spectacularly good.

The superb climate renders the farmer self-supporting with his little patch of luscious fruits, his tapioca, his rice paddy, and plentiful fowl and fish from the many rivers. Hunger is almost unknown. But if Malaya were to go into an economic tailspin, political action from the Chinese could go out of control. They smolder at the discriminations against them, and want their proportionate share of political muscle. The right-wing Malays in turn are close to fanatic, and sometimes advocate driving *all* Chinese out of Malaya.

The Tunku knows better than anyone else that the goal of racial harmony and a multiracial government is generations away. Presently he is implementing plans to bring the Malays' education up to Chinese standards and simultaneously to instill in the Chinese a fealty to Malaysia. At present, the Malays have the police, the army, and the government. The Chinese have the most soothing shade of green in the world—the money.

The Federation of Malaysia was created in 1963. The merger included Malaya, the self-governing city of Singapore, and the three British protectorates in Borneo: Brunei, Sarawak and North Borneo. Singapore, 75 percent Chinese, is influenced by hot-eyed leftist agitators. The Tunku feared Singapore might become another Cuba. The Federation might have been able to dilute the communist influence, since Singapore and Malaya are indispensable to one another.

To Sukarno, the Federation was an outrage and an "aggression." His battle cry, "Smash Malaysia" soon echoed throughout Asia. Before forming Malaysia, the Tunku had allowed himself on various occasions, to be lured to meaningless conferences with Sukarno. During our private talks the Tunku said: "I went in the interests of peace, just as I would go anywhere to solve problems affecting my country. I realize now that Sukarno was puffing and bluffing. I go to him no more."

When I arrived for the private interview, I learned that the Tunku had been up early enough for golf at seven. Entertaining the Kys apparently hadn't taxed his energy. I told him I had been especially interested the night before when he spoke of Singapore. Wasn't Singapore behaving like a fractious, over-spirited nephew?

He said he was sure Singapore and Malaya could work together in harmony, even though Singapore had slipped out of the Federation.

Had Indonesia's attempts to fan small fires into conflagrations influenced Singapore's break from the Federation? The Tunku thought not.

We sat for a while in his palatial residence, then walked around the landscaped grounds. In a little summerhouse his wife was preparing his lunch. She loves to cook for him and sometimes prepares dishes for state dinners. (She had prepared his favorite for the eight-course banquet the night before. It was fried pigeon, a dish of tiny, defeathered bird, mouth agape, resting in a nest of crisp, braided tapioca that tastes somewhat like American French fries. Mme Ky, sitting on the Tunku's right, had declined it, saying, "I have many little birds in my home in Saigon. I could not eat one.")

We continued the interview. "What do you think of Foreign Minister Bhutto's severing Pakistani diplomatic relations with Malaysia? What possible reason could there be for this unprecedented action between members of the Commonwealth?"

"Nothing logical."

"Meaning Peking had a hand in it?"

"Undoubtedly. It is inconsistent for Pakistan to accuse us of betraying fellow Moslems, when they are playing footsie with the communists, who are against all religions. To compound the ridiculousness of the picture," he continued, "India and Pakistan are embroiled in an undeclared war, yet do not break off relations. No, when Pakistan insulted us, they were following a directive straight from Peking. A move in the power-politics game."

The reasons the Tunku gave for his optimism about Malaysia's future emphasized "the very nature of the Malayan people."

"The Malayans are a happy people, eager to do what's right. Rather than cripple our economy, the ruptured trade with Indonesia has stimulated it. Except that we must now spend ten times as much for guns as we formerly did."

I asked if Sukarno's critical problems in his country might result in an Indonesian civil war.

"It would follow," he said. "The dastardly assassination of six top army generals, all staunch anti-communists, has boomeranged already. The people are crying for revenge."

What motivated Sukarno's fixation about confrontation with Malaysia?

"As a nationalist, he must be patriotic to some degree, but he is an inordinately envious man. Envious of the popularity of other world figures among their peoples. His irrational policies are bewildering. It was a spectacularly foolish decision for him to withdraw Indonesia from the United Nations."

"Mr. Prime Minister, you enjoy a fine reputation at poker. Power politics requires similar skills, does it not? Isn't it all a big poker game?"

"A certain amount of bluffing goes on among diplomats, as in a card game, but there the similarity ends. I play poker for relaxation. It is a great game if you do not lose too much money. International intrigue is more like chess."

Then I asked who he considered to be among the greatest leaders of this century—would he name five? He came up with Churchill, de Gaulle, Gandhi, Kennedy, and Nehru—"not necessarily in that order."

On the third night I skipped one state dinner in order to go out with the soldier friends I'd mentioned to General Ky—the men with whom I'd shared some nightmarish adventures in Kasanga and Kindu during the worst of the Congo anarchy. Lieutenant Colonel Ungku Nasaruddin, the former commandant of the Malayans serving with the UN in the Congo, was now a brigadier. Nasaruddin, a graduate of the Royal Military Academy at Sandhurst, is a handsome, imperturbable fellow with great velvet-brown serious eyes. Since he is a cousin to Sultan Abu Bakar of Pekan, the royal town of the state of Pahang, Nasaruddin also bears the title of Prince.

He and Bustami, now a captain, had rounded up eight of the veterans of the Congo fighting to join me at the best Chinese restaurant in Kuala Lumpur. They ordered a feast.

We went through eight rolls of Polaroid color film. Even the kitchen help came in to get into the act. "She turned down a state dinner to be with us," my friends kept repeating in characteristic modesty. Before the evening was over, Bustami gave me a beautiful kris—a special kind of curved Malayan short sword with a hand-carved holder and handle.

Flying home to Saigon, I managed another chat with General Ky. I asked him what he thought might weaken the Peking-Jakarta axis.

We also discussed Sukarno and his years of promoting phony "neutrality." I asked why Sukarno wanted the world reduced to two distinct camps.

"The Red Chinese are more realistic," said Ky. "They prefer that some nations stay uncommitted. They know the camp of the 'imperialists' might be larger if all countries were forced to declare themselves one way or another."

I told Ky I had had a little experience with the Red Chinese myself. First in New Delhi. . . .

In April, 1960, on a visit to India, Premier Chou En-lai and Foreign Minister Chen Yi were officially headquartered in the fabulous Rashtrapati Bhavan, once the Viceregal Lodge of the British Raj, which is surrounded by 330 acres of grounds with magnificent fountains, a profusion of flower beds, formal gardens with pools, terraces, and statues.

All Chou En-lai's meals in Rashtrapati Bhavan were first sampled by official food tasters. Additional police were brought to New Delhi from neighboring cities. Chou's bird-in-a-golden-cage existence was tantamount to polite house arrest, although with a flick of a switch he could communicate with Mao Tse-tung in Peking. Adjoining his mirrored marble bathroom was a bedroom containing a huge bed reputed to be the "biggest and best in the East." It was the same one Khrushchev had declined, saying, "I'd get lost and roll right out of it."

Chou's wing—the one reserved for heads of state—was sealed off from the rest of the building. He was guarded by the thirty-nine Pekingese henchmen who had accompanied him, and a twenty-four-hour cordon of nervous Indian secret-service men. Even so, I thought it was worth trying to get a private interview in advance. And I did manage to slip past the Indian security. The Chinese bodyguards soon discovered that I was a contemptible American and tossed me out like a hot rice cake.

So I had to wait for the formal press conference, which took place in a large room where flocks of sparrows, flying in and out the open windows, were chirping and roosting on the crystal chandeliers and immense framed portraits of Lord and Lady Mountbatten. Though Chou speaks English, he insisted on interpreters, and went through three before the interview concluded. He caught the first two in nuance errors and sometimes even spelled out the words for them.

Chou wore highly polished black oxfords, black silk socks, and the high-necked tunic devised by Dr. Sun Yat-sen. Between dozes,

Chen Yi cooled himself with a big black fan—but awoke with a start when anguished Indian newsmen shouted queries about the Sino-Indian border hassles.

Chou's reception in New Delhi was described as "warm but not warmhearted." Actually it was as chilly as the frozen plateau of Ladakh, India's Himalayan waste which China had just requisitioned —a 35,000-square-mile real-estate grab. (India has always feared China more than Russia.) Most of the Chinese visit was spent shuttling around the Himalayas and conducting sentimental border surveys, with a special hankering for Mount Everest, as if anything under 25,000 feet was an absolute pimple.

I saw the Chinese leaders again on the next leg of their trip— Katmandu. Among many civic receptions honoring the Chinese statesmen was one held at the football and soccer stadium. The local band arrived early, mounted on bicycles, rickshas, jeeps, and ponies, with tubas, oboe-like *sanayi,* and other musical instruments in tow or slung around the musicians' necks. Accompanied by students skirling on the bell-mouthed *sanayi,* Himalayan children burbled welcoming songs to the VIPs.

Chou, Chen Yi, and company sat in an enclosure atop a long flight of stone steps. Here in Katmandu the guards were more relaxed than in India. When the two Chinese leaders nodded and smiled in my direction, I edged up the steps one at a time and focused my Rollei. Both Chou and Chen Yi obliged with grins as I shot pictures from six feet. They seemed to remember me from the New Delhi press conference, where I'd sat on the floor with the photographers in the front row. This time, as in India, I was the only woman in the press group.

On every occasion the Lord Mayor of Katmandu and other Nepalese officials, with what could only be interpreted as a topping example of spot sarcasm, addressed Chou and Chen Yi: "O vigilant sentinels of Asia."

For the next few years I watched for another chance to make my path cross the Chinese leaders'. It came in 1964, when the US ally Pakistan invited the Chinese to come calling. Understandably, Chinese blood was set to churning; here was a prestige plus. Another aspect of Pakistan's motive was crystal clear—a propaganda windfall in the boiling conflict with India over Kashmir.

When I arrived in Pakistan, I found Red China's gold-starred red flag fluttering everywhere. Overhead, banners proclaimed CHINESE-PAKISTANI FRIENDSHIP. Posters welcomed the Chinese Premier, though his name was spelled "Chaw En-lai."

In most countries he visits, Chou is introduced as "the dynamic premier who charms world statesmen." His friends say they are fascinated by the enormous subtlety and profundity of the man. Even his detractors acknowledge him as one of the world's most able diplomats.

The persuasive, wanly handsome Chou is Red China's chief spokesman, propagandist, and agile manipulator in the delicate arts of diplomacy. His nimble mind, glib tongue, slim expressive hands, and trim figure serve him well. His grandfather was a mandarin, one of the powerful caste of scholar-bureaucrats of imperial days. Chou is known for his ruthlessness in cutting down obstacles and has been described as brilliant, pitiless, strong, urbane, self-possessed, and one of the master dissemblers of the age. He speaks knowledgeably of Moscow, Berlin, Paris, and London, and handles dialects of his own country expertly, including Cantonese and Shanghai.

A one-time friend has said of him, "Chou's as slippery as they come. Probably bathes in olive oil. He can disappear while you're shaking hands with him. He wouldn't admit Sunday was Sunday unless it would help him. He ought to be shot."

Others have called him a Chinese Talleyrand, tricky and audacious. In party intrigue he makes few gaffes. His political savvy and agility in ducking firing squads earned him the sobriquet *pu tao wong*—a weighted toy that always lands upright.

If those nuclear bangs in Red China mean the Chinese have exploded their way to a seat in the UN, Chou probably would arrive, bomb in hand, so to speak, to represent his country. That old schmaltz could throw New York hostesses into a tizzy.

In China, as in no other country on earth, the people have been propagandized into a frenzied hatred of American leaders. Our presidents are called everything from hoodlums to bloody-fanged butchers. I remember all too well how on President Eisenhower's 1960 Far East journey, as we sailed with the Seventh Fleet from Manila to Formosa, communist shore batteries unleashed a contemptuous and massive bombardment on Quemoy, Tatan and Ehrtan islands. The Red Chinese News Agency broadcast a sarcastic description of their "welcome to Gangster Eisenhower" and called the US President a "thug," a "rat running across the street—everybody wants to step on him," a "warmonger," and a "god of plague." The bulletin included comments attributed to their "heroic Red Chinese gunners" as they rhythmically jerked their lanyards and shrieked:

"Eisenhower. . . . go back. . . . Fire!"

"Get out of Asia. . . . Fire!"

"Eisenhower is a mad dog. . . . Fire!"

And yet Chou En-lai, the man who masterminds such onslaughts, is a man so affable and mild in manner that many Westerners who knew him early in his career were convinced that he was merely pretending to be a communist. They've since learned that no one has labored longer or more effectively to deliver China to the Marxist camp. During General Marshall's negotiations with him, the General trusted Chou too much. Subsequent checkups revealed that 85 percent of Chou's military reports to General Marshall were false. And in the 1930's Chou once told a friend: "Why should I worry about Chiang Kai-shek's party? I know it as I know my own. The Kuomintang was founded by Borodin, the same Russian comintern agent who originated the Communist Party."

Once, when Chou was asked how he, born into wealth and culture, could become a communist, he replied: "When I was young I hated to climb out of a warm bed on cold winter mornings. My teacher suggested that I leap right out, that I soon would feel warm for having had the contrasting dash of cold. In communism the experience is like that. Chilly at first, but then warmer because of the contrast."

The highlight of the Pakistani tour came in the garden city of Lahore, a two-thousand-year-old city drenched in intrigue and splendor. Chou and Chen Yi were being honored at the ultra-exclusive Gymkhana Club, where membership requires both money and generations of prestige. Perfumed ladies, in silken saris of burning colors, and aristocratic gentlemen created a party-perfect atmosphere. Said one old fellow, "This is the first time outsiders have been feted at our club." Chou and party beamed at him; they were clearly impressed.

Preceding the luncheon the Pakistani and Chinese officials were introduced and made speeches from a small dais in the reception room. Pakistani Foreign Minister Z. A. Bhutto smiled and said hello to me as I joined the photographers shooting pictures of the group. Suddenly Chou stood up and approached me, holding out his hand. "I remember you," he said, "from Katmandu four years ago." He stepped down from the foot-high platform to talk for several minutes. Jacques Nevard, of *The New York Times,* thoughtfully and gallantly picked up my camera to record the tête-à-tête.

Then Marshal Chen Yi, seated beside his young-looking doll-like wife, waved and spoke to his interpreter, who turned to me. "Marshal Chen Yi wants you to know that he remembers you, too."

Before I could think what I was saying, I blurted out, "Oh, I was sure he would remember. He's a girl watcher," and immediately wanted to bite my tongue off, because by then the interpreter was translating to the portly Chen Yi, who just reared back and roared, slapped his knee, and rocked a little, very pleased that I had implied he was a flirt.

Only moments before, Chen Yi's moon face was bunched up in fury as he addressed the group heatedly about US imperialists and capitalists—which I guess surely includes me. Anyway, their friendly greetings to me smoothed the way for subsequent chats at airports and receptions.

Moving among the crowd later, Chou and Chen Yi were in an expansive mood as they drank their whiskey neat, and declared, "This is not a friendship of expedience. If China had Formosa and Pakistan had Kashmir, we would still be friends. Peace and friendship for all is the only sane course in international relations."

The luncheon was followed by an affair out of *The Arabian Nights* —a citizens' reception at Lahore Fort, a former royal residence of the successors to that luminous monarch of the past, Akbar the Great. The Moguls lived in legendary pomp, still reflected in the fort's marble pavilion of marvelously intricate patterns of inlaid precious stones, carvings, and murals depicting elephant fights and polo matches.

The Chinese were feted with all the trappings and fanfare accorded a high presence. Balloons floated, multicolored lights twinkled, and an exuberant fifty-piece orchestra was ensconced on a concrete platform in the center of a vast pool. Luxurious shamianahs sheltered gaily decorated tables bearing cookies and cakes. Drinks in gold-edged crystal goblets were served by a retinue of turbaned, white-clad waiters.

Suddenly someone signaled the orchestra to hush. Sitting together, Jacques Nevard, Richard Critchfield, and Paul Hurmusus, of the *Chicago Daily News,* and I hushed up along with everybody else. Then Mogul officers atop the fort lifted their silver trumpets. Buglers on the roof of an opposite building echoed their notes and elegant Chou made his entrance, followed by Chen Yi, whose hands were folded below a stomach that looked like he'd swallowed a medicine ball.

Chou led the group step by measured step over the long red carpet toward the center shamianah. You don't often get the *jambon* out of an actor, and Chou, as one of the leaders of a country controlling one-seventh of the earth's surface and one-fourth of its people, has a vastly larger audience than during his theatrical days. (Due to his smooth face and manner, in his youth Chou had been much in demand to play female leads in musical comedies, a common practice in the Orient.)

The setting was fit for an emperor and that was exactly the way Chou entered the fort. Dark eyes electric with pleasure, he ever more slowly paced his way over the thick Persian carpets, acknowledging the thunderous applause with bows to right and left.

Outside, barefoot children of many shades peered through the fence and scrambled like monkeys up the gate and grillwork for a better look at the spectacle. These little Pakistanis were unmindful of the Chinese proverb: "Where there is an excess of ceremony, there is sure to be deceit."

My Vietnamese colleagues were interested when I told them that I had had talks with Chou En-lai. For the rest of the trip we sat swapping stories. I told them that I have a friend who was once a roommate of Chou's and that Dana Adams Schmidt, (*The New York Times*) and I sat all one afternoon listening to the roommate's personal sketch of the young Chou. Among other things:

"Chou was a very entertaining companion, had a fine eye for the girls—a real ladies' man. And he had no false modesty. In the steam room or shower, he used to strut around, rather proud of his physique. He had a good sense of humor, too. But his jokes in Chinese were shady rather than earthy. One remarkable thing about the man is that during all the time I roomed with him, he never once lost his temper."

With regard to Chou's temper nowadays, in Ceylon in 1964 I had a chance to observe it firsthand.

Very little had gone according to his wishes on his visit to the island country, then governed by the world's first elected woman prime minister of an independent nation, Mme Sirimavo Bandaranaike. (Her refusal to be cowed by Chou En-lai was once explained by a close associate: "Madame can thin her jaw. She will not have anyone wave a big stick at her.")

Madame's aim was to bring India and China to the conference table, a diplomatic tightrope act then as now. Chou included in his entourage Soong Ching-ling, the widow of Dr. Sun Yat-sen, founder of modern China. This sister of Mme Chiang Kai-shek, a black-haired lady of seventy-six, broke with the family after the civil war.

Around Colombo, some of the posters greeting Chou read: WILL THE CHINESE TREAT CEYLON BUDDHISTS AS THEY DID THE BUDDHISTS IN TIBET?

In reply to Mme Bandaranaike's request that China vacate all its seven manned posts in Ladakh, Chou alibied that he could make this decision only after consulting with his government.

Though it was flatly denied to the press, a spokesman with rare access to Ceylon affairs insisted that Chou had put out feelers about using Ceylon's ports as transshipment centers for goods going to Africa, South Asia, and Europe, and that this preliminary approach had proved quite futile. (Trincomalee, on Ceylon's northeast coast, is one of the few natural deep harbors in that part of the world. That it would make an ideal submarine base is lost on neither Western nor Eastern strategists.)

Mme Bandaranaike's advice to Chou was: "Don't talk about US imperialists. Discuss colonialists and imperialists *in general*." The collision course continued throughout their conferences. Logically, only a tepid joint communiqué could result. The harangue over its wording lasted for hours.

Release of the communiqué took place, as always, at the visit's end. No reporters were allowed, so I quickly obtained photographer's accreditation (both are seldom allowed) and slipped into the room with a handful of local still and TV cameramen, all of them Chinese or Ceylonese.

The atmosphere was electric with tension. Completely out of harmony with Chou En-lai, Mme Bandaranaike sat in her brilliant orange sari and put pen to her copy of the scarlet-backed communiqué, so different from what Chou had hoped to accomplish. Untypically, he had failed to incorporate into it any of his own significant issues. Sullenly he affixed his signature to each page as quickly as an aide could flip them.

From the moment Chou had entered the room, in barely controlled fury, there had been an economy of smiles, these directed at the aides and cameramen. Chou was slightly contemptuous; Madame was about two hundred pounds of pure, ho-hum aplomb. Her attitude was a unique offense to Chou's ego and the sweat pebbled his brow under the hot TV lights.

In spite of the fact that Madame was the hostess, it was Chou who summoned the refreshments. With a jerk of his right arm he motioned a waiter in from the wings with a tray of glasses partly filled with orange soda pop. Tossing off a half-hearted toast followed by a hollow laugh, he skipped the sweet cakes and, leading his entourage, stalked out of the room and down the stairs to a waiting car, to depart from Colombo an hour and a half ahead of schedule. "Bad weather reports" served as his excuse.

Waiting for me at the bottom of the stairs when the meeting was over were Lou Rukeyser, *Baltimore Sun* (he's now with *ABC* in London) and Paul Hurmusus. They couldn't have been more solicitous of my health nor more generous about inviting me to ride back to the Galle Face Hotel in *their* taxi.

In the back seat of the shared limousine, each prime minister sat as close to an opposite window as possible, Madame's chin in her hand as she gazed out at the press, Chou staring straight ahead and scowling as if he had swallowed a bad oyster. The old charm had been lost on *this* lady.

Chairman Mao Tse-tung's writings are instant best sellers in China. His stories and poems deal with the elements, with riddles, nature, and bugs. One of his most recent poems had boggled Western translators' reasoning and conjecture. Loosely, it went:

"On this small earth tiny flies are breaking their heads against the wall, uttering mournful, bitter sobs. Climbing ants boast of the importance of their realm. The four stormy seas voice their anger . . . five continents tremble. All insect pests must be exterminated. Not one enemy must remain alive."

To whom was Mao referring? The Russians? Khrushchev? Americans? I tried to get in one last question before Chou's car pulled away.

"The Chairman's poem about destroying all insect pests," I hollered. "Mr. Prime Minister, do you think he means *everybody?*"

With the unmatched tranquillity of an Oriental, Mr. Prime Minister just sailed away in his big, capitalistic Cadillac.

As soon as Prime Minister Ky's plane landed at Tan Son Nhut and I had said good-bye to all my colleagues, I discovered there was no way to reduce the overwhelming amount of red tape necessary for a reentry into Vietnam, even though my papers had just been renewed the week before and I had been traveling with the head of state. When everything was finally stamped, sealed, and made out in quadruplicate, I took a taxi over to the Pan Am office before it closed. My friend, adviser, even banker, Tom Bready, permitted me to hide my money and valuables in his office safe when I was out of town.

Director of Pan American World Airways for Vietnam, Cambodia, and Laos, Tom was thought of by some of us Americans as the "unofficial mayor of Saigon." His English secretary, Grace Rasmussen, cheerfully shared with him the responsibilities of providing a haven for correspondents with problems.

Tom had lived many years in the Orient and his own family was very much at home there. Once his fifteen-year-old daughter, Barbara, had been in the audience when a movie theater full of Americans was bombed by guerrillas. Nine stitches had to be taken in her head.

"How is she?" I asked Tom.

"Oh, fine. Somebody asked her the other day if she intended to go back to the movies over here. She said, 'It depends on what's playing.' "

After I had answered all the questions about my trip to Kuala Lumpur and was about to walk out the door, he called me back.

"Forgot something. Do you know the latest songs on the Asian Hit Parade?"

I didn't.

"Well, they're 'Every Little Breeze Seems to Whisper Disease' and 'The Rain in Laos Falls Mainly in the House.' "

Nine

EASTER MISSIONS

FLYING ITSELF IS NOT INHERENTLY DANGEROUS BUT LIKE THE SEA
IT IS TERRIBLY UNFORGIVING OF INCOMPETENCE, CARELESSNESS, OR
NEGLECT

It was Easter Sunday. The visors of Smash and Nails's helmets were
painted red, the squadron color, with a death's head stenciled in white.
Nails began his preflight walk around the plane, checking the bombs
slung under the wings, four 750-pounders. He noticed that the ground
crew had painted the bombs like Easter eggs—polka dots and flaming
colors. Chalked around were messages: FOREIGN AID TO HO CHI
MINH, HAPPY EASTER, and NORTH VIETNAM CARE PACKAGE.

"Hey, Smasherino," yelled Nails, "get down off that gahdam wing
and take a look at this. Easter eggs."

What always fractured Smash were the little tags on the bombs.
Attached by wire, they bore the emblem of AID (Agency for International Development). Across the top were four white stars on a
blue background. Below, in a hands-across-the-border spirit, were
fingers clenched in a muscular handshake. Beneath that were red and
white vertical stripes. The idea of these tags on death-dealing explosives to be dropped on an enemy who would never read them was to
Smash "bureaucracy gone berserk."

Everything checked out and the two strapped in and taxied out to
the end of the runway. They were leading a flight of four aircraft to a
special extraction mission near An Khe in the Central Highlands.

"A hundred twenty nautical miles to the target," Smash said. "Pick
up a heading of a hundred seventy degrees after takeoff. Should take
us exactly twenty-two and a half minutes to get there."

Smash threw in the half-minute just to keep Nails on his toes, to
make him think he had the world's greatest navigator. It is impossible
to compute time in the heat of combat while looking for a Forward
Air Controller. Seldom does anyone pay much attention to the time,

anyway. The job is to find the FAC, then the VC, and put the bombs on them.

Nails keyed his mike button and transmitted: "Da Nang Tower. This is Gory Zero One. Over."

"Gory Zero One. This is Da Nang Tower. Over."

"Roger. Da Nang Tower. Gory Zero One flight of four. Number one for the active. Over."

"Gory Zero One. Wind is one five zero degrees at ten knots. Cleared for takeoff."

The Canberras taxied onto the active runway. Nails released the brakes and began his takeoff roll, announcing as usual, "Stoney Burke coming out of chute number five."

Fifteen seconds later the number-two man, Captain Gerald Christeson, released his brakes and began his roll down the runway. The number-three, Captain Doug Weber, was deputy lead. As they flew to their rendezvous with the FAC, Nails roared his favorite bawdy ballad over the hot mike:

> Mary Ann Burns was the queen of all the acrobats,
> She could do tricks that would give a guy the fits.
> She could blow green peas from her fundamental orifice,
> Do a backward somersault and catch them on her tits.
> She's a great big sonofabitch twice the size of me;
> Hair on her armpits like the branches of a tree.
> She can swim, fish, fight, fuck, roll a barrel, drive a truck—

Nails stopped singing for a minute. "Hey, Smash! How about that 'roll a barrel' part? Did you ever know a sug who could roll a barrel?" He coughed his throat clear. "Hard part coming up,"

> Mary Ann Burns is gonna marry me-e-e-e-e-e
> In a pig's asssssss ho-o-o-o-o-le!

"Hey, Nails," called Smash, "how about 'Danny Boy'?"

"Naw, that one always makes me feel like a queer. Besides, it belongs to that Brand X outfit. Old Danny Farr's a hell of a good man but he ought to be wearing one of our red shirts."

"Yeah. Who ever heard of a combat outfit with yellow for their color?"

Nails's boys of the 13th alternated tours of duty at Da Nang with the men of Danny Farr's 8th Bomb Squadron. As the only crews flying B-57s in the area, they were all like brothers, but kept up a healthy rivalry.

The Charlies' special hatred for the B-57 Canberras was often evident in the testimony of VC defectors. When the VC were interrogated by American-South Vietnamese intelligence as to why they defected, many replied that the primary reason was overwhelming American and Vietnamese air power.

"There is no place to hide. You keep us always on the move. Our tactics have to be modified because we are always looking over our shoulders. We could not stand the pounding from the air."

And when intelligence showed defectors the silhouettes of aircraft, most of them immediately pointed to the B-57 as the most despised. "The screaming bird," they would say. "It is the worst. It stays over the target so long. And it never runs out of bombs."

Weapons so dreaded have a psychological assist—for example, the Stuka dive bomber of WW II, with its deadly accuracy and awesome scream. The J-65 engine of the B-57 also has a weird whine all its own. And the VC have a contemptible word for the Canberra —*can sau,* which means "caterpillar," the little creature that they consider the most loathsome thing in all Vietnam.

("Butterflies we like, they are beautiful," a waitress once told me, "but a caterpillar is like—what do you say in America?"

"A rat fink?")

It was time to switch to combat frequency and contact the FAC. An Khe would be coming up in about five minutes. When Nails switched the radio to the Forward Air Controller's frequency, it became clear that this was no ordinary mission. Friendly ARVN troops were besieged by a large unit of VCs.

The strike was in support of a helolift of friendlies from Highway 19. The huge US Army choppers made trip after trip from An Khe to the battle area ten miles west to pick up Vietnamese soldiers and lift them to safety.

Active on both sides of the road, the Viet Cong were throwing everything they had at the ARVN, and there was a solid wall of crossfire as the Vietnamese boarded the choppers.

The FAC directed the B-57s south of the road as F-100 Supersabres worked the north side. Low cloud coverage made dive bombing impossible today. The Canberra does its most accurate work when it can dive in from six thousand feet and pickle the bombs at three thousand, but the bird is an extremely stable platform for level bombing at low altitude. However, if it flies below 1,700 feet it can pick up shrapnel and fragments from its own bombs. The ceiling was down to 1,500.

Nails had to get under that to drop his ordnance and cover the troops being evacuated on the highway. At this altitude the chances of being blasted out of the sky by his own bombs were greatly increased. But the friendlies were in desperate need of air support. So Nails elected to drop from 1,200 feet and immediately pull into the overcast. There was no need for the FAC to fire smoke rockets. Nails and Smash could see the choppers picking up troops on the road.

Nails began his first bomb run as Smash called off the check list. All switches were properly positioned so two 750-pounders would drop from the wings. Nails put his armament-select switch on internal-external. He punched the pickle button as the gun sight passed through the target, an area of heavy concentrated ground fire.

Tracers arced toward the friendlies. Then many VC guns switched their axis of fire and neon-red tracers began winging skyward toward the oncoming Canberras. The heavier-caliber guns joined the onslaught, firing at Smash and Nails.

As the Canberra bombs exploded, the aircraft shuddered, then clawed for altitude. Smash said, "Son of a bitch. I thought they had us that time."

Actually it was the concussion from their own bombs.

Nails looked up and said, "Thanks again, Hube."

The three other planes in the flight made their first run. The fire fight on the ground decreased considerably. It was Nails's and Smash's turn again. They let go with the remaining two 750-pound general-purpose bombs from their wings. Again the aircraft lurched from the concussion.

"I think we may be just a little too close to our work," said Nails. "These gahdam fuel gauges are going ape. Looks like we're hit in the main tank. I think we've got a hell of a hole in there. May have to punch out. I doubt like hell we can make Da Nang. Let's get out over the gahdam water."

"Rog," answered Smash. "I'll take my chances with the sharks rather than the VC. Those bastards would really like to get their hooks on a couple of Grimy Rapers, especially us two keen guys."

Nails pulled off the target and headed for the South China Sea. He switched his parrot to an emergency squawk position, which shows up on the ground radar screens as an aircraft in distress.

Chris dropped his bombs and pulled off the target to fly chase on his crippled leader. Weber and Ed Cook continued to pound the target until the friendlies were evacuated. Again the VC had lost the objective.

Nails headed his plane for the coastline. The gas gauge continued to drop. Smash checked his ejection seat and tightened his straps. Neither mentioned it aloud, but they couldn't ignore the fact that a water ditching didn't rule out Viet Cong altogether. The Charlies prowled along the coast in junks.

Nails was on the radio transmitting the international distress call. "Mayday. Mayday. Mayday. We are over coordinates fourteen-fifty north and one-zero-nine-ten east. Is anyone reading Gory Zero One? Over."

Smash got on the hot mike. "Looks like we might have to make a nylon letdown, huh, Nails? Over."

Da Nang Tower answered the call and informed the B-57 that help was on the way from two Marine F-4s, who would supply air cover for the bailout.

The fuel gauge read zero as the aircraft coasted out over the water at seven thousand feet. Chris was riding high on the left wing. The two Marine F-4s dropped out of the overcast and took up a position high on Nails's right wing. Smash figured to himself that this was a hell of a way to lose an aircraft after all the crap they had flown through on Doom Pussy sorties up north.

Up in Doom Pussy Land there are not just various automatic weapons chewing you up but everything from crossbows to surface-to-air missiles. The VC's trick of arranging lights on the ground to simulate truck convoys has proved fatal for attacking planes sucked into these flak traps. As the planes start their run on the "trucks," enemy antiaircraft batteries unleash a barrage of tracers like a thousand angry geysers spewing hot lead, and suddenly the Doom Puss is breathing down your neck.

Now what had started out as a relatively easy mission had turned into a bucket of worms. A rescue helicopter loomed over the horizon. What a hell of a sight, thought Smash. The Air-Sea-Rescue troops were doing outstanding work both north and south of the demarcation line, risking their ass every day to pluck fliers out of all sorts of situations.

Nails depressed the mike button to broadcast what he thought would be his last transmission before abandoning aircraft. "This is Gory Zero One. My engines will be cutting out any second. We'll be going for a swim. The RESCAP birds are on top of the situation."

Thirty seconds later Nails transmitted into the blind for anyone to hear: "The gauges are showing zero but the engines are still turning. It's apparently a gauge malfunction. Hello. Da Nang Tower?

This is Gory Zero One. I'm heading home. Give me a straight-in GCA to runway three-five."

The escort birds stayed on Nails's wing down to the final approach at two hundred feet. Nails punched the mike button to speak to the two Marine escort planes.

"Thanks a lot for the company, Jarheads."

The Marines were flying close enough to see into Nails's front office. As they advanced their throttles for a go-around, a Marine pilot saluted and transmitted on the air, "See you on the ground, babe."

The half million bucks' worth of Uncle Sam's aerial hardware was rolling down the Da Nang runway instead of pranging into the South China Sea.

Smash and Nails jumped into the air-crew van and headed for the Doom Club. They had a date with the Doom Pussy that night.

Aircraft number 926, which flew the day mission as Gory Zero One, would be out of commission for several days. Three gaping holes in the fuselage would be difficult to repair. The electrical wiring system had been shot away, causing the fuel gauge to malfunction. The ground crews regarded the battle damage and wondered what had kept the grand old lady airborne.

Even if it hadn't been against the rules, there was no time for booze that day. Just a salami sandwich and a quick shot of iced tea.

At the Doom Club were Captain Doug Weber from Hamden, a suburb of New Haven, Connecticut; Lieutenant William Blaufuss, Los Angeles; Captain Francis Hyland, Erie, Pennsylvania; Captain Russ Hunter, Wethersfield, Connecticut; Captain Joe Krasniewicz, Pine Island, New York; Captain Ernie Kiefel, Harrisburg, Pennsylvania; Captain Neil Suggs, Delhi, Louisiana; Lieutenant Denny Jenkins, a navigator from Mesa, Arizona; and Lieutenant George Lyddane. The group quickly took up the popular pastime of ribbing Smash.

"Ever hear about the time Smash and a couple of friends were in Taipei touring the citadels of freedom, or what are delicately referred to in Saigon as massage parlors? Well, the troops marched into the parlor. Those pretty little sugs came about to Smash's belly button. After the boys were kimonoed, well wined, and massaged, arms linked with the girls, they all marched around the room in pairs as the hand-wound gramophone scratched out a tinny record of 'Sweethearts on Parade.' With an Oriental lisp they chirped out the lyrics:

Two by two
We go marching through,
Sweethearts onnnnnnn puh-ra-a-a-a-ade.

"Every time they passed the window, Smash's sug would make him wave to her parents sitting across the street, as she was so proudly doing. Smash's kimono hit him somewhere between Mexico and the border, but he'd had his gourd stuck in the bourbon bottle so long he didn't care. The finale always found all the guests on the balcony so the family could make a head count on how good business was. Smash was off key but booming out the lyrics like a buffalo with his leg caught in a bear trap.

" 'Sweethearts on *puh-rade!* ' "

Captain Arthur Kono, from Seattle, Washington, the Japanese-American member of the 8th Bomb Squadron, joined them. "Come on, do it for us, Smash. Either that or read us some Mercy Belle letters." By now Mercy was practically the 13th's pinup girl.

"Forget it, willya? Things aren't going so damn good."

"Go on, show 'em the latest. Might as well," Nails pressed him. Smash fished the letters out of his pocket. "Yeah. Might as well. You've seen all the rest."

The men gathered around closer.

HELLO YOU BIG DOLL,

Why don't you write more often? Is it my lack of finess?

I honestly believe people tend to be more realistic and a truer person in letters than in actual contact. Listen, my sex partner, just come home to me. Haven't had anyone to wash my back in a long time. I'm sure I would enjoy some in the shower, too. Sounds like a winner to me. I'll drop the soap just to see what it's like being violated. I am anxious to find out how much I can satisfy you, and how gratifying the *complete* act will be. You beast!

To me you would be sexy in a towel. Take a snap in a towel and send it to me. The more I can see the better I like it.

I don't know the meaning of the word "frigid." You better believe it, dad. I think I'd like it on the kitchen table. Then you can walk right into it. Mmmmmmm boy.

"What was it that English dame said? 'Anything goes as long as you don't do it in the street and frighten the horses,' " Nails said.

"She sounds like a round-the-clock hell-raiser," Marty added.

Smash read on:

You be sure to sit on a piece of metal under that parachute. God, I shudder to think of their shooting it off. I think of you constantly. Doesn't the idea of putting me in bed and never letting me go appeal to you? If I ever do catch you I certainly will know what to do with you. I've got you under my skin, Major.

When could you get over here? I've got my fingers crossed and also my legs. I'm sure you have the combination to uncross them, so come home and use your combination. You have lots of girl friends, I bet. Young ones. Old ones. Married ones. Single ones. Have a blast, dad. Someday. Oh boy. *Some*day!

Nails, looking over Smash's shoulder, said, "Here comes the moment without price. Here comes the snapper."

I have only one gentleman friend. (Married of course.) We have a standing date twice a week unless things get bothersome and we need additional meetings. It's quite hush-hush and he's of a very high caliber. Also, I have to have my outlets and do not like a variety of men. Too many loud mouths. And besides I am very, very particular. He's about your size and loves sex and good booze. Not a miser and not too showy either. He reminds me of you in many ways.

Write on MacDuff. It gripes my very soul to think about you and your women but it also pleases me that you seem to be such a virile man and so much in demand. You cause me to have mixed emotions about sex. I know you don't giggle or go to the library and I admire you. I can learn to love you as I am hell on wheels in bed. Or out. So there!

Your true, blue, faithful, passion flower.

MERCY BELLE

"Smash, you gotta donate those to the War Library," Nails said.

"A few jars of ice-cold booze and Mercy Belle would be some jackpot over here in the combat zone, huh?" said Harry Brahm.

"What're you going to do, Smash?" asked Doug Weber.

"Whadda *you* think? The jig is *up*. And the moon is down. She was cheatin' on me. She shouldn't have told me about it. It woulda been a lot classier if she hadn'ta told me about it. She's bollixed it up good now."

"Mercy was writin' real picturesque letters." Denny Jenkins sighed.

"A rare spirit," agreed Doug.

Back on the flight line they briefed the mission with the crew of the C-130 flare ship. The fireball sun sank behind the smoke-purple mountains that embraced Happy Valley. Then, two Canberras taxied onto the active runway. The Valley was a VC stronghold west of the base, formally known as Da Nang AFBRVN. The flare ship, Aztec Zero One, had been airborne for thirty minutes. Bud Childress was Nails's wingman. The two big birds, heavy with bombs, climbed out together to rendezvous with Aztec Zero One.

Nails completed his level-off check at thirty thousand and serenaded Smash over the hot mike with an old RAF number:

> O-O-OH, the hippopotamus, so it seems,
> Very seldom has wet dreams,
> And when it D-U-U-U-Z-Z-Z-Z, it comes in streams
> As it revels in the joys of copula-a-a-shun.

He was interrupted by Bud's transmission: "Cheetah Six One, this is Six Two. I've got the C-130 rotating beacon in sight. He's twelve o'clock low."

"Rog," replied Nails, "let's start a descent. Speed boards out. Now—we'll join this aerial circus up at fifteen thousand."

The incongruous formation was two B-57s, a Marine F-10, and a C-130. They proceeded to a predetermined point on the vital highway deep in Ho Chi Minh territory. The truck convoys full of supplies for the VC down south roll only at night. The job of the four-ship formation was to blast three convoys into oblivion. It is difficult to locate trucks at night. They roll with lights blacked out or dimmed, then hit for the woods when aircraft are heard overhead.

Twenty minutes of road recce produced nothing in the way of rolling stock. Then the C-130 commander came over the air loud and clear: "Convey sighted dead ahead. Will be dropping in three minutes."

The B-57s peeled off and set up a pattern one thousand feet below the C-130 flare ship.

"Dropping. Dropping. Dropping," announced the C-130 pilot. Seconds later a necklace of twelve brilliant white flares suspended by small parachutes began lighting up the landscape.

As Nails started his attack from his base-leg perch, all hell broke loose from automatic weapons on both sides of the road.

"Break right. Break right, Big Mama," cried Nails as he picked up speed on his dive-bomb run.

The lumbering flare bird racked up in a forty-five-degree bank to the right. Antiaircraft fire was exploding all around the C-130.

"Where the hell *are* you guys? They're hosing my *ass* off!"

Nails was halfway down his bomb run with 20-millimeter cannons chopping up the gun positions. Bud was turning base-leg to final as he deepened his voice to broadcast: "A stranger from another planet . . . coming in faster than a speeding bullet . . . more powerful than a locomotive . . ."

Not to be outdone, Nails pulled off the target through blistering ground fire and launched into his tension-easing contribution:

"Mighty Mouse is on the wa-a-a-a-ay

"Mighty Mouse will save the d-a-a-a-ay."

Quickly getting into the spirit, the 130 flare ship jock came on. "Sir, don't you cats realize war is a mighty grim business? Or shall I pull up alongside you and explode?"

A winding mountain road was visible, a river, a bridge, and just below that Nails spotted a batch of trucks as he climbed back into the sky. A nice, juicy convoy that seemed to stretch out to the end of the lighted area. The vehicles were pulling off the side of the road for concealment as Smash called off the last part of the check list and Nails rolled off his perch into a screaming dive.

The bomb-release light winked four times on the instrument panel, signaling that the wing bombs had released. Their faces sagged as the bird pulled out of the dive with four Gs on the wings, and swept upward toward the relative safety of the higher altitude. The bombs detonated and one of the nine trucks blazed skyward with secondary explosions.

The 130's flares gradually died and the sky grew black. Then suddenly other more terrifying forms of radiant energy—searchlights scanning in all directions, familiar white star-bursts of antiaircraft fire, and red tracers.

"Man, we really stepped on our foreskins this time," yelled Nails.

Before Smash had time to answer, *Whummmmppppphhhh!* The Canberra lurched over on its side in a ninety-degree bank with the nose rising sharply in a pitch-up. The aircraft was hit and diving for earth. Nails pushed the control full forward and to the left as the altimeter started to unwind. Not a word was said but Smash could hear Nails's heavy breathing as he exerted his strength on the control surfaces.

He rolled straight and slowly eased the plane's nose upward just as the dark form of a mountain loomed ahead. A navigator must either bring along a change of underwear or trust his pilot as a cub trusts its mother. Sitting tandem to the front-seat driver, when the situation is dicey, he can do nothing but sweat it out.

"Granite cumuli," muttered Smash. "A big rock in the clouds."

Nails pulled the wheel back sharply to avoid the trees. Smash heard a crackling sound, looked out to see tips of treetop being sheared off by the B-57's wing and breathed a sigh of relief as the plane shuddered, then climbed back into the sky amid a shower of bullets.

"That Doom Puss is a mean sonofabitch tonight, Smash. They blasted our butt off and I think we just about lost our elevator control. We're heading for the barn."

Out of the corner of his eye Smash saw a brilliant flash on the right wing, which was suddenly engulfed in sparks.

As quickly as they had appeared, the sparks were gone. A flak burst had exploded just off the wingtip, silhouetting it in the bright light and creating the illusion that the wing was on fire.

By this time Nails had the bird in a climbing right turn, watching Bud make his pass under the second load of flares.

"Six Two, drop all your ordnance on this pass," called Nails. "We've got little or no elevator control and need you to escort us home."

The flare ship had moved the illumination farther down the road, revealing many more vehicles frantically trying to get into the woods. The ground fire was withering and as Nails watched from above, Bud's plane bounced to and fro like a dinghy at high sea. As it dived downward, glittering in the flare light, then veering upward, it seemed to scratch for altitude.

Bud's pass was deadly. The four 750- and 500-pounders went off directly down the road at intervals of 150 feet, blowing pieces of trucks and cargo in all directions. There were two orange secondary explosions, then several blue ones, leaving a third of a mile of the road a blazing inferno.

"That'll teach old Ho Chi Minh he'd better ship by Railway Express," growled Chuck Turner, Bud's navigator.

"Gahdam, you guys do good work," countered Nails.

"Rog," replied Bud in an overly calm voice. "We waxed their tail pretty good but I'm afraid they zapped our ass even worse. Our left wing is shot up."

By this time both planes were out of range of the guns and on a heading for home plate.

"It looks like we both got it pretty bad. Let's milk these mother bears home."

Later, over Da Nang, it appeared that Nails's control problems were less serious than Bud's battle damage. The aircraft had a huge dent in the leading edge of the right wing. Also, Bud's elevator controls were sloppy. But they were operable, using trim.

But Bud and Chuck's plane was losing fuel rapidly. Holes in the wing could be seen streaming a plume of JP-4.

"You make a straight-in approach and go in first, Bud," said Nails.

As the Tower cleared Cheetah Six Two for a straight-in approach, Bud and Chuck went through their before-landing check list. Everything had been accomplished up to the lowering of flaps. The aircraft was at five hundred feet and one mile out.

"Flaps down," announced Bud.

The sky lit up. The change of airflow sucked raw fuel into the hot section of the engine. The explosion took off the left wing.

The craft rolled over on its back. The canopy was blown and two ejection seats were shot from the now inverted cockpit. Nails looked up and said:

"Please, Hubert?"

Chuck's chute never opened. He was too close to the ground. He thudded into the jungle still strapped in the Canberra seat he had flown in so many times.

Bud's canopy blossomed in the moonlight, then collapsed in a streamer into a deep canal. Seconds later not a ripple could be seen on the murky surface.

That night at the Doom Club the Grim Reapers downed drink after drink until closing.

"Splendid frigging way to spend Easter," mumbled Nails.

Down on the flight line the maintenance crews picked leaves out of Cheetah Six One's engine intakes. They read the rule book. They know the guys aren't supposed to fly *that* low.

Said one flight-line guard: "Did you hear about the time Smash and Nails flew so low they got their engine combing gored by a water buffalo? The Major says they were flying a little too low on their napalm passes. They did a veronica, and a few flourishes, he says, but the bastard carabao got them, and there wasn't a dang thing he could do about it. Major Nails says several FNGs* believe it."

Four days later Bud's body was found two miles down the canal. The Doom Pussy was still licking her chops.

---

* Fucking new guys.

Ten

THE NOBLE TWAPS

It seemed I was spending most of my life hanging around Tan Son Nhut scrounging a ride somewhere. This time it was back to Da Nang and Nails's promised B-57 mission.

A C-130 Hercules, the four-engine turboprop cargo aircraft built by Lockheed at their Marietta, Ga. plant, was scheduled to go out shortly. This plane is popular with hitchhikers because of its speed and reliability. The crew recently had arrived from Hickalulu, where they had been hauling helicopters for the Gemini recovery in Africa.

Operations was a beehive of incoming and outgoing crews. As usual, somebody was having a tussle with the telephone system. A perspiring lieutenant's face was scarlet with frustration as he grappled with the mysteries of wartime communications in Vietnam.

"Listen, Tiger. I've been trying for a day and a half to get Mockingbird. You've given me Penguin. You've given me Papaya. You've given me Backache. It's *Mockingbird* I want. What's my priority? It's crucial. That's what it is. Listen, Tiger, I've been fighting VN, VC, VD. Am I gonna have to take you on, too? Omigod! They've cut me off again."

He banged on the hook a few times. "Hello. Hello, Tiger? Lissen. This here is Lyndon Johnson speakin'. Would you all be so kind? Hello, Mockingbird? *Typhoon!* I don't *want* Typhoon. I don't even *know* anybody at Typhoon. Operator? Tiger? Will you get off the line and get Typhoon off the line? No, *not* tycoon, you neblish. *Typhoon! Typhoon!*"

Three pilots who flew the Voodoo 101s were in ops, where they had run into a former flying buddy.

"Well, hi, Al. Haven't seen you since Frankfurt. When'd you get in?"

"Yesterday. What are you flying in this war?"

"Photo Recce, 101s. So damn sneaky pete we're not supposed to talk about it."

"Like it?"

"Of course. Haven't you heard? We go up alone, unarmed, and scared shitless."

The Voodoos cross into North Vietnam to survey targets and photograph recently bombed areas. Each Voodoo has six cameras. Top speed is 1100 mph but most of the picture-taking is done at 600 miles an hour or less. They fly in pairs so that if one goes down the other can help in rescue operations.

To evade heavy antiaircraft fire, guided missiles, or MIGs, the Voodoos like to fly just above treetop level and blend in with the foliage. Mountains, trees, and solid objects at low levels help protect them because it confuses the SAM (Surface-to-Air Missile) radar systems. Flying at low levels doesn't allow enemy gunners the aiming time offered by high-flying aircraft, which even at supersonic speeds seem to creep past gunsights. Because fighter-bombers cannot make their bomb runs at such low altitude, they lose twenty-five planes to the Voodoos' one.

A FAC pilot that I knew walked in. "Hello there, young lady. When are you going with us again?"

"Soon as I get back from Da Nang."

"Did you hear what happened outside a little while ago?"

"No, what?"

"One of the FAC boys was waiting on the runway to take off. There was a helluva crosswind from the right on the takeoff roll. The bird weathervaned into the wind and damn near ground-looped on him. He stomped the left rudder to straighten it out. His left hand was on the throttle and the mike button was depressed as he muttered to himself: 'Oh, God.' A fighter jock entering the landing pattern picked it up and immediately transmitted in a hallowed tone: 'Yes, son?'"

"Well, I've got one for you. There was a crazy guy up in Da Nang flying his last mission. To rib the jet pilots, he rigged a tin can, some rubber bands, and his handkerchief together to make a drag chute for his FAC. When he landed for the last time, here was this ridiculous little toy chute straining at his tail. But what panicked everybody was the next bit. When the FAC came to a stop, it sagged just forward of the tail like a sway-backed mule, and broke in two. That's really getting the last ounce of service out of man and machine, huh?"

"OK, we're off," called the C-130 captain.

We scrambled into the van and drove out to the aircraft.

I rode on the flight deck with an extra pair of earphones clamped on my head. Any routine flight in Vietnam can be anything but routine. At Qui Nhon we couldn't establish radio contact with the tower. To avoid a head-on collision, an airborne Army pilot intervened and passed the word around to other airborne craft and helicopters that the C-130 was next to land. Without radio contact you have to rely on "biscuit guns" beamed from the tower. Green light gives clearance to land and red light indicates a dangerous situation and "take it around and reenter the traffic pattern."

After unloading mail, passengers, and equipment, we found ourselves facing another C-130 unloading on the runway. Our pilot harangued the other to shake the unloading up so we could get off. This went on for about thirty minutes.

Waiting for the matching of wills to be over, two other passengers aboard, the *Life* reporter-photographer team of Bill Wise and Enrico Sarsini invited me to step down to the edge of the runway for lunch. Enrico always tugged along a duffle bag with about sixty pounds of canned goods. To brighten up the menu—Vienna sausages and canned peaches—Bill surprised me by pulling out of his pocket some plastic disposable containers of sealed-in martinis, sent along from New York by samaritan Dick Pollard.

Finally the other crew started their engines and backed around a revetment. We three picnickers hopped aboard and our plane took off.

As soon as we were able to contact Peacock Control at Pleiku, they advised us to get up and out fast as the sandbars below were thick with shooting VC.

There was turbulence; the weather was marginal with thunderstorms in the mountainous area. We went in to Kontoum, unloaded tons of fuel, and I photographed the hundreds of ARVNs sitting on the ramp waiting to be transported south. Kontoum is the end of the Ho Chi Minh Trail and the weather is usually delightful because of the altitude. But today visibility was miserable.

"Let's haul ass," barked the pilot, climbing fast, "before we get our butt in a crack. Da Nang GCA can talk us in. Besides, there's other aircraft in the area too damn close."

GCA: "Coming in you will fly a four-and-a-half degree glide slope if you desire to reduce ground fire probability."

Pilot: "Rog."

GCA: "Ceiling four hundred broken. Four and a half miles to touchdown. Begin descent. Turn right to three five seven degrees."

Pilot: "We're going to have a pretty strong crosswind."

After GCA talked us down safely, the crew chief turned to me.

"My mother writes that sixty percent of the people at home act like they don't know a war is going on."

Warrant Officer Fred Tucker was at the airport when we landed and I caught a ride with him in his jeep to the Press Center. Technically called the Da Nang Command Information Bureau, it is a subunit of the command information bureau in Saigon, and since Da Nang is subordinate to the command in Saigon, is usually referred to as SUBSIB. Tucker, the Marine who had taught me to throw knives, was stationed at SUBSIB with I Corps. He drove as though his machine were a juiced-up golf cart. When we came barreling into the gravel courtyard, he yelled, "Hang on, babe. We don't have any brakes."

With that he threw out an anchor attached to a rope. He had found both before the Navy lost them (sometimes called requisitioning). It caught around a leg of the water tower centered in the courtyard and we came to a jarring halt.

Specialist 5 R. L. Breland was a powerfully built Negro whose Marine buddies called him "Hoss" after the character in the television show *Bonanza*. Hoss got along fine with everybody, including the Vietnamese working at the Press Center as maids, gardeners, and sentries. I took a Polaroid picture of him in color standing beside his jeep. The result pleased him greatly and he promptly sent off the print to his wife, Susan, back in Columbus, Georgia.

I later hitched a ride into town with him to pick up some uniforms that were being altered. My two-piece tiger-pattern camouflage suit, originally manufactured for ARVN, was so snug I couldn't bend over, and my Marine fatigues were so big the pants wouldn't stay up.

The Indian tailor had deftly put gores in one and cut down the other. Hoss decided to buy some miniature commando suits for his two little sons. The tailor's children posed as models as Hoss squinted his eyes and looked them over.

"Now Ronald is tall for five and Reggie is on the plump side," he mused as he tried to guess how much his boys might have grown during his absence.

While the tailor toted up the bill, Hoss talked about his family. "I sent Susan some C-rations so she could see what I'm eatin' here. She's crazy about 'em."

Hoss drove rather slowly on the way back. I asked why. He has a remarkable record for not letting anything get his goat, but he screwed up his face with distaste.

"I got a ticket for speeding the other day."

"In *Da Nang?*"

"Yup. In a radar trap. The provost marshal set up a new rule about driving too fast. It contradicts everything we'd ever been told before. The old instructions were not to be a sittin' duck for VC hand grenades or snipers by creepin' along at fifteen or twenty-one miles an hour."

He shrugged. "I'll go along with that in town, but not on those trips to the Air Base. I may get a few more tickets, but my tour is almost up. I'm aimin' to get home to my wife and kids all in one piece."

Back at the Press Center we sat on the veranda talking about food again. Several Marines and an Australian joined us. A Marine named Stewart, who had seen WW II action, shuddered as he recalled the peanut butter and crackers that stuck to the roof of his mouth during the Normandy invasion. And above all he remembered Spam.

"Five years after the war ended my wife served Spam one night for dinner. I told her, 'Honey, once every five years isn't bad. It's all right. Of course, I'm not gonna eat it. But I forgive you if you don't do it again for another five years.'"

I went into the press office to call Smash at the Da Nang Air Base. He said Nails would be in from a trip to Clark the next day and he thought my mission might come off the day following. When I left to join the men out on the veranda a few feet away, AP's Ed Adams was going through the everlasting struggle. Not the least of the problem was constant interruptions by the Tiger operator asking, "Working?" to which you reply *instantly,* "Working," signifying that you're not finished or that it isn't a personal call. I never did learn which, but that reaction to the word got to be such a reflex that you'd blurt out the answer if asked in your sleep.

"Come on, Tiger," pleaded Eddie, "I'd like Weasel, Quail, or Danger. *Any* one of 'em. I don't care in which order. *Working. . .*"

It seemed almost as crazy as that scene of Mort Sahl in the 20th Century Fox movie, "In Love and War," when he picks up a ringing field phone in the middle of a battle and shouts, "World War Two. Good morning."

As Eddie joined the group, the phone rang again. Word had just come in that Al Chang had been shot in the head. We got the details later. During his twenty-one years as a combat photographer for the US Army, Al had taken pictures of Korean, American, and Vietnamese wounded. He'd never been hit. It seemed ironic for him to get it now, as a civilian photographer in the thick jungles near the Courtenay Rubber Plantation, forty miles east of Saigon.

Later he told us, "As we pressed deeper into the jungle, we could hear the thud of enemy fifty-caliber slugs ripping through the foliage, and the crack of automatic weapons. Suddenly it seemed to be coming from all sides. I was flat on soft ground, my chin pressed into the dirt behind a tree, when a paratrooper called across to me, 'Hey, Al, those tracers are going right past your head.'

Then he did the most human thing in the world, lifted his head to have a look.

"That's when they zapped me. It felt like a sledgehammer."

Eyewitnesses later told me Al had kept on taking pictures like an automaton for a few minutes after he'd been hit.

"It took us two hours to get out of that deathtrap," Al continued. "And I finally knew what it's like to be on the other side of the damned pictures."

Once in a while the Marines have their inning with hostile newsmen. Museum Pier is close by the Press Center at Da Nang and sailors aboard LSTs off Museum Pier shoot at anything floating by on the water—a gunnysack, a dead dog, or any suspicious object that could be a bomb.

As we sat on the veranda nibbling peanuts and sipping drinks, firing broke out. One reporter, who was employed by a small Midwestern television station, was plainly nervous at being in a danger zone. He was thin and tall and much given to kissing women's hands. After one Broadway bit part, he'd given up the stage and, not much of a reporter, he was quite content to be a "reader" on camera. His safari-type uniform was always freshly pressed and the custom-made boots shone as if each precious moment on camera was a New York opening night.

As the shots rang out, Major Mike Styles, a Marine with briny wit, and Warrant Officer Fred Tucker were having a ham and cheese.

Fred recognized the customary firing. "The sailors are at it again."

Terrified, the tall actor-reporter came on the run from his quarters and, flying through the screen door, belly-dived in front of a row of slot machines.

Styles, sandwich in midair, suggested in a spirit of helpfulness, "Why don't you crawl over in front of the two bit machine? It's never been hit yet."

Another reporter, who worked for a larger outfit, produced a program which some critics considered a vicious attack on Marine battle tactics—a one-man attempt to torpedo the legend of Marine

valor and fighting spirit in one show. A few days later this same reporter scowled when a Marine colonel happened to pass in front of
his television camera, blocking the view.

"Colonel, I'm going to take care of you," the reporter growled.

The colonel, Jim Williams, instantly unbuckled his gun belt and
let it drop to the ground. "*Any* time you're ready."

"Oh," said the reporter. "I didn't mean physically. I'm going to
take care of your career."

Two little dogs, mutts named Puma and Tiger, fat, sassy, and
loyal, really bossed the Da Nang Press Center and chewed on every
toe they could find in a rubber tire sandal. An Australian who had
recently joined us often sat around holding Puma in his lap and telling stories about his father who had seen action in the Gallipoli
Campaign. One of the best was about an incident that occurred
when the elder Australian stopped off at Shepheard's Hotel in Cairo.

The Australian's father had faced a court martial for getting
caught tonking stark naked through the hotel corridor in pursuit of
a young girl.

"But," the reporter said, "my old man had quite a lawyer. The
bloke cleared him by quoting an Army regulation which reads: 'An
officer may wear any costume appropriate to the sport in which he
is at the moment engaged.'"

Two pleasant surprises were on tap, this trip to Da Nang. The
Marines in the office could hardly wait for me to adjust my veil in
the coeducational can. In my honor they had screwed on a hook and
eye inside the door.

"Did you notice? Did you notice?" they all wanted to know.

The other surprise was initiation into the TWAPs.

On the candlelit veranda of the Press Center, they plumped onto
my head a battle helmet belonging to Eddie Adams, the Head
TWAP, and handed me a big, lighted red candle to hold as they
proceeded with my initiation.

"We are paying you the singular honor of welcoming you," droned
Joe Gallagher of UPI, "the first woman member ever to be admitted
into the noble order of TWAPs. To be eligible one must be an accredited member of the press who has participated in at least one
combat patrol. Members wounded in battle must show their scar at
the bar, and you must swear to believe and uphold what the TWAPs
believe in."

In a somber tone Eddie took over: "The organization known as
TWAPs was, until tonight, composed of twenty members. Within
our group are representatives of CBS-TV, ABC-TV, Associated

Press, United Press International, *Life* magazine, *National Geographic,* Reuters, the *Los Angeles Times,* the *Detroit Free Press, Leatherneck* magazine, NBC-TV, and now the Mutual Broadcasting System. Our homes range from Korea to New York to Hong Kong to Tokyo and into some lesser-known towns such as Refugia, Texas, Great Snoring, England, and now, Olney, Illinois."

TWAPs stood for "Television, writers, and photographers." Tiger and Puma, the two puppies, were the mascots. The bylaws of this absurd circle were composed before they had thought of taking in women members.

1. I agree that when pinned down by Viet Cong fire, I shall run up and down hills, shouting, yea, screaming, *"Bao chi,"* which, in Vietnamese, means "Press."

2. I agree that I will never hold intercourse with any commissioned Public Information Officer, Technical Information Officer, or Information Officer.

3. I agree that if found having intercourse with any member of the same sex, I shall be forced to turn in my patch and membership card. I understand, however, that I may "screw" any member professionally.

4. I understand that if asked by another member:

a) Are you a TWAP?

b) Will you work with me?

I shall reply:

a) Working.

b) In a pig's ass I will.

If I should not reply in this manner, I sacrifice to the other member a drink of his choice.

5. I understand that the TWAPs is composed of the cream of journalism, never admitting that the Marines suffer anything other than "light casualties" regardless of the number of regiments hit.

6. The symbol of office of Head TWAP is an engraved C-ration can opener. Any member succeeding in wresting this symbol from the Head TWAP will reign supreme until he loses said symbol.

7. Members suffering from the Far East Two-step, known in Egypt as the Pharaoh's Revenge, may leave any formal or informal gathering at a brisk trot at any time without adhering to parliamentary procedures.

8. Members suffering from any form of "social influenza" are required to inform all other noble members of the name and address of the carrier. This is for the protection of other noble TWAPs.

9. Members must use originality in the field. TWAPs utilize the motto "Stick with Me" only at the bar, not on assignments.

Eddie concluded his speech. "We've met here under adverse conditions, yet have found deep satisfaction and humor while forming the TWAPs, and the friendships gained have overcome any animosities or jealousies that derive from competing with other newsmen in the gathering and releasing of stories, films, or photos. We've had a lot of laughs with our organization and have settled some differences.

They presented me with a membership card, and a dappled beret with a naughty insignia attached, featuring footprints upside down. I normally resist becoming a joiner but this was different. Very different.

The night after my initiation I happened to caution one of the young Vietnamese helpers that Ton Ton, the petite Press Center maid, must not wash my newly tailored uniforms in hot water.

A burly Marine, whose mouth turned down at the corners, making his face look like an old Elkhart, interrupted. "Miss, have you *seen* any hot water in Da Nang?"

One day at the Press Center, two German entertainers rolled in aboard a jeep. They were Manfred and Ernst, the Happy Wanderers, two students whose wanderlust had brought them to Vietnam to sing for the soldiers, Vietnamese, and Montagnards.

Manfred hailed from Bremerhaven, Ernst from the island of Helgoland, where the people speak German, Danish, Old English, Swedish, and Frisian, a West Germanic language.

Visiting twenty-two countries en route to Vietnam, Manfred and Ernst had set off with twenty dollars in their jeans and a tankful of petrol. They had been in the war theater five months.

As they were entertaining at a Special Forces camp one night, the VC attacked the base. The boys hid in mortar holes and Ernst later received a Purple Heart for his wounded guitar.

Every night that they were at the Press Center they sang for us: Spanish folk songs, German yodeling, religious numbers in both Yiddish and Hebrew, and, perhaps best and most surprising of all, an impressive repertoire of Southern spirituals. In the background VC artillery could be heard booming, and jets streaked overhead from time to time. Puma and Tiger nibbled on my toes as I turned on the Panasonic and taped two shows on the veranda of Da Nang's Press Center. Then we all joined in for "Kentucky Babe" and turned in for the night.

A few days later, Jim Wilson and Robin Funk rolled into the Press Center in the CBS jeep, unloaded their gear, and went into the bar for a beer. I joined them to hear about the day's happenings.

They had been out with the First Cav in Happy Valley. The group they were with got hemmed in by Viet Cong. Five Americans were dead and ten wounded and the Med-EVACs couldn't let down because of the sniper fire. As the choppers hovered overhead waiting for their chance, one of the wounded, who was leaning against a paddy dike, started singing, "Things go better with Coca-Cola. . . ."

"It broke the tension," said Jim. "Everybody howled."

Robin and Jim were such skillful technicians as sound engineer and cameraman that they scarcely needed a TV reporter.

Once, when they were traveling with Marines in a helicopter, a tail rotor was sheared off on the side of a four-thousand-foot mountain near Da Nang and they started to go into a horizontal spin, but the pilot managed to crash land near the helipad.

The day before, they had been shot down while riding in a Med-EVAC over Happy Valley.

The CBS bureau chief, Sam Zelman, was a rare bird in that he was liked by all his staff. Quiet and industrious, Sam normally let no frustrations get him down. He *coped* with them. For example, because there were only four trunk lines at the Caravelle switchboard, Sam had been out to wangle a private wire.

"Did Sam ever get his telephone?" I asked.

"He sure did," replied Robin. "When he first asked for an outside line, he was told to go to the director of the government telephone agency. Write a letter, they told him. So he did, then waited a respectable two weeks before bugging them again. Finally he was told he'd have to come see them in person, that no letter had arrived. Then it developed that the letter had been rerouted to the technical commissioner of the telephone agency, which would rule on the technical feasibility of his request. Sam learned this on his *third* visit to the director.

"Three or four weeks passed. About the sixth week Sam was told it was out of their hands, that phones installed in hotel suites had to be wired and handled by hotel personnel. Well, that was a pip, since Sam had *started* the whole screaming bit with the hotel manager, who had then sent him to the telephone company. In a few days the hotel electrician showed up and cased the place and told Sam he would eventually get his phone.

"Two months later they really did begin wiring and installed a bright-pink instrument labeled WESTERN ELECTRIC, MADE IN USA. At fantastic expense to CBS, at last Sam had his direct line and could dial. For the first time a private line to outside, or so he thought. It turned out to be a direct line to a Vietnamese operator at the telephone company who couldn't even speak English. So Sam has the only pink phone in Saigon and he says that like most things pink, it's more attractive than it is useful!"

Jack Foisie and Simon Dring of Reuters shortly joined us. Simon was skinny as a pencil, a tall young man who wore his tiger-pattern camouflage hat with the unstarched brim flapping over his eyes, and drove his jeep like a madman.

There were always notices at the Press Center entrance headed: ATTENTION: ALL DRIVERS AND SIMON DRING.

When we went swimming in the South China Sea, Simon and Tim Page would roar around in Simon's jeep axle-deep in the water and play tag with the fish.

Mike Styles hollered that a poker game was being formed and I filed inside for that. I don't get to play often but the longer the session the better. Once, on the last leg of President Eisenhower's South American tour, I started for the powder room on the White House press plane but ran into a game in the lounge. When the Secret Service boys, reporters, and White House luggage officials saw my eyes light up, they invited "the lamb" to sit in. We played for the whole seven-hour trip. I never did make it to the powder room but it was worth it.

You pay strict attention in a card game with the Marines. They don't play like a bunch of old women matching cards—everybody in every pot and the queens with the hang nails wild. They play poker. Five card stud and five card draw.

Styles is a shrewd card player who makes funny cracks which tend to get your mind off the play. So it took me till seven in the morning to win a few hundred.

George Esper was in the game and when it broke up he showed us a long sheet of paper some wag had prepared to send on ahead to the families of men returning to the States:

HEADQUARTERS
AIR FORCE REHABILITATION CENTER
SOUTHEAST ASIA
DA NANG AB, REPUBLIC OF VIETNAM

Issued in solemn warning, this _____ day of _____ 196__. To the friends, relatives, and neighbors of _____:

1. Very soon the above will once again be in your midst, *de-Americanized, demoralized,* and *dehydrated,* ready once more to take his place as a human being with freedom and justice for all, and engage in life, liberty, and the somewhat delayed pursuit of happiness.

2. In making your joyous preparations to welcome him back into respectable society, you must make allowances for the crude environment in which he has suffered for the past _____ months. In a word, he may be somewhat Asiatic; suffering from advanced stages of Viet Congitis, or too much Ba Muoi Ba beer.

3. Therefore: Show no alarm if he prefers to squat rather than sit on a chair, pads around in thong sandals and towel, slyly offers to sell cigarettes to the postman, and picks suspiciously at his food as if you were trying to poison him. Don't be surprised if he answers all questions with, "I hate this place" or "Number ONE." Be tolerant when he tries to buy everything at less than half the asking price, accuses the grocer of being a thief, and refuses to enter an establishment that doesn't have steel mesh over the doors and windows.

4. Any of the following sights should be avoided, since they can produce an advanced state of shock: people dancing, television, and "round-eyed women." In a relatively short time his profanity will decrease enough to permit him to associate with mixed groups, and soon he will be speaking English as well as he ever did. He may also complain of sleeping in a room and refuse to go to bed without a mosquito net.

5. Make no flattering remarks about exotic Southeast Asia, avoid mention of the benefits of overseas duty and seasonal weather, and, above all, ask before mentioning the food delicacies such as "flied lice." The mere mention of these particular subjects may trigger off an awesome display of violence.

6. For the first few months, until he becomes housebroken, be especially watchful when he is in the company of women, particularly young and beautiful specimens. The few American girls he may have seen since arriving overseas were either under thirteen years old or married to personnel who outranked him, therefore his first reaction upon meeting an attractive round-eye may be to stare. Wives and sweethearts are advised to take advantage of this momentary shock and move the young lady out of his reach.

7. Keep in mind that beneath his tanned and rugged exterior there beats a heart of gold. Treasure this, for it is the only thing of value he has left. Treat him with kindness, tolerance, and an occasional fifth of good whiskey, and you will be able to rehabilitate this hollow shell of the man you once knew.

8. Send no more letters to the above-named individual after _____ for he is leaving the tropics in _____ days, and heading for the land of the "Big PX."

9. Future address will be: _____

_____

CLARENCE D. WELSMIRE
MAJOR, USAF
COMMANDER

Eleven

HIGH FLIGHT

Nails picked me up at the Press Center in the faint glow of false dawn. It was Sunday. The day would be lovely to some, lethal for others.

We ate a substantial breakfast at the Doom Club. I knew it was wise to venture into the air on a full stomach, and keep the liquids to a minimum, but I was so thirsty that I drank three large tumblers of orange juice.

Nails seemed pleased at my interest in planes and my eagerness to go on the mission with him. I was as absorbed in the task before us as if I had been trained for it. But then I've never been able to develop the knack of doing anything lightly.

"It's a real kick, your curiosity," he said, as we got back into the jeep. "My former wife never wanted to listen to airplane talk or hear about my work."

When we got down to the flight line to suit up, we found that a sickening accident had just happened. Willie Peter had exploded prematurely in a Caribou, and three Australians, horribly burned, were being carried from the field to ambulances.

The Southeast Asian sun literally beats a man to his knees. We didn't linger long outside but went into the 13th's operations. As Nails checked with Chris Christeson on the mission, I walked into an adjoining room, where the F-104 guys were chewing the fat after a debriefing.

They itched to tangle with the MIG-17s and 19s, the Russian-built aircraft which do not have the speed and maneuverability of the 104s. The MIG-21s would be another matter, but none were known to be in North Vietnam at the time, though they were rumored to be in Red China. The 104s usually flew MIG CAP for strike air force or other aircraft, but recently pylons had been put on their wings and 750-pound bombs mounted on each. Overnight they had gone from support to strike.

They could carry 1,000-pounders on each wing, had bombed and strafed in both North and South Vietnam, and were capable of firing rockets. They had 20-millimeter Gatling guns, which fired up to 6,000 rounds per minute and were equipped with sidewinder air-to-air missiles. With tanker taps, some of their missions went seven hours and fifty minutes. That's a long time to sit in a jet airplane.

Captain Steve Korcheck of Chicago and Lieutenant Colonel Harlan Ball of Bartlett, Nebraska, were with the 436th TAC Fighter Squadron of the F-104 jet Starfighters.

Steve was a powerfully built young man, bursting with enthusiasm about his jet. "A lot of the guys say the 104s are ugly and crazy-looking. Just the same, they usually ask to sit in them and look around at the gadgets. I love the bird. It's like a sports car to me."

Captain H. E. Sargent, Jr., of Apple Valley, California, joined us. "You mean you're going to do a story on the 104s? You seem to spend a lot of time with those Cranberry guys."

"I'm not twins, or I would have been here before. Let's tape a show right now," I suggested, so they ran through their debriefing again.

Then Nails stuck his head in the door and said it was time to get into our flight duds. We went down the line to the hangar and Sergeant Raymond W. Bezio carefully checked me out on parachute-ejection procedure and survival gear in case we had to ditch.

Sergeant Bezio was a personal-equipment technician, who inspected all parachutes. He took them to and from the shops for repacking every ninety days, and every thirty days inspected them for broken threads, hardware erosion, tears in the pack, or anything else unusual that could be detected by visual inspection.

It is important to listen to men like Bezio. Many have been injured more severely from assuming the wrong position or not tucking in their elbows before ejection than from hitting the ground after bailing out.

He showed me the plastic case, called a Blood Chit, which contained a map of the area, an oblong piece of silver a downed pilot could use for bartering, and the Blood Chit itself—a numbered piece of silk cloth worth five hundred dollars to any person who would safely guide a downed American airman out of enemy territory. He fitted me into a helmet, the HGU-2A/P protective type, which provides maximum impact and piercing protection. The shell liner is built up with fitting pads to conform to the wearer's size and head shape. Today's helmets are considerably lighter than the former neck-cricking type.

During ejection the protective helmet prevents head injuries caused by buffeting, which occurs between time of ejection and separation from the seat. When buffeting causes the head to strike the protective helmet, the installed fitting pads absorb this force and reduce injuries. The helmet also provides protection from flash fires and adequate retention of the oxygen mask when exposed to windblast from egress. Since one might land on hard and rocky terrain, the requirement for head protection on landing impact is almost as great as during punch-out.

Bezio showed me how to lower the visor connected to the helmet, then selected an oxygen mask best fitted to my face measurements. Inside was an adjustable microphone for communication with the pilot.

The sergeant loved his "boys."

"Fourteen of 'em have bailed out in my chutes. Every last one of 'em was rescued and made it back to Da Nang," he said proudly.

Bezio was from Greenfield, Massachusetts. His face was lined and he had been in the Air Force a long time. He was a square-jawed, rip-roaring, copper-bottomed, two hundred-proof, authentic patriot. What a contrast he seemed to the malcontents who demonstrate in the street or burn their draft cards. The flag, his country, and "his boys" were a shining thing to Bezio. "My folks taught me," he said, "never to knock my name, my country, or my religion."

Bezio accepted the idea of my going on a mission with Major Nails as naturally as if the Canberra drivers took up a lady correspondent every day. Bail-out procedure he explained clearly and in detail. The "next of kin" handle on the left of the seat locks the shoulder harness, the right handle blows the canopy, and the trigger fires the ejection seat.

"The chute will open automatically. On the right of your back pack is a round yellow knob. Pull this. It will release the life raft attached to you by static line. Before hitting the water, pull the two lanyards on each side of the upper chest, which will inflate the life preserver that keeps you afloat. If you seem certain to descend over land, never mind inflating them. Now, this is very important. As soon as you hit the land or water, disconnect yourself from your parachute by flipping the safety fasteners covering the release rings. Hook your thumbs in these rings and pull hard. The chute could pull you under the water or drag you dangerously on land."

Nails told me that Captain Curt Farley of Chester, Pennsylvania, and Lieutenant Fleming Hobbs from San Antonio, Curt's navigator, would be flying as wingmen.

Our target was just outside Hue, the beautiful capital of central Vietnam. A few miles from the demarcation line of North and South

Vietnam, Hue is a politically restless Buddhist stronghold that produced the fifteenth-century Vietnamese hero Le Loi as well as Ho
Chi Minh.

As Nails finished preflighting his aircraft with a detailed walk-
around inspection, I told him, "King Hussein does this for himself,
too. I flew with him three times when I was in Jordan last summer."

Captain Ed Cook, a nondrinking, practicing Mormon from Ingle-
wood, California, preflighted topside, then helped me fasten my leg
straps and tighten them securely. I thought again how this was no
exercise for anyone afflicted with claustrophobia.

Ed rechecked my oxygen mask, secured my helmet, and climbed
off the plane. Nails put on his black flying gloves—his "warrior's
gauntlets"—and glanced back at his hitchhiker. I upped my thumb in
the traditional sign of confidence and we taxied for takeoff carrying
maximum bomb load.

What I could see through the canopy was breathtaking: the bluest
of skies, pure white fluffy clouds—and the red-nosed B-57 flying just
off the tip of our wing, as Nails gestured to Farley for a level-off. Incongruous that we were on a mission of death and destruction.

I thought it must have been a day like this that inspired RCAF
Pilot-Officer John Gillispie Magee, Jr., to write his "High Flight."

> Oh! I have slipped the surly bonds of Earth
>   And danced the skies on laughter-silvered wings;
> Sunward I've climbed, and joined the tumbling mirth
>   Of sun-split clouds—and done a hundred things
> You have not dreamed of—wheeled and soared and swung
>   High in the sunlit silence. Hov'ring there,
> I've chased the shouting wind along, And flung
>   My eager craft through footless halls of air.
>
> Up, up the long, delirious, burning blue
>   I've topped the wind-swept heights with easy grace
> Where never lark, or even eagle flew—
>   And, while with silent, lifting mind I've trod
> The high untrespassed sanctity of space,
>   Put out my hand and touched the face of God.

I felt more at home in the sky than I did on the ground. I was flying
with the Iron Duke of Da Nang, who was sentimental enough to get
misty-eyed over his daughter's letters. Vietnam was where the action
was and we truly were in the thick of it. Best of all, I found that I
could move my seat. Only an inch, but even that made a great deal of

difference. Psychologically it relieves the hemmed-in feeling to know that you can wiggle a little bit.

I had been quite adamant about no burp cup beside my seat. "If it's not there, I wouldn't dare" was my philosophy. Cook had placed a plastic bag on the floor beside my seat, which was directly behind Nails's, tandem style. "It's for the helmet," he lied.

On the hot mike Nails made a few cracks which caused me to blush. Just as I was hoping I could believe him when he said it was private and confined to our ears alone, another voice came in over the radio. The FAC pilot instructed:

"Follow the river south of Hue. Take the west fork and follow it. Let me know when you reach the fork, drop your delays, and I'll take you to the next target. Drop your bombs on my smoke and we'll move on to the next one," announced the FAC pilot on the radio.

Nails: "Do you want all the delays?"

FAC: "Roger. I'm circling a little cleared area. I've got you in sight. Recommend attack east to west."

I looked down at the little aircraft, lolloping and bobbing along so far below us.

All the bravado seeped out of me when Nails began the first dive and, in the absence of Smash, called out the altitude himself: "Sixty-five hundred, fifty-five hundred, forty-five hundred, thirty-five hundred, pickle and *pull.*"

There's a special timbre about a man's voice when he's being shot at. It has its own unique urgency, no matter how many times it's happened before.

Nails had patiently explained how to counteract the Gs, the force encountered when pulling out of a dive. There is a tendency for body fluids, mainly blood, to accumulate in the lower regions of the body. The blood vessels, the veins in particular, will expand to accommodate this additional volume, and the net result is that the upper body is deprived of sufficient blood supply. This has a particular effect on the brain and eyes, causing grayout, blackout, or unconsciousness. Such pooling of the blood in the lower extremities is called venous pooling. To combat it, one tightens the muscles, lowers the head, raises the legs slightly, and grunts.

"Tighten up your gut muscles," Nails had put it.

It is advised to yell or grunt audibly to make certain the vocal cords are not completely closed. If you hold your breath, a reflex could cause sudden unconsciousness.

We carried 500-pound general-purpose bombs, 4,800 rounds of 50-caliber, and eighteen 500-pound delays. We released at slant range. Some of the delayed bombs were fused in tail only. Instantaneous bombs were fused in both nose and tail and would go off on impact.

We were shallow dive bombing and shallow strafing at 400 feet now, slashing at the target at 450 miles per hour. The FAC had seen trails heavy with traffic and honeycombed with tunnels and caves. The delayed-action bombs we seeded were to surprise any VC passing through later. Our ground forces would go in after the delayed bombs had exploded.

The high *ping* of static on the radio sounds exactly like a bullet hitting metal. These *pings* startled me at first, but I knew it was difficult to spot ground fire in daylight. "If you're not looking when they're hosing you, you can get a bad hit without even seeing it," Smash had said. Well, there was no use worrying about what I can't see, I decided.

Sergeant Bezio had cautioned me that in the event of a bail-out over land, every leaf could be a booby trap. Almost invisible wires were strung everywhere. Some were fastened to hand grenades, others to hard balls planted in overhead branches and embedded with bamboo needles. When activated they could put out a man's eyes.

Ninety out of a hundred casualties come from booby traps. They are the biggest killer in this war. Nothing is too crude for the Cong; they have a diabolical genius for booby traps. Bezio said that at night in the jungle it was not wise to move, speak, scratch, or light a match —not even to burn off leeches, which get in through the eyelets in your boots or inside your pants.

Knife-sharp punji sticks soaked in filth—human excrement or rancid animal fat—that can give a man gangrene within hours. "They plant them everywhere. The fat is an erratic poison, not always effective," Bezio said, "but if it doesn't kill you, it can make you so sick you'll *wish* you were dead." Then he added, "We don't give you ponchos, because the rain makes too much noise falling on it. It's better to sleep on the ground. Sorry about the ants and mosquitoes."

I marveled at the thoroughness that went into survival kits. The MD-1 contained items for emergency signaling, food procurement, first-aid treatment, personal hygiene, and protection against the elements. The components were: two kinds of radio for contacting rescue aircraft, sea-marker dye which makes a large green cloud in the water to facilitate rescue, a plastic water bag, a signal mirror, waterproof matches, flares, a whistle, shark repellent, rations, two small E & E (escape and evasion) kits containing fish hooks, water purifier, various medicines and bandages, aluminum foil to cook in, sunburn preventive, and a desalter kit.

Over the second target, Viet Cong infiltration routes, barracks, and ammunition dumps, Farley and Nails alternated, five passes each, dropping 500-pound bombs, then made six strafing passes, firing the 50-caliber wing machine guns. Nails continued his monologue into the microphone: "forty-five hundred, thirty-five hundred, twenty-five hundred, pickle and *pull*."

As the VC spit tracer bullets from below, Nails broke left.

"Hang onto your ass, sug," he warned on the hot mike.

The jet screamed up to a safer altitude and, out of ammo, we headed for home plate. The FAC pilot would assess the damage.

"Look at Farley, he's flying upside down to be sure he's dropped all his bombs," said Nails.

I looked over and thanked God it was Farley instead of us, because I was beginning to feel queasy. A gulp of orange juice came up in my throat. I forced it right back down. Up it came again. Stubbornly I swallowed a second time.

Nails, who claimed he knew what I was going to do or say before I did it, inquired, "What's going on back there, Pee Wee?"

"Oh, shut up," I replied, furious with myself because this time about two tablespoonsful had got away from me and into my oxygen mask. Now what to do?

I took off the mask, then spied the plastic bag sly Cook had said was to encase my helmet after the flight. I emptied the orange juice into the plastic container, cleaned the mask with a Kleenex, and furtively folded the evidence of my humiliation into the lower leg pocket of my flightsuit.

The base photographer waited on the ground to shoot pictures. As the ground crew dearmed the wing guns and pointed out to Nails the three hits the aircraft had taken, I saw an oil can on the ramp. Not wanting anyone to know how woozy I felt, I went over to sit on it. Someone approached me from the rear, leaned over to growl in my ear.

"You little heathen. *You* little heathen, out bombing Viet Cong on a Sunday. You better get your tail over to chapel and have a talk with the chaplain."

It was Nails, of course. We climbed into a waiting metro truck that would transport us to the hangar to deposit our gear.

"How did it go?" asked Bezio.

I decided to come clean.

"Where shall I put this?" I asked, surrendering the telltale plastic bag.

"Why, hell, it's just enough for a couple of screwdrivers," cracked Nails.

"I was doing fine until you made that last pass over the target, Big Chief Straight Arrow."

"Maybe it wasn't Farley flying upside down." Nails laughed and gave me a backside-fracturing pat on the rump. It has never been my favorite show of friendship or affection. But Nails was a man who did what he pleased, and only what he pleased. If he didn't like a person or a situation, he cut out. Just put on his baseball cap or whatever sky piece he favored at the moment and left.

He had supreme confidence in himself but candor prevented it from being offensive. He made up for it by being so blasted entertaining. He lived every minute of his life and was rarely willing to waste a second's time on phonies.

"How about a drink in the trailer?" he asked.

A breather seemed an outstanding idea. I was still a little giddy from the mission and could tape my shows later. Doug Weber had said he would carry them to Saigon for me.

Nails poured champagne into jelly glasses, told a few jokes, and slapped his favorite red baseball cap on my head. Then he put on his red Go to Hell commando hat which he had bought to go deer hunting back in Utah with The Moose. It was wide-brimmed, sort of a cross between what is worn in the bush and a New York fireman's trappings.

I told him I like crazy hats myself, that once at Maxwell Field, when a particularly stuffy visiting general was going to call on my husband—and we had been so informed by an even stuffier colonel who was terribly impressed with brass—a few officers who usually hung out at our place around Happy Hour agreed to wear whatever headgear I indicated for the general's arrival.

Since I had a fashion show scheduled for the Air Force wives next day, I'd been able to commandeer a batch of eighty-dollar numbers from a store in Montgomery. When the general walked in, five men in uniform sat around reading or playing cards. On the head of each was a flowered chapeau with huge cabbage roses or eighteen-inch feathers shooting straight forward. It was one of the great moments of my tenure as an Air Force wife. And it would be impossible to forget the expression on the face of the colonel escort, who has never spoken to me again.

"You're still wet around the belly band of your flight suit," Nails said. "You're welcome to take a shower if you like."

"That's a number-one idea."

Nails was in unusually good spirits, which for him amounts to near explosion point. Currents of optimism flecked through the air. He danced around the little room throwing punches.

"Did you know Jack Johnson made love before every match he fought?"

I would have thought it more logical for boxers to stay celibate during training. To conserve their strength.

"No. Why ever did he do that?"

Nails looked at me as if I were feebleminded.

"He was a *very ardent man.*"

I didn't dally in the shower. I never do. I'm not a lover of bathroom rituals. It's kind of lonely in there.

And I left my hat on throughout. After checking the water temperature, I twisted the shower nozzle so that the spray struck me at chin level. I didn't get a drop on the hat.

When it was Nails's turn, he went in and made sure I could hear his little ritual of checking what he considered the only four things that mattered. Crossing himself with his forefinger, he chortled, "Spectacles, testicles, wallet, and watch."

As he belted out "Bill Bailey, won't you please come home?" I noticed he had left a book by Dr. Marian Hilliard where I couldn't fail to notice it. It was open at a page where she had painted a portrait of a woman in love:

"The sex drive of the normal woman is capable of giving her great radiance. It's the force within her that makes her gentle with children. It's a power that can knock the cover off a golf ball or take her straight down a perpendicular ski trail. It's part of the passion she feels when an animal is mistreated. It's in the understanding she can give another human being who is desperately lonely."

As I thought this over and weighed the tactics at *my* disposal, the air was rent with an ear-shattering roar from the john, followed by a bellow.

"Call me a doctor!" howled Nails as he came lumbering out, sort of draped in a big towel, his deer-hunting hat awry. "I've been torpedoed!"

How it got into an air-conditioned trailer remains wholly mysterious, but a great ball of a bee had stung Nails right on the end of his tyrooger (pronounced with a soft *g*). A painful and dastardly thing.

I located Hightower's number in the registry and fortunately found him in. He rushed right over and I retired to one of the bedrooms while the good doctor removed the stinger. This war was getting daffier by the minute.

"I'm sorry about your credentials getting impaired," I said to Nails a few days later as he drove me to the flight line for a mission.

"They sure make 'em stubborn where you come from, Miss Peach-out-of-reach."

"Heaven forfend that you should be out of action long."

"When it comes to sex, you talk like a frightened dryad," he growled.

"You're just odd for variety in your women and food. Onions for breakfast. Gad!"

"I'm handsome, though."

"You just about get by."

"You'll keep me in mind?"

"All the time. While you're hopping from flower to flower, like—you'll excuse the expression—a bumblebee."

"Now don't give me that heartache."

Tacked on the Da Nang Press Center bulletin board was a notice:

CAPTAIN KY, REPUBLIC OF VIETNAM, G-5, DESIRES TO INFORM THE PRESS THAT THERE WILL BE AN EXECUTION TODAY. I WILL BE AT THE PRESS CENTER AT 16:30 HOURS TO ESCORT ANYONE WHO WISHES TO ATTEND.

To accommodate the press of many nations and a few thousand spectators, the event was booked for the soccer field.

Five Viet Cong guerrillas, four men and one woman, had fomented an anti-American demonstration. They were caught by alert security men at 11:30 A.M. and condemned within hours. Three had received the death sentence: one man and the woman were sentenced to twenty-five years at hard labor.

Huge crowds outside the soccer field, possibly infiltrated by Viet Cong agents, made it a very touchy situation. Tanks and armored cars rolled toward the entrance. The tanks had their long guns elevated. Inside the field, standing by, were a Buddhist chaplain, named Han Dao, and a Catholic Priest, Father Dinh Huang-Loi. The Buddhist's face was inscrutable. The priest, who spoke Latin, French, and innumerable dialects, sighed, "There is much to be done for my country."

The press, not trusting Captain Ky's timetable, arrived an hour early. At first pictures were forbidden. Signs were posted everywhere: NO PICTURES ALLOWED. Major Huan, Prime Minister Ky's press secretary, finally relented on that score, though there were to be absolutely no pictures of the actual execution.

A canvas-covered van wheeled onto the field with the prisoners inside. The press kept inching closer to them. The condemned peeked out through the slits while the military police argued with us incorrigible working stiffs. Vietnamese soldiers raced over to poke the prisoners' heads out of sight and relace the canvas openings.

"When are they knocking them off? It's getting late," complained a well-traveled newsman.

One MP carried a walkie-talkie or what looked like one. I was astonished periodically to hear bizarre rock-and-roll music issuing from it. The frisky American photographers got into a scrappy argument with the military about the boundary lines for the press. Not content with Major Huan's concession to let them shoot *some* pictures, the cameramen were working their way practically into the prisoners' van. They couldn't really be blamed for trying.

Suddenly, over the public-address system, a spokesman for Premier Ky announced that the execution was being postponed for security reasons. The crowd gradually dispersed.

A few hours later I received a phone call from Major Huan, who was at the Kong Khang Hotel in town. He and a friendly government public-relations official informed me that I was to stand by, the execution would take place at nine o'clock that night. I was evidently being given the grisly privilege of being the only foreign reporter to eyewitness the death of the three guerrillas.

There were thirty-six soldiers with carbines, twelve for each of the condemned. They carried out their orders with accuracy and dispatch. Within hours the hate-filled VC announced that they would reply in kind and, just as advertised, they murdered a captured American sergeant and captain. I wound up a broadcast that night:

"Prime Minister Ky, the resolute leader of the Republic of Vietnam, says he will continue to punish traitors. There is little doubt that both sides will carry out their grim promises with equal intensity."

Next day I was scheduled to go on a combat strike in an F-105-F two-seater version of the Thunderchief, the jet that is the mainstay of the fighter-bomber operations against targets in North Vietnam. On the flight line I heard a woman's voice shout my name. I turned to see tiny Dickey Chapelle piling out of a C-130, which had carried her from Saigon to Da Nang. I adored and respected this girl, whose integrity forced her to report only stories she had "eyeballed," to use her phrase. Official government handouts, she complained, "have all the authenticity of patent-medicine ads." We often had talked of going on assignments as a team. She was the only gal I knew who was ready to go anywhere.

This was Dickey's seventh war. She had been imprisoned and kept in solitary confinement by the Hungarian government when she had slipped into that country to report on the 1956 uprising against communism. She'd covered the Algerian rebellion, on the side of the Algerian guerrillas, and marched with Fidel Castro before he became prime minister. Dickey had been in Vietnam in 1961–62 and also had reported on the action in Laos. She was a qualified parachutist and one of the few civilians in the Republic of Vietnam to have gone through the rugged Special Forces training course.

"Hi, there, girl," she called. "I hear you conned Colonel Jim Williams out of permanent quarters for women at the Press Center. Great."

"You going out with the Marines on patrol?" I knew that Dickey had patrolled with them so often that she almost was a Marine. She even carried her pack of cigarettes in the top of her socks like they did. When it came to their colorful four-letter language, she could cuss with the best of them, though she usually saved these expletives for the generals.

Dickey's aim in reporting was "to tell the folks back home how cruel war can be." Dickey and danger were never very far apart.

"Yup. I think I've arrived just in time to get in on an operation."

"I expect to leave for Saigon tomorrow, Dickey, so the room's yours. It's far too small to get another cot in there."

"Where you headed in that gear?"

"It's taken months, but I've finally been OK'd for a mission in a 105. A two-seater. A trainer."

"Good for you. Sounds like a dandy story."

"Dickey, it's ridiculous for me to be giving you advice. But be careful. The Viet Cong have traps set everywhere. It's a dirtier war than when you were here before."

"Oh, I suppose my luck will run out someday. But if you're scared, really scared, you don't belong over here."

It was the last time I ever saw my friend.

Captain Sol Horner lined up on the runway. It was a flight of four. Two elements had taxied from the sandbag revetments at Da Nang, followed by two more at a separation of a thousand feet. The leader gave the signal to cut in the afterburners and a nod of the head to start the takeoff roll. Both ships in the first element went into afterburner and began their takeoff roll.

Horner rotated his aircraft at takeoff speed. His wingman, Captain Gordy McLeod, on Horner's right, followed suit as we became airborne together. Numbers three and four duplicated the maneuver. When all four craft were safely airborne, the lead element started a turn to take up a heading toward the target. This day it was Xom Bang barracks.

Republic's F-105 Thunderchief is a marvel of design, ingenuity, and electronics. All components and equipment are miraculously integrated, a highly tuned machine. A Mach-plus-two aircraft, it has a range of 2,000 miles without refueling; a wingspan of 34 feet 11 inches; and a length of 64 feet 3 inches. Its ceiling is 52,000 feet-plus and it can carry a bomb load of 8,000 pounds of nuclear or conventional weapons in its bomb bay, plus 4,000 pounds of bombs, incendijel, rockets, or Bullpup or Sidewinder missiles on wing pylons and under the bomb bay.

Horner asked if I was OK. I was so thrilled at the sensation of speed, I replied, "It's beautiful."

A fantastically sophisticated and expensive wagon strapped to their bottoms, today's fighter pilots must attend to as many as one hundred cockpit instruments and switches, an instrument panel of electronic wizardry. The afterburner injects fuel into the hot exhaust gases to give extra thrust.

After the throttle snapped into the AB notch and the flame shot from the tail of the plane, I could feel a kick in the pants from the afterburner and suddenly we were supersonic, with the planes moving in perfect concert. I tried to ignore the unrelenting humming in the earphones.

The dual-cockpit 105 is a model used primarily for training, but it is as useful in combat as the single seaters. Within minutes we were over the target and the enemy was waiting for us. As we approached the area, the flight commander gave the signal to commence the descent to target to make the bomb run. Horner started his roll in at twenty thousand feet.

The Thud-five emptied two tons of bombs on the communists, who opened up with everything they had. Horner began his climb to a higher altitude. Two Phantom jets flew cover for the 105s. Then we heard a violent explosion. Both Phantoms had been blasted out of the sky by Soviet-installed SAM-2 surface-to-air missiles. They came from semimobile missile launchers well concealed in the foliage below.

These were the same birds that had brought down an American U-2 over Cuba in 1962. Riding a radar beam en route and blasting the aircraft with a proximity-fused high explosive or a nuclear bomb, they can pluck a plane from the sky at 80,000 feet and thirty-five miles away.

The radar locked on our wagon. We both saw the missile coming at us. There was a bright flash as the booster fell away. It looked like a thirty-foot telephone pole as it went by straight up through the formation. Two more whizzed through the sky, missing their targets and exploding harmlessly.

The next one we didn't see—the one that tore away the right wing of Sol's aircraft and sent us into a spin.

On the hot mike Horner ordered, "Bailout. Bailout. Bailout."

You never believe it will happen to you, I thought, as I positioned myself in the seat and followed the instructions given to me on the ground such a short time ago. I raised the left arm rest, the right arm rest, and squeezed the ejection trigger.

The seat and I were shot out of the jet, the lap belt opened, and I separated from the seat. The chute made a cracking noise as it opened automatically by the lanyard attached to the seat that fell away. As the chute deployed, the jolt was sharp but comforting. I was enormously relieved to see Horner's orange-white canopy blossom five hundred yards away. The jet, out of control, rolled over, trailing smoke, then spiraled to earth.

On the ground I discovered I had wrenched my back during ejection but could walk. Horner had slipped his chute so that he would land close to me. We could hear trucks on the road below and VC yelling commands.

McLeod's Thunderchief screamed earthward, cannons blazing. It was reassuring to us below to have him up there, along with the other two thud-fives flying cover.

"If their fuel holds out, I think we'll be OK," said Sol.

He assembled the survival radio from the pouch sewn to the leg of his flying suit. He checked me out on its use and continued flashing the signal mirror. The radio would provide the signal tone to lead in the rescue troops.

Sol and I could now hear the VC cutting through the underbrush, two to three hundred yards away. We could also hear the *snick* of released safety catches on rifles.

"Show me how to use that .38 in case you get hurt," I suggested. He did, then handed me his jungle knife just as a Canberra zoomed overhead spitting 20-millimeter cannon shells. I recognized the bat wings at once.

"Sol, I know a screwball Cranberry pilot. I kind of wish he was here now."

The B-57 dived for the treetops, its 20-millimeter cannon's high-explosive ammo glittering along the ground as it sprayed the line of men.

The VC doggedly continued to beat their way toward us. Sol, like the other combat fliers, had a price on his head. The VC knew the rescue routine and had Red Chinese machine guns to clobber the incoming rescue choppers.

We could hear the *chook chook chooking* of the helicopter. The VC were now within fifty yards. Horner fired his .38 tracer ammunition in the direction of the advancing VC to let the Canberra and the rescue-chopper crew know in which direction the enemy fire was originating.

As the gunner on the helicopter blazed away and the pilot let down, Horner threw me over his shoulder and sprinted toward our rescuers. The chopper crew chief and the door gunner sprang out of their ship to cover Horner. Their AR-15s spurted slugs at the enemy as Horner raced through the clearing like a broken field runner. The VC bullets chopped up the dirt steadily. Ten yards from the helicopter Horner stumbled and fell. He was hit. He tried to get up, fell again.

The gunner scooped me up and placed me aboard. The crew chief lifted Horner and staggered to safety with him as the pilot impatiently hollered, "Jesus Christ. Load up, man. Let's get out of here."

In a great cloud of dust the big bird ascended vertically, the VC still firing.

I cradled Sol in my arms. He was hit through the lungs. The pinkish blood foamed up. Deep crimson stains trickled from both corners of his mouth.

"Sorry about this milk run, sweetie. But I guess you can make a story of it."

His head dropped forward and the sharpest Negro pilot in Vietnam died in my arms.

Twelve

CLUB 21 AND THE SENATOR

I was flown on a C-130 hospital plane to Clark Air Base, where I shared a room with Captain Mary Ware, a nurse who had contracted a severe case of malaria.

Mary had been exposed to mosquito-borne parasites in the area around Da Nang. The mosquitoes are allied with the Viet Cong, who forbid antimosquito spraying in their territory. Newly arrived US personnel are not protected by the partial immunity of those who have had malaria and recovered.

US servicemen weekly take a prophylactic tablet containing 300 milligrams of chloroquine and 45 milligrams of primaquine. Mary had the new and resistant strain of parasites. Doctors were forced to give her, intravenously, heavy doses of quinine, the oldest antimalarial of them all. This procedure can prove fatal, but there was no choice with pernicious malaria threatening her brain. In Mary's case she responded, survived, and was exhorting the doctors to let her return to active duty in two weeks, instead of the usual thirty-day convalescent period.

Because of my sprained back the doctors put me in traction.

Mary was anxious to get back on the floor because there never are enough nurses.

"God," she said, "I've never seen anything to equal these guys who are brought in here. They don't complain; all they want to do is get back in the war. They don't even bellyache when they receive heartbreaking letters from home. Would you believe that some wives write basket cases, saying, 'Don't come back. I don't want to be saddled with a cripple'?"

"It must be chippies they met just before coming overseas. Families couldn't write things like that."

"Bad enough to get your legs or arms shot off without being told you're not wanted."

Mary was well enough to go for daily walks. One afternoon she left, saying she'd be back in an hour. A few minutes later the Nail stood in the doorway. I had on the red baseball cap he'd given me. As he ambled in I said, "Well, hello, Tom Terrific."

"You have neat ears and sexy knees."

"Was that you and Smash spraying the hated Cong?"

"Who else? Did you know that slender knees on a woman are almost as rare as perfect ears?"

He was leaning in close.

"What are you going to do? Kiss me?"

"No," he replied.

"Oh, why not?"

"Because I like it too much. I wouldn't sleep."

With his left boot he drew the curtain around the bed as if it were nature's secret laboratory. Nails was sound asleep with his head on my shoulder when Mary returned from her walk, accompanied by the head doctor, Colonel Swansdowne. When he peeked around the curtain, the good doctor looked as if he might have a stroke standing up.

In his sleep Nails was smiling like a seraph right off the Sistine ceiling. I was awake but felt no compelling urge to lead off the conversation. Finally, in a voice that sounded like a choirboy getting his manhood, the Colonel managed, "Major. You know better than this. My God. And her in traction yet."

Nails left quietly.

The next day he brought Smash along, and another roommate, Bear Bryant, who was with the 8th Bomb Squadron and a close friend and former Dirty Thirty flying buddy of General Ky. They told me that when I got out of the hospital they were going to throw a three alarm jamboree at Canberra House. "We'll get you all dolled up in your black pajamas and go dancing," said Nails.

"We have a new Mercy Belle letter," Bear said.

Smash hauled it out of his pocket.

MAJOR SMASH CRANDELL
13TH BOMB SQUADRON

DEAR SIR:
   This is to inform you that I may be slow, but no letters for all this time? I get the message. Excuse the phone calls and silly letters. What did I do? Please have the courtesy to inform me. Thank you for your friendship.

I truly appreciated and coveted our written relationship. And I did look forward to the physical.

Thank you for your attentions in the past.

Sincerely,

MERCY BELLE MEATY

P.S. Truly . . . wha hoppen? Is it what I told you about my friend the politician? Well, say la vive. Get them Cong, baby. Jesus. What I could have done to you. Well, say la damned guerre, baby.

P.P.S. How is Nails? Do you think he would want to write to me?

"I think she's out of her capsule," Bear said. "Maybe she just talked a great act."

"Listen, my good ass," Smash snorted. "The worst piece of poontang I ever had was—was—absolutely *magnificent!*"

Senator John Goodwin Tower, Republican, Texas, the son of a Methodist minister, was, at thirty-five, the youngest Senator in the 87th Congress, the first Republican to be elected to the Senate from Texas since Reconstruction, and the only Republican Senator ever elected by popular vote from any of the former Confederate states. As a member of the Armed Services Committee and the Joint Committee on Defense Production, he was interested in seeing the war firsthand.

Tower was accompanied on his tour of Clark Air Base and Vietnam by Charlie Kirbow, chief clerk on the powerful Armed Services Committee, and Lieutenant Colonel Bob Old, liaison for USAF to the Senate. Bob was a former flying buddy of Nails's.

"One of the real reasons Senator Tower wanted to come on this trip," said Old, "was because he sits on the committee day after day and recommends policies that would cause this country to pursue more vigorously a military course of action in Southeast Asia. Tower feels that if he's making these decisions on policy, a trip over here would improve his outlook. He wants to hear what the troops have to say."

One of Senator Tower's first acts was to dismiss a press man assigned to him, bypassing yards and yards of publicity.

He talked to one young soldier from Texas who had attended high school in Tower's home town. "But I was there in 1943, a little before your time," the Senator told him.

"Oh, no, sir," replied the lad quickly, "I was born in 1942."

Tower had served three years in WW II in the South Pacific aboard an amphibious gunship. When he visited the *Ticonderoga* he said, "I left the Navy as a Seaman First Class and get piped aboard now like an admiral. Nice."

The Senator went for a practice bombing mission in Nails's Canberra. Captain Gerald Blake, one of Nails's best pilots, took Kirbow along as he flew wing on the exercise. Kirbow, a former Navy pilot, took over the dual controls for a couple of passes. His modesty couldn't conceal his satisfaction. "I guess you don't forget, even after fifteen years."

Senator Tower was profoundly shocked on his tour of the hospital at Clark to visit the wounded. The extent of their sacrifices for their country affected him deeply. He stopped beside a patient who had the arm muscles of a stevedore.

"How are you?" he inquired.

"They shot off my legs, Senator."

Tower reached for the man's hand. "Good luck, soldier," he said, and moved on.

That night Nails took the Senator around to the Club 21 and introduced him to all the boys of the 13th. He sang, swapped jokes, and drank with them. They explained the encircled names on the ceiling.

Navigator Charlie McLaughlin tended bar and never let anybody's drink get within an inch of the bottom before he was screwing another into his fist. Tower was flattered at being taken backstage. His pleasure reminded me of the story about Fritz Kreisler meeting a champion wrestler. Next day the renowned violinist ordered a bathrobe with his name embroidered across the back, an exact replica of the one worn by his new friend.

Nails and Tower got along so famously that they dropped by the Senator's place at the BOQ for a nightcap. It was there that the tough little political scraper broke down and wept as he recalled how he had felt at what he'd seen in the hospital wards.

"They were so young. So damn brave and uncomplaining. That fellow who lost his legs. It was hard enough to control my emotions, let alone try to match his dignity. The people back home have got to be made to realize these men's sacrifices. In a way it's been a privilege to witness it. You think you understand but you don't really, until you've seen for yourself."

No one could have appreciated what he was saying more than a squadron leader dedicated day after day to getting his men back alive and whole. The war talk continued until six-thirty in the morning. The Senator was a little weary at the early takeoff for Hong Kong.

"How does that Nails do it? He's four years older than I am. Flies all day. Up all night. Next time I come, if he's in the area, I want you to have him locked up. He's too damned entertaining."

He sent Nails an autographed photo of the two of them in their flying suits. Inscribed on the picture was: "Many thanks, friend." A thank-you letter followed:

HONG KONG

MAJOR NAILS NORELLI
COMMANDER
13TH BOMB SQUADRON
APO US FORCES 96274

DEAR NAILS,

I would normally wait until my return to Washington to express my gratitude and appreciation to the many nice people who so willingly gave their time to be helpful to me during my trip. In this case, however, I was so impressed by the devotion to duty and esprit de corps of your fine group of young men that I feel compelled to write to you now.

I want to thank you again personally for allowing me to monopolize your time Wednesday evening. I can't recall when I've had a more enjoyable and rewarding experience.

My visit with you and the officers of the "21 Club" and the conversations I had with them confirmed my earlier impression that all those guys would follow you into hell if necessary. This is the rare leadership quality which is required in so many but found in so few today.

May I again commend you, your officers, and your men for the fine job which they so willingly and professionally perform for our great country.

The American people owe you and all your kind an eternal debt of gratitude.

With warm personal regards, I am
                    Sincerely,
                    JOHN G. TOWER U.S.S.

Before all the 13th left for Da Nang, and after some of the 8th had returned, Smash took me to the Club 21 one night. In a little ceremony, they pulled out one of the bar stools, and asked me to climb up on it. Then they handed me a lighted candle and told me to write my name on the ceiling. A few nights before we sadly had encircled Little Mo's name. The VC had got a bead on his Canberra and shot

him out of the sky. His navigator parachuted to safety and was rescued. Little Mo never ejected.

Smash and his roommates at Clark lived in General Douglas Mac-
Arthur's old four-bedroom quarters, which the boys now called Canberra House. It was an ideal spot, with a large patio front and back,
and spacious grounds.

As I sat typing reports and working on this book, Smash came in
for lunch, first heading for the kitchen and a bottle of San Miguel.
When he joined me at the table in the screened-in dining room, it
was time to clear off the carbons, notebooks, dictionary, and typewriter. The day was brilliant with sunshine and off to the left was the
magnificent panorama of Mount Arayat rising majestically into the
cloud-flecked morning sky.

The area around Canberra House, like all other strategic sections
of Clark Air Base, was guarded by alert, wiry Negrito guards, the
"little blacks" who fought so fiercely and savagely against the Japanese during WW II.

When the enemy occupied the island, the Negritos refused to surrender and slashed and mauled the army of occupation at every opportunity, taking a heavy toll of the Japanese. Their ability as
guerrillas is unparalleled and they can penetrate even the heaviest
army defenses undetected. As a gesture of gratitude, the United States
provides lifetime jobs and quarters for the Negritos on Clark Air
Base. They are employed as guards on the perimeter and at important
locations around the base.

An area was set aside for their nipa huts and families. Tourists
readily purchase their handicrafts of knives, blowguns, bows and arrows.

Before WW II the Negritos used blowguns and other primitive
weapons. Now they're as skilled with shotguns carrying buckshot, the
best weapon for the patrols because of the high grass and scrub brush
around the base.

The Negritos are proud of the dark-blue denim military uniforms
provided for them. These are always heavily starched and worn with
elan. Interlopers rarely enter the base for the wrong reasons; the loyal
Negritos would show them no mercy.

Smash once talked with a guard when he returned home one night.
The friendly little fellow with the gold teeth told Smash that a prowler
had been found attempting to break into a house down the street
and had been shot by another guard.

"Did he kill him?" Smash asked.

"Oh, yes. When we shoot him, we kill him," the guard answered simply, as if there were no other way.

As Sammy served our lunch, I heard voices in the back yard below. The Negrito guard was talking to Bryan Mulligan, the five-year-old son of a neighbor.

Bryan had a small American flag. "All of those red and white stripes mean states?" he asked.

"That's right," answered the guard with his slight accent. "They stand for the original thirteen states. The white stars on the blue background represent the states of the Union as they are today."

Bryan interrupted. "And George Washington and Abraham Lincoln?"

The Negrito corrected him. "No, Bryan, those are not states. They were American Presidents. American Presidents are all very great men and those were two of the greatest."

I listened attentively, fascinated at the irony of a Philippine Negrito giving US history lessons to a little American boy.

The guard continued, "Another fine American President was John F. Kennedy. He was riding in the back of an open automobile in Texas and a very bad man hid in a window above the street and shot him with a rifle."

"I wish none of our Presidents had died," interjected Bryan. "Then we could have a whole bunch of Presidents instead of just one."

"No, son, this is not the American way," answered the guard. "It would be nice if all those men could still be alive, but in a democracy there can only be one President. You should be proud to be an American."

"Oh, I am. I think I'll go tell my mom what the stars on the flag mean," said Bryan and skipped off through the bushes.

I turned to Smash. "I think everyone should remember the record of Filipinos during the discouraging days of Corregidor, Bataan, and the infamous death march. At the risk of almost certain death, many Filipino hands slipped morsels of food or cigarettes through prison fences to Jap-held American prisoners. General Carlos Romulo once told me of a Filipino schoolteacher whose classes were rudely interrupted by a group of Japanese soldiers, bayonets on the ready, guns on full automatic, ordering that the American flag be lowered.

"The teacher refused and the soldiers machine-gunned him on the spot. His bullet-ridden body slumped to the floor as they took down the flag and left him to die. After the war, a reporter interviewed the schoolteacher, who had somehow miraculously survived the attack.

'What crossed your mind when you were given the ultimatum?' the newsman asked.

" 'In that moment,' replied this symbol of Filipino guts, 'I realized what a privilege it was to live up to the pledge of allegiance that I had talked about all my life.' "

Nails walked into the dining room. It was, for him, a quiet entrance. We hadn't even heard him drive up.

"Your friend Dickey Chapelle was killed this morning. Word just came in at headquarters."

I rushed to the phone to call Captain Monty Bodington, information officer at Da Nang. In the early morning of the second day of Operation Black Ferret, Dickey, with a flower in her helmet, had set out with a forward group of Marines near Chu Lai.

Crossing a cane field, her foot brushed a trip line of almost invisible catgut, and a booby trap exploded shell fragments that hit six Marines and the girl reporter from Milwaukee, Georgette Louise "Dickey" Chapelle. The shrapnel caught her in the left side of her neck and she bled to death. The lethal trap had been made from an M-26 grenade wired to an 81-millimeter mortar round.

Generals and colonels and enlisted men who had known Dickey in Korea, and even in WW II, and loved her deeply ordered an extra round of drinks that night. In an unusual tribute to a civilian and a woman, her body was flown home accompanied by a six-Marine honor guard, and as the GIs have a way of putting it, "under a fifty-star flag."

Wrote Ernest G. Ferguson, *Baltimore Sun,* in his eyewitness account:

> Dickey wanted to be up front with the lead units. The blast came just as she and several Marines moved through a line of low brush, among a field of hundreds of punji sticks set by the Viet Cong to pierce the boots and shins of advancing Marines.
>
> She was badly hurt, hit in the throat. Then a chaplain moved up and gave her the last rites of the Catholic Church. He said he had no idea what her religion had been. A Marine handed me Dickey's hat, one side turned up Australian style. I carried it back to the graves-registration unit at B Medical Company at Chu Lai. It still bore the Marine Corps emblem given and pinned on in Washington by the commandant of the Corps, General Wallace M. Greene, Jr., the two pairs of paratroopers wings she had earned, and a sprig of pink flowers she had plucked as she moved down off objective 'A' this morning. . . .

Bob Considine wrote for King Features:

> Dickey Chapelle was the kind of war correspondent who made you
> sorry you had been born a man.
> She, a delicate woman, had more guts under fire than probably
> any male correspondent who ever went to war, pencil in hand, and
> heart in mouth. There wasn't a dangerous scrap anywhere in the
> world since the biggest war of them all that didn't have Dickey in-
> volved. Involved is the only word. She went with the expendables,
> parachuted into action with them. A thousand bullets and chunks
> of iron somehow missed her.
> When Dickey went to war, she went to war. Nobody saw much
> of her around headquarters, or at the senior officers' mess. She ven-
> tured where angels and men twice her size and half her age feared
> to tread, not with any aura of bravado but simply because she felt
> that if a newspaper or radio chain hired her to cover a war, it de-
> served war coverage, not a rewrite of a headquarters mimeographed
> handout.
> We cannot guess what the sight of her, sprawled dead on the
> ground with a Navy chaplain praying over her, did to the beats and
> the draft card burners.

Beverly Deepe wrote for the *Overseas Press Club Bulletin:*

> . . . Dickey's first love was the Marines. It wasn't that she was a
> mascot or anything like that. She was a Marine. The Leathernecks
> at first had wondered what they should do about a woman in their
> midst but Dickey had said to one of them, "Don't worry about it,
> sonny. I'll take care of things myself." The system they devised was
> flying a little red flag on the outdoor latrine. It meant "Female in-
> side."

Hungarian Freedom Fighters sent a bouquet of red roses to be
placed on her grave, and a lone red rose came from Tony, her former
husband and still her friend.

I knew that Dickey had been where she wanted to be, where the
story was, but the full impact didn't hit me all at once. I didn't cry
until I saw the AP Radiophoto of Chaplain John McNamara administering last rites to little Dickey, crumpled on her right side in the
weeds and dirt like a broken doll.

By Christmas, the 13th was back at Da Nang and Americans at
home were finding ways to show their support of US policy in Vietnam
—everything from "Operation Fruitcake" in Richmond, Virginia, to a

mass march down New York City's Fifth Avenue. Young and old citizens stood up to be counted with gift-collection campaigns, blood-donor drives, and "letters to soldiers" (all somewhat more subdued, I hope, than Mercy Belle's).

Sixty-five thousand members of veterans' groups, labor unions, student and civil organizations marched, sponsored by City Council-man Matthew Troy, Jr., of Queens and the *New York Journal-American*. The parade was headed by five New Yorkers who had won the Congressional Medal of Honor.

There were innumerable other expressions of solidarity on the home front. This fervor of the home folks was appreciated but a prob-lem arose when the good women in the US decided to send packages at Christmas time. Soldiers were literally inundated with every con-ceivable mold of cookie. By Christmas week, 1,410,000 of these homemade goodies had been airlifted into Da Nang alone. Colonel Scott, Colonel Walter Eisenbrown, Commander of the 6252nd Com-bat Support Group, and Lieutenant Colonel Hugh Baynes, the com-mander designated to succeed Harry Howton in the 311th, were go-ing crazy looking for places to store them.

"Cookies," said Colonel Scott, shaking his head. "It was a real fine gesture, but gee whiz."

And there was also the great soap opera. A member of an advisory team, Captain Roy A. V. Holck, happened to write his brother, Wilbert S. Holck, Honolulu's deputy city clerk, that the villagers of Soc Trang were desperately in need of soap.

Wilbert Holck promptly called a friend, Samuel A. Ching of Colgate-Palmolive in Honolulu, and Ching said he could scare up 500,000 hotel-size bars if the city clerk could figure out how to get them there. A veteran of WW II and Korea, Wilbert realized the logistics were getting out of control, but telephoned a former master sergeant who telephoned his former commanding officer, Colonel Millard Gray at Fort Shafter, near Honolulu, and exacted a promise from the USAF that they would ship the several thousand pounds of soap. Now all that remained was getting them to the C-118 at Hickam AFB.

Holck had another brother, Captain Frederick Holck of the Hawaiian National Guard, who advertised for volunteers among his buddies and eventually they toted the soap to the aircraft. The Navy cooperated handsomely at the Saigon end and that is why the little kids in Soc Trang play in the village with scrubbed faces and clean hands.

All week the Da Nang Air Base Men's Chorus had been entertaining at Vietnamese children's hospitals and many other outposts. I slipped into the chapel on Christmas Eve to hear them. It was a very fine choir, composed of the following chorus members:

DIRECTOR
Captain M. E. Bodington

ACCOMPANIST
Gina Phan Van Thiet

Lieutenant Colonel Leo I. Beinhorn, MACV, Da Nang Press Center
Captain James H. Darnauer, 311th Air Commando Squadron
Sfc Edward L. Diggs, 178th Signal Company, USA
Captain W. D. Eschenlohr, 6924th Security Squadron
Captain Creighton W. Frost, Detachment 7, 38th Air Rescue Squadron
Airman Second Class Leslie W. Fry, 6252nd CAMRON
Captain John H. Green, Jr., 6252nd Supply Squadron
Airman Second Class Paul R. Hammond, Detachment 7, 38th Air Rescue Squadron
Airman First Class Maxie J. Harris, 6252nd Transportation Squadron
Master Sergeant Nathaniel Jones, 6252nd CAMRON
Major Thomas A. Julian, 311th Air Commando Squadron
First Lieutenant John R. Levis, 6252nd Air Police Squadron
Captain Jerry J. Mallory, Protestant Chaplain
First Lieutenant Walter D. Meyer, Detachment 9, 30th Weather Squadron
Airman Second Class Duane R. Nygaard, 6252nd Air Police Squadron
Lieutenant Colonel Arthur G. Phillips, 6252nd Air Police Squadron
Airman Second Class Jerome J. Renne, 15th Aerial Port Squadron
Staff Sergeant Joe N. Sanders, 6924th Security Squadron
Airman Second Class Gerald L. Thelen, Detachment 5, Air Postal Squadron

Families of some of the missionaries filed in to hear the program. I was in a row alone. One attractive group sat directly in front of me. Their little blond three-year-old daughter spent the evening on her knees with her back to the entertainment, staring at me, her chin cupped over the back of the pew. Captain Monty Bodington, who sang a glorious tenor, led the chorus and sometimes asked the audience to join in the stirring numbers.

We Wish You a Merry Christmas
Carol of the Drum
Silent Night
Oh, Holy Night
The Twelve Days of Christmas
O Little Town of Bethlehem
A Star Was His Candle
O Come, All Ye Faithful
Joy to the World
Hark, the Herald Angels Sing
It Came upon a Midnight Clear
The First Noel
God Rest You, Merry Gentlemen
Silver Bells
O Christmas Tree
Angels We Have Heard on High
Jesu Bambino
Lo, How a Rose E'er Blooming
The Lord's Prayer
The Hallelujah Chorus

By the time the men got to Handel's magnificent "Hallelujah Chorus" I was ready to weep over a weather report. My eyes were about F-11 from doing just that. The little blond tot by now had her fingers wrapped around one of mine and she looked so much like Lindy at that age that I had a severe case of homesickness.

Very little later I was back at the Press Center. Major Macho, Styles, Tucker, and the other Marines had done their best to decorate the place. There was a tree of sorts that somebody had driven miles to find and had broken the law to chop down, and some candles and colored balls and wreaths.

With everybody pretending they didn't miss their families or home or anything else, I stood at the bar with George Esper and some Marines and bellowed the new lyrics to "Jingle Bells."

Jingle bells, mortar shells,
VC in the grass—
You can take your Christmas
And shove it up your ass.

Soldier-in-grease-paint, Bob Hope was loved by the fighting men in Vietnam just as he had been by US troops in three other wars. He was solidly behind them, too. "Westmoreland ought to be backed to the hilt," said Hope. "Why fight a limited war? We ought to throw everything at the enemy. Not worry about Red China. We should do it now. Lock it up."

He arrived in Da Nang during holiday week and, with Carroll Baker, Joey Heatherton, and the rest of the company, performed in the driving tropical rain to a typical roaring GI audience. After the show Smash took one of Hope's engineers to the trailer so he could grab a shower before they pressed on for the next performance.

Day and night, troops actually headed elsewhere had been overrunning the trailer. A few feet behind it a shack called the Mars Station had been built to facilitate one of the most popular Christmas activities. Inside were two technicians assigned to put through the soldiers' calls to their families back home. A notice had been posted in the enlisted men's and officers' clubs explaining about the Christmas-week bonus of free calls. Because Nails and Smash's trailer appeared a more likely place than the sagging shack nearby, there was a steady stream of men knocking on the trailer door and asking, "Is this the Mars Station?" In order to get some sleep, Nails and Smash finally printed a sign and tacked it on the trailer's front and rear entrances:

NO. THIS IS NOT THE MARS STATION.

In one of the trailer windows was a smaller placard:

CHRISTMAS! BAH! HUMBUG!

The cream of General Ky's VNAF were assigned to fly with the B-57s. Each VN pilot flew with an American navigator and vice versa. Strikes had been called off during the holidays but the Viet Cong violated the truce eighty-three times.

At eleven o'clock Captain Nguyen Bien, a pilot with over a thousand combat missions, attended services in the base chapel with us—Bien, the Buddhist, Nails, the Mormon, and Smash and me, Methodists. Then we packed a picnic lunch and went to the beach for a swim in the South China Sea.

We rode the breakers on rubber life rafts but didn't venture out too far. One soldier had been drowned the week before. The currents are treacherous during the monsoon season.

Nails and I paddled to a calm spot. "What are you going to do after the war?" he asked.

"Haven't thought much beyond that. I'd like to stay on here for a while, maybe go over to Thailand one of these days and do some pieces about the fabulous guys flying out of there. Right now wild Caucasian ponies couldn't drag me out of this profession."

"Smash and I put in for an extended tour, but they turned us down. Claim we're pressing our luck. Twenty-five years in the service is up for both of us the end of this month. Guess we'll retire."

"Then what?"

"I'm not sure about Smash. I've had some interesting offers. I'll sort them out before I leave."

Most fliers dream of commanding a combat squadron; it's a great thing to have on your record. But when a crew and aircraft are lost, the brass at headquarters (in this case at Clark in the Philippines) lay the blame squarely on one individual. Who else but the squadron commander? No matter if he is blameless or that mechanical failure, ground fire, or a bolt of lightning was involved. Traditionally, command must be rejiggered.

When the 13th lost a second crew, Nails was called to Clark. His immediate superior there, Colonel Jim Hill, a double jet ace, went to bat for him all the way. Outcome: Both were eased up to important-sounding posts in headquarters at Clark.

Back at Da Nang, Colonel Scott, on-the-spot boss of Air Force strikes and the logical judge of how best to run his operation, was unhappy, to say the least. He considered Nails the best of his squadron commanders and told him so. "You can serve with me anywhere, any time."

It is to Scott's credit that policy has since changed. The decision regarding who will or will not lead a squadron in Da Nang no longer sifts down from Clark. It rests with the commander of the 6252nd TAC Fighter Wing.

Bad as he felt about losing his squadron, Nails didn't wear out a lot of carpet over it. Then, when the 8th rotated to Da Nang, foul fortune began plaguing them, too. Nails called me in Saigon.

"Farr lost a bird last month. Jere Joyner was shot up and air-evaced out. A couple of others were shot up almost beyond repair last week. Bear Bryant and Tom Walker were both killed last Thursday. Bear was hit in a dive-bomb pass. He never pulled out. They went straight in and no chutes were observed."

I didn't have to ask what Nails was thinking. There was foundation to the rumors of a shortage of the bigger bombs. Bear had only 100-pounders. They don't keep the Charlies' heads down.

"What about Bear's things?" I asked.

"I haven't packed his gear yet. And Rosie won't go near his room. If I don't get home by dark she goes to the neighbor's house to sleep. She makes my bed and cleans the bathroom before I go to work and then she won't even go down the hall the rest of the day. I guess she'll be OK once I get all Bear's belongings packed up and shipped out.

"Yesterday two 57s ran together returning from a strike. Danny was fired on the spot and Gerry Hamilton now has the squadron. *He* lost two more before he'd even been informed he was the new leader. I sent Danny a singing telegram complete with music: 'Anything Nails can do, you can do better . . . tra la la. You can do anything better than me.'"

Smash wrote me a letter. "Yep. The 8th finished up their tour in a blaze of something other than glory. If this keeps up, before very long B-57s are going to be an extinct bird like the passenger pigeon."

Actually, the 13th felt miserable about their sister squadron and Danny's bad luck. Wakes were held at the Club 21, encircling the names of the fallen. Nails was sent to the States on a secret mission and took an extra few days to go hunting out in Utah with The Moose. One day a cable arrived at the Caravelle:

MEMO TO THE ALPINE MILKMAID: IF YOU WANT TO TAKE THAT LONG-OVERDUE R & R IN HONG KONG I'LL MEET YOU THERE. NAILS.

The good air of Hong Kong revived me as I rode the ferry to the Mandarin Hotel. The management had assigned me a suite about the size of an indoor rifle range, very elegant after the cow dung, jungle mud, and bucket seats of war. There was indirect lighting, a huge iron ice bucket from Taipei painted pale green, extravagantly embroidered upholstery on the furniture, and a Thai silk spread on the honeymoon-size bed.

I left the hotel to go shopping for a sloping straw coolie hat and had the Doom Pussy patch stapled to the crown. Back in the suite, as I unwrapped my parcels Nails breezed in. He ordered champagne and got to the point. "I've made a deal with Bill Lear. He's offered me a pilot-salesman job. He does business all over the world. So I'll be flying his jets for a while. Fine birds."

Bill Lear, Sr., was one of the greats in aviation history and now a tycoon who manufactured executive jets. They were coming off the line at the rate of thirteen a month and Bill was doing a million dollars' worth of business before taxes. His Lear Jet cruised at 540 mph, had a ceiling of 45,000, and could be landed with the brakes on in a little over 750 feet.

With his usual exuberance Nails added, "If you ever get tired of riding around on commercial planes, maybe Bill would let you come along with me. We could zap into revolutions, floods, or the Casbah. You could write your head off. What I've got in mind right now is a hunting lodge in Utah, a hidey hole in Majorca—"

"A villa in Rome, a flat in Paris, and a house in Georgetown," I said helping him along.

"That's the idea. Then all the Cranberry crews could have a few places to RON whether I'm there or not. New York, too, of course. But I guess your place would do for the time being."

At that moment the phone rang. It was the wife of Los Angeles Mayor Sam Yorty, returning my call. They had arrived in Hong Kong the day before and I planned to do a story on them. Before hanging up she asked if I'd heard the latest bulletin on the radio. Defense Secretary McNamara was en route to Vietnam. Here was my cue to get back to Saigon and I hadn't even unpacked yet. Riding the vehicular ferry from Hong Kong to Kaitek Airport in Kowloon, I asked Nails, "By the way, how's Smasherino?"

"Someone saw him in Bangkok the other day. He's on leave for a few days. They said he was leaning on a lamppost looking glassy-eyed. I think maybe he misses his front-seat driver. I'd like to work him in on this Lear deal if we do retire at the same time."

In the lobby at Tan Son Nhut Airport, giant crossbows, masks, baskets, bundles, and duffle bags were stacked everywhere. A group whose tour of duty was up were going home. Harry Howton, Nails, and Smash were among those being rotated. Harry was being reassigned to Hurlburt Field, Florida, while Smash and Nails had decided to retire and be prosperous civilians.

I suddenly thought of those who would never return. One was Colonel Chuck Honour, whose chopper had hit a power line a few miles northeast of Tan Son Nhut with seven aboard, including Chuck's pretty fiancée, Second Lieutenant Elizabeth Jones, an Army nurse. Captain Charles M. Smith, Jr., oldest son of Merriman Smith of *UPI,* was piloting the craft.

I shall always remember Chuck's ramrod-straight bearing, his good nature, and the way he loved his boys. Besides, he had let me fly copilot three different times. A captain later had told me, "The Colonel's got the only twelve-foot neck over here. If anything had happened to him, you'd have been a glob of hardware flying sideways."

Maybe. But Chuck had checked me out fairly well, even to auto-rotate landings. If you lose all your power you autorotate (fall through the air), picking up a gain in kinetic energy which causes the blades to build up power even though there's none available from the engine. This can be turned to advantage to stop the chopper. Then, twenty or thirty feet from the ground, you pull on collective and soften the landing.

Harry came over to talk and as we stood there, some of our trips together washed over my mind. At Kham Duc, where the final approach takes you over a ridge perpendicular to the runway, engineers had cut a fifty-meter notch in the hill for the birds to come in. But still it had been necessary to fly a crazily steep final; and at Gia Vuc, I remembered that the field is a narrow, rolling former pasture full of ruts and mudholes. "If we miss it," Harry had said, "we'll just fly up the valley about five clicks till we get shot at. Then we'll know we missed it and come around again. Then we got to be careful landing so we don't hit that buffalo fence, and if an engine fails to reverse, you may be introduced to the actual performance of a mine field in full operation. *Real* sporty."

"Aren't you going to find Florida a little humdrum?" I asked Harry. He had a fairly acute case of the whips and jingles from getting martinized at all the going away parties of the past week.

"I'm gonna concentrate on Mama San and southern cooking," he drawled.

As the day of departure had drawn closer, Smash and Nails savored the shock of being short-timers. "I'm getting so short I'm afraid to start a long conversation," Nails said.

They walked over. "When do you think you'll be heading for home?"

"Well, I'm glad I won't be on this flight, with you three twitching all over your seats and your feet up against the seat in front of you at every landing." I've yet to see any pilot relax with someone else up in the front office.

Nails slipped his arm around me, at the same time nodding to Smash, who then fished a little parcel out of his pocket. "Something from the guys in the thirteenth," he mumbled.

When I unwrapped it I found a woman's cigarette lighter, with the Devil's Own Grim Reaper insignia soldered on the front. Before I could thank them, Nails said, "Turn it over, sug."

The reverse side was engraved with my name at the top, a little halo in the middle, and at the bottom:

LAST OF THE GREAT BROADS

"Well, let's go climb on that gold bullet out there waitin' to carry us home," Harry said.

I tucked the preposterous piece of flattery into a pocket of my jump suit and zipped it shut. I wouldn't ever want to lose that. We all vowed to meet again some day, somewhere.

Harry and Smash walked toward the plane steps, then turned to wave once more.

With his thumb and forefinger, Nails tilted my chin up and winked. "Now, don't let your Munsingwear seize on you."

I didn't move until the plane was out of sight. It was very, very hard to believe they were gone.

Thirteen

WHAT MAKES CHARLIE TICK?

In the early spring of 1966, one of those political ploys least understood by the average American suddenly erupted. The Buddhists, in short, took to the streets. The pretext that brought them out was the sudden clash between Prime Minister Ky and his spunky general, Nguyen Chanh Thi, in command of I Corps, which embraces five provinces in South Vietnam. The two had been the closest of friends and rivals. But six months after our trip to Kuala Lumpur, Prime Minister Ky had no choice but to sack his longtime friend, who, Ky felt, was still acting like an insubordinate, oldstyle warlord.

This was exactly the sort of incident the militant and politically minded clique of Buddhists had been waiting for. It happened to suit their purposes especially well in and around Hue and Da Nang. The venerable leader, Tri Quang, who photographs rather like Yul Brynner playing Dracula, made the most of it. Indeed, it got so bad that Ky had little other choice but to go into Da Nang with loyal troops and reestablish law and order—a job made harder by the wave of suicides by fire set in motion by the leaders of the pagodas.

As Vu Van Thai, Vietnamese Ambassador to the United States once said: "After the overthrow of Diem, the Buddhists were in a dilemma. They couldn't withdraw from the political action they had instigated, and as a church they could not formally enter politics."

The more militant Buddhists are not subject to any discipline from other Buddhists the world over—those well known for their dedication to decency and peace. The Vietnamese Buddhists' extremist tactics profoundly embarrass their brethren elsewhere.

When Buddhists had burned themselves in political frustration to protest against President Diem, the Western world was dutifully appalled. The news was little less shocking now, though the pattern was far clearer. It was evident that a few high-ranking venerables cared more for power than for their nation's welfare. And American officials with access to the facts were convinced that the faction committed to Ky's overthrow was headed by the prestigious Buddhist leader Thich (Venerable) Tri Quang, who could surely have prevented the chaos, and who instead threatened more immolation epidemics if he didn't get his way. Yet he carefully labeled the suicides "spontaneous."

Any impartial observer of recent history knows that a Buddhist confrontation with communism can only precipitate disaster. Strategist Quang stated that he gladly would talk to the Viet Cong if they were to occupy a place in the Vietnamese government. He wouldn't be talking long; he would be listening.

String-puller Quang has been called a "mystery man." He served with the communist-front groups working hand in glove with Ho Chi Minh's Viet Minh army and twice was arrested by the French Colonial Office for these connections. He also quarterbacked the "suicides by frying" from his headquarters in the Xa Loi pagoda in Saigon, thereby influencing the West against the late President Diem. By subterranean intrigues and unscrupulous methods, he seeks not merely a participating position, but a key role in any future South Vietnamese regime. He has overlooked or ignored the fact that he is the leader of only one of a number of Buddhist sects, most of which steer clear of politics. Other religions in Vietnam are: Catholic, Confucianist, Animist, Taoist, and there are a few Mennonites and Baptists, and devotees of the Hoa Hao and Cao Dai religions.

Quang had survived the wrath of President Diem in September, 1963, only because Ambassador Henry Cabot Lodge did not deny him asylum in the American Embassy. Also, Lodge went along with President Kennedy's decision that Diem's government was not to be supported. As the late Marguerite Higgins wrote: "Quang wanted Diem's head, not on a silver platter, but wrapped in an American flag."

In 1966, the power-intoxicated Quang warned Lodge that Ky must go and that the Buddhists must be admitted to power. Both Lodge and the Johnson administration decided to stick with Prime Minister Ky.

The Buddhist rioting was the cue for the Viet Cong to intensify their weapons of terror and harassment. They went to work at it with the same fervor they might have devoted to a spring military offensive. Few would dispute that VC agents were closely embroiled in the campaign against Prime Minister Ky, primarily in Da Nang and Hue. Their error was in underestimating Ky's prompt and effective counteractions.

In some instances the press has portrayed Quang with an absurdity reminiscent of former errors made in China back when ambitious old Mao Tse-tung was usually described as a lovable agrarian democrat. Quang scarcely could be called a pure-minded advocate of democratic processes. His practices denote otherwise. His attempts to subvert Vietnamese armed forces in the Da Nang and Hue area and gain control of the Army's Buddhist chaplains so that they could take their orders from him simply could not be tolerated by Prime Minister Ky's government.

As the riots intensified, students carried banners suggesting that the Americans Go Home. Out of a student body of two thousand, barely two hundred took part in the burning of the US Information Service library while the Hue police chief and twenty of his men stood idly by half a block away. A delegation of Buddhists then marched to the steps of the American Consulate and were met by James Bullington, the vice consul. The student leader protested that President Johnson's reply to Quang's letter was unsatisfactory. Quang had appealed to the American president for aid in overthrowing Ky, and Johnson had refused.

Bullington told the students, "I do not appreciate threats. If you have anything to say, say it. But do not threaten me."

As one American official put it, "The time to leave is not when these people get into worse trouble."

Reporter Richard Critchfield says: "Press coverage has played into the hands of Buddhism's political kingmakers. I don't think Tri Quang would have really existed without the American press. He has fooled an awful lot of people for a long time into thinking he speaks for all the Buddhists of South Vietnam." As for what Madame Nhu called "the barbecues," an expression she picked up from the US press, Critchfield says: "My impression is that these just aren't voluntary suicides."

After Ky had sent government troops to Da Nang to contain agitators, the militant group of Buddhists blundered spectacularly when they enticed forty members of the press corps into a pagoda and trapped them there.

Critchfield, whose overall coverage of the Vietnam war won him the Overseas Press Club award for the best daily-newspaper or wire-service reporting from abroad, filed an account of the pagoda "incident," which appeared on the front page of the *Washington Evening Star.*

The collapse of the myth that the Buddhist represented a just but repressed popular cause probably began Sunday night in Da Nang when veteran Associated Press reporter Robert Poor staggered into the American press camp livid with anger and bleeding from a chest wound.

"The Buddhists trapped us in the pagoda and then opened fire when we tried to get out," Poor shouted with rage.

During the previous hour the scales had fallen from the eyes of some forty American and foreign newsmen, who spent some of the most frightening moments of their lives within Da Nang's besieged Tinh Hoi pagoda.

In a kind of shock treatment that stripped bare the almost incredible cynicism toward human life of Buddhist monks and rebel political commissars, newsmen were enticed inside for a fictional urgent announcement, then were told it was too dangerous to leave for the remainder of the night after Buddhist forces provoked a heavy fire-fight with surrounding paratroopers and tanks.

The press unmistakably were being held as "eyewitness hostages" in a place of unutterable horror, full of corpses, Buddhist flags, and swarms of flies. The senior bonze held a press conference. "I fear the paratroopers will attack us tonight or at dawn," he said. "I want the press to be here to see it."

The rebel fanatics then started shooting at any rebel soldiers who tried to surrender to Ky's forces.

The newsmen then were shown wailing women lying on stretchers, their wounds unattended. It was a hideously callous display for press photographers. One outrageous touch was added when someone propped a crying baby against the body of a dead woman for the photographers' benefit.

"It was the most callous use of human suffering toward political ends I have ever experienced," said one photographer.

"It was just a show for us," said NBC's Ron Nessen. He ordered his cameraman to stop filming.

Tim Page was wounded by a grenade blast as he and other newsmen ran out of the pagoda. Tim was pulled into a doorway a few yards down the street. He kept murmuring through the blood-soaked mosquito net bandaged around his head wounds, "Don't take me back to the pagoda. Don't take me back to the pagoda."

Critchfield's dispatch continued:

If Prime Minister Ky's battalions had indeed launched a bloody all-out assault on the pagoda it would have been an epic news story to reporters who survived to describe or photograph it. But a compulsion to stand up for human decency swept the newsmen there in the darkness of Tinh Hoi, and their fright became mixed with almost uncontrollable anger.

Despite the real risk of being mowed down by the Buddhist rebels, the newsmen turned their backs on the monks and, waving handkerchiefs and undershirts, marched out the pagoda gates with rebel machine guns trained at their backs. After trying to stop the first group with sniper bullets and a grenade, and injuring three, rebels let others pass without firing.

Looking back now with relative calm, the truth is the real civil war in Da Nang probably ended as the reporters marched down the dark street away from Tinh Hoi. The rebel leaders and senior bonzes might have defied Ky's troops and triggered a bloody showdown after slipping away themselves at the last moment. But if the pagoda was to be destroyed and scores of women and children and soldiers massacred, the enormity of such carnage would require the monks' being positive in advance that the press would fix the blame on Ky's forces and not themselves.

The Buddhist extremist minority, led by Quang, had failed in their attempt to blackmail the American President, win over the American press, and sway world opinion. The grisly shows of flaming suicides subsided, the effect of stage-managed riots and gruesome rebellions began to pall on world spectators.

It was not easy, but Prime Minister Ky had landed on his feet yet again. So Thich Tri Quang, who makes Barnum look like a dim-bulb amateur, resorted to fasting. And then cabled President Johnson to pray for him.

It had been six weeks since Harry, Smash, and Nails had flown back to the land of the big PX, all-night generators, and ninety million round-eyes. I was on my way to Thailand. It is a welcome relief for combat reporters to get out of intrigue-ridden Saigon with its mood of *bo pang nhan*—"it doesn't matter." The majority of war correspondents prefer to be with the fighting men. Jack Foisie expressed it best. "It may sound corny," he said, "but it's refreshing to get out where people say what they mean."

Of all the nations in Southeast Asia, Thailand alone has remained independent since the thirteenth century. She has never been dominated by a colonial power. The Thais terminated alliances with England in the last century and with the Japanese during World War II, and are now one of the United States' strongest allies. It has been their long-standing practice to go along always with the major power in Asia. Were the US to pull out of Vietnam, the Thais would almost certainly go over to the only other power in the area, Communist China.

In the event of a US withdrawal, Laos undoubtedly would be lost. If Thailand, Burma, and Cambodia were to acknowledge the reassertion of China's historic authority over the area, they might maintain some semblance of independence, but Malaysia could scarcely be counted on to continue as a pro-West bastion. And Indonesia might again find itself dominated by a Sukarno-type pro-Red China hierarchy. Of even more importance, North Vietnam could no longer play off Peking against Moscow. These are the main reasons why President Johnson's administration has accepted and reaffirmed President Eisenhower's 1954 domino theory, which maintained that if *one* Asian nation flipped over to the communists, the others would have no choice but to follow.

Today's strong and stable Thailand figures prominently in the headlines. Only thirty years ago it was still called Siam, and Southeast Asia was referred to as "the Farther Indies." Now more American servicemen are stationed in the Pacific than in Europe. The Thais do not doubt for a minute that if Peking topples any one country in Southeast Asia, the remaining nations would succumb to Chinese influence. They believe unreservedly that Communist China is on the march in Asia and do not question Mao Tse-tung's pronouncement that their country is next on his list of candidates for "wars of liberation."

Chinese Foreign Minister Chen Yi has publicly stated that "we hope to have a guerrilla war in Thailand before the year is out." To emphasize this threat, Peking announced in December, 1965, that it had merged two Thai revolutionary groups under the name of the Patriotic Front of Thailand, which sounds like a playback of the beginnings of the Vietnam conflict. US Embassy officials in Bangkok term it "aggression by seepage."

Thailand, in fact, has a huge Achilles heel on its remote northeast region, where a third of the population lives and where eleven million peasants there endure grinding poverty; some families' incomes are an annual ten dollars, in stark contrast to the opulence and affluence of the capital, Bangkok, headquarters of SEATO. Tourists who ride in taxis, listen to tinkling temple bells, stay in air-conditioned hotels, and admire the parasols, lampshade hats, and caparisoned elephants in Bangkok seem unaware that communist agents and guerrillas, like termites, gnaw away at the Thailand-Laos border, already two-thirds controlled by Reds.

Rich in corn, tin, rice, and rubber, Thailand has one of the highest standards of living in Southeast Asia. But she has neglected her three-thousand-mile frontier. In the north, Thailand merges with Laos and Burma, where thousands of pro-Peking Chinese exiles woo the Meo tribesmen. Along the northeast frontier communist infiltrators merely wade across the muddy Mekong and disappear into spidery trails on either side. The isolated and unlettered peasants eagerly believe what Red agents tell them—that the Bangkok government steals their rice and that Americans rape women and torture children.

Newsweek refers to the dirty and disagreeable war that threatens the whole Indochina peninsula as "the Battle of Time and the River." The Mekong, the world's tenth largest river, marks the border between Burma and Laos; it flows down the frontier of Thailand for 850 miles, then cuts across Cambodia and into the delta of South Vietnam. Originating in the Himalayas at 16,700 feet above sea level, it courses through the plains of Red China's Yunnan Province toward the South China Sea. Some consider it the key to the war that we fight in Southeast Asia. If Laos collapsed totally, the path to the rice bowl of Southeast Asia would be wide open. Whoever controls the Mekong's 2,600-mile course holds the key to victory. No one recognizes this better than the Red Chinese.

Thailand is riding the crest of an unprecedented economic boom, but reluctant as her leaders are to admit it, the country is also geared for war and is playing a critical role in the Asian battle. All American air strikes against the Reds in Laos take off from Thailand air bases, and US planes based in Thailand account for at least 80 percent of the strikes over North Vietnam.

Touchy about its tradition of being the only country in Southeast Asia never colonized by the West, Thailand has not relished publicity of her cooperation with us. The fact that she not only firmly sides with us but has permitted air bases to be built and strikes to originate from them has been a badly kept secret. The pattern of this friendly policy was assured when Thailand contributed troops to the UN fighting forces in Korea, one of the first countries outside the US to do so. When Thailand joined the US-sponsored SEATO (Southeast Asia Treaty Organization) in 1954, Pote Sarasin, former Thai ambassador to the US and currently Minister of National Development, was elected the first secretary general. When the Laotian crisis peaked in 1961–62, Bangkok and Washington formed a defense agreement and President Kennedy sent five thousand troops to Thailand. We now have thirty-five thousand there, two-thirds of them Air Force under the command of Major General Richard G. Stilwell, chief of the Military Assistance Command—Thailand.

Swimming champ Mao Tse-tung frequently and publicly had announced that northeast Thailand was Red China's next target. There was plenty of material there for a reporter, but much of it classified. A borderline case was Air America, the world's shyest airline, never advertising and rarely discussing its operations. Referred to as "Gray Ghosts," the planes are unmarked and the crews' awards for heroism are presented in private ceremonies.

The airline ferries supplies and ammunition to remote government outposts in the northeast, where the Viet Cong have been infiltrating for years. Air America has lost more than twenty aircraft and fifty fliers to the enemy. One crew was shot down and executed by the Charlies. The airline's activities are irregular and very hush-hush. The crews wear unmarked gray uniforms and are close-mouthed about their work. For obvious reasons of diplomacy, in areas where overt US military forces cannot be employed, operations of this type must be developed.

The history of Air America dates back to misty beginnings on the Chinese mainland in the days following the defeat of the Japanese by the combined forces of the US and Chiang Kai-shek. It started at that time as China National Airways Corporation and was partially owned by Pan American, with US companies involved in the management and flying end of the airline. The more colorful fliers of those days included Billy MacDonald from Columbiana, Alabama, whom other pilots knew as the gent who flew a DC-3½ out of a rice paddy in 1937—with about six tons of human fertilizer hanging onto the fuselage.

As Harry Howton once told me, "Billy and me were just a couple of southern boys trying to make a living."

The pilots who made CNAC came from a varied background. Many of them were former mercenaries of the famous AVG group recruited in the US by Claire Chennault, the legendary Flying Tiger who, during WW II, was made a general and led the 14th Air Force to victory on the mainland.

Following the end of the war, Civil Air Transport, or CAT, was started by Chennault with the help of the US government, some war surplus transport planes, and a boost by UNRRA, United Nations Relief and Rehabilitation Agency. In 1948 CAT became the principal flag carrier for the Nationalist Chinese Government during its battles with the Communist Chinese, who were pouring down from the northern provinces.

During the last bitter months of 1949, when the tattered legions of the Generalissimo were pushed into the sea from Canton, CAT flew day and night evacuating Chinese Nationalist forces to havens like the islands of Hainan and Formosa. CAT became the principal flag carrier for the Free Chinese Government and the covert arm for the United States, for special operations involving night penetrations, drops of agents on mainland China, agent pickups, and leaflet drops.

CAT also participated in Korea from the beginning of that war. (Harry and Nails had told me of running into CAT crews in Pyong-yang in the fall of 1950, "when we were streaking for the Yalu and everybody was gonna be home by Christmas.") In Korea, as well as providing support for State Department agencies, CAT flew as a military airlift contractor—operating out of US military bases in Japan, Okinawa, and Taiwan, while its commercial arm maintained a regular scheduled civilian operation all the way from Seoul to Bangkok.

As the French-Indochinese war moved into its last phases, CAT furnished air crews and flew C-119s in support of the French as a part of a US Military Aid Program. The aircraft were originally USAF; the pilots were mostly Americans, and they performed airlift and any other missions that were requested by the French in their Indochina war operations. The C-119s flown by CAT were heavily used. In the last major battle of the Indochina war, at Dien Bien Phu, a number of pilots were lost including the boys' notorious old pal, Earthquake McGoon, the jovial giant whose pilot's license read, James P. McGovern.

As the US has become more and more involved in South Vietnam, CAT and its subsidiary companies, Air America, Southern Air Transport, and Air Asia, have provided overt airlift support for the US State Department and other US agencies in Vietnam. They fly a variety of aircraft, ranging from single-engine turboprop Swiss-built Porters to borrowed or civil-purchased C-46s, C-47s, Caribous, and C-123s. Like the old Bird & Sons flying outfit recently bought by Continental Airlines, they also operate in Laos and Thailand, supporting in-country AID projects and other operations.

The personnel are contract crews, many of them ex-military. The pay is good but hard-earned. The men are paid by the flying hour, and after base pay, which is equal to a pretty good month's flying pay for an Air Force pilot, they earn overtime. In the overtime area the money becomes interesting. Aircraft maintenance and repair facilities are based primarily in Formosa.

About nine thousand Nationalist Chinese and Filipino employees work at the huge maintenance base for the combined airline operations at Tainan and Kaoshung on the southern tip of Formosa. One of the unique features is that the original maintenance base for the airline was, and still is, a floating machine shop, housed on a converted LST brought down from Shanghai in the last days of the Nationalist-Communist War.

On paper Air America belongs to the Pacific Corporation, a Delaware holding company whose board chairman is retired Admiral Felix Stump, former US commander in the Pacific. Its field headquarters remains on Taiwan, where the huge repair facility is located. The fleet of aircraft numbers about 150, including the little single-engine Helip Couriers and Pilatus Porters, which can land in a little over two hundred feet. There are Huey helicopters and a Super Constellation with interesting humps on its fuselage.

The four hundred or so pilots are reluctant to talk to the press except to say, "As long as we get paid we don't care what they put in the back." Service for the US military between South Korea, Japan, and Okinawa is scheduled. The rest is "irregular."

The US supported the Laotian royalists in the communist-agitated civil war. To help the Meo tribesmen and royalist troops clobber the communist Pathet Lao, Air America planes made weapon and rice drops by the ton. The pilots say, "A hell of a lot of those kids would give you an argument if you told them that rice didn't grow in the sky."

When VC infiltration increased in the northeast, Air America activities were stepped up considerably in Thailand by flying supplies and ammunition to the outposts. There were tales of outstanding courage concerning their helicopter crews, who rescued downed airmen in North Vietnam and ferried them to safety.

Air America has been called the stepchild, cousin, and brainchild of the Central Intelligence Agency. The managing director of the airline, George Doole, Jr., was an old friend of my family, since we had all lived in Istanbul at the same time. There was a chance I might get a story out of him.

The Thai Airways International Plane set down at Bangkok's Don Muang Airport at 5:50 P.M. After going through the ritual of customs and passport inspection, I stood beside my gear to hail a taxi.

"Well, good evenin', ma'am. Let's go into town and get our batteries recharged with a little vodka therapy," said a familiar voice
from just behind me. Before I could turn my head to verify, two
big arms clamped tight about my waist and swung me around as if
I were a principal in the Ice Follies. It was Harry the Hog Hauler,
all decked out in an unmarked uniform.

"Hmmm, couldn't resist the sharp joy of combat after all?" I
asked, recovering my breath, and looking him over.

"Those desk jobs are for sea gulls," Harry said with a grin, then
helped me pile the gear into a taxi. As we settled back for the
eighteen-mile trip into town, Harry announced, "Nails and Smash
got in two days ago. They're in Tainan for maintenance. Ought to
be back tomorrow."

We took my baggage to the Erawan Hotel, then slipped over to
the New Lunar Club, a favorite hangout for American soldiers. A
trio of men at a corner table were winding up a verse from "Cats on
the Roof Top":

> Oh, the donkey in the meadow's a funny bloke,
> He very seldom gets his poke,
> But when he d-u-u-u-z-z-z-z, he lets it soak
> As he revels in the joys of copula-a-a shun.

After Harry ordered for us I asked him to fill me in. "What happened to the Lear deal?"

"They put it on ice for a year. The scratch is pretty good over
here, too. And us keen, stouthearted fellows get a kick out of fighting the bad guys," Harry replied. "And as ole Nails says, even Hubert pays off, but not every day."

It wasn't too surprising that the big Mormon airplane driver, the
Duke of Da Nang, spoiled, sentimental rogue of quicksilver moods
and high passions, the rebel who so enjoyed breaking the rules, was
back, or that Smash had come with him. As Harry had said in the
beginning, it's usually the same ones who turn up when there's trouble and their country is involved.

For Harry, Smash, and Nails, duck hunting, families, and promis-
ing civilian careers could wait for a while. There was fundamental
unfinished business over here.

EPILOGUE

We are fighting a war in Asia so that the South Vietnamese will not be prevented by force from establishing something they have never yet known although it has long been an American birthright: a government of the people, exercising their right to have a voice in their own destiny.

After one hundred years of French occupation and exploitation, the Japanese occupied the country in 1940. At the end of World War II the French returned to continue their colonial regime. Under Ho Chi Minh, the Communist Party formed a guerrilla army called the Viet Minh and fought the French for ten years. Defeated in 1954, the French evacuated a partitioned Vietnam. The communists then took control of North Vietnam above the Seventeenth Parallel and the Free Republic of Vietnam was formed in the South. In a population of fourteen million, 80 percent are industrious but illiterate peasants with no conception of—or background in—self-government.

The Viet Cong, or Communist Party, then tried to take over the balance of Vietnam by force, deceit, blackmail, revolution, tyranny, terror, and, the most difficult to combat, infiltration. To deceive the outside world, the Viet Cong hid behind the claim that the struggle was a civil war, an indigenous uprising of social discontent. The facts are that Le Duan, presently First Secretary of the Communist Party of North Vietnam, went south to set the stage for guerrilla warfare long before the outbreak of hostilities. From Hanoi, Ho Chi Minh manipulated this underground movement made up of thousands of cadres which the communists in the North had ordered into hiding when war with the French ended in 1954. Hanoi provided large quantities of military equipment as well as thousands of cadres to assist in the conspiracy and struggle.

There is no question that the Viet Cong can be defeated, but building a solid peace must be accomplished by the South Vietnamese themselves. Our aim is to help them build a genuinely popular, stable, cohesive government. Then these proud people may be stirred to preserve and defend such a precious accomplishment.

South Vietnam potentially is one of the very richest countries. The Vietnamese are a talented, charming people. With peace, they should prosper and become strong. The present churning confusion is nurtured by shortsighted power blocs, loyal to their own areas, clans, and religions. These rival groups think of themselves first, victory second.

The education problem in Vietnam will be staggering. It has been suggested that after the battles are won, some hand-screened American soldiers might be allowed to transfer to the Peace Corps and remain in the area. This could be an effective program against expansionist communism.

President Johnson's policy makers think that he should repeatedly remind the American people that we are over there to prevent the spread of communism to unwilling and helpless peoples, rather than because of commitments of SEATO, which some State Department officials consider almost a ghost of a treaty. Our presence in Vietnam is not alone a humanitarian impulse. We are determined to maintain a balance of power in that area, and properly so, since the outcome will be a turning point in the Pacific. It is far more than one isolated conflict over communist ambitions.

Progress in the humanitarian area is encouraging. Between 1962 and 1965, seven million textbooks for schoolchildren were distributed throughout South Vietnam. The goal for 1966 is to double that by an additional seven million. Thanks to President Johnson's action in giving Deputy Ambassador William Porter full authority to force military cooperation on all civilian programs, there has been a sharp reduction in the bottlenecks that used to cause some ships to wait in port for a month before unloading non-military commodities. White House aide Robert Komer's appointment as "construction czar" was another welcome way to speed up reconstruction programs.

But it is hard to imagine the propaganda war subsiding. One reporter made world headlines when he first broke the story that American troops were using gas. No matter that it was harmless and that General Westmoreland employed it *in the interest of saving lives* of innocents. (Tear gas can smoke out of tunnels both the Viet Cong and the civilians behind whom they hide.) Headlines around the globe in communist, neutral, and even some friendly nations branded American military "barbarians" for using tear gas. The

British were "horrified," yet their troops have used these gases in Cyprus and elsewhere in their military operations. Police in scores of countries use riot gases on crowds—precisely to avoid wounding the rioters.

A resourceful reporter has dozens of contacts who tip him off to stories. If the tipper happens to be a VC-sympathizing infiltrator into the Saigon hierarchy and the story provides fodder for America's critics and enemies, it is regrettable, though not necessarily a reflection on the newsman's lapse in self-imposed censorship, private convictions, or integrity. A hard-working correspondent takes his tips from the best sources available.

But what a beautiful setup for the enemy—a guaranteed worldwide outlet usually precipitating a flood of anti-American demonstrations around the earth.

It is the shocking stories that hit the front page. Good news is no news. Who would care to feature in print that in WW II the War Department mulled over the idea of using poison gas on Iwo Jima in order to take that fearfully defended island. It was quite the spot to use poison gas, if ever. But when the idea came to the attention of the late Fleet Admiral Chester W. Nimitz, he nixed it, saying, "I decided the United States should not be the first to violate the Geneva Convention." It was a tough decision for the Admiral to make at the expense of many gallant Marines. The exact casualty figures on Iwo Jima were 17,252 Marines wounded, 5,931 killed.

In Saigon I had many long conversations with Mr. Nguyen Van Tuoi, publisher-editor of the *Saigon Daily News*. A passionate humanitarian who deplores the idea of Vietnamese shooting Vietnamese and the daily bombing of his country, he fervently anticipates the day when all combatants seat themselves at the conference table. We discussed the Red Chinese movements of army units into North Vietnam and the fact that these troops man Chinese antiaircraft batteries and maintain a key supply railroad connecting mainland China with Hanoi.

The nineteenth century was a period of humiliation for the Chinese by foreigners. Two wars were fought by the British to foist the introduction of opium upon China. And the French, in 1883–95, forced the Chinese to enter into treaties which cost them suzerainty over North and Central Vietnam and Laos. Many Sinologists feel that the appeal of the Chinese Communist movement in 1920–21 was built on these wrongs.

"How rhetorical," I asked Tuoi, "was Defense Minister Lin Piao's pronouncement that the rural areas of the world will surround and conquer the cities of the world, meaning that the underdeveloped nations, in joint rebellion, will eventually triumph over the developed countries? Isn't that a long-range blueprint for destruction of the United States?"

"Mao Tse-tung," Tuoi replied, "has preached that since 1936 in such basic documents as *Strategic Problems of Chinese Revolutionary War.*"

Some Far East analysts dismiss all this as Confucian pragmatism and refer to the unrealistic picture the Red Chinese have of the outside world. They think war with China is avoidable and far from imminent and point out that in the past Mao Tse-tung has been known to reverse his course quickly when he bumped up against an insurmountable obstacle. They say that we should help the Chinese to become more sophisticated.

In the interests of finding a solution, Secretary of State Dean Rusk refers to the "pragmatic genius of the Chinese people"—people whom Americans have known and befriended for more than a century in educational, missionary, and trade relations, and as allies in a great war. Rusk says the United States does not assume that there is anything "eternal" about the "state of hostility" between Red China and the United States.

It would be useful if we could get a clear and close-range picture of the other side. Mr. Tuoi granted me permission to reprint excerpts from a poem published in his paper in October, 1965. At a time when the war was being criticized inside and outside the United States, the thoughts and feelings of one young man fighting with the Viet Cong had been expressed in this poem. The simple verses were found in an envelope in the pocket of a uniform on a body slain at Duc Co. It was addressed to the soldier's mother, Mrs. Tran Thi Phan, in Hai Dong, North Vietnam. The translator, Ton That Thien, a widely read Saigon newspaper columnist, repeated to me the well-known line *"Traduttore, traditore!"* and asked me to remember that Oriental poetry does not go easily or with exact effect into English.

In an early stanza of the poem were the two lines:

> For peace we were fighting,
> For peace we accepted suffering.

After a number of other stanzas of homesick reminiscences, it read:

Here, too, at dusk, the sniffing buffalo slowly treads his dusty way home
While his little master plays a plaintive tune
On his bamboo flute,
The way our boys at home also do. . . .
Why burn and destroy? Why was I ordered to pull
The trigger that would make of a child an orphan and his mother a widow?
There were times when my hands shook like the willow
On laying the mine that would spill
The blood of people like you and me, our kin.

Like the poem, diaries have been recovered from bodies left behind by Viet Cong. And North Vietnamese captives have, at times, talked of the harrowing journey south. Harassed by snakes and insects—and sometimes by wild animals and such diseases as malaria —troops must carry seventy-five-pound packs as they trudge up forty-five-degree slopes and wind their way through the slimy mud of the jungles and mountains of Laos and Cambodia. Defectors also tell of critical food shortages.

Some of the ammunition to supply the communist troops must be carried on the backs of porters over tortuous trails—an eight-hundred-mile journey. A pair of 81-millimeter mortar rounds fired by the North Vietnamese represents a three-month hike over the trail by a carrier.

Senator Wayne Morse of Oregon is widely quoted in North Vietnam. The communists there claim that Morse's anti-Johnson stand on Vietnam speaks for the majority of Americans. Another Senator with an unerring instinct for the spotlight, who is ever eager to air his views as whilom hero of the dissenters and a prime objector to the President's Vietnam policies, is Senator Fulbright of Arkansas. One of his more eccentric outcries occurred during his lecture at Johns Hopkins University when he cited a press report that "American soldiers are turning Saigon into a brothel."

Since Fulbright has not been to Vietnam in recent years, he has been spared the firsthand sight of lonely men, sweat-drenched in a stinking jungle. And the shock of seeing a sniper pick off your best friend at dawn. And the craze for water when you've emptied your last canteen hours ago.

Before passing judgment on battle-fatigued men, Senator Fulbright might have given a little more thought to the subject. Is it for him to have simulated vapors over life today in Vietnam? Saigon has always been a loose-living town; perhaps it is more so today. There is no denying that some of the night scenes on the formerly fashionable Rue de Catinet would shock a dock walloper, not the least of these being a nine-year-old boy offering his ten-year-old sister.

But not every American in Vietnam seeks out women of negotiable virtue; and when you're on the scene you tend to become more preoccupied with the fighting men's courage. In World War II hanky panky was not unknown in London. "My God," the GIs used to say, "if the lights ever go on in Piccadilly!"

Time printed the following piece on May 20, 1966:

> Not everyone in Fulbright's own Arkansas cities of Little Rock and Hot Springs patronizes prostitutes either, though there is an abundance of whores, ranging from massage-parlor employees ($5) to $200-a-night hotel call girls. And at Little Rock Air Force Base, every airman so inclined knows that he has only to call Franklin 4-2181, ask for "Rocket" or "Houston," and find out if the "ice is on." The price of ice starts at $15 a dish.

Senator Fulbright has reminded us that World War I German soldiers wore belt buckles engraved *"Gott mit uns"* and he has likened America's "arrogance of power and fatal presumption" as similar to that of Napoleonic France and Nazi Germany. Yet he deplores anyone's practicing "policy-making by analogy," particularly those who would equate North Vietnam's attack on South Vietnam with Hitler's invasion of Poland, and a conference with the Viet Cong "as comparable to another Munich."

The normally patient Senator Jacob Javits of New York expostulated that Fulbright was "challenging the very foundations and motives of US policy without offering viable alternatives."

Barry Goldwater had a few words to add. Recalling a Fulbright suggestion that Harry Truman resign the Presidency after the sweeping Republican Congressional victory of 1946, Mr. Goldwater said: "Senator Fulbright could do no greater service for his nation and the American fighting man in Vietnam than to resign as Chairman of the Senate Foreign Relations Committee. In fact, his title lends a phony official stature and impetus to his expressions of guilt that his country is militarily powerful enough to defend freedom."

Goldwater further declared in his address to the Republican Women's Conference in Washington, D.C.:

No American has the right or the justification to describe his nation as immoral, imperialistic, and arrogant. That goes double for doing it in time of war and in a fashion that lends support and aid and comfort to our enemies. I don't care whether the American is a misguided Vietnik or Chairman of the Senate Foreign Relations Committee.

To wage a limited war against carefully selected targets, to curry favor with a domestic political group to whom the word "escalation" is the greatest of all evils, not only flies in the face of history, but is an unforgivable disservice to the men who are doing the fighting.

The dissenters have received bolder headlines than the defenders, except in the cases of the American President and, to some extent, Vice President Humphrey. Asian tours have convinced Humphrey that United States policy in Vietnam is on the right track and that the issue over there is the classic power tactics of communism. Far-left liberals are infuriated by Humphrey's stand. Heaping rude and bitter criticism on him, they shout that *they* are the "conscience of the people." Such pomposity is not easy for Humphrey to contend with.

In the findings of the US Senate Internal Security Subcommittee on the Communist Youth Program, the various sessions revealed that the Party definitely had fomented campus riots in 1964 and 1965 in its attempt to round up and organize students to agitate against the war in Vietnam. The committee stated that the agitators who subtly incite student protests and the defiance of law try very hard to make the demonstrations appear spontaneous.

But "the stamp of the Communist Party may be recognized in every phase of the rallies—from planning to the final effort at proselytizing young people."

One of the last letters the late Ambassador Adlai Stevenson wrote was to his friend Paul Goodman. In this important document, recently published in *The New York Times Magazine* section, Stevenson clearly endorsed heading off Red China in Vietnam and elsewhere in Southeast Asia. He referred to the vast areas of Asia—including some of India and all Southeast Asia—over which the aggressive Chinese dynasties of the past had claimed sovereignty. With regard to the behavior of the new communist dynasty, Stevenson pointed out that Tibet had already been swallowed, that India had been attacked, and that the Malays had to fight twelve years to resist a Chinese "national liberation" that they could and did receive from the British by a more peaceful route. He commented on the apparatus of infiltration and aggression already at work in northern Thailand and called attention to current Chinese maps showing, to the world's chagrin, the outermost limits of the old empire.

Stevenson did not think the idea of Chinese expansionism fanciful nor the effort to check it irrational. He ended his letter with: "If one argues that it should not be checked, I believe you set us off on the old, old route whereby expansive powers push at more and more doors believing they will open, until, at the ultimate door, resistance is unavoidable and major war breaks out."

In late 1965 the French press expressed some interesting views on Vietnam. Formerly, most French news media had claimed that the US-Saigon alliance could never hope to win. They have changed their tune. The military analyst of *Figaro* now scoffs at the idea of an American military defeat. And the big-circulation *Paris Match* weekly recently printed an article declaring that the United States, unlike France at Dien Bien Phu twelve years ago, cannot lose, and that the communists would be well advised to keep in mind two characteristic American traits: power and patience. Psychologically, America is equal to the task. Materially, she can try out a hundred different keys on the same door. The door eventually opens.

C. L. Sulzberger's column in *The New York Times* zeroed in:

A DISTORTED MIRROR OF WAR

Unfortunately, because the conflict is both technically unfamiliar and charged with emotion, one sometimes finds but faint resemblance between what actually happens and the mirrored impression and there is often scant connection between the real Vietnam and heated discussions of its reflection here. One of our adversary's most effective weapons is propaganda, deployed against us among our friends and even among ourselves.

The United States has never before engaged in so complex a military-political enterprise. We are forced to combat a subtly evolved new form of strategy with which our enemies are as familiar as we are ignorant. We are handicapped by lack of national tradition of governing experience among those we would help. We have accepted self-limiting rules not applicable to our adversaries.

Americans find it hard to comprehend a commitment which cannot be easily explained in either pragmatic or idealistic terms. . . .

Many major simplifications bandied about in public debate are incorrect. . . .

It is not right to say that the Viet Cong controls the majority of

South Vietnam's people and territory. The population majority demonstrably opposed the guerrillas and a vast chunk of the underpopulated country is simply no man's land.

It is not right to say that South Vietnam is a Buddhist nation and the Buddhists are against us. Less than half the population actually practices Buddhism and probably less than half that half belongs to the Unified Buddhist Church, which is itself riven by factions.

It is not right to say we are fighting all alone. We receive tangible military support from South Korea, Australia, New Zealand, Thailand, and token support from others including the Philippines.

And it is not right to say that no other Asian land sympathizes with us. The American position is far better understood than certain governments wish to advertise, for fear of embarrassing their own diplomacy.

President Johnson has been criticized for not specifying our Vietnam aims in precise terms, yet I doubt these differ from those objectives stated by President Kennedy on September 12, 1963. Kennedy said: "We have a very simple policy in Vietnam. We want the war to be won, the Communists to be contained, and the Americans to go home. That is our policy."

Those least informed are strangely unable to resist debating the issues. Private citizens visit the area for three days or a week and become instant experts. Even thoughtful people find themselves slipping into the use of slur and innuendo; the more emotional the argument, the more the arrogance of ignorance creeps in to compound the bewilderment of anyone sincerely interested in learning or understanding.

One fanatical group is soliciting donors to volunteer their blood and money for Viet Cong soldiers—not to be given to the Red Cross, but shipped straight to Hanoi. Whether they are sincerely committed to the North Vietnamese cause, are anti-US administration, or sly propagandists is their secret. But only a mechanical man, made of metal and wires, could fail to react, one way or another, to such stunts.

When our former USAF Chief of Staff, General Curtis LeMay, reorganized the Strategic Air Command in the late forties, his men chose as their motto: "Peace is our profession."

General LeMay has always insisted that the best way to maintain peace is to be stronger than anyone else. And as he has lately said so well, it is time now for all of us to realize how right George Washington was when he said:

"If we desire to secure peace, it must be known that we are at all times ready for war."

GLOSSARY

ADF—Automatic Direction Finder
AFBRVN—Air Force Base Republic of Vietnam
A.I.D.—Agency for International Development
ARVN—Army of the Republic of Vietnam
ASPCA—American Society for Prevention of Cruelty to Animals
BAR—Browning Automatic Rifle
BX—Base Exchange
Charlies—Viet Cong
CA—Combat Assault
CABOOM—Clark Air Base Officers' Open Mess
CO—Commanding Officer
DFC—Distinguished Flying Cross
D.O.—Director of Operations
DOOM—Da Nang Officers' Open Mess
DZ—Drop Zone
E.O.D.—Explosive Ordnance Demolition
FAC—Forward Air Controller
G-2—Government Intelligence
GCA—Ground Control Approach
H and I—Harassment and Interdiction
ISO—Informational Service Officer
JUSPAO—Joint U.S. Public Affairs Office
KBA—Killed By Air
LZ—Landing Zone
MACV—Military Assistance Command Vietnam
MedEVAC—Medical Evacuation
NCO—Noncommissioned officer
P's—Piasters
PACAF—Pacific Air Force
PSP—Pierced Steel Plank
PTAT—Post Telegraph and Telephone System
PTT—Saigon's Only Radio Station

PX—Post Exchange

R and R—Rest and Rehabilitation

RON—Remain Overnight

SAC—Strategic Air Command

SAMs—Russian Surface to Air Missiles

SATS—Short Airstrip for Tactical Support. It is transportable, quickly assembled, and has a portable catapult of launching and recovery capability.

SEATO—Southeast Asia Treaty Organization

SLAR—Side Looking Airborne Radar

SLICK—Troop-Carrying Helicopter

SOP—Standard Operating Procedure

TAC—Tactical Air Command

USO—United Services Organization

VC—Viet Cong

VNAF—Vietnamese Air Force

Willie Peter—White Phosphorus